A Gift to the Children

TO HELP THE CHILDREN

By purchasing *CHRISTMAS FOR THE WORLD: A Gift to the Children*, you are blessing the life of a child in need. All royalties and publisher's profits are earmarked for Humanitarian International—a non-profit organization established in Salt Lake City. From the sale of each book, at least $3.50 will go towards purchasing food, clothing, medicine, and other essentials for poverty-stricken children in Eastern Europe. Control of all proceeds are being audited by independent accountants, and 100% of all donations are guaranteed to reach programs that directly help the children.

If you wish to give more assistance to the needy children, please send your donations to Humanitarian International, in care of this publisher. All donations are greatly appreciated.

CHRISTMAS

FOR THE
WORLD

A Gift to the Children

Edited by:

Curtis Taylor
and
Stan Zenk

 ASPEN BOOKS
Salt Lake City, Utah

ACKNOWLEDGEMENTS

The following publishers have generously given permission to use stories from copyrighted works: Peregrine Smith Books: From *The Girl From Cardigan*, "The Wind, The Cold Wind," by Leslie Norris; from *Mr. Wahlquist in Yellowstone*, "The Red-tailed Hawk," by Douglas H. Thayer; *Network* magazine, December 1990: "Christmas Vigil of Mothers at the Gates of the Pershing Missile Site, Mutlangen, Germany," by Emma Lou Thayne; Deseret Book Company: From *Frost in the Orchard*, "Friends and Loved Ones Far and Near / Merry Xmas From Our House to Yours," by Donald R. Marshall.

CONTENTS

PREFACE

It all started with kitty litter.

A small, smudged-up letter arrived last year, postmarked St. George, Utah. We didn't recognize the name of the sender. In the envelope was a faded copy of a short story written by Maurine Whipple in 1939. We read the four or five pages of the story and set it aside; it didn't seem complete, and besides, book publishers don't publish just one short story.

We opened it again a few months later, for no good reason, and an idea suddenly clicked: what if a more complete version of this story existed? And what if we joined it with other Christmas stories by other LDS authors? Maurine Whipple was, in many people's opinion, one of the finest writers the Church had produced. Her one novel, *The Giant Joshua*, is still taught in university classrooms—50 years after publication. We made a phone call to the mysterious sender of the story.

We'll never forget the trip that followed. On the way down I-15, hail alternated with rain, which was replaced by a string of unbelievable rainbows. Somewhere between Fillmore and Cedar City, we pulled out a new essay by Eugene England and read it out loud. Our eyes filled with tears as we read the words describing genuine charity among members of another church in Africa. The essay solidified the idea and international cause behind this collection of stories. That essay now introduces this book.

We pulled into St. George and met Maurine. She was in top form, regaling us with one episode of her life after another. After eighty-eight years, she had compiled an amazingly colorful stock of such episodes. She didn't remember this particular story very well, except that it had been rejected by the Church magazines just before World War II. She said that "that woman," Veda Hale, had found it somewhere. That woman, the mysterious letter sender, was waiting for us across town.

Veda Hale had spent a year working on a biography of Maurine Whipple. After searching much of St. George and the BYU Archives for information, she had stumbled upon a gold mine—sort of.

A former neighbor had found a couple of old boxes of Maurine's old stuff and put them in her garage for safe-keeping. They had been in "safe-keeping" for two decades now, and the neighbor's cats were using them for litter. Veda took them home and began the unpleasant task of going through them. Buried in the litter was over 400 pages of Maurine's original manuscripts—short stories, novel excerpts, and the unfinished sequel to *The Giant Joshua*. It was also in this box that she found the completed version of Maurine's Christmas story.

Now we had to go back to Salt Lake and try to put an anthology together. We went to another great LDS author, Orson Scott Card. He was under contract to write four books by the end of the year, he said, and couldn't help us. We begged. He said he had a writers conference to attend and a promotion tour to embark on, and he couldn't possibly find the time. We begged again. A story showed up. He said he finally found the time while not sleeping at the writers conference. Other doors opened, and a fortune of great writers came in. We were amazed: Leslie Norris agreed to participate. One of the finest writers from Great Britain, he currently teaches at Brigham Young University. Though not LDS, he has become a favorite of many LDS readers (and writers), and this collection would seem incomplete without his touch. Other great writers came on board. Douglas Thayer, Linda Sillitoe, Herbert Harker, Carol Lynn Pearson, Don Marshall, Susan Evans McCloud, Michael Fillerup; and the list went on. Any one of the writers could have written the book him or herself. All were please to participate and donate their royalties to an important cause.

During this process, arrangements were made with Humanitarian International for the profits and royalties of this book to go toward the needy children of Eastern Europe. Many of the other authors had championed the causes of international brotherhood and charity for years, and here was a chance to do something about it. We sought financial sponsors. The advertising agency, Hurst and Phillips donated their time and energies in advertising it. They contacted KUTV, in Salt Lake City, who graciously agreed to run the advertisements at reduced rates—again, so more aid could be given to the children. Distributors were contacted, stores were approached, displays were made, and soon the project became a full-blown cause. We found ourselves hanging on by the shirttails.

Now the work is done. Everybody from typesetters and printers to store clerks and advertisers have made it possible, and in retrospect, we have many people to thank.

We are appreciative of the talent and generosity of the authors. Without their work, none of this could have been accomplished. We appreciate the gifts of the various sponsors who allowed us to bring this cause to the public. We appreciate the bookstores, many of whom donated their profits. Without their participation, all of this would have died in infancy. Summed up, we are grateful for all the gifts and services, all the donations and encouragement, we have received. Hundreds of talented and generous people have made *Christmas For the World* possible.

However much is given to the children through this project, we know that this effort will have been worth it. We have all grown in some way by our participation. We have felt the joy of giving. Although this project has it origins low in the earth (in the kitty-litter, actually), it has grown to become something greater than any one of us. It has blossomed into a unified act of charity. We may never know the children who are benefitted by this cause, but we will always know that in trying to help, we ourselves have grown.

Curtis Taylor and Stan Zenk
October, 1991

Eugene England is professor of English Literature at BYU and teacher of the Family History Writing Class in his Provo, Utah Ward Sunday School. He is married to Charlotte Hawkins England, and they have six children and nine grandchildren. His most recent books are Converted to Christ by the Book of Mormon *(Deseret Book, 1989);* Harvest: Contemporary Mormon Poems *(Signature, 1989), edited with Dennis Clark; and* Beyond Romanticism: Tuckerman's Life and Poetry *(BYU, 1991). A collection of essays will be published by Bookcraft in 1992. He writes personal essays, poetry, and criticism of American and Mormon literature and Shakespeare. He is presently at work on books about the poet Leslie Norris and about Shakespeare and is editing a collection of Mormon stories.*

INTRODUCTION:

THE SPIRIT OF MERCY AT CHRISTMAS

by Eugene England

My faith in the Restored Gospel of Jesus Christ was formed in Primary, most often to the sound of music. The simple, lovely songs we sang still move me deeply, when I hear or even think of them. They are inseparably entwined with my feelings about what is most precious in my life, my testimony of Christ's mercy and the love of my family. One of those songs is particularly precious because it connects all my emotions about Christmas, about Christ's birth, with my certain hope Christ will, in his great mercy, come to earth again to give final meaning and resolution to my life and to human history. That song is Mirla Thayne's "When He Comes Again" (*The Children's Friend,* March 1956).

The song asks two important questions that the Book of Mormon gives unique answers for: "I wonder, when He comes again will herald angels sing?" and "I wonder, when He comes again will I be ready there?"

The author does not give us an answer to the first question in the song itself. She shows she probably knew the answer, because she must have been reading the Book of Mormon carefully in order to ask, "Will daylight stay the whole night through? Will songbirds leave their nests?" We know from the Book of Mormon, though the information is missing from the Bible account, that on the night the Savior was born

1

daylight indeed stayed the whole night through—and songbirds probably did leave their nests, because "at the going down of the sun there was no darkness" (3 Nephi 1:15). But we also know something marvelous from the Book of Mormon about the angels who appeared on that same night to "shepherds abiding in the field," bringing "tidings of great joy, which shall be to all people" (Luke 2:9-15). We learn that those "herald angels" will also come to earth before Christ's *second* coming. Why will they come and who will hear them?

Helaman tells us that the herald angels appeared in America as well as Bethlehem, but not just on the night of Christ's birth. Two years before, "Angles did appear unto men, wise men, and did declare unto them glad tidings of great joy" (Helaman 16:14). And *eighty* years before that, Alma testifies, "The voice of the Lord, by the mouth of angels . . . doth declare it, that they may have glad tidings of great joy; and he doth sound these glad tidings among all his people, yea, even to them that are scattered abroad upon the face of the earth, wherefore they have come unto us" (Alma 13:22). Alma makes clear why these herald angels are appearing: "For behold, angels are declaring it unto many at this time in our land; and this is for the purpose of preparing the hearts of the children of men to receive his word at the time of his coming in his glory" (v. 24).

It seems that God sent his angels not only to announce the glad tidings of the birth of his Son, our Savior. He also sent angels, beginning at least in 82 B. C., to prepare the hearts of those who would be able to receive Christ when he comes again to judge the world and reign as Lord of Lords. And he apparently will send angels for that purpose right up until the Second Coming.

Who among us can hear such angels and have their hearts prepared for the glorious coming of Christ? Alma teaches in the passage above that people in all lands will receive the angels. Later he makes clear that God "imparteth his word by angels unto men, yea, not only men but women also. Now this is not all; little children do have words given unto them many times, which confound the wise and learned" (Alma 32:23). Not everyone will hear, of course, but it seems that men and women and children all over the earth may *already* be hearing, right now.

What determines if we can hear? Luke gives one key when he quotes the actual words of the "heavenly host": "Glory to God in the highest, and on earth peace, good will toward men" (Luke 2:14). Those who can hear are those who can give glory to God and for love of him can proclaim *peace and good will* on earth and act to bring it about.

Christ gave another crucial key when he taught his disciples that when he comes again he will separate the sheep from the goats by only one measure—not by our learning or our skills, not even by our beliefs, but by our humble service to God's children: "I was an hungred, and ye gave me meat: . . . I was a stranger, and ye took me in: . . . I was sick, and ye visited me: I was in prison, and ye came unto me. . . . Inasmuch as ye have done it unto one of the least of these my brethren, ye have done it unto me" (Matthew 25:35-40). In other words, those who can hear the herald angels are those who truly show mercy—those whose hearts have been softened by Christ-like love and can open to the sounds of the angels.

The Book of Mormon bears exactly the same witness. King Benjamin teaches that the *only* way to be saved by Christ's Atonement, that is, "for the sake of retaining a remission of your sins from day to day, that ye may walk guiltless before God—I would that ye should impart of your substance to the poor, every man according to that which he hath, such as feeding the hungry, clothing the naked, visiting the sick and administering to their relief, both spiritually and temporally, according to their wants" (Mosiah 4:25-26). Only those who are giving mercy can receive mercy, can open themselves to Christ.

Sister Thayne ends her song with the same witness as Christ and King Benjamin when she answers the child's question, "I wonder when He comes again will I be ready there?" with the child's own conviction: "When that blessed day is here, He'll love me and He'll say, 'You've served me well, my little child, come unto my arms to stay.'" I am thrilled with the Book of Mormon witness that herald angels continue to appear to merciful men, women, and children all over the earth—to prepare our hearts for the time Christ will come again.

At Christmas I remember Christ's first coming, in a manger, and his constant teaching that if I am to greet him in joy when he comes I must "renounce war and proclaim peace" (D&C 98:16) and must love and serve others as he has loved me (John 13:34). I want, even as I celebrate the birth of our Savior, to join my faith with that of Alma and his people: "Now we only wait to hear the joyful news declared unto us by the mouth of angels, of his coming; for the time cometh, we know not how soon. Would to God that it might be in my day; but let it be sooner or later, in it I will rejoice" (Alma 13:25).

To be able to rejoice in the coming of the Lord, to look forward with hope and peace rather than fear to that "great and dreadful day," I believe there are some very specific things I can do. Christmas, and the whole holiday period that comes to an end with New Year's Day—the end of one year and the beginning of another—provide an exceptionally good time for me to repent and make new resolutions. In recent years, I have been moved to resolve to stop worrying so much about mere fairness and justice and instead to share what I have with my loved ones, even when they don't "deserve it," and to give what I can, even to my enemies.

I was impelled to this resolve by the call of President Ezra Taft Benson, in the First Presidency Christmas Devotional of December 5, 1985, to let Christ's impartial love for all humankind, which we celebrate so intently at Christmas, empower us with similar love throughout the year. At that same time Elder Dallin H. Oaks proclaimed that Christmas has its best effect as it reminds us of the place of sacrifice in salvation and moves us to forgive, "to heal old wounds and restore relationships that have gone awry."

One of the areas where relationships have most gone awry and where old wounds continue to fester dangerously is in relationships between races, between religions, and between nations—in Ireland and the Middle East, in South Africa and Korea, even still between the United States and communist countries like Cuba, Vietnam, and China. Many people have often wondered if there isn't something in Christmas—in the birthday celebration for the "Prince of Peace"—that might heal those wounds and end that real and potential violence. And, in fact, the First Presidency of the Church, in their Christmas message of 1981, reminded us that "To all who seek a resolution of conflict, be it a misunderstanding between individual, or an international difficulty among nations, we commend the counsel of the Prince of Peace, 'Love your enemies . . . .'" Elder Oaks reminded us in that 1985 devotional that Christmas is the particular time to "eliminate arrogance and provocation," to "subdue criticism and de-emphasize differences among people," to "extend the true hand of fellowship to all."

Our Church leaders have not merely exhorted us to show such mercy—both at Christmas and throughout the year, they have also led the way. Not long after that 1981 Christmas message, when many Latter-day Saints participated on February 24, 1982, in a National

Fast for Poland, the First Presidency donated large amounts of food and medicine to be sent to relieve suffering in that Soviet Block country, which too often we had thought of as an "enemy." The Church continued to help with such efforts for Poland and then became increasingly involved in efforts to relieve the famine in Africa, culminating in a special Church-wide fast in January 1985. Much of the $6.6 million raised was spent on both immediate relief and on long-term water development in Ethiopia, even though that country too was seen, and still is, as an "enemy" because of its communist government. Another $3.8 million was raised through the Church after the First Presidency invited members to join the National Day of Fasting to relieve world hunger in November 1986.

The fund established by these fasts, and from the continuing contributions of Church members that are earmarked for such international relief, continues to be administered by the Church. I have learned that I can contribute to it regularly. I want to be one of those who, in the words of Elder Oaks, "look beyond their own family and, touched by the spirit of giving, fulfill the needs of countless individual lives made bitter by want, illness, loneliness."

I have found that it is fairly easy to be kind, even generous, to the people who are much like my own family and friends, who live near me and go to Church with me—or to send a contribution to help meet a disaster in our nation or that of a friendly ally, such as for the 1985 earthquake in Mexico or the one in 1989 in San Francisco. The challenge I have is in reaching out in mercy to those I don't know—the Baptist widow down the street who needs her house painted, the old couple in a shabby tenement in Salt Lake, living without adequate food or heat or medical care, the struggling single parent across town—or to those, like the Poles or the Ethiopians, who are perceived as my enemies in some way.

But our leaders have challenged us to continue moving in that direction. In October General Conference, 1990, Glen Pace of the Presiding Bishopric, asked us to resist our usual focus on justice—wherein we ignore or even take satisfaction in the suffering that seems to be "deserved" by people in the last days because they have ignored the Lord's warnings. He reminded us of the unconditional quality of mercy taught us by the Lord: "Of you it is required to forgive all men" (D&C 64:10):

Our forgiveness must be manifest by reaching out to help mend wounds even when they are the result of transgression. To react in any other way would be akin to setting up a lung cancer clinic for non-smokers only. (*Ensign*, Nov. 1990, p. 9)

Elder Pace expressed particular concern that as Latter-day Saints, aware of the prophecies of destruction and suffering before Christ's coming, we not smugly remove ourselves:

We must all become players in the winding-up scene, not spectators. We must do all we can to prevent calamities, and then do everything possible to assist and comfort the victims of tragedies that do occur. . . .
. . . I fear some members suffer from action paralysis, waiting for the Church to put its stamp of approval on one organization or another. The Church teaches principles. Use those principles and the Spirit to decide which organizations you would like to support. . . .
We must reach out beyond the walls of our own church. In humanitarian work, as in other areas of the gospel, we cannot become the salt of the earth if we stay in one lump in the cultural halls of our beautiful meetinghouses.

Elder Pace himself helps direct one such way we can reach out in mercy. The mechanism set up by the Presiding Bishopric's Office to handle the contributions from the special Church-wide fasts continues in place. Contributions earmarked simply for "World Hunger" can be made through LDS wards and branches or sent directly to Church headquarters. One hundred percent of these contributions (the Church takes *nothing* for administration) will continue to be transferred directly to front line relief and development, directed by such agencies as the Red Cross, Catholic Relief Services, CARE and Africare (which for instance, is building a dam in Ethiopia sponsored by the Church).
The Lord has assured as that "the earth is full, and there is enough and to spare" (D&C 104:17), and research by organizations combatting hunger, like Oxfam, has constantly confirmed that the world produces plenty of food for its population—if we would share it effectively. One dollar, for example, can buy 20 gallons of surplus milk, enough to feed ten children for a week. When I fast two meals each

week and give just $10 to the Church fund for world hunger, I am feeding 100 children. And if these children are my "enemies" in Ethiopia or Russia or wherever, perhaps I am helping to reduce some of the hatred and violence that too often make Christmas only a temporary cease-fire before we go back to hating and killing.

I pledge to fast and to send that offering. That is one way I can respond to what I hear the prophets calling me to do. It is one way I can be true to Christ and can answer that question I loved to sing as a child, "I wonder when He comes again will I be ready there?" It is a way to prepare my heart to hear the herald angels sing.

Another way is to follow the example of merciful people. Emma Lou Thayne, the eminent Mormon poet and essayist and constant laborer for peace, has written about one such example, experienced by her friend Jan Cook:

She and her husband were for three years in Africa, in "deepest Africa, where *The Gods Must Be Crazy* was filmed." His work had taken them and their three small children there, and any meetings attended were in their own living room with only themselves as participants. By their third Christmas, Jan was very homesick. She confessed this to a good friend, a Mennonite; Jan told her how she missed her own people, their traditions, even snow. Her friend sympathized and invited her to go with her in a month to the Christmas services being held in the only Protestant church in the area, saying that there would be a reunion there of all the Mennonite missionaries on the continent.

It took some talking for Jan to persuade her husband, but there they were being swept genially to the front of the small chapel. It felt good, being on Christmas in a church again. The minister gave a valuable sermon on Christ; the congregation sang familiar carols with great vitality. Then, at the very end of the meeting, a choir of Mennonite missionaries from all over Africa rose from their benches and made their way to stand just in front of Jan and her family. Without a word, they began singing. Without a leader, without music, without text, they sang, "Come, Come Ye Saints." Every verse.

Disbelieving, totally taken by surprise, Jan and her husband drenched the fronts of their Sunday best with being carried home on Christmas. . . . When they finished, Jan's friend said simply, "For you. Our gift."

Jan's Mennonite friend had sent to Salt Lake City for the music to the hymn that she knew Jan loved, had had it duplicated and distributed to every Mennonite missionary in Africa; they in turn had learned it very carefully to bring the spirit of Christ to their own reunion where foreigners to their faith would be waiting to hear. ("The Gift," *Exponent II*, Fall 1982, p. 6.)

Orson Scott Card was born in Richland, Washington and grew up in Santa Clara, California and Mesa, Arizona. His science fiction and fantasy writing has been awarded major prizes, including the Hugo Award, the Nebula Award, and the World Fantasy Award. His novel Saints *is a favorite among many Mormon readers. He is a former* Ensign *editor, and runs his own publishing company—Hatrack River Publications—which specializes in funny and truthful Mormon fiction. He is currently a counselor in the Greensboro Stake Mission Presidency, and he and wife, Kristine Allen, are the co-chairhumans of the Activities Committee in their ward. The couple has three children, Geoffrey, 13; Emily, 11; Charlie Ben, 8.*

CHRISTMAS AT HELAMAN'S HOUSE

by Orson Scott Card

There were times when he wanted to give up and live in a tent rather than fight with the contractors one more time, but in the end Helaman Willkie got the new house built and the family moved in before Christmas. Three days before Christmas, in fact, which meant that, exhausted as they all were from the move, they *still* had to search madly through the piles of boxes in the new basement to find all the Christmas decorations and get them in place before Santa showed up to inaugurate their new heat-trapping triple-flue chimney.

So they were all tired, weary to the bone, and yet they walked around the house with these silly smiles on their faces, saying and doing the strangest things. Like Joni, Helaman's 16-year-old daughter, who every now and then would burst into whatever room Helaman was in, do a pirouette, and say, "Daddy, daddy, I have my own room!" To which he would reply, "So I heard." To which she would say, hugging him in a way calculated to muss his hair, "You really do love me, now I *know* it."

Helaman's old joke was that none of his children had ever been impossible, but they had all been improbable more than once. Twelve-year-old Ryan had already been caught twice trying to ride his skateboard down the front staircase. Why couldn't he slide down the banister like any normal boy? Then at least he'd be polishing it with his backside, instead of putting dings in the solid oak treads of the stair. Fourteen-year-old Steven had spent every waking moment in the game room, hooking the computers together and then trying out all the software, as if to make sure that it would still work in the new house. Helaman had no evidence that Steven had yet seen the inside of his own bedroom.

And then there was Lucille, Helaman's sensible, organized, dependable, previously sane wife, kissing all the appliances in the kitchen. But the truth was that Lucille's delight at the kitchen came as a great relief to Helaman. Till then he had been worried that she was still having doubts about the house. When the movers left, she had stood there in the main floor family room, staring at the queen-sized hide-a-bed looking so forlorn and small on the vast carpet. Helaman reassured her that in no time they'd have plenty of furniture to fill up the room, but she refused to be reassured. "We're going to buy a truckload of furniture? When our mortgage is bigger than the one on our first store back in 1970?"

He started to explain to her that those were 1970 dollars, but she just gave him that how-stupid-do-you-think-I-am look and said, "I took economics in college, Helaman. I was talking about how I *felt*."

So Helaman said nothing. He had long since learned that when Lucille was talking about how she *felt*, none of the things he could think of to say would be very helpful. He couldn't even begin to put into words what *he* felt—how proud he had been of this house he had caused to exist for her, how much he needed to know that it made her happy. After all their years of struggling and worrying to try to keep the business afloat, and then struggling and worrying about the huge debts involved in starting up the branch stores, he knew that Lucille deserved to have a fine house, the *finest* house, and that he deserved to be the man who could give it to her. Now all she could think about was the huge amount of money the house had cost, and Helaman felt as though someone had taken the very breath out of him.

Until she came into the kitchen and squealed in delight. It was exactly the sound his daughters made—an ear-piercing yelp that gave him headaches whenever Trudy and Joni got excited for more than a minute at a time. He had almost forgotten that it was hereditary, that they got that glass-shattering high note from Lucille. She hadn't been surprised and happy enough to make that sound in years. But she made it now, and said, "Oh, Helaman, it's beautiful, it's perfect, it's the perfect kitchen!" It made up for her reaction to the family room. If it hadn't, he would have despaired—because he had worked hard to make sure that the kitchen was irresistible. He had kept careful track of everything she had ever admired in magazines or home shows; he had bought all new appliances, from the can opener and toaster to the microwave and the breadmaker; he had brought those all into the house himself and had his best crew install everything and test it so it ran perfectly. He had inventoried every utensil in her old kitchen and bought a brand new replacement; they had chosen new silverware and pans and dishes for daily use, and he had arranged it as close to the way she had her old kitchen arranged as possible, even when the arrangement made no sense whatever. And he had kept her out of the kitchen—with tape across the door—all the time he was doing it, and all during the move itself, until that moment when he told her she could tear away the ribbon and walk through the door. And she squealed and kissed all the appliances and opened all the drawers and said, "Just where I would have put it!" and "I can't believe there's room for everything and there's *still* counter space!" and "How did you get them all out of the old kitchen without my seeing you do it?"

"I didn't," Helaman told her. "I bought all new ones."

"Oh, you're such a tease," she said. "I mean, here's the old garlic press. I've never even used it."

"Now you have two of them."

And when she realized that he meant it, that he had really duplicated all her utensils and put them away exactly as she had always had them, she started to cry, which was a sign of happiness even more certain than the squealing.

So yes, they loved the house, all of them. Wasn't that what he built it for? For them to feel exactly this way about it? But what he hadn't expected was his own feeling of disappointment. He couldn't match their enthusiasm; on the contrary, he felt sad and uncertain as he walked through the house. As if after all his struggling to cause this house to exist, to be perfect, now that it was done he had no reason to be here. No, that wasn't quite the feeling. It was as if he had no *right* to be here. He strode through the house with all the rights of ownership, and yet he felt like an interloper, as if he had evicted the rightful occupants and stolen the place.

Am I so used to struggling for money all my life that when I finally have visible proof that the struggle is over, I can't believe it? No, he thought. What I can't believe is *me*. I don't belong in a place like this. In my heart, I think of myself in that miserable three-bedroom tract house in Orem with the four makeshift bedrooms Dad built in the basement so all his six kids could have rooms of our own. Well, I'm not a wage man like Dad, and my kids will not be ashamed of where they live, and my wife will be able to invite any woman in the ward into her home without that look of apology that Mother always had when she had to bring chairs from the dining room just so there'd be enough places for her visitors to sit.

Yet even when he had told himself all these things, reminded himself of the fire that had burned inside him all during the building of the house, he still felt empty and disappointed and vaguely ashamed, and he just didn't understand it. It wasn't fair that he should feel like this. He had *earned* this house.

Well, what did he expect, anyway? It was like Christmas itself: The gifts were never as good as the preparations—the shopping and hiding and wrapping. He felt as he did because he was tired, that's all. Tired and ready for it to be the day after Christmas when he could get back to running his little empire of five Willkie's stores, which sprawled on their parking lots in choice locations up and down the Wasatch Front, beaming their cheery fluorescent lights to welcome people in to the wonderful world of discount housewares. This had been a record Christmas, and maybe getting the accountants' year-end reports would make him feel better.

Then again maybe it wouldn't. Maybe this is what it is, he thought, that makes all those lonely women come to see the bishop and complain about how they're so depressed. Maybe I'm just having the equivalent of postpartum blues. I have given birth to a house with the finest view in the Darlington Heights Ward, I'm sitting here looking out of a window larger than any of the bathrooms, the twinkling lights of Salt Lake Valley on Christmas Eve spread out before me, with Christmas carols from the CD player being pumped through twenty-two speakers in nine rooms, and I can't enjoy it because I keep getting the postpartum blues.

"They're *heeeere!*" sang out Trudy. So the new love of her life (the second in December alone) must be at the door. At eighteen she was their eldest child and therefore the one nearest to achieving full human status. Unlike Joni, Trudy stilled spelled her name with a *y*, and it had been more than a year since she stopped drawing the little eyes over the *u* to make it look like a smile in the middle of her signature. At church yesterday she had fallen in love with the newly returned missionary who bore his testimony in a distinctly Spanish accent. "Can I invite him to come over for the hanging of the stockings?" she pleaded. In vain did Helaman tell her that it would be no use—his *own* family would want to have him all night, it was his first Christmas with them since the 1980s, for heaven's sake! But she said, "I can at least ask, can't I?" and Lucille nodded and so Helaman said yes, and to his surprise the young elder had said yes. Helaman took a mental note: Never underestimate the ability of your own daughters to attract boys, no matter how weird you think your girls have grown up to be.

And now the young elder was here, no doubt with so many hormones flowing through him that he could cause items of furniture to mate with each other just by touching them. Helaman had to get up out of the couch and play father and host for a couple of hours, all the time watching to make sure the young man kept his hands to himself.

It wasn't till he got to the door and saw *two* young men standing there that he realized that Trudy had said *they're* here. He recognized the elder, of course, looking missionary-like and vaguely lost, but the other was apparently from another planet. He was dressed normally, but one side of his head was mostly shaved, and the other side was partly permed and partly straight. Joni immediately attached herself to him, which at least told Helaman what had brought him to their door on Christmas Eve—another case of raging hormones. As to *who* he was, Helaman deduced that he was either a high school hoodlum she had invited over to horrify them or one of the bodacious new boys from the Darlington Heights Ward that she had been babbling about all day. In fact, if Helaman tried very hard he could almost remember the boy as he looked yesterday at church, in a lounge-lizard jacket and loosened tie, kneeling at the sacrament table, gripping the microphone as if he were about to do a rap version of the sacrament prayer. Helaman had shuddered at the time, but apparently Joni was capable of looking at such a sight and thinking, "Wow, I'd like to bring that home."

By default Helaman turned to Trudy's newly-returned missionary and stuck out his hand. "Feliz Navidad," said Helaman.

"Feliz Navidad," said the missionary. "Thanks for inviting me over."

"I didn't," said Helaman.

"*I* did, silly," said Trudy. "And you're supposed to notice that Father said Merry Christmas in Spanish."

"Oh, sorry," said the missionary. "I've only been home a week and everybody was saying Feliz Navidad all the time. Your accent must be good enough that I didn't think twice."

"What mission were you in?"

"Colombia Medellin."

"Do I just call you Elder or what?" asked Helaman.

"I've been released," said the missionary. "So I guess my name is Tom Boke again."

Joni, of course, could hardly bear the fact that Trudy's beau had received more than a full minute of everyone's attention. "And this is *my* first visitor to the new house," said Joni.

Helaman offered his hand to Joni's boy and said, "I know a good lawyer if you want to sue your barber."

Joni glared at him but since the boy showed no sign of understanding Helaman's little jest, she quickly stopped glaring.

"I'm Spencer Raymond Varley," said the boy, "but you can call me Var."

"And you can call me Brother Willkie," said Helaman. "Come on in to family room A and we'll tell you which cookies Joni baked so you can avoid them and live."

"Daddy, *stop* it," said Joni in her cute-whiny voice. She used this voice whenever she wanted to pretend to be pretending to be mad. In this case it meant that she really *was* mad and wanted Helaman to stop goading young Var.

Helaman was too tired to banter with her now, so he pried her off his arm, where she had been clinging, and promised that he'd be good from now on. "I was only teasing the spunky young lad out of habit."

"His father is *the* Spence Varley," Joni whispered. "He drives a Jag."

Well, *your* father is *the* Helaman Willkie, he answered silently. And I'll be able to get you great prices on crockpots for the rest of your natural life.

The family gathered. They munched for a while on the vegetables and the vegetable dip, the fruits and the fruit dip, and the chips and the chip dip. Helaman felt like a cow chewing its cud as he listened to the conversation drone on around him. Lucille was carrying the conversation, but Helaman knew she loved being hostess and besides, she was even worse than the girls, waiting to pounce on Helaman and hush him up if he started to say anything that might embarrass a daughter in front of her male companion for the evening. Usually Helaman enjoyed the sport of baiting them, but tonight he didn't even care.

I don't like having these strangers in our home on Christmas Eve, he thought. But then, I'm as much a stranger in *this* house as they are.

By the time Helaman connected back to the conversation, Joni was regaling her fashion-victim boyfriend with the story of the marble floor in the entry way. "Father *told* the contractor to lower the floor in the entry way or the marble would stand an inch above the living room carpet and people would be falling down or stubbing their toes forever. And the contractor said he wouldn't do it unless Father accepted the fact that this would make them three days late and add a thousand dollars to the cost of the house. And so Father gets up in the middle of the night—"

"You've got to know that I warned them while they were putting *in* the entryway floor that they needed to drop it an inch lower to hold the marble, and they completely ignored me," said Helaman. "And now it had the staircase sitting on it and it really would have been a lot easier to just install a parquet floor instead, but I had promised Lucille a marble entryway and the contractor had promised *me* a marble entryway and—"

"Father," said Joni, "I was going to tell the *short* version."

"And now he said he wouldn't do it," said Helaman, and then fell silent.

"*So*," said Joni, "as *somebody* was saying, Father got up in the middle of the night—"

"Six in the morning," said Helaman.

"*Let* her tell the story, Helaman," said Lucille.

"And he got the chainsaw out of the garage," said Joni, "and he cut this big gaping hole in the middle of the entry floor and you know what? They realized that Daddy *really meant it.*"

They laughed, and then laughed all the harder when Helaman said, "Remember the chainsaw if you're ever thinking of keeping my daughter out after her curfew."

Even as he laughed, though, Helaman felt a sour taste in his mouth from the chainsaw story. It really *had* cost the contractor money and slowed down the house, and when Helaman had stood there, chainsaw in hand, looking in the first light of morning down in the hole he had just made, he had felt stupid and ashamed, when he had *meant* to feel vindicated and clever and powerful. It took a few minutes for him to realize that his bad feelings were really just because he was worried about somebody walking in without looking where they were going and falling down into the basement, so he wrestled a big sheet of plywood over and laid it *mostly* over the hole, leaving just enough of a corner that the contractor couldn't help but know that the hole was there. And then it turned out that *that* wasn't the reason he felt stupid and ashamed after all, because when he'd finished he *still* had to come home and take a shower just to feel clean.

Of course, while he was thinking of this, they had gone on with the second marble story, only now it was Trudy telling it. "So this lady from across the street comes over and Mom thinks she's going to welcome us into the neighborhood, and so she holds the door open and invites the woman inside, and the first thing she says is, 'I hear you're going to have marble in the foyer of your new house,'" and Mom says yes, and then the woman—"

"Sister Braincase, I'll bet," said Var.

"Who?" asked Lucille

"Sister Barnacuse," said Var. "We call her Braincase because she's going bonkers."

"How compassionate of you," murmured Lucille.

"*Any*way," said Trudy, "whoever she was—Mrs. Barnacuse—said, 'Well, I hope it isn't that miserable *fox* marble.' And Mother just stands there and she's trying to think of what fox marble might mean. Was it a sort of russet shade of brown or something? She'd never heard of a color called *fox*. And then all of a sudden it dawns on her that the woman means *faux* marble, and even though the marble in the entry *is* real, Mother says to her, 'No, the marble *we* have is *faux*.' As if it was something to be proud of. And the woman says, 'Oh, well that's different,' and she goes away."

Var laughed uproariously, but Tom Boke only sat there with a polite missionary grin, which Helaman supposed he probably perfected back before he really knew the language, when he had to sit and listen to whole conversations he didn't understand. Finally the young man shared with them the reason for his failure to laugh. "What's foe marble?" he asked.

"Faux," said Lucille. "French for false."

"It means fake," Ryan said, in one of the brief moments when his mouth wasn't full of chips. "But ours is real. And our toilets flush silently."

"Ryan," said Lucille in her I'm-still-acting-sweet-but-you'd-better-do-this voice, "why don't you go down and pry your brother away from the computer and ask him to come up and meet our guests?"

Ryan went.

"Old Braincase is such a snob," said Var, "but the truth is all the marble in *her* house really *is* faux, but we think the contractor sort of misled her about it and she's the only one who doesn't know that there's not an ounce of real marble in her whole house." Var cackled uproariously.

"How sweet of you not to break her heart by telling her," said Lucille. "We'll keep the secret, too."

"Guided-tour time!" cried Joni. "Please, before we hang the stockings or anything? I want Var to see my room."

"This is the best time to do it," Helaman said to Var. "It'll be the last time her floor is visible till she goes away to college."

Var smiled feebly at Helaman's joke, but Tom Boke actually managed to laugh out loud. I'll count that as my first Christmas present, Helaman said silently. In fact, if you do that again I'll ask you to marry my daughter, just so I can have somebody to laugh at my jokes around this house.

This house this house this house. He was tired of saying it, tired of thinking it. Six thousand square feet not counting the garage or the basement, and he had to take yet another tour group to see every single square foot of it. The living room, the parlor, the dining room, the kitchen, the pantry so large you could lose children in it, the breakfast room, the library, and back to the main-floor family room—giving the tour was practically an aerobic exercise.

Then downstairs to family room B, the big storage room, and the game room with the new pool table and two elaborate computer set-ups so the boys wouldn't fight over who got to play video games. Not to mention the complete guest apartment with a separate entrance, a kitchenette, two bedrooms, and a bathroom, just in case one of their parents came to live with them someday in the future.

Then all the way up two flights of stairs to see the bedrooms—eight of them, even though they only used five right now. "Who knows how many more we'll need?" said Helaman joking. "We're still young, we'll have more to fill 'em up."

But Lucille looked just the tiniest bit hurt and Helaman regretted saying it immediately, it was just a dumb joke and for *that* he had caused her to think about the fact that she'd blown out a fallopian tube in an ectopic pregnancy two years after Ryan was born and even though the doctors said there shouldn't be a problem they hadn't conceived a child since. Not that their present crop of children gave them any particular incentive to keep trying.

No, thought Helaman, I must never come to believe my own jokes about my family. Most of the time they're great kids, I've just got the blues tonight and so everything they do or say or *think* is going to irritate me.

"*Will* you have more children?" asked Tom.

It was an appalling question, even from a recently returned missionary who had gone so native that he was barely speaking English. "I think that's for the Lord to decide," said Lucille.

They were all standing in the master bathroom now, with Ryan dribbling an imaginary basketball and then slam-dunking it in the toilet. Tom Boke stood there after Lucille's words as if he were still trying to understand them. And then, abruptly, he turned to Trudy. "I'm sorry," he said, "but I've got to go."

"Where?" asked Trudy. "We haven't even done the stockings yet."

"I didn't know it would take so long to see the house," said Tom. "I'm sorry."

"*See*, Dad?" said Trudy. "If you'd just learn how to give shorter tours, I might actually someday get to . . ."

But before she could finish affixing blame on Helaman, even though it was Lucille who had insisted on the tour for her daughters' gentlemen callers, Tom Boke had already left the master bathroom and was heading out the master bedroom door.

"Get him, Father," said Trudy. "Don't let him go!"

"If *you* can't keep him," said Helaman, "what makes you think he'll stay for *me*?" But he followed Tom all the same, because the young man had looked quite strange when he left, as if he were sick or upset, and Helaman didn't feel right about just letting him go back out into the cold.

He caught up with him at the front door—Helaman assumed that the only thing that slowed Tom down was the fact that it was so easy to get lost when you came down the back stairs. "Tom," said Helaman. "What's wrong?"

"Nothing, sir."

But the expression on Tom's face declared his "nothing" to be a lie. "Are you going to be sick? Do you need to lie down?"

Tom shook his head. "I'm sorry," he said. "It's just . . . I just . . ."

"Just what?"

"I just don't belong here."

"You're welcome under our roof, I hope you know that."

"I meant America. I don't know if I can live in America anymore."

To Helaman's surprise the young man's eyes had filled with tears. "I don't know what you're talking about," Helaman said.

"Everybody here has so *much.*" Tom's gaze took in the entry way with its marble floor, opening onto the living room, the dining room, the library. "And you keep it all for yourselves." The tears spilled out of his eyes.

Helaman felt it like a slap in the face. "Oh, and people don't keep things for themselves down in Colombia?"

"The poor people scratch for food while the drug lords keep everything they can get their hands on. Only the mafia have houses as large . . ."

The comparison was so insulting and unfair that Helaman was filled with rage. He had never hit anyone in anger in his life, not even as a child, but at this moment he wanted to lash out at this boy and make him take it back.

But he didn't because Tom took it back before he even finished saying it.

"I'm sorry," Tom said. "I didn't mean to compare . . ."

"I earned every penny of the price of this house," said Helaman. "I built my business up from nothing."

"It's not your fault," said Tom. "Why should you think twice about living in a house like this? I grew up in this ward, I never saw anything wrong with it until I went to Colombia."

"I *didn't* grow up in this ward," said Helaman. "I *earned* my way here."

"The Book of Moses says that in Zion they had no poor among them. Well, Darlington Heights has achieved *that* part of building Zion, because no poor people will ever show their faces *here.*"

"Why aren't you home telling your own parents this, instead of troubling *my* house?"

"I didn't mean to trouble you," said Tom. "I wanted to meet your daughter."

"So why don't you just stay and meet her, instead of judging me?"

"I told you," said Tom. "It's *me*, not you. I just don't belong here. Enjoy your new house, really, it's beautiful. It's not your fault that I taught so many people whose whole house was smaller than your bathroom. But the Spirit dwelt there in their little houses, some of them, and they were filled with love. I guess I just miss them." The tears were flowing down his cheeks now, and he looked really embarrassed about it. "Merry Christmas," he said, and he ducked out the door.

Helaman had no sooner closed the door behind him than Trudy was down the stairs railing at him. "I always knew that you'd drive one of my boyfriends away with all your teasing and the horrible things you say, Daddy, but I never thought you'd send one away in *tears*."

"What did you *say* to him, Helaman?" asked Lucille.

"It wasn't anything I said," Helaman answered. "It was our bathroom."

"He *cried* because of your *bathroom*?" asked Trudy. "Well thank heaven you didn't show him your cedar closet, he might have killed himself!"

Helaman thought of explaining, but then he looked at Trudy and didn't want to talk to her. He couldn't think of anything to say to that face, anyway. She had never whined and demanded and blamed like this when she was little. Only since the money. Only since the money started happening.

What am I turning my daughter into? What will she become in this house?

Helaman wasn't feeling the blues anymore. No, it was much worse. He was suffocating. It was desolation.

Helaman's hand was still on the doorlatch. He looked at Lucille. "Do the stockings without me," he said.

"No, please, Helaman," said Lucille.

"Oh, good job, Trudy," said Joni. " Now everybody's going to be mad at each other on our first Christmas in the new house."

"I think I'd better go home now," said Var.

"*I* can't help it if my father and my sister both went insane tonight," said Joni. "Don't go, Var!"

Everyone's attention had shifted to Joni's pleading with Var; Helaman used the break to slip out the front door, Lucille's remonstrance trailing him out into the cold night air until at last he heard her close the door and Helaman could walk along the sidewalk in the silence.

The houses rose up like shining palaces on either side of him. Mrs. Braincase's pillared mansion across the street. The huge oversized bi-level two doors down. All the houses inflated as if somebody had been pumping air into them up and down the street. Christmas lights in ever-so-tasteful color-coordinated displays on the trees and along the rooflines. Every house saying, I have succeeded. I have arrived. I am somebody, because I have money.

He imagined that it wasn't him walking along this sidewalk tonight, but a Colombian family. Maybe a father and mother and their two daughters and two sons. Big as these houses were, would any of them have room for them tonight?

Not one. These houses were all too small for that sort of thing. Oh, somebody might slip them a twenty, if anybody wasn't too terrified of robbers to open the door in the first place. But there'd be no room for them to sleep. After all, they might have fleas or lice. They might steal.

Helaman stopped and turned around, looking back at his house from a distance. I can't live here, he thought. That's why I've been so depressed. Like the day I cut out the entry floor and forced them to redo it—I was powerful and strong, wasn't I! And yet all I had the power to do was get my own way by bullying people. I built this house to prove that I had what it takes to get a house in Darlington Heights. And now I'll never see this house without imagining that poor Colombian family, standing outside in the cold, praying for somebody to open the door and let them come inside somewhere that it was warm.

What am I doing here, living in one of these houses? I hated these people when I was a kid. I hated the way they looked down on my family. The way they could never quite imagine Dad or Mom in a leadership calling, even though they were always there helping, at every ward activity, every service project, bringing food, making repairs, giving rides. Mom in the nursery, Dad as permanent assistant to four scoutmasters, and all the time Helaman knew that it was because they weren't educated, they talked like farm people because that's where *they* grew up, they didn't have money and their car was ugly and their house was small, while people with nowhere near the kindness and love and goodness and testimony got called to all the visible, prominent callings.

Helaman remembered one time when he was thirteen, sitting there in the office of his bishop, who told him how he needed to set goals in his life. "You can't separate the Church from your career," he said. "When Sterling W. Sill had the top insurance agency in the state of Utah, he got called to the First Council of the Seventy. My goal is to have the top agency by the time I'm forty, and then serve wherever the Lord calls me from then on." The unspoken message was, I'm already bishop and I'm already rich—see how far I've come.

Helaman had come out of that interview seething with rage. I don't believe you, he had insisted silently. The Lord doesn't work that way. The Lord doesn't value people by how much money they make, the two things have nothing to do with each other. And then Helaman had gone home and for the first time in his life, at age thirteen he saw his father the way that bishop must have seen him—as a failure, a man with no money and no ambition, a man with no *goals*. A man you couldn't possibly respect. Helaman's prayers that night had been filled with rage. He stayed up finding scriptures: It's as hard for a camel to pass through the eye of a needle as for a rich man to get into heaven; let him who would be greatest among you first be the servant of all; he who would find his life must lose it; sell all you have and give it to the poor and come follow me; they were not rich and poor, bond and free, but all were partakers of the heavenly gift. All those ideas still glowed in Helaman's memory as they had that night, and when he finally slept it was with the sure knowledge that it was his father, the quiet servant without ambition for himself, who was more honorable in the sight of God than any number of rich and educated men in the Church. It was the beginning of his testimony, that peaceful certainty that came that night.

What Helaman had never realized until right now, on this cold Christmas Eve, standing on this street of mansions, was that he had also believed the other story as well, the one the bishop told him. Maybe it was because he still had to see that bishop there on the stand, week after week, and then watch him become stake president and then go off as a mission president; maybe it was because Helaman was naturally ambitious, and so his heart had seized on the bishop's words. Whatever the reason, Helaman had not modeled his life on his father's life, despite that testimony he had received that night when he was thirteen. Instead he had followed the path of the people who had looked down on his father. He had built a house in their neighborhood. He had brought his children to dwell among them. He had proved to them that he was exactly as good as they were.

And that was why he felt so empty, there in his new house, even though his whole family loved the place, even though he had worked so hard to build it. Because the fact that he lived there meant that he was exactly as good as those people who had despised his father, and he knew that it was his father who was good, not them.

Not me.

Lucille even tried to stop me, he thought. She knew. That was why she kept saying, We don't need such a big house. We don't need all those rooms. I don't have to have a separate sewing room—I *like* sewing in the family room with everybody around me.

Helaman had been deaf to all she said; he had taken it for granted that she was only saying these things because she always worried about money and because she was too unselfish to ever ask for anything for herself; he knew that secretly she really wanted all these fine things, these big rooms, these well-earned luxuries.

Only once had she put her foot down. The architect had specced out gold fixtures everywhere, and Lucille had rejected it immediately. "I'd feel like I had to wash my hands before I could touch the faucet to turn it on," she said. Helaman was all set to go ahead anyway, on the assumption that she really wanted them after all, until she looked him in the eye and said, "I will never use a bathroom with gold fixtures, Helaman, so if you put them in, you'd better build me an outhouse in the back yard."

Even then, what had finally convinced him was when she said that chrome fixtures went better with all the towels because they didn't have a color of their own to clash with.

I wasn't listening, thought Helaman. She was telling me exactly what the Spirit told me that night in my childhood, showing me in the scriptures what my goals should be and what I should think about money. And I knew she was right, yet I still went ahead and built this house and now I can't bear to live in it because every room, every bit of wainscoting, every polished oak molding, every oversized room is a slap in the face of my father. I was so angry at those snobs that I had to get even with them by becoming just like them. I don't belong here,

I don't want to live among people who would build and live in houses like these, and yet here I am.

Tom Boke stood in my house and wept because I had so much, and I kept it all for myself. I am the opposite of my father. I had the money to do good in the world, and I used it to build a monument to Helaman Willkie, to win the respect of people whose respect isn't worth having.

He was trembling with the cold. He had to go inside, and yet he couldn't bring himself to take another step toward that house.

It's a beautiful house, said a voice inside him. You earned it.

No, he answered silently. I earned the right to live in a house big enough for my family, to meet our needs, to keep us warm and dry. There is no work in the world that a person can do that can earn him the right to live in a house like *this*, when so many others are in want. I sinned in building it, and I will sin every time I put a key in the lock on that door as if it were my right to take this much of the bounty of God's Earth and keep it for just my family to use.

The door to the house opened and light spilled out onto the porch, onto the bare trampled ground that didn't yet have a lawn. It was Lucille, coming outside to find him. Lucille, wearing a coat and carrying another, looking for her husband to keep him warm. Lucille, who had understood the truth about this house all along, and then loved him enough to let him build it anyway. Would she love him enough to let him abandon it now?

He could not walk back to the house, but he could always walk to his wife, and so he called out to her and strode on trembling, uncertain legs toward where she waited for him.

"Here's a coat," she said. "If you don't have the brains to stay indoors, at least wear the coat. I don't want to have to bury you in the back yard, not till the landscapers come in the spring, anyway."

He took her teasing with good cheer, as he always did, but all he could really think about was the impossibility of telling her what he needed to tell her. It was so hard to think of the words. So hard to know how to begin.

"So can I stay out here and talk to you?" said Lucille.

He nodded.

"The house is too big, isn't it," she said. "That missionary has told you about poverty and you took the news as if you'd never heard of it before and now you feel guilty about living here."

As so often before, she had guessed enough about what was in his heart that he could say the rest himself. "It wasn't the boy, what he said. I was already unhappy here, I just didn't know it."

"So what do we do, Helaman? Sell it?"

"Everybody will think we built a house bigger than we could afford and *had* to sell it."

"Do you care?"

"There'll be rumors that Willkie Housewares is in financial trouble."

"It's not a corporation. The stock won't drop in value because of a rumor."

"The kids will never forgive me."

"*That* is possible."

"And I don't know if I could ever look myself in the eye, if I gave you a kitchen like that and then took it away because of some crazy idea that living here means I'm ashamed of my father.

"Your father loves this house, Helaman, he's been over here a dozen times during the building of it, and if he hadn't promised your sister Alma that he'd spend Christmas with *her* family in Dallas he'd be here with us tonight."

"What about you?"

"Moving is a pain and I won't like doing it twice," she said. "But you already know that I never wanted a house this big."

"But I wanted you to have it. I wanted you never to be like my mother, living in a ward where all the other women looked down on her, raising a family with no money in a tiny house."

"*Our* old house wasn't tiny, it was just small."

"You love the new kitchen. I don't want you to give up the new kitchen."

"You sweet, foolish man, I love the kitchen because you took so much care to make it perfect for me."

"I'll give it all up," said Helaman. "Because I can't live with myself if I stay in a place like this. But how can I take it away from you and the kids? Even if you didn't really want it, even if you never asked for it, I gave it to you anyway and I can't take it back."

"So, will you rent an apartment near the main store and come visit us on weekends? Helaman, I couldn't bear it if this house came between us. Why do you think I didn't try to stop you from building it? Because I knew you wanted it so much, you were so hungry for it—not for yourself, but to give it to us. You needed so much to give this to us.

Well, you *have* given it to us, and the kids and I love it. You meant to build it for the best motives, and as soon as you realized that maybe it wasn't such a good idea, you were filled with remorse. The Lord doesn't expect you to sell it and live in a tent."

"Sell all you have and give it to the poor and come follow me," Helaman quoted.

"That was what he said to a rich *young* man. You're middle-aged."

"And you're just saying whatever you think will get me back into the house where it's warm."

"Well, what *are* you going to do, then? Never come back inside again?"

To Helaman's surprise, he found tears running down his cheeks, his face twisting into a grimace of weeping. "I can't," he said. "If I go back inside then it means I'm just like *them.*"

"So don't *be* just like them," said Lucille, putting her arms around him. "You never *have* been just like them, anyway. You've never run your business the way they do—you've been fair and even generous with everybody, even your competitors, and everybodys know it. There's nobody in the world who resents your having this house—your employees love you because they know you've paid them more than you had to and made less profit that you could have and you work harder than any of them and you forgive them for mistakes, and every one of them is glad for you to finally move out of that house that we've stayed in since 1975. Most of them don't understand why it took us so long to move. You can live in this house with a clear conscience. You're *not* like the rest of these people." She looked up and down the street. "For all we know, half of *them* might not be like the rest of these people."

"It's not about them or what anybody else thinks," said Helaman. "I just can't be happy here. It's like what the missionary said. Tom, right? He said, I just can't live in America anymore. Well, I just can't live in that house."

Lucille stood there in silence, still holding him, but not speaking. Helaman was still full of things to say, but it was always hard for him to talk about things inside himself, and he was worn out with talking, and even though he had stopped weeping now, he was afraid of feelings so strong that they could make him cry. So the silence lasted until Lucille spoke again.

"You can't sell the house," said Lucille. "It won't be a poor person who buys it, anyway."

"You mean I should give it away?"

"I mean we should give it away in our hearts."

He laughed. He remembered the testimony meeting where Sister Mooller, who had more money than General Motors, had gotten up and said that thirty years ago she and her husband had decided to consecrate all they had to the Lord, and so they gave away "in their hearts," which was why the Lord had blessed them with so much more in the years since then. Whereupon Lucille had leaned over to him and whispered, "I guess the Lord really needed that new Winnebago they bought last month."

"Don't laugh," said Lucille. "I know you're thinking about Sister Mooller, but we could *really* do it. Live in the house as if it weren't our own."

"What, never unpack?"

"Listen to me, I'm being serious. I'm really trying to find a way for you to have all the things that you want—to give this house to us, and yet not be the kind of man who lives in a big fancy house, and still keep the family living under one roof."

"That *is* the problem, isn't it." He felt so foolish to have gotten himself into such a twisted, impossible set of circumstances. No matter what he chose, he'd feel guilty and ashamed and unhappy. It was as if he had deliberately set out to feel unrighteous and unhappy no matter how things turned out.

"Let's consecrate this house to the Lord," said Lucille. "We were going to dedicate it tomorrow, anyway, as part of Christmas. Well let's do it tonight, instead, and when we dedicate it let's make a covenant with the Lord, that we will always treat this house as if others have as much right to use it as we do."

Helaman tried to think of how that would work. "You mean have people over?"

"I mean keep watching, constantly, for anybody who needs a roof over their heads. Newcomers who need a place to stay while they're getting settled. People in trouble who have nowhere else to turn."

"Bums from the street?"

She looked him in the eye. "If that's what it takes for you to feel right about this house, and you'll be here at night to make sure that the family is safe, then yes, bums from the street."

The idea was so strange and audacious that he would have laughed, except that as she spoke there was so much fire in her eyes that he felt himself fill with light as well, a light so hot and sweet that tears came to his eyes again, only this time not tears of despair and remorse but rather tears of love—for Lucille, yes, but more then for her. There were words ringing in his ears, words that no one had said tonight, but still he heard them like the memory of a dear old friend's voice, whispering to him, Whatever you do to help these little ones, these humble, helpless, lonely, frightened children, you're doing it for me.

And yet even as he knew that this was what the Savior wanted him to do, a new objection popped into his mind. "There are zoning laws," he said. "This is a single family dwelling."

"The zoning laws don't stop us from having visitors, do they?" said Lucille.

"No," said Helaman.

"And if somebody stays very long we can always tell Sister Barnacuse that they're faux relatives."

Helaman laughed. "Right. We can tell her that we've got a lot of brothers and sisters who come and visit."

"And it'll be the truth," said Lucille.

"This can't be one of those resolutions that we make and then forget," he said.

"A solemn covenant with the Lord," she said.

"It isn't fair to you," said Helaman. "Most of the extra work of having visitors in the house would fall to you."

"And to the kids," she said. "And you'll help me."

"It has to be like a contract," said Helaman. "There have to be terms. So we'll know if we're living up to the covenant. We can't just wait for people in need to just happen along."

"So we'll look for them" said Lucille. "We can talk to the bishop to see who's in need."

"As if anybody in *this* ward is going to need a place to stay!"

"Then we'll ask him to talk to the stake president. There are other wards in this stake. And people you'll hear about at work."

"Someone new every month, unless the house is already full," said Helaman.

"Every month?" said Lucille.

"Yes."

"Like home teaching?" she asked.

It was a sly jab indeed, for she well knew how many times Helaman had come to the end of the month and then grabbed one of his sons and ran around the ward, trying to catch their home teaching families and teach them his famous end-of-the-month procrastination lesson. "Even when I'm late, I *do* my home teaching."

"If you think you can find somebody every month, then that's the covenant," said Lucille. "But you're the one who'll have to take the responsibility for finding somebody every month, because I don't get out enough."

"That's fine," said Helaman.

"And if we find that we can't do it," said Lucille, "that it's too hard or it's hurting our family, what then?"

"Then we sell all we have and give the money to the poor," said Helaman.

"In other words," said Lucille, "if we can't make this work, then we move."

"Yes."

It was agreed, and it felt right. It was a good thing to do. Hadn't his own parents always had room on the floor for somebody to lay out a sleeping bag if they had no other place to stay? Hadn't there always been a place at his parents' table for the lonely, the hungry, the stranger? With this covenant that he and Lucille were making with the Lord, Helaman could truly go home.

And then, suddenly, he felt fear plunge into his heart like a cold knife. What in the world was he promising to do? Destroy his privacy, risk his family's safety, keep their lives in constant turmoil, and for what—because some missionary cried over the poverty in Colombia? What, would there be a single person in Colombia who'd sleep better tonight because Helaman Willkie was planning to allow squatters to use his spare bedrooms?

"What's wrong?" asked Lucille.

"Nothing," said Helaman. "Let's get inside and tell the kids before we freeze." Before my heart freezes, he said silently. Before I talk myself out of trying to become a true son of my father and mother.

They opened the door, and for the first time, as he followed Lucille onto the marble floor, he didn't feel ashamed to enter. Because it wasn't his own house anymore.

Joni was all for having Var stay through the whole rest of the Christmas Eve festivities, but Helaman politely told Var that this was a good time for him to go home to be with his family. It only took two repetitions of the hint to get him out the door.

They gathered in the living room and, as was their tradition on Christmas Eve, Helaman read from the scriptures about the birth of the Savior. But then he skipped ahead to the part about Even as ye have done it unto the least of these, and then he and Lucille explained the covenant to their children. None of them was overjoyed.

"Do I have to let them use my computer?" asked Steven.

"They're *family* computers," said Helaman. "But if it becomes a problem, maybe you can keep one computer in your room."

"It sounds like this is going to be a motel," said Trudy. "But I'm going to college after this year and so I don't really care."

"Does this mean I can't ever have my friends over?" asked Ryan.

"Of course you can," said Lucille.

Joni had said nothing so far, but Helaman knew from the stony look on her face that she was taking it worst of all. So he asked her what she was thinking.

"I'm thinking that somehow this is all going to work around so I have to share my bedroom again."

"We have spare bedrooms coming out of our ears, not to mention a whole mother-in-law apartment in the basement," said Helaman. "You will *not* have to share your room with anybody."

"Good," said Joni. "Because if you ever ask me to share my room, I'm moving out."

"We don't make threats to you," said Lucille, "and I'd appreciate if it you'd refrain from making threats to us."

"I mean it," said Joni. "It's not a threat, I'm just telling you what *will* happen. I waited a long time to have a room of my own, and I'll never share my bedroom again."

"We'll be sure to warn your boyfriends that your husband is going to have to sleep in another room," said Trudy.

"You aren't helping, Trudy," said Lucille.

"Joni," said Helaman, "I promise that I'll never ask you to share your room with anybody."

"Then it's OK with me if you want to turn the rest of the house into a circus."

For a moment Helaman hesitated, wondering if this *was*, after all, such a good idea. Then he remembered that Joni had brought home tonight a boy who was attractive to her only because his father was famous and he drove a Jaguar. And he realized that if he let Joni live in this house, in this neighborhood, without doing *something* to teach her better values, he was surely going to lose her. Maybe opening up the house to strangers in need would give her a chance to learn that there was more to people than how much fame and wealth they had. Maybe that's what this was all about in the first place. He had wanted this house to be a blessing to his family—maybe the Lord had shown him and Lucille the way to make that happen.

Or maybe this would cause so much turmoil and contention that the family would fall apart.

No, thought Helaman. Trying to live the gospel might cause some pain from time to time, but it's a sure thing that *not* trying to live the gospel for fear that it *might* hurt my family will *certainly* hurt them, and such an injury would be deep and slow to heal.

As he hesitated, Lucille caught his eye. "The stockings seem to be hanging in front of the fireplace," she said. "All we need to do now is have our family prayer and bring presents downstairs to put them under the tree."

"You aren't going to make us give away our *presents*, are you, Dad?" asked Ryan.

"In fact, that's why we all got lousy presents for you this year, Ryan," said Helaman. "So that when it's time to give them away, you won't mind."

"Da-ad!" said Ryan impatiently. But he was smiling.

Instead of their normal Christmas family prayer, Helaman dedicated the house. In his prayer he consecrated it as the Lord's property, equally open to anyone that the Lord might bring to take shelter there. He set out the terms of the covenant in his prayer, and when he was done, the children all said amen.

"It's not our house anymore," said Helaman. "It's the Lord's house now."

"Yeah," said Steven. "But I'll bet he sticks you with the mortgage payments anyway, Dad."

That night, when the children were asleep and Helaman and Lucille had finished the last-minute wrapping and had laid out all the gifts for the morning, only a few hours away, they climbed into bed together and Lucille held his hand and kissed him and said, "Merry Christmas and welcome home."

"Same to you and doubled," he said, and she smiled at the old joke.

Then she touched his cheek and said, "All the years that I've been praying for another child, and all the years that the Lord has told us no, maybe it was all leading to this night. So that our lives would have room for what we've promised."

"Maybe," said Helaman. He watched as she closed her eyes and fell asleep almost at once. And in the few minutes before he, too, slept, he thought of that Colombian family he had imagined earlier. He pictured them standing at his door, all their possessions in a bag slung over the father's shoulder, the children clinging to their mother's skirts, the youngest sleepy and fussing in her arms. And he imagined himself holding the door wide open and saying, "Come in, come in, the table's set and we've been waiting for you." And Helaman saw his wife and children gather at the table with their visitors, and there was food enough for all, and all were satisfied.

Maurine Whipple was born January 20, 1903, at St. George, Utah. After graduating with honors from the University of Utah, she taught school at various locations in Utah and Idaho. In 1937 her novella Beaver Dam Wash *attracted the attention of Ford Maddox Ford who introduced her to Houghton Mifflin. They later published* The Giant Joshua, *which was envisioned as the first in a trilogy. It won rave reviews in the Eastern press but was reportedly suppressed by some Mormon leaders. She never published another work of fiction but went on to write features for Life, Look, Collier's, and other magazines. In 1991, over 400 manuscript pages of her later fiction were found—some at BYU Archives but most in a box at a neighbor's home. The neighbor's cats had been using it as kitty litter for years. Included in the box was* Cleave the Wood, *the unfinished sequel to* The Giant Joshua. *Veda Hale, who discovered the manuscripts while researching Whipple's biography, has compiled them for Aspen Book, which will be publishing them next year as* The Unpublished Works of Maurine Whipple. *This story is from that collection.*

A DRESS FOR CHRISTMAS

by Maurine Whipple

Grandma Stapely smoothed the folds of the black knitted shawl nervously—John's and Maggie's present a year ago. This year it was to be a dress. She was sure the package contained a dress. Had not John in his last letter (almost three months ago, it was, but she must not forget her boy was very busy) said that Maggie would "go shopping . . . and find her a nice dress for Christmas." She remembered the exact words. She had never had a real pretty dress all her life. The early years had been too full of building a place to live in and growing food, to think of fancy clothes. But the later years had been hard, too; they seemed as they stretched behind her, one eternal wash day. She did not regret the washings, though, because they had helped to keep John in medical college. Her fine big John; so famous and so busy.

And now he was sending her a dress. She hoped it would be black silk, or maybe grey, or brown silk; she wondered, would she be too daring if she wore blue. She could almost see it, with its soft lace at her throat to cover the wrinkles.

Well, the time had come when she ought to have something she did not actually need; she was eighty. A new dress would make her look younger, too, she thought complacently.

"Do not open until Christmas." The package had come three days ago. How she had counted the hours! But the time was here at last to cut the string, and her fingers ached in their eagerness. Would Maudie ever come! They had dreamed and planned together, ever since Maudie first started to bring the milk in the mornings, and now Maudie must share the joy.

All morning while she worked she had been conscious of the Christmas sounds outside in the street: sleigh bells, the sweet caroling of young voices in the frosty air, calls of boys on new skates to other boys on new sleds, excited little girl voices clucking in maternal solicitude to new dolls in new buggies. All the happy, happy Christmas sounds.

Grandma Stapely undid her apron strings and re-tied them again carefully. With the tortoise-shell comb from the back of her white hair she brushed up the scolding locks and anchored them more firmly. She took out her handkerchief and surreptitiously scrubbed at her cheeks which were already as softly glowing as withered apples. For the hundredth time she moved the spray of holly on the mantle from in front of the china shepherdess back to the clock, and for the hundredth time studied the effect critically, her head on one side like an enquiring sparrow.

With an impatient sigh she turned to the window and flattened her nose against the pane and stared up the frosty street. No sign of Maudie yet. She could just make out the star on top of the big spruce Christmas tree over on the village square. Last night that tree had been alive with lights, and a hearty Santa Claus had seen to it that every child in town shared in the Christmas spirit. The children had had such a good time around the tree, shouting, laughing, singing. She wondered suddenly why it seemed so hard for people to remember the child that might also dwell in an old lady's heart.

The sounds of Christmas. She turned away from the window and sank into the comforting cushions of her rocker. So many women that day with big homes and large families who would cry out before the day was done over the children's noise. She thought there was nothing she would not give to turn back the clock to a young John shrieking with a Christmas puppy on the floor. Sounds of Christmas!

She wet her lips and piped forth a brave but tremulous note into the silence of the room.

"Jingle bells! Jingle bells! Jingle all the—"

But somehow she couldn't make her own old voice sound like a real Christmas sound.

No matter. Maudie would soon be here. She mustn't moon. After all, children had their own lives to lead, she couldn't expect—

At a quarter past eight the timid knock came and the old lady rushed to open the door.

"Merry Christmas, Maudie," she quavered breathlessly.

She took the quart bucket of milk from the girl's hands and unfastened the safety pin which held her coat together.

"Did you get a present, Maudie?"

The girl smiled aimlessly.

Grandma Stapely bustled around her visitor and got her seated on the low stool in the warm place behind the stove. She wiped from the child's red and chapped chin the saliva which was always drooling there, and took gently from her mouth the thread-wound end of the tight braid which she was always biting between her teeth.

"Did you get a Christmas present, dearie?"

"I got these mittens, Grandma Stapely. Be you goin' to open the package now?" "Yes, dearie. But shall we have our usual singin' first, and shan't we have just a wee prayer 'cause it's Christmas? Then we'll see—"

Grandma Stapely sighed. She should have had better sense'n to have mentioned the music now. Seemed like a body couldn't get much real satisfaction out of visitin' with Maudie because her brains could only hold one thought at a time. And when it come to singin'—! Funny, too, with Maudie's voice so queer-like. Real short-sighted of the Lord to give a body such an itch to do a thing and then forget to put in the means to do it with!

Maudie's dull smile had taken on sudden meaning. She stood by the old organ in the corner and looked back at Grandma expectantly.

"All right, dearie. You can have your way. I guess we can wait to see what Maggie and John have sent all the way from the city. If it's a new dress I'll put it on this afternoon and you shall come back over and we'll eat Christmas dinner together like we been plannin'."

Grandma gave the organ stool a turn or two and settled herself before the worn keys. Her feet shoved at the stiff pedals.

"You sure don't have to be at the hotel all day t'day, do you?"

Maudie's pale stare wavered, lowered, and her slack lips puckered together.

"Well, there, there, child, you come down anyway and I'll tell Andy Roberts just what I think of him for makin' you work on Christmas."

The old organ wheezed, bent fingers found the notes to "Rock of Ages Cleft for Me," and Grandma's reedy voice piped the words.

"Let me hide myself in Thee," contributed Maudie. The incredible monotone of her voice rasped on in a sort of exalted fervor. Her wizened little face was shining now and something in the depths of her eyes brought an ache to Grandma's throat. Weeks and weeks of effort. The child listening painfully to each note of the hymn and trying so patiently over and over again. Herself cheering the hurt in the pale eyes.

"Don't you worry, dearie. We'll have this song learnt by Christmas, you wait and see! 'Rock of Ages' by Christmas, and if you've got one song learnt real good, it'll be easy to go on t' the others!"

Grandma knew Maudie had taken to saving her money lately for real singin' lessons. A' course it wan't no use but you couldn't tell Maudie that. The old lady pedaled with all her might and shouted at the top of her lungs as if she'd make Maudie sing by sheer force.

"'Free from sin and make me pure!'"

They finished and Grandma Stapely whirled briskly around.

"Why, child, you're gettin' better 'n better. When we first tried to sing you couldn't even say the words and now you can go through a whole song without stoppin'. A' course, you don't allus get the tune right, but that'll come. Now you pray, and then fer our package!"

Maudie's whole body wriggled with dumb but adoring gratitude as she turned from the old lady and knelt on the floor. She clasped her hands and turned her pasty face with its dim smile upward.

"Our Father who art—who art—"

"In Heaven," prompted Grandma, kneeling beside the girl.

"Make everybody—be good to—Maudie and Grandma—because this is Christmas—and let Grandma's dress be a purty one, please—"

"Amen!" Grandma came to the rescue. "That's enough. I'm sure he'll understand. And *now*—"

The moment had come. Christmas had come! Grandma took the package down from the mantle and held it an instant, savoring the thrill of opening it. There was her name in bold, black ink. She imagined Maggie choosing the dress carefully and wrapping it tenderly and addressing it lovingly. Because they had not forgotten her. Because they did love her.

She pulled the string and took off the brown wrapping paper and sank into the rocker with the gaily wrapped box in her arms. Maudie knelt beside the chair and chewed the string and stared at the box. Such wonderful, shiny paper! All patterned with the cheerful red and green of holly wreaths. Such beautiful red ribbon with that rosette of a bow where the four ends met.

"Ain't it—oh, ain't it purty, Maudie!"

Her fingers trembled until she could hardly untie the rosette. But at last she pushed off the ribbon and opened the crinkly holly paper and drew out the brown pasteboard box underneath.

"See?" said Grandma. She traced the letters with her fingers. "It says, 'Marshall-Field, Chicago.'"

She caressed the box with her hand.

"See, I told you they'd not forget me! Didn't I? Didn't I?"

She stared defiantly at Maudie who chewed on her braid and stared back.

Eagerly Grandma lifted the lid and raised the box to smell the fragrant newness. A thrill to part even the fine tissue paper—

Some of the expectant joy left her face as she saw the light tan color and the thinness of the silken fabric. She shook out the dress and standing up, held it to her shoulders.

Impossible to hide the quaver in her voice.

"Maudie, dear, do you suppose the clerks made a mistake?"

But, no, there was the card; no mistake. She measured the sleeves, elbow length; she measured the neck—low, even on a girl. Instead of real lace trimmings there was ribbon, bright green ribbon, caught in little whorls on the waist and skirt. Her startled eyes measured the length—barely below the knee; and tried to account for the shirring that encircled the waist and rose to a point in front so plainly revealing the bosom.

Grandma avoided Maudie's gaze and walked to the window and tried to swallow the ridiculous disappointment that choked her throat. Silly tears. What ailed her? It was—was a real purty dress. Just a mistake. Anybody might've made it. Maggie'd just forgot she was so old. Too old. The world had no room for the old. She shook her head and smiled brightly.

"I—I'm afraid they forgot I am such an old, old person, Maudie—"

These foolish tears—! That was the trouble with being old. You couldn't manage yourself the way you used.

Maudie's pale gaze focused intently on the tan dress. Her clumsy brain beat frantically against a real problem.

"I know, Grandma Stapely! It's 'cause they don't care about you no more!"

"Oh, no, child," fearfully. "You mustn't say that! Why, when John was going to school he was allus sayin'—" (Maudie knew the time-worn assurance by heart) "—'some day, Mom, I'll send for you to live with me in a fine, big house and we'll spend all our Christmases together!'"

But no matter how she tried, the day had lost its flavor. She was almost glad when Maudie got up to go.

"Be sure and come back t' dinner, dearie." But she thought, I can't help it, I won't want to eat it. It ain't like Christmas, somehow. I won't be hungry. She sat by the window and listlessly watched Maudie shuffle through the snow up the street.

Maudie, eyes unseeing on her trudging feet, was squaring around to her problem. Grandma Stapely was the only friend she had ever known, the only human being who had ever tried to understand or help her, and Grandma Stapely felt bad; she knew Grandma felt awful bad no matter how hard she tried to pretend. Grandma Stapely could not live much longer. She needed folks, she needed folks *now*. That was it. If her famous doctor son understood he would come and make her happy. Maudie knew in the vague, chaotic jumble of her mind, in the tag ends of ideas that made up her thoughts—he'd come, if only he understood.

At the hotel Maudie walked straight through the lobby and pushed open the swinging doors into the kitchen without once raising her head.

Andy Roberts, behind the desk, grinned and then frowned. You never knew what to expect with the Bigler kid. Rum little mutt. You'd think, being s'late on a busy day like this, she'd say something instead of barging through like she owned the blamed joint. But that was what you got for hiring a nut. Of course, the only reason he'd got a kid like that in the first place was because she'd begged so hard. He usually had some boy to do the chorin' around, but for all this kid wasn't more'n ten or twelve an' a half-wit at that, she got more work done'n any dozen boys.

Andy Roberts chewed a toothpick reflectively and ruminated on the whims of a capricious fate. Family smart as all git out, and that poor kid slinkin' amongst 'em like a scairt pup. An' her bein' off on singin' now! Put that in your pipe and smoke it. Her folks had even hadter take her outa school because she got to be the laughin' stock of the town. Jumped up to sing every chanct she got. Darn near die laughin', yerself, at sight of her in church with her mouse-colored braids stretchin' tight the skin on her skull, her big crooked teeth pokin' a hole through her daffy grin, an' that raspy voice of hern, plowin' a straight furrow through the up an' around pattern of the hymn.

Daft little beggar. There was the time she kept a-askin' him was there a real singin' teacher in town? An' did he think the perfessor could learn a body like her to sing, too? The kid a-hoardin' her money fer lessons! It beat all git out. A' course it wan't none of his business an' the fool town could laugh its head off before he'd give her away. Let her take lessons if'n she got a kick outa it. Besides, it didn't do to laugh too much at kids who was fey like his Bigler kid. If anybody wanted a thing so all-fired bad as she did, why who knowed, the good Lord, Hisself, might send her a tune t' carry!

Poor little devil. Let 'er go home early t'day—

Andy Roberts pushed into the steaming kitchen. The breakfast orders were all in and the place jangling with activity. Here was the warm, wet breath of soapsuds and the clink of jostled dishes. Layers of odors of many foods—the faint, tainted odor of last month's cabbage beneath the sharp strong tingle of today's fried steak. A familiar diapason of odors to Andy who chewed his toothpick and stared without interest at the bustle. The kitchen paused a moment to salute its lord and master. All but the dogged figure with mousey braids bent over the pan of potatoes. Andy sauntered over to her.

"How ya makin' out, Kid?"

Maudie rested her pale stare on him briefly, chewed thoughtfully for a moment on the end of her braid, and went back to the paring knife.

Andy shrugged.

"Get off at two if y' wants, kid, seein' it's Christmas."

Suddenly Maudie dropped the half peeled potato and without another look for the nonplussed Andy shuffled out of the room. He stood with his mouth agape and watched her go through the swinging doors.

"Well I'll be damned!"

Maudie had made up her mind.

The hands of Nurse Howard's wristwatch were both exactly on the figure twelve. Christmas day was over, but out in the snowy city festive lights still blazed from hotels and restaurants and drawing rooms. Show windows still carried glittering trees, dolls, teddy bears, and bright toy trucks; behind plate glass, incongruous upon the busy street, the Christ child still slept beneath the ancient beneficence of the Star. Overhead lights traced an intricate network of red and green brilliance against the black sky. Everywhere neon signs filled the night with a kind of garish beauty. At street corners a few Salvation Army lasses still shuffled tambourines. Newsboys still hawked special Christmas editions.

But in spite of it all, Christmas was really over and Nurse Howard was glad. She clutched the chart she was studying in fingers numb with fatigue. Christmas was always a hard day, especially in the children's ward. But she reflected drowsily it had been a good day and she was glad they'd staged all that fuss for the kids even if there was a mess to clean up after.

She patted a yawn, adjusted her white cap, stretched her arms until the joints creaked, and got up from the desk to take up her periodic patrol of the long dim corridor with its rows of human freight stretching into the gloom behind her. Nurse Howard looked and listened and tiptoed. Here a cough, there a childish whimper, a sigh, or a small body threshing under the bedclothes. But every tiny sleeper clutching a Christmas toy. That had been her doing, and now softly pacing in the murky quiet, she felt her heart throb with satisfaction. People said Doctor John had the finest hospital in the city. She hoped sleepily her small bit helped to make that true. Dear Doctor John . . . she knew the nurses called her the power behind the throne, but that was just silly.

At the other end of the ward she came to the huge tree they had had this morning for the kids. A shining star on its top, wreaths of popcorn and the tinsel among its branches, and gifts piled at its feet. Now all the gifts were gone, but the tree with its trimmings still remained somehow forlorn in its holiday finery like an actress who had forgotten to wash off the greasepaint.

Extra work tomorrow taking out the tree, storing all the trimmings in boxes. A job to get everything straight again and routines and schedules running at normal.

Back at the desk, pressing fingers against aching eyelids, Nurse Howard mumbled to herself, "Yes, it means taking the trouble. But just the same it'd break my heart if I thought there had been this day any child *without* a Christmas!"

Abruptly the shrill clamor of the telephone shattered the night. Oh, darn! She reached for the receiver.

"Yes?" She yawned and dug the receiver into her ear.

"Will you tell me that again? I'm sorry but I'm not— But you see, Doctor John's busy and can't be called— Well, yes, he's attending an entertainment— But I couldn't possibly disturb him!— Some other doctor— But it's probably just a silly fancy of the child's and I don't want to call him unless it's absolutely— I see. Funny she'd keep on calling him like that, I'm sure he doesn't know her— But on *Christmas!* What on earth was a child running around alone on Christmas for in the first place?— Well, can't you locate her people?— But how on earth— Of course, if it's that urgent I'll just *have* to call him. Bring the case over—"

When she finally reached Doctor John his voice sounded tired. She thought as she hung up that she was glad he'd had a good Christmas, at least a restful one. She'd simply insisted that he go to this party with his wife. Funny how he'd changed. Used to love to go to all the swell places with her when they were first married. Oh, well, Nurse Howard shrugged, the woman was obviously a fool. She was an orchid and real doctors had no room for orchids in their lives—unless the orchid learned how to be a cauliflower. But to have Doctor John on *any* terms—! The gal he'd married had been a perfumed darling who couldn't appreciate him; he'd worshipped her, and she'd tossed aside his love—

She got up and walked briskly to the far end of the ward beyond the tree. There was a vacant bed here, probably far enough away from the others not to wake them. Let's see, she thought. Lights, and accident bed—screen it off completely—two of those tall ones should do the trick with the wall on the other side—because if the child's dying—. Now the dressing cart wheeled by the bed; better get a new bottle of merthiolate. You never knew what Doctor John might want. For a good many years now she'd been doing just that—foreseeing his wants.

That's how she'd helped him— This year he'd even been mentioned by the A.M.A.—

A little glow flooded her heart at the thought. The nurse from the emergency hospital at the other end of the line had been so nicely deferential—*we would not consider bothering Doctor John if the child weren't so insistent . . . keeps calling for him over and over*—they *knew*, you bet! All the profession knew his worth.

She looked at her watch. One o'clock. Doctor should be here any minute . . . . While she filled hot water bottles her busy thoughts ran on. If somebody could just do something with that wife of his. Surely she was *human*. Even with a perfumed hussy there must be *some* way to her heart! It was just that she wanted Doctor John to be happy—because, well, because he'd do so much better a job if he were happy!

The whine of the elevator. She rushed to hold open the swinging doors for the orderly and to help the tossing, crying figure from the stretcher on to the bed.

The driver of the ambulance drew a hand across his forehead.

"Whew! That was some job. I'd ruther handle ten men than a crazy kid like that!"

Nurse Howard stared at his red face and wide grin. He'd evidently had too much Christmas cheer.

He answered her questions volubly.

"Yes sir, we thought all the accidents for this holiday were done with, when this kid got run over. Ran right in front of the car the driver said, though a' course they all say that. Seemed scairt pink and not to know where she was going. If she wasn't so young I'd think she was one of the drunks!"

He tipped back on his heels and tittered.

"Blamedest thing you ever heard! The nurse said she kept saying, 'Fifteen dollars, all Maudie's!' Then she'd sorta light up and say 'Fer singin' lessons!'— Can you tie that!"

"But what did she say about Doctor John?"

"Oh, I ain't told you the half! She'd moan and cry somethin' about Grandma and then she'd shout, 'Doctor John! Maudie must tell Doctor John!' Then she'd rave about 'real lace' or somethin', and once she sang Rock of Ages clear through. You shoulda heard it."

Nurse Howard finally got him out the door and turned to her patient. The child was bandaged from the neck to heels but she still writhed and moaned. Nurse Howard's hand was cool on the hot forehead; she found herself looking into dim, light eyes behind whose vacant stare some kind of pleading beat.

"What is it, honey? Can't you tell me what it is?"

For an instant the stare focused and tightened and the child cried, "Doctor John! Maudie must see Doctor John!— It didn't have real lace! Grandma wants real lace! Oh—Maudie tried and tried, but all the people—"

The words sank into low, heartbroken whimpers. The pale eyes darted like caged birds in the chalky face and the arms threshed constantly under the covers. The room seemed filled with her struggle to breathe.

Nurse Howard daubed a bit of ointment over the red chapped place on the chin and burned with righteous wrath. A child like that out alone— What had her family been thinking of?

"There, there," she crooned. "It'll be all right. Nurse will make it all right!"

"You'd make the whole world right if you could, wouldn't you Howdy?"

She turned and smiled up at Doctor John. She never got over being a little breathless when he surprised her like that. Sometimes when he was tired or a case had gone wrong, a weary six-year-old looked out of his eyes and she longed to rest his head against her heart. So long suffering, so patient, so tender; with a scalpel in his hand, such a god.

"H'm, is this the patient?" he was saying now as he stripped off his evening jacket. Deft fingers exploring, probing, taking pulse. Handing him gowns, instruments, gauze, rubber gloves, Nurse Howard was thinking, "She might be the wealthiest patient in the world, so far as he knows—or cares."

But at last when everything was done Doctor John looked at her across the bed. He sighed.

"Just a matter of time."

"They said she had something to tell you—"

"I can't imagine what. I never saw her before."

"Well, she kept calling and calling—"

"Oh, I'll wait. She's likely to come out of this any minute. I think she'll come out of it, too, before—"

*   *   *

Maudie's gaze questioned first the kindly face of the woman bending over her; but that face was strange. On the other side of the bed was a tall dark man who seemed somehow familiar.

Something flickered for an instant in the back of Maudie's mind. When she struggled to speak, and her crushed body strained against its bandages, her vague stare glazed over for a moment with the dumb hurt look of a wounded animal. But the flicker persisted. Briefly she fought the pain in her lungs for a deeper breath, closed her eyes and rallied the cumbersome machinery of her thoughts until the flicker ceased to waver and became a clear pin-point of purpose.

"Be you—Doctor John?"

The man nodded his head.

She fought harder up through the pain.

"She—wanted—real—lace—"

The man turned to the nurse.

"Can't you find out what she wants for me? It's late and I—"

The hand on Maudie's forehead was soothing.

"Who was it, dear? Try to think. Who wanted real lace?"

Again the flicker for a moment burned clearly.

"Why, Grandma Stapely! She's good to—Maudie. She's good to—everybody. Please—the purty dress—it ain't right, it ain't got—real lace, it—"

Doctor John suddenly bent closer to the bed.

"Where do you live?"

His voice was strained and urgent, now.

"Tell me, where do you live? Is it in Three Oaks—Three Oaks?" He repeated each syllable carefully.

But Maudie merely continued her mumble.

"She said—Doctor John would come if he knew— She's lonesome— Folks git lonesomer at Christmas— 'n any other time— Grandma's lonesome—"

Nurse Howard wiped the saliva from Maudie's chin.

Doctor John tried to hold the wavering pale gaze.

"Who did you say? Grandma who?"

He took hold of the child's restless hands.

"Try to think: Grandma who?"

Maudie's slack lips suddenly puckered and her tone became anguished.

"Fifteen dollars—fer singin' lessons!— But Grandma's so good to Maudie—"

"Is that your name?" questioned Doctor John. "Maudie who?"

The child's eyes were filling with tears.

"She wanted—a dress—with real lace—"

The man looked across at the nurse in despair.

"Who wanted real lace?"

Suddenly Nurse Howard had an inspiration. Just a hunch but she believed in hunches. She left Doctor John with the patient and walked down the corridor to the telephone. She kept her voice low but insistent. There were ways of handling Doctor John's wife, even if she *had* just got home from an all-night party. The voice at the other end of the line was chilly with indignation.

Back at the bed where Doctor John sat helplessly, Nurse Howard waited with one ear alert for the elevator. When she heard it she went out in the hall to meet its passenger. This time the wife's aloof, blond beauty, her mink and orchids and exquisite perfume made no impression on Nurse Howard whatsoever. "I know too much about you this time, sister," she said to herself as she led the lady back to the ward. "Too much about your carelessness and selfishness, your impatience, your indifference to an old lady's feelings. We'll just see now if you *have* got a heart."

Nurse Howard was very brusque and professional. She placed a chair by the Christmas tree where the first faint light of the winter dawn would gild its tinseled star and reveal all the cherished toys in the childish hands. She placed the doctor's wife so that she faced the screen around the bed in the corner. She motioned to the sleeping children and put her fingers to her lips.

"Wait here," she whispered. It was really a command. "Doctor John will see you in a moment."

The lady's eyes questioned her irritatedly but Nurse Howard deliberately turned her back and tiptoed down the ward to the desk. She had played her trump. If I know anything about women's curiosity it will work, too, she thought, and if that woman has got the sense God gave little green apples, she'll know what to do.

Nurse Howard folded her arms on the desk and pillowed her weary head on them. Only for a moment. She was dead for sleep.

Somewhere a pulse beat: "Real lace, real lace, real lace!" And the room was filled with a voice croaking, "Free from sin—and make me pure!"

The voice faded and became fainter and seemed to change and glow and dissolve into itself like colors running together.

*   *   *

Nurse Howard suddenly straightened and listened. Was she imagining things? But the echo of the childish singing that still hung on the air was as sweet and true as a Christmas bell. . . .

The late afternoon sun streamed into the ward. Grandma Stapely closed up the wonderful story books and patting into place the lace cuffs of her dress, smiled at the eager faces. John and Maggie would be holding dinner for her.

"Will ya come tomorrow, Grandma Stapely? Say you'll come tomorrow!" The ward was filled with childish clamor.

Nurse Howard came in and smiled at the confusion.

"She'll come tomorrow, boys and girls. She always comes tomorrow!"

Walking out into the hall with the old lady, Nurse Howard slipped an affectionate arm about the stooped shoulders in their fine black silk.

"You do them a lot of good, you know. You're so understanding."

"Laws sakes," said Grandma Stapely, "Folks *need* understandin'. Everybody used to say even Maudie was queer-like before she died, but I allus thinks people tapped their heads significant-like at Jesus, Hisself!"

Until someone else steps forward, it appears Lee Nelson is the only man in modern times to have killed a bull buffalo from the back of a galloping horse with bow and arrow—part of the research for his action-packed Storm Testament *series. Lee was born high in the Rocky Mountains in Logan, Utah, and later went to high school in California. After studying at the University of California at Berkeley, he served a two-year mission for the LDS Church in Germany. Later he earned a Bachelor's degree in English literature and a Master's degree in Business (MBA), both from Brigham Young University. He has completed post-graduate work in psychology and has been published in the Journal of Psychology. Lee has been a corporate speech writer, an advertising agency copywriter, publisher of his own magazine, and editor of a large-circulation community newspaper. Since 1979 Lee has had seventeen books published, nine fiction and eight non-fiction. He is best known for his seven-volume* Storm Testament *series of historical novels with nearly half a million hardbound copies in print. Parts of the* Storm Testament *series have appeared in serial form in over a hundred newspapers nationwide and in Canada. In the area of non-fiction, Lee is best known for his three* Beyond the Veil *series books, each volume containing true accounts of near-death experiences wherein the subjects, mostly LDS, were able to see beyond the veil. Lee is a popular speaker and lecturer at schools, colleges, service clubs, youth conferences, Boy Scout awards banquets, historical societies and community celebrations focusing on pioneer heritage. Lee's favorite non-writing pastime is taking his children and friends on wilderness horseback pack trips to remote areas of the West in search of Indian ruins, outlaw hideouts, wild horses and trophy-class mule deer. Lee and his family live on a small farm in Central Utah. The following is an excerpt from Lee's upcoming biographical novel,* Cassidy, *the eighth volume in* The Storm Testament *series.*

BUTCH CASSIDY'S MOST UNFORGETTABLE CHRISTMAS

by Lee Nelson

It was December and Butch had agreed to meet Elzy and Sundance in Santa Fe for Christmas. Mary wanted Butch to stay longer in Wyoming, but if he was going to make it to Santa Fe before Christmas he had to start moving.

He decided to ride a new buckskin gelding he had purchased from Lone Bear. Butch was heading south towards Lander when the storm hit.

When he left Thermopolis the weather had been unseasonably warm, but cloudy. The second day of his journey it began to rain, a drizzle at first, but eventually turning to a downpour. Hoping to make Lander before nightfall, he didn't seek shelter. For Wyoming in December, it was an unusually warm rain, so he didn't worry about getting wet.

During the later part of the afternoon the wind suddenly changed, bearing down hard from the north, bringing with it much colder air. The rain changed to sleet, then to snow. The wind blew harder, and colder. Butch urged his horse into a trot. His teeth began to chatter from the cold.

It was soon dark. Butch's clothes were as hard as rawhide, but he had no choice but to push on, thinking he would soon be in Lander. When he reached the top of the last hill, thinking he would see the lights of the little frontier town ahead of him, there were none.

Earlier the clouds had obscured the tops of the mountains. Apparently he had made a false calculation as to where he was. Now it was too dark to see ten feet in any direction. The matches in his coat pocket were wet and frozen. His feet were numb, already partly frozen, and his fingers, still hurting from the cold, would soon be numb too.

It occurred to Butch that he might be on his last ride. The most notorious bank robber and horse thief in the country was about to freeze to death in a blizzard—unless he found shelter and warmth soon. The problem was that he didn't know which way to go. He couldn't see. If he picked the wrong direction, he might ride for miles, or he might ride in circles all night, or at least until he froze to death.

For the first time in his life Butch began to feel panic. Unless he became very smart, or very lucky, very fast, he would soon be dead.

Butch remembered something Lone Bear had told him when he had purchased the buckskin, that the animal had a keen homing instinct, that if it ever got loose it would head straight home to the ranch where it was raised. Lone Bear had said the horse had been raised somewhere in the Lander area, but Butch couldn't remember anything more.

"I don't know where you were raised old boy," he said to the horse, "but take me there as fast as you can." Butch tied a knot in the reins and dropped them on the animal's neck. Folding his arms and hands across his chest, he nudged the horse with his heels to hurry it along.

In the blackness of the storm Butch had no idea whether the animal was going north, south, east or west. He knew only that it moved with confidence, not seeming to hesitate as to which way it should go.

Butch was surprised when he began to feel drowsy. The pain in his hands and feet began to subside. Then he could hear singing, beautiful music. It reminded him of when he was a boy, and his mother used to play the organ with all the children standing around singing together.

For a minute he thought he was home again, with everything just fine. He wasn't cold anymore. He felt happier than he had felt in a long time.

Then suddenly he was in agony again. The pain in his hands and feet was excruciating. His chest hurt too, like big nails were being pounded into his heart whenever he tried to breathe. For a minute he felt hot. Then he was cold again, his teeth chattering. He could do nothing to control it.

He didn't notice when the horse stopped in front of a gate. He didn't hear the dog barking, or the voice calling to him from a partly opened cabin door. He didn't remember being pulled from the horse and dragged inside.

The first thing he remembered was a man and woman and two small children standing around him, rubbing his frozen extremities with snow which they fetched a handful at a time out of a wooden tub. To get at one of his frozen feet the boot had to be cut away with a knife.

Butch groaned in pain. Every inch of his body hurt. Because of the continuing pain in his chest, the man and woman concluded he had pneumonia. After the woman and children went to bed, the man stayed up all night putting hot aspen branches over Butch's chest and under his arms. Butch had never heard of such a cure for pneumonia, but with time the pain in his chest began to subside. Breathing became easier.

In the dim light of the lantern he could see that he was not in a cabin, but a shack made of rough sawn boards. The walls were not very tight when it came to keeping out the cold north. The lamp flickered from the movement of air through the shack. The wood stove had to be full all the time to keep the room from getting cold. If the fire went out he was certain the temperature would drop below freezing very quickly.

The man said his name was Billy Hancock. He was a young strong man with a thick neck and broad shoulders. He didn't talk much. Butch didn't feel much up to talking either, so the two got along just fine. As the night passed, Butch wondered why this Hancock man was trying so hard to save a half frozen stranger.

Butch was even more surprised when Hancock said he had raised and trained the buckskin gelding Butch had been riding, but that it had been stolen from him the previous spring. Butch wondered why the man had brought him in out of the cold, certainly thinking Butch was the man who had stolen his horse.

"Bought him from an Indian," Butch said, "and that's the absolute truth."

"I believe you," Hancock said, a simple sincerity in his voice that left no doubt but that he believed the frozen stranger.

Looking around the inside of the dimly lighted shack left no doubt in Butch's mind about how poor the Hancocks were. The cupboards were nothing more than upright apple boxes. The dishes consisted of tin plates and cups. There was no glass in the windows, just oil cloth. The children slept in an old wagon box resting on blocks of wood. The door had no door knob, just a wire latch.

Butch's observations were confirmed when Mrs. Hancock got up to fix breakfast. The fare consisted of fried corn cakes and salt pork, nothing more, not even coffee. There was no butter, syrup or honey for the corn cakes. When Butch asked for a glass of milk to wash down his food, all she could give him was cold water.

Mr. Hancock said the cow had died a month earlier, and that as soon as he could find time to go mavericking he planned to get another. He had worked in the mines for a while and was trying to homestead some land to get a start as a farmer.

Mrs. Hancock was a thin tired woman. Butch guessed she was younger than she looked. The frontier life, along with bearing children, had taken a hard toll on her. Watching the Hancocks in their seemingly hopeless poverty made Butch feel glad he was an outlaw.

As Mr. Hancock had been eager to care for Butch during the night, Mrs. Hancock was now eager to please at breakfast. Her first name was Myrtle. She was a thin woman with pale, white skin. An army blanket was draped around her frail shoulders to shield her against the cold air pushing through the many cracks in the walls. She apologized for not having coffee, sugar, syrup and butter. Every time Butch finished a corn cake, or a piece of pork, she was quick to place another on his plate. When he told them his name was George Parker they appeared to believe him.

While the adults were eating, the children finally woke up and crawled out of their wagon box. The boy, Jimmy, was six or seven, and the girl, Loretta, appeared to be about five. Both of them were as friendly as their parents and didn't waste any time crowding around Butch.

"Do you believe in Santa Claus?" Jimmy asked.

Butch began to laugh. The children had caught him by surprise. He was so used to handling questions about bandits, outlaws and Butch Cassidy, that he hadn't been ready for anything like this. Of course, it was December, just before Christmas, time for children to start thinking about Santa. He remembered his own childhood in Circle Valley and how excited the children had been before Christmas.

"Sure, I believe in Santa," Butch said. He leaned forward, placing one of the children on each knee.

"Do you want me to let you in on a little secret?" he asked. Their eyes were wide with excitement and they nodded their heads up and down.

"I've been to the North Pole," Butch whispered.

"You have not," Jimmy challenged.

"You saw how frozen I was when your Pa brought me in last night," Butch explained. "Traveling from the North Pole does that to a man."

"Did you see Santa?" Loretta asked, her blue eyes bright with excitement.

"Yes, I did." Butch said. "And I saw his workshop and all the toys he is making."

"Did he get our letter?" Jimmy asked. "We mailed it from Lander about two weeks ago." Butch looked at the parents. Both looked surprised.

"There were so many letters," Butch said, "I'm not sure if I saw yours, or not. What did it say?"

"We asked for new boots for Ma so she wouldn't have to borrow Pa's when she goes to the outhouse," Loretta said.

"I asked for a new saddle, and a doll for Loretta," Jimmy said.

"I asked for an orange," Loretta added. "I've never tasted one before. Have you?"

Butch looked at the parents. Neither one of them looked very happy. It was obvious they were too poor to buy the things the children were asking for.

"Santa said he got more letters than usual this year," Butch said, his voice very serious. "He was worried that he might not have enough presents to give all the boys and girls everything they ask for."

"We never get everything we ask for," Jimmy said. "Last year we didn't get anything we wanted. That's why I wrote directly to Santa this year."

Billy Hancock didn't want to hear any more. He put on his coat and went outside to do the chores. Myrtle started cleaning up the breakfast dishes. Butch was surprised that even after a filling breakfast he still felt very weak. The cold had drained his strength. He needed time to recover.

He spent the remainder of the day in the shack. Some of the time he slept. When the children were beside him he told them about his own boyhood, and his brothers and sisters. Talking about his childhood made him homesick, but the children were so eager to hear what he had to say that he continued. Myrtle seemed to enjoy the children finding someone else to pester with their incessant chatter and questions. Butch liked the children.

Butch spent another day with the Hancocks before announcing it was time for him to leave. When they refused to accept payment for taking care of him, he insisted they take a $20 gold piece for the stolen horse. Billy agreed to do that. He said he would use it to buy seed for the spring planting. He thanked God that Butch had come along with the $20. Now there would be a summer crop. If the weather cooperated they could now get through another year.

Two days later, after borrowing another horse and a wagon at a nearby ranch, Butch drove up to the hitching post behind the general store in Lander. He had entered town through a back alley, not wanting to drive down the main street. With so many warrants out for his arrest, the fewer people who saw him the better, especially in Lander where so many knew what he looked like.

He knew the store owner, Gus Sweeny, wouldn't turn him in. Butch was a frequent customer at the store, always paying with gold. Sweeny wasn't about to ruin a relationship with one of his best customers, regardless of whether or not the man was wanted by the law.

The first thing Butch picked out was a sweater for Myrtle. Then a pair of boots. He asked the merchant to wrap them up. Then he picked out a saddle for Jimmy, a doll for Loretta, and a new coat for Billy. He asked Sweeney to throw in a ten pound bag of sugar, some butter, honey, coffee, a blue and white checkered table cloth, and four big oranges from California. After paying Sweeny and having the merchant wrap the doll too, Butch threw everything in the back of the wagon and slipped quietly out of town, heading straight for the Hancock place.

Butch didn't think anyone had seen him enter or leave town, but just before reaching the turnoff to the Hancock's farm he noticed two men riding parallel to him on a nearby ridge. As he watched them, not only did they seem to be watching him too, but they were also pacing their horses in order to remain parallel with him.

Butch's first thought was to stop the wagon, unhitch and saddle the buckskin, and head for the woods as fast as the horse could run. It occurred to him that that might be a foolish thing to do in the event the two riders didn't mean any harm.

He decided to do nothing, at least not until he was absolutely sure the two riders were following him. When he reached the turnoff to the Hancock place he left the main road, acting like he hadn't noticed the two riders.

For a minute they disappeared behind the ridge, Butch hoping he would never see them again. But as he approached the shack he saw the riders again, this time much closer. They came over the top of a hill directly above him and were riding straight for the shack too. There was no way he could outrun them in the wagon, and there was not enough time to saddle the buckskin. He certainly didn't want to have a shootout with the two strangers.

Even though Butch had been an outlaw for some time and had stolen countless numbers of cattle and horses, and robbed banks and trains, he still had not killed a man, and had no stomach for it. It was one thing to take money from the rich and powerful, but shedding a man's blood was something he wanted no part of.

Destiny had seemed to bring him to the Hancocks. He wondered why. It didn't seem right that they had saved his life just so he could go back to prison. Perhaps his life had been spared so he could provide a happy Christmas for the Hancocks.

At any rate he intended to finish what he had set out to do. He pulled the team to a halt in front of the shack.

Myrtle was the first one out the door, the old army blanket wrapped around her shoulders.

"Merry Christmas," Butch said, tossing her the sweater and boots, still wrapped in clean white paper. Soon the children were scampering from the house, and Billy was walking up from the barn. Butch handed down all the presents.

"You'll never believe this," Butch explained, "but I ran into Santa up the road a bit. And boy was he mad."

"Why?" Loretta asked, concern on her little face.

"The runner on his sleigh was broken," Butch explained, a serious expression on his face. He noticed the two men he had seen on the hill were directly in front of the team. He ignored them.

"He said the broken runner was going to make him late getting around to all the boys and girls on Christmas Eve," Butch continued, "so he asked me to help him out by running some things over to the Hancocks. Told him I'd be glad to help out."

By this time Loretta had torn the wrapping off the doll and was hugging it tightly. Jimmy had thrown his new saddle over the hitching rail and was climbing aboard.

"You didn't need to do all this," Billy said as Butch handed him the sugar, oranges and other food stuffs.

"You saved my life," Butch said, simply.

"You didn't have to do all this for us," Myrtle said.

"This is my way of saying thanks," Butch said, pulling the team to the right so they could pull the wagon alongside the two strangers. He noticed one of them was wearing a badge on his coat.

"Sorry, Santa didn't give me anything for you two," Butch said in a happy voice, pulling the horses to a halt.

"Maybe he did," the marshall said, his voice deep and strong. "All I want for Christmas is to catch an outlaw. I have a warrant for the arrest of Butch Cassidy."

Butch was surprised the marshall hadn't reached for his gun. The man beside him hadn't either. Butch guessed he could probably beat them both, if he went for his gun first. He had checked the cylinder before going into town for the presents. He knew his gun was ready to fire. Even if he wasn't fast enough to get both of them, it would be better to die than return to prison.

"Should have brought a bigger posse, if its Butch Cassidy you're after," Butch said, stalling for time, still not sure what he was going to do.

"Marshall, would you like to come in for a cup of coffee," Myrtle called from the doorway to the shack.

"Thank you, in a minute," the marshall said, not taking his eyes off Butch.

Billy walked up to the marshall. Loretta was in her father's arms, holding tightly to her new doll.

"Marshall," Billy said, "I think I know where Cassidy's camp is. I'll take you there after we have a cup of coffee." It was obvious to Butch that Billy and the marshall already knew each other. Did Billy know the real identity of George Parker?

"Do you know where Cassidy's camp is?" the marshall asked, still looking at Butch.

"I sure do," Butch said. "Right where Billy intends to take you. But I can't go with you. If I don't get this wagon home by dark, there's a farmer up the road who will swear out a warrant for my arrest."

Butch tapped the reins on the horses' backs. They started forward, pulling the wagon in a wide circle then back up the lane towards the main road.

"Hope you get your man," Butch called back to the marshall.

"Me too," the officer responded.

"Coffee's ready," Myrtle called from the shack.

According to Kathryn H. Kidd, she was born, she's lived, and she hasn't died yet. Somewhere along the line she decided writing was an easy way to make a living, so that's what she does. Her books include Paradise Vue, The Alphabet Year, *and a children's book,* The Innkeeper's Daughter. *Also in the quest to make a living, she is working on a science fiction trilogy with Orson Scott Card. She lives in a suburb of Washington, D.C., with her husband extraordinaire, Clark L. Kidd. On Sundays she masquerades as a spiritual living teacher in the Sterling North Ward Relief Society.*

VOUCHER AND THE CHRISTMAS WARS

by Kathryn H. Kidd

It took the new church budget system to finally end the Christmas Wars in the Old Mountain Home Ward, allowing Voucher Christiansen to achieve the immortality she had long felt she deserved.

There are many ways to achieve immortality. You can bat .400, for example, or invent a better mousetrap, or find a cure for the common cold. Voucher didn't have those talents in her genes. She had grown up on a Payson onion farm, but she aspired to greatness. Maybe she could have invented a better onion ring, but Voucher set her sights higher than that.

Voucher wasn't the name on her birth certificate, of course. Her Christian name was Ethel. She got the name Voucher because she couldn't make a grocery list without bearing her testimony about it. Everything Voucher saw or did was testimony fodder. "I bear you my testimony that Formula 409 works better than any of that Amway stuff," she'd say to a disbeliever. "409 picks up stuff that Amway can't touch." After a few hundred testimonies from Ethel, none of them borne on Fast Sunday when they could have done anybody any earthly good, one tired soul told her, "You'll vouch for anything, won't you?" Thus the name Voucher was born.

Voucher defied family tradition by going on a mission. She ended up in Sweden, where she met and later married a sturdy Swedish student who also had aspirations that were greater than his pocketbook. The two of them moved to Mecca—Salt Lake City,

Utah—where Erik started his own business and Voucher popped out the requisite 3.7 children.

Life plodded onward, and after a progression of business successes the Christiansens were finally able to buy a house in the Old Mountain Home Ward. The Old Mountain Home Ward was and is a status symbol of sorts, boasting a membership list that reads like a Who's Who of Salt Lake City. We always like to brag on the famous people who live in the ward, even the ones who spend more Sundays floating in Bear Lake than snoozing through Sunday School. They're good-hearted folks; they just have their priorities skewered up. But they're still part of our congregation, and one of these days they'll get tired of Bear Lake and come back to church.

We brag about a lot of our members, but nobody ever bragged about Erik and Voucher. The Christiansens were guppies in the Amazon River of our ward, constantly battling piranhas on their upstream swim. They wanted to prove they belonged. Eventually Voucher found the means to do it.

The highlight of the Old Mountain Home Ward social season was the annual Christmas party—an event that was more exclusive than any governor's ball because only people who lived in our tiny geographical area could attend. Back in the old days, when every family contributed money to finance their own ward's activities, our ward Christmas party cost enough to send the entire population of a third-world nation through Harvard. Our Christmas party wasn't always as big as the one Voucher inherited, I'm sure. The first Christmas party, long before I was born, probably cost a reasonable amount of money. Whoever was called to be in charge of the party probably hung crepe paper streamers, red and green ones to match the season. The refreshments may have been hot chocolate or some sort of mystery punch—cider without the kick, or eggnog without the brandy. That first chairman may have even sacrificed decorations and food in favor of a program that inspired ward members to remember the true spirit of Christmas.

Next year, of course, the chairman would have wanted to make the party just a little more memorable. Maybe she hung balloons in addition to the red and green streamers, or maybe she served eggnog *and* cider instead of just either-or. She couldn't do much with the program, of course. Much to the dismay of Christmas program organizers everywhere, there are only so many things you can do to illustrate the true spirit of Christmas. Her only opportunities for creativity had to come from the decorations and the desserts.

By the third year, however, the snowball would have been rolling. The program became almost an afterthought, assigned to a lesser ward member so the party chairman could concentrate on the *real* concerns of theme and decorations and refreshments. Each party was bigger and better than the one before. It *had* to be. The entire reputation of the party chairman was riding on the line, and the only way one chairman could succeed was to demolish the memory of the Christmas party that had preceded hers. Thus the Christmas Wars began.

The year I was party chairman, I outdid all the parties of Christmas Past. I trucked in live reindeer, who left homemade souvenirs all over the gym. I was a hero for a solid year, as ward members debated the pungency of reindeer doody and pointed out hoofmarks in the basketball court. Then the next party chairman flew in Santa on a hot air balloon, and the reindeer were immediately forgotten.

The year before Voucher, the theme had been "A Candy-Coated Christmas." The chairman, who ran a covert catering service out of her home, made a village of gingerbread houses that were tall enough for children to walk through. Before the party was over, the children spontaneously attacked the village like army ants, devouring the gingerbread walls as well as the candy decorations. The party chairman, who had planned to use the gingerbread village as the focal point for all her illegal holiday jobs, threatened to sue the ward over that one.

After the gingerbread fiasco, the ward was painted into a corner. The next year's party had to be bigger and it had to be better, but the gingerbread village was virtually untoppable. So when Voucher actually volunteered to chair the ward Christmas party, Bishop Hensel must have done handsprings in his office. He must have thought Voucher was being noble; maybe he thought she was an answer to prayer. What probably didn't dawn on him was the bald truth that being chairman of the Christmas party was as big a status symbol as a person could achieve in the Old Mountain Home Ward. Voucher had waited patiently for the bishopric to *give* her this honor; when they didn't, she took matters into her own hands.

Voucher and Erik had scads of money, although she never bore her testimony about where they got it. They just *had* it, and that was the important thing. Even though our Christmas party budget would have wiped out the national debt, a good Christmas party—a *proper* Christmas party—was bound to cost far more than whatever the bishop set aside for it. Voucher had the funds, as well as the inclination, to supplement where the ward budget left off.

Voucher had no idea when she volunteered to host the Christmas party that the budget system would change and that, for better or worse, this was the Christmas party that ward members would remember for time immemorial. Volunteering to do the party in 1989 was serendipity on her part—the same sort of serendipity that seemed to drape itself over Voucher like a blanket of Utah smog. But even without that knowledge, Voucher planned a party that no one would ever forget. She started dropping little hints about it in April, piquing the interest of people who thought they might have to top her *next* year. Some of the hints were self-explanatory—"sleighs", for example, and "trees, zillions of trees." But then somebody heard her say "pillar of salt," and that opened a bird's nest of theories with a different set of feathers.

Brother Call put it all together one Sunday, during a Priesthood lesson on the law of consecration. "Sodom and Gomorrah," he whispered in wonderment and delight. "We're gonna have an X-rated Christmas party." The men brightened, totally forgetting the law of consecration as they contemplated more temporal pleasures. Brother Call's Sunday revelation guaranteed that the Christmas party would have even a higher percentage of male attendees than it usually did.

Voucher only fueled the fire. One day she mumbled, "I bear you my testimony we'll have a *lot* of salt," and the people in earshot could only interpret her emphasis on the quantity to be a confirming pun that the Sodom and Gomorrah theory was right on the money.

Once the wheels were in motion, Voucher could no more be stopped than a dropped egg could be prevented from splattering all over the kitchen floor. Maybe nobody could stop the egg from breaking, but the bishop could—and did—change the crash site. Like it or not, I was his chosen target.

Bishop Hensel called me in to his office on a Thursday night in the middle of October, when I was long since finished with my Christmas shopping and was planning for Valentine's Day.

"DeNeen," he said, "I've heard rumors that the ward budgets are going to be handled differently next year, and we may have to start scaling things down. If that's true, I want to go out with a bang. Since Christmas is the last big event of the year, I want the Christmas party to be the biggest extravaganza anyone's ever seen. Voucher's doing the decorations and the refreshments—I'm sure you know that. But nobody ever does much with the program. They stick us all in the chapel for an hour, squashed next to each other like smoked oysters in a can while some high school's acapulco choir sings 'Jingle Bells' without a piano."

"A capella choirs *never* use pianos. If they did, they wouldn't be a capella choirs."

The bishop only shrugged. "It's a stupid idea. Christmas songs weren't *meant* to be sung without a piano. Those programs bore me stiff—and I'm not the only one. *Watch* the crowd. *Nobody* cares about the program; everyone squirms in their seats till the choir shuts up and we can eat. It's a royal waste of time. This year, I want the *program* to be the climax. I want a Christmas play that everyone will talk about for years to come." He leaned forward in his chair, resting his pot belly on the rim of his desk. "What do you think?"

What I *thought* was that Voucher wouldn't sit still while anyone else stole her thunder, but I didn't put that idea into words. Whenever the bishop looked that excited, he had his mind set on something. He was hatching a plot somewhere, and I was right in the middle of it.

When I didn't open my mouth, Bishop Hensel opened it for me. "We want you to put on the Christmas play. You're a writer; we know you'll write a dynamite script."

"I'm not a writer," I said.

"You do the Sacrament Meeting program on Sundays."

"*That's* not writing. That's *typing*. I *type* the Sacrament Meeting program."

"Writing, typing—same difference. We don't want a long play, DeNeen: Thirty minutes or so should do it."

The bishop was a man who knew how to keep people from saying no—he never asked them to do anything. He told them what he wanted and when he wanted it. Then, when their mouths were open to say, "Not in *this* lifetime," he'd add something along the lines of, "I was so inspired when your little Hortense played 'Having My Baby' on the violin during Sacrament Meeting last week. Your child has a genuine talent, and I was so proud for both of you." Hortense's proud parent would think, By golly—Hortense *was* good, and the bishop's a perceptive man to notice. Of *course* I'll climb Mt. Everest in my underwear, if that's what he wants me to do.

Sure enough, just as I opened my mouth to say no way to the Christmas play he chimed in, "I do believe you're losing weight, DeNeen. You're looking awfully good."

I'd gained fifteen pounds in the past six weeks, but I *had* bought some new make-up to paint hollows into my cheeks. He really *was* a perceptive man.

I sighed. "Where are we going to *have* this play?"

"On the stage, of course. That's what the stage is for. You'll have to work around Voucher's decorating crew as you do your rehearsals, but that shouldn't be a major obstacle. You'll also have to work around the fire department. They're still fine-tuning the sprinkling system in the cultural hall, but everything will be just fine by the time you have your Christmas play."

The Old Mountain Home Ward had a brand-new sprinkling system courtesy of Brother Hagers, who was a pyrophobe if I'd ever seen one. The system was supposed to be top-of-the-line, but it had such a nervous disposition that people secretly thought it was a K-Mart blue-light special. The fire department spent so much time adjusting those sprinklers that the full-time missionaries had their hooks in two of the fire crew.

I wasn't worried about the fire department, but Voucher was another matter. If Bishop Hensel thought Voucher would let my play be the climax of the Christmas party rather than her food and the decorations, there must be two Voucher Christiansens. But that was the bishop's problem. I went home and fretted about my play, trying not to wonder whether I'd be working with the Voucher Christiansen the bishop knew or her evil twin, who customarily attended the Old Mountain Home Ward meetings in her place.

I had never written a play before, mind you, and I didn't think it would be easy. But the bishop was right—anybody could write a play. It just took a little time, and a pencil with a good eraser. To my surprise, the play practically wrote itself.

I spent a week fine-tuning the script. I wrote the story of Christmas from a manger scene's point of view, with all the porcelain pieces jockeying for position underneath the Christmas tree. I'd been in the ward long enough that I did the casting as I wrote the script, infusing the personalities of my chosen actors into the lines that the cows and shepherds and camels would speak. The Virgin Mary had to be played by none other than Annabella Keats. Annabella was a tiny girl with a heart-shaped face and the voice of an angel. Nobody looked more like a Virgin Mary than she.

Barry Lyman, the high school football star, would make a sturdy Joseph. And I had a ten-month-old son who was just perfect to play the Baby Jesus.

But the star of the show was none of these. The name of the play was "Pedro, the Reluctant Wise Man." Pedro, the title character, would be the focus of all our attention.

The Old Mountain Home Ward sported the perfect Pedro. He was Sheldon Eliason, the fattest man who had ever lived in our ward boundaries. Sheldon was so fat he had to lose weight to play Santa Claus. He wore so many rolls of blubber that he once lost a taco chip for several days, finding it between hunks of flesh only when he felt his skin getting tender and raw. Life had played a cruel trick on Sheldon, who exercised relentlessly and still looked like the statue of Bob's Big Boy outside the JB's Family Restaurant. But the same trick of fate that turned Sheldon into a giant tub of flab had also given him a voice that was so resonant it could raise goosebumps on a bowling ball.

"Pedro?" he asked, when I passed out the scripts at our first cast meeting. "I thought the wise men were named Shadrach, Meshach, and Balthazar."

"Not *our* wise men," I said. "I want ours to represent wise men from all over the world. Ours are Pedro, Olaf, and Chun-King."

John Ushida, who suddenly realized he had not been chosen to play Olaf, rolled his eyes.

"And while we're talking about our names, that brings up another point. When we're all together, I want everyone to call everyone else by their play names. Don't say Annabella—say the Virgin Mary. That way she'll feel like she *is* the Virgin Mary, and she'll do an even better job the night of the play."

"What about the animals?" asked Joseph. "What about the shepherds? We have *duplicate* shepherds and animals."

"Call 'em by their real names and *then* their stage names," the Herald Angel suggested. "You can have Kimberly Camel and F.W. Shepherd and Scooter Sheep."

The cast nodded agreeably. The Herald Angel was already earning his wings.

"Sister Albacore," called the Virgin Mary. "Sister *Albacore*. Your little boy needs you."

"That's not my little boy," I said. "That's the Baby Jesus."

"The Baby *Jesus*?" said Sally Cow. "Isn't Frankie a little *old* to be a Baby Jesus?"

"He's awfully *ugly* to be a Baby Jesus," said Olaf under his breath, and I decided to keep my eye on him. He may have been a bad choice for a Wise Man.

"He's awfully *squirmy* to be a Baby Jesus—that's for sure," said the Virgin Mary. "He's over in the flower box eating artificial dirt."

I retrieved Frankie and swabbed wood chips from his mouth with a Kleenex. It wasn't *my* fault he had started crawling early. The Baby Jesus took after his father—*not* his mother, who would have been sitting placidly in her swaddling clothes until the script called for her appearance.

I couldn't organize the rehearsal and watch a baby too. Fortunately, there was the Virgin Mary. I put the Baby Jesus in her arms and said, "Here you go. He's your little boy for the play. Why don't you get to know him?"

"But I don't *like* children, Sister Albacore. Children don't like *me*."

"Nonsense," I said, just as Frankie started to whimper. It was true; there was an instant personality conflict between the Baby Jesus and the Virgin Mary.

"I'll take the Baby Jesus," said Joseph, who was the oldest of eight children. "Kids like me fine."

I passed off Frankie to Joseph and explained the premise of the play. The manger figurines, sitting under a family Christmas tree, would get all caught up in the trappings of Christmas. The Virgin Mary would want to be placed in the forefront; the Herald Angel would naturally want a Christmas tree light behind him to make him stand out from the rest. Cows and sheep would refuse to stand next to each other, immortalizing the feud between sheepmen and cattle ranchers that still raised tempers in parts of Utah. Every porcelain figurine would have his own agenda and own complaints, and I'd written a great score of songs to highlight the various conflicts. Only after a single Wise Man, Pedro, refused to participate in the manger scene at all would the rest of the figurines remember what Christmas was all about. Then they'd all join together in a rousing song and dance, designed to promote the true spirit of Christmas and warm the hearts of young and old ward members alike.

It was an extraordinary Christmas play, and I was justly proud of it. I let everyone study their scripts for a few minutes to get a feel for what was going on. I leaned back in my chair, waiting for compliments, but the only comment came from Pedro—and his observation wasn't a compliment at all.

"What's this about a can-can?" he asked, looking balefully up from the pages of his script.

"We're supposed to do a *can-can?*" Chun-King looked appalled. He had probably never danced a step in his life, but I didn't need professional dancers. He'd look fine in the chorus line.

"It's right here on page fourteen," Pedro said. "DeNeen, why do you have a can-can in a Christmas play?"

"If you'll read the script, you'll see the can-can is completely appropriate," I said. "The song you're singing when you dance it is called 'Can't-Can't'. Let me sing a few bars. Hit the piano, will you Gracie?"

"Sorry, DeNeen. I can't play that fast. Not without practice."

"Then I'll have to do it without the piano." I cleared my throat and did the first verse:

> *"CAN'T have a manger scene with two wise men you*
> *CAN'T have two wise men, you can't—*
> *(Two wise men doesn't cut it!)*
> *CAN'T have a manger scene with two wise men you*
> *CAN'T—that's not a manger scene!*
> *(No, not a scene at all!)"*

"You see," I said when I finished, "It *has* to be a can-can. With a little practice, you'll do just fine."

"I can't," said Pedro, and Chun-King chimed in with, "He can't-can't." "I can't lift my legs that far off the ground. People my size just don't *move* that fast. Can't we do a conga line instead?"

"Take my word for it. People are going to love you."

But Pedro lumbered to his feet and handed me his copy of the script. "I wish I could, but it's impossible," he said. "You'll have to find another Pedro."

The Herald Angel, sitting in the corner, raised his hand. I tried to ignore him—we couldn't even have a play without Pedro, and his departure was far more important than any question the Herald Angel could ask—but the Virgin Mary said, "Sister Albacore. Sister *Albacore*. We have a hand raised over here."

I sighed. "Yes, Herald Angel?"

"Why don't you have the rest of the cast can-can *around* Pedro? They're trying to convince him to stay in the manger scene anyway. He shouldn't even be *part* of the dance."

Pedro brightened. He reached out and took his script right from my fingers. The shepherds cheered.

"You're right," I said, vastly relieved. I noted to myself that the Herald Angel had been aptly chosen.

The cast members were so intent on studying their roles that they left the first read-through without even complimenting me on the script. That was no problem; I'd earn my kudos later, when the cast members were taking their bows after the play. Maybe they'd even chip in for flowers for the writer-director. *That* would be nice. I hoped the flowers would be roses—long-stemmed ones, tied with a ribbon to match the petals. I made a mental note to write an acceptance speech, just in case the cast members surprised me that way.

But standing between me and unmitigated triumph were twenty-three cast members, a costumer, set builders, and a whole cartload of behind-the-scenes people—all of whom had to perform their roles before I could receive my reward. There was also Voucher Christiansen. Her specter hung over "Pedro, the Reluctant Wise Man" like the Ghost of Christmas Future.

Whenever the phone rang after that first rehearsal, I expected to hear Voucher's voice on the line. I left on the answering machine and screened the calls, but none of the callers bore that Utah twang mixed with Swedish accent that distinguished Voucher from the rest of humanity.

Voucher was just about the *only* person who didn't call. The people who *did* call me were the cast members, and the cast members' mothers or spouses, and my costumer, and everyone else who was involved in the play, none of whom had caught the vision of "Pedro, the Reluctant Wise Man." Every member of the cast and crew seemed to need individual reassurance that the play was as terrific as I knew it was.

The first protest came from the costumer, who balked when I told her the cast members needed to be dressed in white.

"White is ugly," she said. "It's drab. It's plain."

"White is the color of porcelain," I explained. "These are porcelain figurines."

Camille sniffed. "If we make them *ceramic* figurines, we can put color in the costumes."

"I don't *want* color in the costumes. If you put color in 'em, how will people know they're figurines and not people?"

"You can mention it in the script."

Honestly. The people around me had no artistic sense. As patiently as I could I said, "Camille, if the costumes are white, everyone will *know* the figures are porcelain. I won't *have* to put it in the script."

No sooner had I hung up the phone than it rang again. It was Annabella's mother, complaining because Annabella's solo was being done to the tune of "Proud Mary."

"It's a pun," I explained. "The Virgin Mary's problem is going to be pride. She wants to sit at the front of the manger scene where everyone can see her. 'Proud Mary' is the perfect tune to use."

"But it's not a *Christmas* song."

"Neither is 'Ahab the Arab,' and we're using *that*."

Annabella's mother sighed. "Who *wrote* this play, DeNeen?"

"I did."

"Oh," she said, and she didn't protest anymore.

But other people did protest. The sheep didn't like the donkey chorus of "sheeparestupidanimals" that underscored their tap dance routine. It was the bass line—it provided the beat for the whole arrangement—but the sheep wanted the donkey chorus out. The donkeys, on the other hand, didn't think there should be any roosters or pigs in the play. They especially didn't like the part where Krista Cow jumped over a moon-shaped Christmas tree ornament as her way of standing out from the other manger scene characters.

Naysayers were everywhere. I had no idea how artistically ignorant the members of the Old Mountain Home Ward were until I wrote that Christmas play. To a person, my cast members were just as prideful and petty as the porcelain figurines they had been chosen to represent.

Just when I started thinking that things couldn't *get* any worse, things deteriorated. Voucher heard about the Christmas play, and World War III erupted in the night sky over the Old Mountain Home Ward.

The missile Voucher fired came in the shape of Voucher herself. I was improvising the dance steps for the Chicken Ballet one evening when she knocked hard enough on my door to dislodge my Thanksgiving wreath. She looked furious when I opened the door, but she opened her eyes and dropped her jaw to stare at me instead.

"What in the *world* are you wearing?"

"You can recognize all of it, Voucher. That's a rubber glove filled with water under my chin—those are my wattles. The feather dusters are my wings, and the flippers on my feet are the closest I can get to webbing. I'm *obviously* a chicken."

"Chickens don't have webbed feet. It's *ducks* that have webbed feet."

"Well—they'd dance the same. I'm working out the choreography for the Chicken Ballet, and I wanted to do it in character."

"Since when are you a choreographer? Since when do you have any interest *whatsoever* in the performing arts?"

"Since the bishop called me to do the Christmas play—*that's* when." I straightened the Thanksgiving wreath on my door and sighed. "You might as well come in, Voucher. Have a seat."

Voucher sat, and I stood over her. Voucher stood up again.

"Have a seat, Voucher," I said.

"Not until you do."

"I can't sit down—not with this chicken tail." I turned around and showed her my fanny. Before I could stop her, she pulled the feathers off my rear.

"*Now* you can sit down."

I sat down, and Voucher followed suit. She was as mad as I'd ever seen her, though, and if her body was sitting on my divan, her voice was standing on tiptoe.

"What. Have. You. Done. With. My. Christmas. Party?"

"Not a thing the bishop didn't call me to do. He wanted me to do the program; he wanted it to be a play. I'm only following his orders."

"And where are you having this play?"

"On the stage, of course. That's where we always have plays."

"Not *this* play. It would *ruin* my Christmas decorations."

"Are you using the stage?" I asked.

"Of course not. That stage is a white elephant. I'm going to camouflage the curtains with a winter scene. Nobody will know the stage is there."

"Then if you aren't using the stage, there isn't a problem. Make your camouflage portable so we can open the curtains for the play. When the play's over, we'll shut the curtains and put your camouflage back in place."

"You. Don't. Understand. I've been planning this party for a whole *year*, and the *last* thing I want is for people to drag chairs into my cultural hall."

I felt a tiny pinprick of sympathy for Voucher. After all, I'd been chairman of the ward Christmas party myself. It was a tradition in our ward (and in the Old Mountain Home Ward, traditions were just about etched in stone) that the Christmas program consisted of some insignificant performance designed to bore the congregation almost to insentience. Then the chairman of the Christmas party would usher the stuporous ward members into a wonderland of her own creation, full of glorious decorations, where a sumptuous feast would jolt them back to life. The idea that all Voucher's efforts were going to decorate an auditorium to house somebody *else's* achievement was humiliating.

By this point, however, I'd spent a lot of time in my own preparations. As much as I might sympathize with Voucher, I had a terrific play on my hands. I'd written the play, I was directing the play, and I was even choreographing the play. My chicken suit bore silent testimony to the work I'd put into "Pedro, the Reluctant Wise Man." I was prepared to knock the tennis shoes right off old Sister Vigory, who always wore Reeboks because she fell down in anything else.

"Well?" Voucher demanded, and I realized she had proposed a suggestion while my mind wandered. "You *can* use the Primary room for your play—can't you?"

"The Primary room doesn't *hold* everybody, Voucher. If we have the play there, we'll have to do it three or four times for everyone to see it."

"That. Can. Be. Arranged."

We were clearly at an impasse. I stalked over to my closet, walking as haughtily as my flippers would allow, and found a cape to drape over my chicken suit.

"Where are you going?" Voucher asked suspiciously.

"It's Tuesday night. The bishop's in his office. Let's go talk to him."

"You're going *out* dressed like a *chicken*?"

I knew what Voucher was after. She wanted to shame me into wearing civilian clothes over to meetinghouse. But this was war, and my chicken suit was important ammunition against Voucher. "Are you embarrassed to be seen with a chicken?" I demanded. "I'm not embarrassed to be seen with *you*. Let's go."

Voucher followed me. She went in her own car, driving two blocks behind me as if my chickenhood were contagious. When we got to the meetinghouse, she wouldn't even walk to the bishop's office with me. She drove around to the rear parking lot instead of going through the front door.

We reached the bishop's office simultaneously, and Voucher let out a horrendous cackling sound to announce our arrival. There were no witnesses; Bishop Hensel couldn't help but think the person in the chicken suit was the one doing the cackling. Score one point for Voucher.

The bishop opened his door in record time. He bit his lower lip when he saw me and quickly fixed his gaze firmly on Voucher. After a brief hesitation he released his lower lip from his teeth and said, "Voucher! DeNeen! It's wonderful to see you."

Voucher scowled. I smiled cheerfully to offer the bishop a contrast, but he didn't look in my direction. He ushered the rest of the bishopric out a side door and led us into the sanctum of his office. Voucher didn't give him time to ask why we were there.

"My. Christmas. Party. Is. Ruined."

Bishop Hensel widened his eyes in practiced innocence. "I can't imagine how it *could* be, Voucher. From what I hear, you're going to put on the best Christmas party our ward's ever seen."

Voucher preened. You'd have sworn she was the one wearing the feathers. "Well, it *would* have been," she conceded, sobering. "That play is going to ruin everything."

Bishop Hensel's jowls quivered and his brows knitted in concentration. "That's sad," he said. "That's not what I wanted at all."

"It isn't?"

Bishop Hensel shook his head. His jowls followed his chin to and fro. "Of course not. You're the chairman of the Christmas party, Voucher. That play is going to be a jewel in your crown."

"*My* crown?" Voucher asked.

"*Her* crown?" I asked, and the bishop gave me a quick warning look before he bit his lip and looked toward Voucher again. That was it. Bishop Hensel was reeling Voucher in like a trout hooked to a lure. I was not to throw pebbles in the water.

"It *is* a jewel in your crown, Voucher. Picture this. You lead everyone into the darkened cultural hall and sit 'em in front of the stage. The play begins. DeNeen's play is the appetizer for your Christmas party, Voucher. Once you get 'em all excited about the play, they'll be in a frenzy to see what you've done to top it."

Voucher risked a tentative smile.

Bishop Hensel raised his hands to shoulder level, spreading his fingers to punctuate his words. "I can see it now. The play ends and the curtain falls. Everyone sits, transfixed with anticipation, waiting for you to give the signal to turn up the lights. Then you raise your hand, and the lights go up. *It's a miracle!*"

Voucher's smile widened into a grin. Avarice glistened in her eyes. "I'll *do* it!" she said. "I'll bear you my testimony we're going to have the best Christmas party the Old Mountain Home Ward *ever* saw!"

The bishop smiled cheerfully at Voucher and then extended his smile to me. "By the way, DeNeen," he said, staring at my chicken suit, "you have a rubber glove strapped to your chin."

"She's creating a ballet for chickens," Voucher said. "It's part of the Christmas play."

"Glad to hear it," said Bishop Hensel, and he ushered us both outside together.

Voucher strutted off, happy as I'd ever seen her. The bishop was a master at human relations, and I'd just seen the performance of a lifetime. I'd have no more trouble from Voucher.

But I wasn't as happy as Voucher was. Standing alone in my chicken suit, I realized that "Pedro, the Reluctant Wise Man" *would* be a jewel in Voucher's crown—not just mine. There was nothing I could do about it, either: The harder I worked, the better she was going to look.

As I realized this, I learned a nasty thing about myself: *I didn't want to share the glory.* My play was the greatest thing the Old Mountain Home Ward had ever seen, and I wanted every scrap of the credit for myself.

Sighing, I went home and got back to work on the Chicken Ballet. Bishop Hensel had defused Voucher's opposition, making me the winner of the first skirmish. But I was in imminent danger of losing the war.

* * *

The more I worked on my play, the more I realized I had a work of art on my hands. "Pedro, the Reluctant Wise Man" wasn't destined to be performed once and then sink into oblivion. Quite the contrary—my play had at least as much potential as any of the Mormon musicals I could name. I forgave Bishop Hensel for telling Voucher my play would be a jewel in her crown. She could *have* the glory—for now. I set my sights on a distant reward. I envisioned a day when "Pedro, the Reluctant Wise Man" would be performed in wards all over the Church. And the author's name, printed on the front of every script that would sell for $2.95 apiece at Deseret Book, would be not Voucher Christiansen, but DeNeen Albacore. I could be as famous as the guy who wrote "Saturday's Warrior"—whoever he was. If Voucher's Christmas party was her shot at immortality, "Pedro, the Reluctant Wise Man" would be mine.

I redoubled my efforts, embellishing the script and adding two more numbers to the play. I brought in an innkeeper (although none of the manger scenes in my collection even *had* innkeepers), so he could sing a great song to the tune of "Ruby, Don't Take Your Love to Town". That was a thigh-slapping highlight of the show, sure to excite the audience.

But the crowning achievement was the new opening I wrote, featuring a flying entrance for the Herald Angel. The play would begin with the porcelain figurines milling around on the stage, murmuring against one another. The Herald Angel would swoop on-stage, singing a song about the joy of Christmas. It was a terrific song, sung to the tune of "Tie a Yellow Ribbon 'Round the Old Oak Tree." I was especially proud of the rousing chorus:

"Oh, Christmas is a happy time for you and me.
There is joy and peace;
There is gaiety.
It is the Christ Child's birthday—that's the centerpiece, you see.
And that's why I like Christmas 'round the old
('Round the) Christmas tree!"

The Herald Angel's song would be ignored by the cast members—all except Pedro, who would stand apart from the other cast members to watch the Herald Angel's entrance. In fact, the Herald Angel's attention would be distracted by the murmuring below. Even he would be drawn into the fray, forgetting the Christmas spirit as he tried to seize the best spot under the tree for himself. When Pedro made his appeal to the manger pieces, he could reprise the Herald Angel's song instead of speaking the lines I had written. That would offer a poignant moment, as the Herald Angel realized even he had forgotten the true meaning of Christmas.

When I showed the changes to the cast, the Herald Angel sighed. "Do I *have* to sing this?"

"You *get* to sing it," I corrected. "Everybody loves 'Tie a Yellow Ribbon.' This is an inspired choice to open the play, don't you think?"

The Herald Angel looked unconvinced. "I already have a solo later on," he said. "Nobody but Pedro has two solos. Maybe we'd better keep the beginning of the play the way you had it."

"Nonsense," I said. "This will grab the crowd's attention. Think what flying did for *Peter Pan*! People are going to love you!"

"I'm acrophobic, DeNeen. I don't think I can sing and fly at the same time. Can't someone *else* do the flying scene?"

"You're the only Herald Angel. It *has* to be you."

The Herald Angel said, "You're the director, DeNeen," with such fervor that I hoped he could sustain the drama on opening night. He was such a good actor. He had no reason to feel so insecure.

But the Herald Angel *did* feel insecure. I realized it was up to me to offer a little friendly encouragement.

"Picture yourself," I said, spreading my fingers for emphasis and hoping I was as convincing as Bishop Hensel. "When the curtain rises, the porcelain figurines will be huddled underneath the Christmas tree—all of them except the Herald Angel. Then, the spotlight turns on you. You fly above them all, with your beautiful white robes and those glorious wings, singing your heart out. I get chills whenever I think about it."

The Herald Angel shook his head. "Mormon angels don't have wings."

"Manger scene angels *do* have wings."

"Manger scene angels are all girls, if you want to get right down to it," he said.

"I've already compromised on that. Our Herald Angel is going to be a man—"

"*That's* a relief, since I was still a man the last time I checked."

"—but you've got to have wings."

The Herald Angel sighed. "If I have to have wings, I hope they'll at least flap. I hate those little wimpy wings that don't *do* anything."

"Take it up with Camille," I said. "She's the costumer. Tell her I said it's okay. You can flap your wings to your heart's content, as long as you remember to sing while you're doing it."

The Herald Angel smiled weakly and got to work on his new solo. The script was perfect, and I had the cast pretty well under control. Even the costumes were coming along fine, although I didn't want to be in Camille's shoes when the Herald Angel demanded flappable wings. Now all I needed to do was ride herd on the set decorator and the electrician, and "Pedro, the Reluctant Wise Man" would be ready to go.

The set decorations were no problem. Virgil Fenton was more than happy to build the set, seeing as how his daughter Krista was our lead cow. He constructed the set to my exact specifications, covering the floor of the stage with cotton batting to simulate snow. He also produced giant Christmas tree limbs to hang over the set, weaving half a billion fuzzy green pipe-cleaners together to form the needles. He created a half dozen giant ornaments to hang down from the Christmas tree branches, too. Each was a work of art, although I believe he spent extra time building the moon-shaped ornament that Krista would leap over during her solo. Then he invented a mechanism that would help Krista do her airborne scene. We were lucky: Krista was pretty small, for a heifer. Virgil would have to find another means to make the Herald Angel fly.

Our electrician was just as cooperative as Virgil, but not nearly as talented. The Old Mountain Home Ward didn't *have* a whole lot of electricians, focusing instead on doctors and lawyers and Assorted Famous Utahns. The play was less than a week away before we learned that Harley Downey, who was a proctologist by day, was a home handyman on weekends. He agreed to do our electrical work, but when I met him on stage after rehearsal one night to show him what we needed, he shook his head mournfully.

"That's hard—really hard," he said. The Herald Angel, who had hung around to inspect the set decorations, nodded in solemn agreement.

"It shouldn't be too much of a challenge," I said. "Most of the lights will be your standard floodlights and spotlights. All we'll have to do is aim them in the right direction and turn them on at the right time.

The only real problem will be putting those giant colored lights on the Christmas tree branches. Do you think you can manage it, Harley?"

"I guess so." Harley's words got lost somewhere between his lungs and his teeth.

The Herald Angel cleared his throat. "I hate to meddle, Harley, but have you ever *done* electrical work before?"

"Of *course* I have," said Harley, whose voice sounded a lot better when he was somewhat irate. "I installed a ceiling fan once."

"Did it work?"

"Of *course* it worked."

"Isn't that the fan that fell down in your living room?" asked the Herald Angel.

"Well, maybe. *But it worked right up till the day it fell down.*"

Having thus been reassured, I left Harley to his electrical work, concentrating instead on those last few practices. Every night I worked with a different soloist or dancing group, making sure the words were enunciated and the steps were executed with just the right degree of professional enthusiasm.

The dress rehearsal went pretty smoothly. The major problems were mechanical, as the costumes steadfastly refused to perform the way they were intended. The humps kept sliding off the camels during their dance routines, and Krista Cow's udder flew off during her over-the-moon solo, narrowly missing the Baby Jesus in his crib. The Herald Angel's outfit still wasn't ready, so he made his flying entrance in his wife's white nightgown and no wings. Our costumer would have a busy twenty-four hours before the play premiered.

The flying scene lacked the fluidity I'd remembered from Mary Martin's performance in *Peter Pan*. The chain that hoisted the Herald Angel up to the top of the stage made the crick-crick-crick sound of a roller coaster climbing inexorably up to the top of the track. The Herald Angel turned up his singing volume to mask the sound of the special effects, and the wonder of seeing him in the air compensated for the jerky movements that got him to his airborne destination.

But all those tiny details would be corrected by show time. Only one thing mattered to me: My play was a masterpiece, just as I knew it would be. The debut of "Pedro, the Reluctant Wise Man" would only be the premiere of thousands of performances of my first Mormon musical. When Bishop Hensel called me to write this play, I hadn't even known I was a writer. Now I knew my destiny, and the first of many successful productions was just a few short hours in the future.

Everything was finished. The cast and crew could do no more. Tomorrow we wouldn't even have access to the meetinghouse, because Voucher had sequestered the building to erect her secret decorations. I only hoped Voucher's end of the Christmas party would be a fitting end to my beginning. If it were, there would be enough jewels to adorn *both* our crowns.

I spent a sleepless night and a fretful day. Finally, with zero hour approaching, I joined the cast as they assembled in the Primary room for a final pep talk before the play began. As my cast members trooped in, I was dismayed to see that they still hadn't grasped the concept of being porcelain figurines. Most of them were wearing make-up; their bodies, covered by costumes, were stark white, but their faces were painted with all manner of rouge and foundation and eye shadow.

I rooted through the Baby Jesus's diaper caddy and found a container of Wet Wipes. One by one I cornered my cast members and removed the offensive color from their faces. It wasn't a popular move.

"We already looked like ghosts," said Rooster Bob. "Now we look like *dead* ghosts."

"Now you look like porcelain manger scene pieces," I corrected. "Trust me."

The words were barely past my lips when the Virgin Mary arrived. Her diaphanous robes hung in stark contrast to her orange parka, and she was shod in white jogging shoes and socks instead of the sandals I hoped she'd wear. But her face was so red it looked like a stop sign. Even the Virgin Mary didn't fathom the vision of my Christmas play.

I pulled two Wet Wipes from the container and marched over to the Virgin Mary, only to see that a thousand Wet Wipes wouldn't have washed any color from her cheeks. The Virgin Mary wasn't wearing makeup. She had hives—hundreds of hives. *Millions* of hives. Her face looked as if it had been stung by a herd of killer bees, with nasty red welts everywhere but on her lips and eyelids. There were even hives in her ears and on her hands. Every square inch of the Virgin Mary's body was plastered with those puffy red blotches.

The Virgin Mary giggled. "I'm nervous, Sister Albacore. I always get hives when I'm nervous. Don't worry. They'll be gone by tomorrow."

An improvement in the Virgin Mary's skin by tomorrow wasn't exactly a comfort to a director whose play began in twenty minutes. I pulled Johnson's Baby Powder from the Baby Jesus's diaper caddy and squirted puffs of it on every visible inch of the Virgin Mary's skin. It didn't help, and I was frantically thinking of an alternate plan when the Herald Angel appeared. His wings, which barely fit through the door, were composed of seventeen hundred white ostrich feather dusters that had been liberally sprinkled with sequins and glitter. Joseph sneezed. Two of the piglets sneezed. A shepherd sneezed four times in a row, and the Herald Angel sneezed in empathy with all of them. His feathers quivered when his body shook, filling the air with a cloud of glitter and dust. I heartily wished that Camille had used *new* feather dusters for the Herald Angel's wings—not feather dusters that had apparently seen hard use in Oklahoma's Dust Bowl. I broke out the Sudafed tablets and passed them out to one and all. The Virgin Mary's hives were forgotten.

I asked Chun-King the Wise Man to offer a prayer on our efforts. Chun-King bowed his head and cleared his throat.

"Dear Lord," he said, in a voice that carried straight up to heaven, "we're down to the wire right now. You know we've worked long and hard to support the bishop by being in this play, even though most of us didn't want to do it. We aren't asking much tonight except that we don't want to make fools of ourselves. Please help us not to make fools of ourselves—and if you can't manage that, please fill the ward members with compassion, we pray. Amen."

Chun-King's prayer wasn't much of a pep talk. Of *course* none of the cast members would embarrass themselves by forgetting a line or missing a step. We'd rehearsed so often and so thoroughly that I was sure the cast members were performing "Pedro, the Reluctant Wise Man" in their dreams. I knew *I* was. So I clapped my hands for attention and said that. I reminded the cast to smile as they sang and raise their voices as they spoke. I also told them to have fun. The work was done; now was the time to reap the rewards of our efforts. We were going to be proud of the work we did together.

Chun-King shrugged. Joseph sighed. Olaf the Wise Man cleared his throat. Two of the shepherds rolled their eyes at each other. I had never seen so many pessimists assembled into one room, but I was optimistic enough to counteract all their fears. We had a terrific play on our hands. Nothing in the world could destroy our achievement.

I ushered the cast through the back door of the stage, making sure the Herald Angel was firmly fixed in his flying harness before I whispered last-minute instructions to the lighting crew. I needed to direct from the audience, so I left the Baby Jesus with his favorite stuffed octopus and a kiss, abandoning the cast in place on the stage. Then I went out the back door to enter the cultural hall from the main entrance. I could have sneaked down the stairs of the stage to find my front-row seat, but I wanted to enter the Christmas party the traditional way. I wanted to see what Voucher had wrought.

Voucher had created a vision of total darkness. As far as I could see, she had decorated the cultural hall to look like the inside of the Bat Cave. The only illumination came from coach lamps that marked a single lighted pathway through the gloom. The ward members, who seemed to arrive simultaneously, groped their way down the pathway to get to their seats. I joined the crowd and shuffled forward so as not to trip in the darkness.

As my eyes adjusted to the lack of illumination, I saw dim gray mounds on either side of the pathway. They looked like snowdrifts. I reached over a retaining rope and touched a drift, fully expecting to retrieve a handful of snow. Instead I brought back grains of gravel.

"It's rock salt!" somebody behind me whispered. "*Tons* of rock salt!" Sure enough, when I tasted the "snow" for myself I confirmed that Snelgrove's ice cream factory could have stayed in business for a year with the rock salt that graced the floor of the Old Mountain Home Ward. There was enough salt in our cultural hall to resalinate the Great Salt Lake.

I stepped over squirming bodies until I found my reserved seat in the first row. Then I waited patiently for the bishop to greet the ward members and open the evening with prayer. Finally the "amen" was said, and someone backstage opened the curtain. On went the floodlights, illuminating the colorful set and my pale cast of porcelain nativity scene pieces. I had never beheld such a beautiful sight, and I fully expected to hear gasps of delight from the congregation. Instead, there were giggles.

"I thought this was a *Christmas* play," said a woman, speaking in a stage whisper. "This looks like Hallo*ween*." I recognized the voice and vowed that the next time Jan Bosworth came visiting teaching to *my* house, *somebody* wasn't going to be home to greet her.

Chip Bosworth didn't even bother to whisper his answer. "It *is* Halloween," he said. "It's 'The Night of the Living Nativity Scene.'" His observation was greeted by sniggers and snorts.

I turned around and shushed the audience, and most of them stopped laughing. As soon as the play began, everyone would know why all the cast members were dressed in white.

But the play hadn't even begun before something awoke the Baby Jesus, who had slept peacefully through virtually every rehearsal but immediately came to life now that all eyes were on him. He threw his stuffed octopus straight into the air, where it knocked the cock's comb right off Rooster Bob. Then the Baby Jesus started screaming. He held out his arms to the Virgin Mary, expecting to be picked up and comforted. The Virgin Mary froze in her tracks.

"Pick him *up*!" Pedro hissed to the Virgin Mary.

"*I* can't pick him up," she hissed back. "He hates me. *You* get him, Joseph!"

Joseph threw the Virgin Mary a look that was colder than Voucher's ersatz snowdrifts, but he picked up the Baby Jesus and cuddled him. The Baby Jesus stuck his finger in Joseph's nose and stopped crying. The audience clapped, and I heaved a sigh of relief.

Then, at my signal, the play began. The cast, minus the Herald Angel, milled around under the Christmas tree, each in turn positioning himself in front of the others. Then the Herald Angel's motorized pulley started grinding, and the Herald Angel started his relentless ascent to the top of the set.

"He's flying!" shouted a little boy a few rows back. "He's Superman!"

I smiled. Already, one critic liked the play. From where I sat, things were looking pretty good.

Still rising, the Herald Angel began his song. He accompanied the words with a flurry of wing-flaps, and a hubbub of appreciation rose from the ward members. Then I saw that appreciation was not what was causing the hubbub. The Herald Angel had never flown in costume, and he couldn't see what was painfully obvious to the rest of us: His oversized wings were grazing the Christmas tree lights that Harley Downey had jury-rigged to the oversized Christmas tree branches. I could only pray that the Herald Angel was near the crest of his flight.

But the Herald Angel continued his rise, still singing his heart out. Suddenly one of his feather duster wings caught in a string of lights. The Herald Angel flapped all the harder to disengage himself from the electrical wire, but the light string remained firmly tangled among his feathers.

The Herald Angel stopped singing, and the taped accompaniment merrily continued without him. He gave the light string a yank. "Damn!" he said when the light string didn't give, and the audience laughed. He pulled harder, managing to create enough slack that finally he could free his wing.

But before the Herald Angel could pick up the singing where he left off, sparks flew. The Herald Angel's desperate yanks had shorted out the Christmas tree lights, and the stage was briefly illuminated in a shower of sparks. The multi-colored lights died for good even as the sparks faded. Only then did the Herald Angel shrug and find his place in the musical score. He finished up with a great burst of energy and even remembered to flap his wings as he descended to the ground.

Just as I began to hope the play could be salvaged after all, several members of the audience started screaming. "Fire!" "Look! Fire!" *"Fire on the set!"* Sure enough, in the corner of the stage, errant sparks had ignited the cotton batting "snow" on the ground. Smoke rose from several other locations, where sparks caused the cotton batting to smoulder.

Quicker than I could say "Smokey the Bear," my cast members stamped out the fires and then tromped all over the rest of the cotton batting, just for good measure. Pedro even waddled to the front of the stage with the plug from the Christmas tree lights, showing the audience that the source of the fire had been extinguished along with the flames. I sent a quick prayer of gratitude heavenward. The emergency was over.

But the sprinkling system didn't know that the crisis had ended. Wisps of smoke activated the sprinkler system on the stage. The heavens opened, drenching camels and piglets and the disgruntled Virgin Mary along with the rest of my ill-fated cast. The audience cackled and cheered, but the laughter and merriment stopped fast. The sprinklers for the stage were on the same circuit as the sprinklers for the cultural hall, and the first set of sprinklers triggered the second. Suddenly we were in the midst of a rainstorm.

"Turn off the water!" Voucher screamed from somewhere behind me. *"TURN OFF THE BLESSED WATER!"*

Somebody turned on the lights then, and as my eyes adjusted to the sudden brilliance I thrilled to the view in the cultural hall.

Voucher's year of planning had resulted in the most glorious scene ever to grace a Mormon gymnasium. Rock salt snowdrifts were everywhere, and Voucher had trucked in a forest of trees that peeked out from the artificial snow. There were ski tracks and cabins and rustic snow forts, as authentic as the scenery on any movie set. There were also "snowflakes," represented by thousands upon thousands of asterisk-shaped styrofoam pellets. It was a miraculous vista, right up until the moment the rain hit the rock salt. Then, like the Wicked Witch of the West, the entire panorama began to dissolve.

Voucher flapped her arms as though she were trying to join the Herald Angel in flight, but the sprinkling system paid her no heed. The only result of her waving was that she drew styrofoam snowflakes to herself like magnets. Her arms her legs turned white with styrofoam and globules of salt.

Still the rain fell.

As if they were all inspired in the same instant, the members of the Old Mountain Home Ward dashed for cover. They stampeded through salt that was rapidly turning to liquid in a vain effort to save their shoes from saline poisoning and their hairdos from Hurricane Voucher. Like rats leaving the Titanic they escaped, whooping in excitement and amazement and wonder.

Somebody shoved a baby in my arms before sprinting through the rock salt toward safety. I looked down and saw the former Baby Jesus, who was transformed by the deluge into my all-too-human son, Frankie. Frankie smiled at me and cheerfully spit up all over my dress before turning his face toward the ceiling. Frankie always did like the rain.

In minutes the cultural hall was cleared. I saw the bishop, way across the gym under the clock, shaking his head as he surveyed the scene. The gym was deserted except for a few hardy ward members who, apparently realizing they couldn't get any wetter than they already were, meandered up and down the pathways of Voucher's winter wonderland. I joined the stragglers, inspecting each of the creations that had occupied Voucher's thoughts for more than a year. Here was a skier, skis akimbo from her recent fall on the slopes. Over there were some children sticking a carrot into a snowman that was taller than they were—and as ugly as any snowman a five-year-old child knew how to build. Behind a cabin, a father assiduously chopped firewood for his winter store. Each figure in the tableau was cheerfully oblivious to the rain falling from heaven and the snow turning to brine underfoot.

Two of the wanderers, who met each other at the intersection of two pathways just a few yards ahead of me, were dressed in white robes that marked them as members of my tormented play. I squinted through the rainstorm and made out Chun-King and Rooster Bob. As they approached one another, Rooster Bob called out in a hearty voice, "Your prayer was answered. Except for the Herald Angel, none of us had *time* to be humiliated tonight."

"God answers prayers in mysterious ways," Chun-King agreed. Rooster Bob fell into step with Chun-King, and the two of them disappeared around a bend in the path.

I ended my promenade at the refreshment table. Voucher had outdone herself there. In addition to the hors d'oeuvres and the requisite red punch and the cups of wassail, she had made hundreds of miniature sleighs out of meringue and candy. Even though the rain was melting them like slugs on a salt lick, the sleighs were nevertheless magnificent creations. I picked up a sleigh and took it home, where I tried to dry it in the oven. It crumbled into dust, denying me even one souvenir of Voucher Christiansen's efforts.

By the time someone thought to shut the sprinklers off, there was enough salt water on the floor of that gym that all of us could have floated like corks, if we were so inclined. But floating like a cork wasn't what Voucher had in mind. Immortality was. As she stood forsaken and forlorn in the gym, with styrofoam pellets clinging to her like albino leeches, it was too early for Voucher to know that her wish had been granted. She asked for renown and got notoriety instead, but the results were the same. Voucher Christiansen's name would be remembered. Her Christmas party was the celebration to end all celebrations—the one Christmas party that would never fade from our memories, no matter how many years passed us by.

Thus was Voucher's Christmas gala the apex of her church career. And mine too, as it turned out. I've looked all over the Salt Lake Valley, as far north as Logan and even down to Provo, but I still haven't found a theatrical troupe to sponsor "Pedro, the Reluctant Wise Man."

If I could only get it performed once, I know it would be a big success.

Elouise Bell says that she first came to BYU about the time the glaciers were leaving. Currently Professor of English and Associate Dean of General and Honors Education, she has received the Karl G. Maeser Distinguished Teaching Award, and Alcuin Award for General Education, a Maeser General Education Professorship, and a "Cougar Groomer Award" from the student alumni association. Other recognition which she prizes include a First Place award from the Utah chapter of the Society of Professional Journalists for her Network column "Only When I Laugh," and the Susa Young Gates Award for service in support of human rights and the cause of women in Utah. In recent years, she has traveled the West performing her one-woman show, "Aunt Patty Remembers," based on the journals of Mormon pioneer Patty Bartlett Sessions. Sister Bell filled a mission to France "earlier in the century"; from 1973 to 1978, she served on the General Board of the Young Women. A collection of essays, Only When I Laugh, *has been published by Signature Books and is now in its third printing.*

A GENEROUS HEART

by Elouise Bell

December 21, 1962, La Rochelle

Well, I have penned my cheerful half-truths to the folks, the bishop, and the Mission President. I think that entitles me to record a few full-truths in my own journal; and future grandchildren can take the hindmost.

I never understand people's attitude about truth-in-journal-keeping. "Oh, I can't put *that* in," they say. "I wouldn't want my grandchildren to know I did *that*, or felt *that*!" Bizarre! And naive. First of all, if any grandchildren ever do read these journals, it will be for about five minutes on some rainy Sunday afternoon when there's nothing better to do. These pages will add up to a minor blip of interest in a flatline of boredom. On the other hand, to me, right now, this journal is a lifeline. Sometimes it seems the only link to sanity and my real life, which apparently is in deep freeze somewhere else.

Second point: if these future heirs *do* read Grandma's journal, won't it be a dandy surprise if they find a human being coming

83

through its pages? I want my grandchildren to know I had blood in my veins, tear ducts in my eyes and spit in my mouth. I *don't* want them to believe I was some anemic—

Well, I seem to be off on a tirade again. That's what comes of not giving a discussion for three weeks: all my rhetoric gets dammed up and then comes flooding out to swamp my defenseless journal. I may never break any records for number of converts, but I'm certain to be the only missionary in this century to amass fifteen volumes of journals in a two year mission. Who do I think I am anyway; Parley P. Pratt? Or was that Wilford Woodruff who did all the writing?

Christmas in France. Sounds so glamorous on paper. "Oh, Grandma, tell us what it was like to spend Christmas in France!" And I'll probably oblige, and make a great heart-warming story out of the whole dreary business, and we'll all chuckle with faith-promoted tears in our eyes as we gobble down our flash-cooked turkey or whatever we'll be eating for Christmas dinner in 1995. And my granddaughters will write in their journals, "I hope I get to go to France on *my* mission," and the full cycle will start off again: dreams, reality, disillusionment, transfigured reality, the passage of time, the reshaping of reality into folklore, and new dreams born out of folklore. Only right now I'm in the less popular, less publicized part of the cycle. The folklore, when it finally ripens will last me for decades—as will the testimony; let's be fair—I'll be telling and re-telling Tales from My Mission as long as memory hangs in there. The questions is: can I make it through the fiery furnace of here and now?

A fiery furnace might be welcome, actually. Just for a few minutes. Everybody talks about how great La Rochelle is! "Branch parties on the Ile de Re. Walks on the beach. Lovely evening breezes off the quai." That's what you hear at missionary conference up in Paris. Well, all of that is like a preview of coming attractions at the moment, the moment being December. No boats to the island. The beach glowers dark, gloomy and cold. The stiff breezes from the sea slice inside my coat and make me ache and shiver. Those famous tenth-century battlements may be filled with delighted tourists in season; out of season, they are grey frigid tombs, about as much fun to visit as an abandoned graveyard. An abandoned *non-Mormon* graveyard.

Aggh! When we start talking about graveyards, we're carrying honest journal-keeping too far! Go to bed, Sister Gloom! And a Merry Christmas to you, you old sourpuss!

December 22, 1962, La Rochelle

The branch party was tonight. Sigh. Well, I award myself a few points for Making an Effort, and a bandelo badge for Being a Good Sport. My harmonica and I provided accompaniment for a game of musical chairs that came very close to erupting into laughter once or twice. Sister Adams' popcorn was a pan-rattling success; apparently popcorn is not a standard item of French cuisine—the barbarians!—and the children in the branch (all four of them) were properly impressed when the handful of corn exploded into a couple of large bowls of fluffy stuff. (The parents took one dubious taste and maintained a diplomatic silence thereafter.) Frere Delacroix did his "lisping baby" poem once again; I think even Sister Adams, she of the quicksilver memory, knows it by heart now. The elders favored us with several songs about snow, sleighbells, and Rudolf. No snow *ici*, but my fingers are permanently stiff, and at night, we pile *all* our clothes on top of us—coats, sweaters, skirts, *let tout*—in an effort to stop shivering long enough to fall asleep. In the morning, that great load having been on top of us all night, we are a chiropractor's dream.

Sister A. and I explored the subject of morale in study class this morning—our morale. She is convinced that if we would Do Something for Someone Else, it would raise our spirits. I agree with the principle totally. It's the translation into practice that gets complicated, as always. Which is why, I'm convinced, the Brethren wisely call the very young to serve on missions. Nineteen is just the right age. So many things are black or white then. Mental reservations are at a minimum. Alas. Was I foolish to come on a mission at twenty-seven? I hold on to the idea that my five or six extra years can somehow, somewhere, bring a contribution to this mission, but so far, that too is mere theory, rather than practice.

In any case, Sister Adams and I went down the roster of our little branch, looking for Someone to Do Something *for*. But half the members have gone elsewhere for the holidays, and who can blame them? Some are off to family in Lyons or Bordeaux, or, in the case of the Tomanos, to Milan. (Footnote: All the missionaries agree that the addition of Italian converts totally changes the character of a branch. For one thing, smiling becomes a bilateral activity between missionaries *and* members. Not to mention what Italians do for congregational singing!)

Of those left in port, it's hard to think of a candidate for our charity. Certainly not the snooty Bardieu sisters in their big house facing the sea, tending their snuffling little Pekinese, that arrogant spoiled mop who has the run of the manse which neither missionary nor member has ever seen from the inside. No, not les Bardieu. Le Famille Arnaud are comfortable and serene, as always, Papa Arnaud's two Lambretta dealerships thriving. Doing Something for them would be like sewing a ruffle on the flag. There is no question of our Doing Something for that strange young man the elders baptized last month; what *is* his problem, anyway?

There *is* old Soeur Fanchard. But of course we do something for her every week: do her shopping, accompany her to the clinic, bring her church magazines. And we already have Christmas gifts in mind for her: Sister A.'s mother is knitting a shawl; I'm making a tape of myself reading *Le Petit Prince* since she loves it so much, and can't read any more. A gift surely motivated by vanity, I confess, since she compliments me on my French with repetition born of either sincerity or growing senility. But she is a stalwart soul, bless her. I must learn from her the lesson Hemingway never did learn, despite all his talk: grace under pressure. Soeur Fanchard has more reason to complain than any of us, but I have yet to hear the first word of self-pity or gloom from the woman. Go thou to thy prayers, Sister Hobbs, and learn from thy betters.

December 23, 1962

We sang "Though Deepening Trials" in study class this morning, but all it did was establish an especially depressing mood for the whole day. Poor Sister Adams. She tries to do her crying out of earshot, but in this tiny place, that's impossible. We were determined to get in a good morning of tracting, convinced that the holiday spirit would soften at least a few hearts so that we could deliver the message we came to this place to share. We set out with vigor, much prayer, and many scarves.

By the time we had ridden fifteen minutes on our scooters out to our tracting area, we were frozen numb, barely able to feel the handlebars under our senseless fingers. Sister A.'s whole lower jaw was immobile, despite being bundled up. When we knocked on the first door, believe it or not, someone answered! Sister A. started to give the door approach, but found her mouth was so numb it really didn't work.

When she tried to speak, she sounded like a drunken robot whose batteries had run down. The amazed woman at the door didn't even bother to say, "Cela me n'interesse pas." Or anything else.

We kept at it all morning. I could feel Sister Adams' misery thickening, congealing, as we trudged up one staircase and down another. She pulled a smile out of somewhere each time we knocked on a door, but otherwise, under her wool headscarf she looked like a poster child for Save the Refugees. I tried to kick my way through my own gloom long enough to think what I might possibly do to cheer her even a little. I couldn't come up with a thing. Tried jokes. Tried singing. Tried my imitation of Sister Whatcott's atrocious French. Received a wan, blurred look of appreciation for my effort.

Just as we were puffing to the top of one more staircase, a door burst open and two children pelted out. First, a little girl, blonde and pink, maybe four or five, straight off a Renoir canvas: dressed lovingly in an emerald green coat with white fur collar and a white fur muff which she held out before her like a chalice, her hands tucked within, invisible. Behind her, a boy, somewhat older, and beautiful beyond envy, the way some European boys can be, their faces exquisitely balancing the best of male and feminine grace.

"O, Maman," squealed the girl to the woman behind them, who was double-locking the apartment door. "Comme j'*aime* le Noel!"

The mother, laughing, bent to lay her cheek beside the child's pale curls; then they all ran down the stairs, *Maman* trailing a whiff of Chanel. We could have been two drain pipes for all the notice they took of us.

Sister Adams' face, a moment red from the exertion of climbing, was now white. I remembered the framed photograph by her bed, the big tribe of grinning brothers and sisters. Angie, the baby sister, would be about four. I busied myself with the tracting book so that I didn't have to look at my companion's face.

So far, we have not come up with anyone to play Santa Claus for. Frankly, considering the shape we're in, I would say that's just as well.

December 27, 1962

Sophia Tolstoy (Mrs. Leo) wrote that anyone reading her journals would think she led a miserable life, when actually she was "the happiest of women." It was just that she turned to her journals when she was low, whereas when she was happy, she neglected them altogether. Move over in the confessional, Sophy; I'm a sister under the notebook.

Actually, I haven't forgotten about my journal. I've just—what? Hesitated to break the spell, maybe. I've lived the last three days in a—a magical bubble that nothing can touch. No, that's backward. It's more as if this magical bubble reaches out and touches everything and makes it part of me. And I guess I've been afraid that words might shatter it all.

But I decided you needed to hear about this, you grandkids out there in the next century, wherever, whoever you are. You listening? All right, then.

Two days before Christmas Joyce Adams and I were in a pitiful state, as chronicled above. On top of everything, on the morning of the 24th, we learned that there was a major postal *greve* in effect, a strike. No mail. No cards, no letters, no packages.

We were slumped at the little wooden table by the window, trying to absorb these glad tidings, staring out at newspaper scraps flitting down the street ahead of a scolding wind. Suddenly I saw Madame Seurel on the pavement. Hoisting her full skirts, she marched up the stairway towards our door. What now? What could our landlady want? Maybe to tell us that the heat and the electricity were also on strike. At that point, I would have believed any and all bad news, up to and including an Algerian invasion force rolling onto the beaches of La Rochelle.

Was not, however, prepared for *good* news.

"Mais certainement!" said Madame in her husky, non-nonsense voice. "Certainly you will join us this evening. Surely your religion, your calling, does not require that you sit alone, two foreigners in a rented apartment on Christmas Eve? No, I did not think so. This is a time for joy. In a manner of speaking, we have a *duty* to rejoice on this occasion."

I tried to say thanks but no thanks. Our exchanges with Madame S. had always been strictly business, very asocial transactions: we'd hand over a check, she'd return us a warning about not taxing the water heater; we'd murmur about how cold the apartment was, she'd give us a quick summary of the corruption at the hydro-electric plant down in Rochefort. She was never unkind; she was just very—French. This invitation disoriented us, both of us.

"We will come for you about nine. You will go with us to Mass, of course."

I saw Sister Adams, already shaking her head, begin to mouth the word *non*. I faked a large and very unconvincing cough to cover her response. Madame continued with the agenda.

"Then, to our home, and festivities. The children have their little preparations made, and our cook, well, she is from Marseilles, but nonetheless. . . . Now dress warmly, warmly, hear? You Americans think the whole world is California ("Cally-forrn-ee-ah"), isn't it so?"

By this time, Sister Adams had stammered out, "Mais, mais—"

"But what?" said Madame. "You have other plans for tonight, perhaps?" She looked Sister Adams full in the face. Sister A. had no resources for lying. The elders had been invited to dinner by two bachelor investigators they had met at the municipal swimming pool. We had no intention of joining *them*.

Madame had more than her ration of Gallic astuteness.

"It is perhaps forbidden to attend a religious service other than your own?" she asked. Blank look sent my way from my companion. Thunderous ticking of the clock: one, two, three.

"Non, non, non! Mais, non! Of course not!" I broke in, booming in my awkwardness and confusion. "Very kind, very kind on your part. It is all right with Messieur, this kind invitation?" We'd never met Messieur.

"As a matter of fact, it was his idea. It is settled, then. Until nine!" And she was gone.

We'd been softened up by our loneliness, by the cold, by our low spirits and the final coup of no mail. How else could we explain our accepting this invitation? Definitely uncomfortable, we spent the rest of the afternoon looking at each other, making what-do-you-think? What-have-we-let-ourselves-in-for? Don't-look-at-*me* faces. We took the money we had been planning to spend on our dinner that evening and bought a huge box of chocolates ("the children"? How many? Was this enough chocolate?) and a modest bouquet of flowers for our hosts. Even as we made these preparations, I couldn't believe we were going to spend Christmas Eve with strangers. Sister Adams seemed in shock.

"But Sister! A Mass? We're going to a Catholic *Mass*?" Poor Sister A. She'd heard just enough about incense, bells, Latin, and "priestcraft" to be traumatized. I didn't need psychic gifts to know what she was thinking: all the misguided Us/Them missionary put-downs about the Catholic Church were buzzing around in her head.

Her pale freckled face looked very anxious, but definitely not depressed any more. Panicked, yes; depressed, *non*.

At nine sharp, a knock comes at the door. For one nervous moment, Sister A. grabs my hand. I give hers a squeeze and then firmly unlatch myself from her and open the door.

"Good evening, Misses, and a very joyous Christmas to you. I am Paul Seurel. You will accompany me, please?" A smile, dark hair falling straight over his nice forehead, an expensive midnight blue overcoat on this very young man.

On the street below, the Family Seurel waits, stamping in the cold, puffing breath-clouds into the night. Messieur turns out to be handsome in a thick-set way, shorter than Madame, but from his manner, I decide that he would consider any more height to be a bit ostentatious on his part. He seems to be as much the host in this frigid street as if he were in his home.

"Sister—we call you sister, that is correct?—Sister Adams. What a fine name, Adams! Many great countrymen of yours named Adams, I believe?" How did M. Seurel know that genealogy was the golden key to unlock Sister A.'s timid tongue? In an instant she is tracing her connection to John Quincy. Messieur walks attentively at her side, bending his ear to catch her stumbling French. For a moment, he takes her arm, but, perhaps sensing her tension at the gesture, he soon releases it and simply walks close. As we pass under a lamplight en route to the church, I see Madame nod ("Go on!") to the smallest Seurel, a curly-headed boy. He immediately moves up beside Sister A. and, looking straight ahead, slips his hand into hers.

Mass. As advertised. Unknown language. Chanting down the aisles. Swinging, smoking censers. Priests and little priests, or maybe apprentices, in robes of many colors. Sister Adams looks sideways at me, Ruth amid the alien corn. Then Jean-Michel of the curly hair smiles up at her. "C'est beau, n'est-ce pas, Soeur Adams?" And for a moment, I think she sees it all as he does: light, color, music, mystery, fine clothes, family packed close on the long pew, not so different from the many Adamses packed close on the long pew in the Spanish Fork Seventh Ward chapel. She bends far over to whisper in his ear, "Oui, Jean-Michel, it is very beautiful, your church."

Much standing up, sitting down, kneeling. We remain fixed, our arms folded across our chests in our best Primary behavior. No one seems to mind our departure from the norm. Then, from the rear of the church, comes a sound that lifts the hair on the back of my neck. In a loft or gallery above the great doors roosts a choir of boys. Among them I spot Paul Seurel, nearly anonymous in a white robe. His face is empty of everything but the music he is part of. Music that feels like cool, cool water being poured down upon my head, my neck, over my shoulders. Music that anoints me. Balm of Gilead.

This music reaches so far within me that I no longer feel misplaced. I turn towards La Mere Seurel, seeking her eyes. I must see her eyes. She returns my gaze proudly, then apparently sees my tears, and her own eyes fill. She does not turn away from me, just lifts her solid chin still higher and takes a very deep breath. I do not look away, either.

At the Seurel home, my dominant first impression is of a great deal of dark furniture and woodwork, set off by an enormous amount of Christmas glitter. Beautifully wrapped presents everywhere, little intriguing packages on end tables and coffee tables and mantlepieces, great beribboned boxes under the tree, beside easy chairs, piled on a long desk. Silver tea and coffee sets gleaming on their own tables. Our box of candy nestles beside several others, gold and silver and red and green foil catching the lights from the tree and the fireplace. The fireplace. Huge. Tall enough so that Jean-Michel, as he tells me, can stand erect inside it (in summer, of course). Great logs blaze. On the hearth, a roughly made wooden box filled with straw.

There are enough people in the house to make a very respectable branch. We are the only non-family guests. A Seurel daughter, who whispers modestly to me that she'll be eighteen next month, takes us around for introductions. Everyone's name seams to be Jean, Jeannene, Jeannette or Jean-Paul. Whatever the names, all are very polite and welcoming. Sister Adams even receives compliments on her French.

Two or three times, Sister Adams decides she must be a Daniel, even if we no longer seem to be in the lion's den she had expected. "We are missionaries," she begins as an ice-breaker with one Seurel. "We are here with a message for all people—" Jean or Jeannene smiles brightly, and then waves to an uncle across the room or rushes to kiss yet another great-aunt who has just tottered in on a silver-headed cane. A few minutes later, Sister A. corners Paul, and tries again: "In our church, we believe—" Paul listens courteously, tossing his hair out of his eyes, which dart around the room, scouting for comely female cousins, I would guess.

Le Pere Seurel, having observed all this, comes up. He hands Sister A. a glass of punch.

"Sweet cider," he makes clear. "No alcohol, absolutely not. To your health, good sister. Tonight you are our guest. Please enjoy yourself. On another occasion, perhaps you will be so kind as to explain your creed to us; that would be most gracious of you. But tonight, we must rejoice in those truths we share, rather than the points upon which we differ, is it not so? Ah, and the little ones are ready to illuminate those truths in their own unique way. Come, have a seat."

Everyone takes a seat around the hearth, aunts and grandmothers on the long sofa, others in chairs, on stools, on the floor. We are front row center in matching arm-chairs. Paul leans against a polished credenza. A little blonde cousin flounces out her short skirt and sits on a large pouf in front of him, within easy whispering distance.

It is, of course, the pageant we all expect and never tire of. Jean-Michel has the big role. He enters, leading, with one hand, a slightly taller sister and, with the other, the family St. Bernard, patiently resigned to being a donkey for the occasion, wearing a folded towel as a saddle. At the crucial moment, the little girl demurely turns her back to us, and when she faces us again, she holds an exquisite doll, swaddled in what appears to be Paul's silk neck-scarf. She places the Child in the box of straw, and then stepping back, crosses her hands over her chest and frowns deeply as she portrays for us "pondering these things in her heart."

Jean-Michel then stands up very straight, hands tight to his sides, and begins to sing, "Il Est Ne, Le Divin Enfant." For the second time that evening, my hair prickles from my scalp.

At the midnight supper, I lose count of the number of courses, though I try to keep track. A story-teller is known by her details, after all.

Le Pere Seurel directs the conversation, and Sister Adams and I are the hub around which the wheel of talk revolves. His conducting skill is marvelous; truly a maestro, he cues now one motif, now another solo. He inquires about our schooling; then the talk is directed to Paul's aspirations and hopes for a medical scholarship. We are asked about our fathers' occupations; then Cousin Bertrand is invited to tell about his exciting new job in the Ministry of Transportation. Is it quite true that Utah has a great deal of snow—but is it not a desert province?—and can it really have excellent skiing? Young Uncle Francois, of the splendid mustache, is urged to recount the story of how he almost made the French ski team a few years back. Francois is a skilled raconteur, and laughter rings out again and again. Sister Adams and Jean-Michel, seated beside each other, seem to be playing a little game trading olives back and forth between them. I realize, eaves-dropping, that in our four months together I have never heard Sister Adams laugh before. She has a lovely, musical laugh; what if I had never found that out? As for myself, I am at the right hand of Madame Seurel, who apparently has confused me with a starving Armenian child. I say no to nothing she offers me.

After dinner, there is music. Paul sings a haunting folk-song in a strange dialect. I have the eerie experience of not quite understanding any one word of the lyrics, yet knowing precisely what it all means. Two cousins perform a flute and violin duet. Then we all sing Christmas songs. Le Pere Seurel smiles broadly and nods, congratulating Sister Adams and me for knowing the French words to "Silent Night" and "Bring A Torch, Jeannette, Isabella." By this time, Jean-Michel is camped on Sister A.'s lap more or less permanently. Her soft laugh breaks out again and again.

It is one a.m. before we leave. As we gather our wraps, I see Sister Adams peer thoughtfully into her huge handbag, where the corner of a tract is visible. She hesitates. I concentrate totally on bundling up: she will have to make this decision on her own. I hear a loud zip, and turn to see the handbag slung over her shoulder, no pamphlet in sight.

Both host and hostess are at the door to say good-bye. Paul and Uncle Francois will see us home. We try to stammer our thanks. Papa Seurel gently interrupts us.

"But no. Surely you understand the gift you have given us, this night of all nights. Surely you realize—for you are educated women, and symbolism is not lost on you—you understand Who you represent, as you have allowed us to share our food and our hearth with two strangers? In these comfortable days, to be allowed to give, to have one's gift *received* with a generous heart—well, perhaps you understand the rarity of such a circumstance. Is it not so?" His smile is like Paul's singing.

"It is so, Brother Seurel," says Sister Adams, every freckle aglow in the frugal light of the entry hall. "Perhaps we do understand, after all. Even so, this is a Christmas Eve which . . . about which . . . we will tell our children, and our . . . the children of our children." And after shaking his hand in both of hers and kissing Madame Seurel soundly on each cheek, she leads the way out the door.

Perhaps some day she'll let me read the story of this Christmas as recorded in *her* journal. I think I'd like that very much.

Carol Lynn Pearson is a native of Utah and is currently residing in Walnut Creek, California. She began her career as a performer and then became a writer. She earned a Masters degree in theater arts at Brigham Young University. Carol Lynn twice won best actress award at BYU, toured with the USO in the Orient, and performed in the Utah Shakespearean Festival. She is a popular speaker and has been a talk-show guest on the Oprah Winfrey Show, Geraldo, Sally Jesse Raphael, Good Morning America, and was featured in People magazine. Carol Lynn is the author of four books of poetry which have sold over 250,000 copies. She has also authored several novels, musical plays, and screen plays, including Cipher in the Snow. She is the winner of numerous international awards. Her most recent creative project is a one-woman play that she wrote and performs, Mother Wove the Morning. Carol Lynn has four children; one is serving a mission in Argentina.

CHRIST CHILDREN

Let us make you a child again
For Christmas.
Let us put you in the cradle
As we put Jesus in the manger
Pre-crucifixion and sweet
With just born eyes that meet
The wonder of star and smile.

For a little while
Let us make you children again.
Here there are no nails
In your innocence.
Here there is over you
A sky bursting bright
And under you the breast of a mother
Softer than hay.

You will not stay
I know
And Jesus will have to go
To Golgotha:
His little hands were born to bear a cross.
And you, my darling,
Came to the same sad world
Where trust is lost
At the hands of those who
Know not what they do.

At the end of the story
The Christ will rise
And so will you.

But let us make you
Children again for Christmas
(The Christ children that you are)
Touched only by swaddling
And the light of a star.

Carol Lynn Pearson

Dean Hughes always wanted to be a writer when he grew up. He finally accomplished the first part: he is a full-time writer. But, he says, he has never grown up. He has written more than forty novels for children and young adults. He lives with his wife, Kathy, in Provo, Utah. They have a married daughter, Amy Russel, and two sons, Tom and Rob. All three are college students. Dean is a bishop, and he will soon publish his first adult book, a true crime work entitled Lullaby and Good Night. *Still, he resists the pressure; he has no intention of growing up.*

SUN ON THE SNOW

by Dean Hughes

Gary flipped the gearshift to neutral and opened the door. "We're in a mess," he said as he swung down from the truck. Dennis stayed inside. He really didn't need this today.

Dennis watched Gary walk around the truck, check the back tires, and then come forward and crouch by the right front wheel. When he stood, he looked at Dennis and shook his head, even smiled a little. Dennis rolled his window down. "What now?" he said.

"I don't know. We're in up to the axles, all the way around. The tires got down through the snow and into the mud."

Dennis decided he better get out. But he was a little put out. He had to correct and hand back a set of term papers by tomorrow. As he stepped down, his foot sank into the mud. He took a long step and then pulled, his shoe making a sucking noise.

Gary laughed. "I hope your shoes are tied," he said.

Dennis tried to laugh. "I guess it wouldn't do any good if I pushed and you rocked the truck back and forth."

"No way. We'd just sit and spin."

"Well, then, I'd say we're in deep trouble."

Gary turned so he was leaning with his backside against the fender. He crossed his arms. He had on a big parka but no hat. His fine blond hair had blown in the breeze, a lock in front standing up. He looked like a kid—tall and lean and freckled.

97

"This isn't trouble, Dennis. This is a diversion. When you've got real troubles, something like this is fun—it gives you something else to think about for a while."

Dennis nodded. He knew that had to be true. "Do you think about it a lot?"

"Sure, I do." Gary slipped his hands into his pockets. He looked down, scraped one boot against the other to clean away some of the mud.

"Doesn't that just make it worse?"

"Yeah, sure, but I can't help it." He looked out across the snowy hillside. "I keep trying to picture what happened. I have an idea she looked one way, then the other, and started across, and the truck came over the hill from the direction she looked first. I see all that, and then I think, 'If the guy had been going a couple of miles an hour slower, or if he had taken another second or two to get in his truck—or, you know, anything like that—she'd be alive now. Just one second might have made the difference.'"

Dennis didn't know what to say. That had been his problem from the beginning. "I guess the worst is missing her."

"Yeah." Gary stared ahead, didn't speak for a time. "Yesterday, I started to feel good about something. And then all of a sudden I said to myself, 'Wait a minute. You can't do this. Your little girl's only been dead ten days. You can't start feeling good yet. It wouldn't be right.'" He looked over at Dennis. "Do you know what I mean?"

"Sure. But no one expects you to go around with a long face forever. Life goes on."

"That's what everyone says." Gary laughed. "No. It does. It does. Look, we're going to have to walk out of here. The only thing I can think to do is call Brother Stewart. He lives closer out this way than anyone else in the ward—and he's got that cattle truck. He could get back in here close enough that he could get a chain on my bumper and pull us out."

"Okay." Dennis let his breath out. His afternoon was shot; there was no getting around that. "Where can we call from?"

"Back on the main road, up about a mile or so, I saw a couple of farms."

"Okay, let's go." Gary nodded, and then he walked around his truck and cut the engine.

The two started back down the snowy road. Dennis wished he had worn a big pair of boots. He just hadn't expected anything like this.

"Dennis, I don't remember volunteering to look after this welfare project, do you? I guess we must have been called by revelation."

"Actually, I did volunteer. I thought beekeeping might be kind of interesting."

"Now that's the professor talking. 'I thought it might be interesting.' I'm sure the Bishop asked me because I've kept a few bees over the years. No one told me it was 'interesting.'"

"Gary, don't give me that. You love that image—the *practical* man. But I know darn well it's cheaper to buy a jar of honey once in a while than it is to keep bees."

"Hey, I gotta sound like a hick. I'm surrounded by all you professors in the ward and I make a living slinging hamburgers. If I try to sound any other way, you guys would all laugh at me."

But that was the other topic. Dennis hesitated, and then he asked anyway. "How's your business doing, Gary?"

"Bad."

"I guess things get slow at Christmas, don't they?"

"It's not just that. I can't compete with McDonald's and all the others that have come in. Somebody's going to go broke this next year—maybe two or three places. If I can hang on, maybe it won't be me. But I don't think I'm going to make it."

Dennis hadn't realized things were quite that serious.

"I don't like to admit it," Gary said, "but a couple of times lately I've caught myself saying, 'How come me, Lord?'"

"It doesn't seem fair, does it?" Dennis knew he ought to have something better than that to say, but he could think of nothing. And that was his problem lately. He felt as though he were sliding down a whole mountain of questions, and he couldn't find any answers to grab onto. How could he help Gary when he couldn't help himself?

"But I don't really think that way—most of the time," Gary said. "In fact, the truth is, this whole thing has been good for me in some ways."

But Gary didn't explain. Dennis found himself, in the silence, wanting to say something meaningful, but all he could come up with was, "I guess it's the tough times that help us grow."

"Well, yeah," Gary said, seeming to pass off the remark. But in a few seconds he added, "It was strange. When I first picked her up out of the weeds, I knew she was gone. But I panicked, you know. I put my hands on her head and commanded her spirit to come back. I prayed. I almost went crazy—all the way to the hospital in the back of the ambulance. But then . . ."

Gary stopped. He wasn't losing control. He just seemed to be gathering his thoughts.

"This might sound stupid to you. I don't know," Gary finally said, "but I was standing there, and the doctors were working on her. And I knew she was dead. But I wouldn't admit it. And then I felt someone put a blanket over my shoulders. It was nice and soft, you know, and I really appreciated that the nurse or someone would do that. So I just turned a little to say thanks, but no one was there. And then I looked down at my shoulder, and there wasn't any blanket."

Now tears did come into Gary's eyes.

Dennis nodded, and he felt a warm sort of vibration pass through him. It was a sensation he knew well, but one he hadn't felt for a long time. He was immediately thankful for it.

"And then some words came into my head," Gary said. "I said, 'Accept this.' I didn't . . . *think* it. I just heard my own voice inside my head. 'Accept this.' I don't know how else to describe it. I stood there with that warm blanket all around me, and then I heard my own voice say that."

"I've had some things like that happen to me, too. Once, especially, in the mission field."

Gary nodded, and he seemed satisfied. "So anyway—now—I keep saying, 'Accept this,' and it seems to help. Sometimes I catch myself saying it over and over—sort of subconsciously or something." Then he laughed. "Hey, don't tell anyone, okay? They'll think I'm nuts."

"You're not nuts, Gary. You're way ahead of anyone I know. I couldn't believe it when I heard that you and Jenny spent that first night trying to console the truck driver."

"No. That wasn't anything special. You would have done the same thing. That poor guy was really hurting."

But Dennis wasn't sure what he would have done. He wasn't sure about anything. It was strange, suddenly, to envy Gary, who had so much to deal with.

The two men walked. The sun was bright on the snow, but the frozen fields looked like graveyards to Dennis. He knew the warmth of the sun was a deception; winter was only just setting in. And what

Dennis felt was shame. He knew he should be doing more to help Gary, but he had actually dreaded this little trip. He knew they would have time to talk; he also knew he had nothing to say. But he wanted to do something. "What are you and Jenny going to do for Christmas?" he asked.

"I guess we'll spend the day with my folks."

"Why don't you come out for a while? Maybe Christmas Eve."

"Okay. Maybe. I don't know what Jenny will want to do."

"Do you dread Christmas now?"

"Well, no. We had her presents bought, and, you know, we have a lot of memories. That stuff is hard. But Christmas feels good to me right now. I'm sort of forgetting the usual stuff, and keeping my mind on . . . Christmas. I'm seeing things a little different from the way I used to."

"That's good, Gary. We all need to do that," Dennis said. But he meant much more than he was saying.

"You know, Dennis, we talking about 'passing on to the other side.' But it's one thing to know what you believe, and it's another thing to pick up your beautiful little girl and find out she's turned into . . . nothing. Just flesh. There was a short time, like about fifteen minutes, when everything seemed gone. It was like I'd fallen into a black hole with no way out. And I just wanted to scream and curse. And then he put that blanket around me. I still start fighting the thing, you know. I think about that one lousy second that might've made the difference. But then I just go back to that blanket. And I tell myself, 'Accept this.' And then I'm okay."

They reached the paved road soon after that, and they started north. Dennis loved the Missouri countryside in summer, but everything looked so harsh now. Everything lay dead under the snow, all white except for the fence lines and the tree-filled creek bottoms. The cottonwoods and oaks looked like black etchings—skeletons. Dennis told himself that it was all very pretty, if he thought about it right, but it was so harshly white and black and, somehow, fierce. He only felt really human again when the colors, the life, came back with the spring.

Gary and Dennis chatted as they walked along, talked about their options should they not be able to reach Brother Stewart, joked about some of the guys in the ward who might like to take up beekeeping. Eventually they came to a long lane that led to a farmhouse. Somewhere, out in the distance, Gary could hear a cow bellowing—persistently. He wondered why it would do that.

When Gary and Dennis reached the house they decided to knock on a side door and avoid getting mud on the front porch. When the door opened a heavy, dark-haired woman looked out at them. "Hi, boys, what do you need? You ran out of gas, I'll bet—or you got yourself stuck somewheres."

Gary laughed. "Now why do you say that? Do we look stupid or something?"

"Yeah. A little." She laughed, her jowls quivering. She had dark hair in front of her ears and along her jaw, a sort of beard. "You look like teachers from over at the college."

"Hey, *I'm* not," Gary said. "But I got my four-wheeler stuck up to the axles—so maybe I oughta go apply."

"Yeah, I think you could get on." But she asked, seriously, "Where's your truck?"

"About a mile south, and back in on Pedersons' land. We've got some beehives in there we were going to check on. What we were thinking is that we could call a guy we know and get him to come and pull us out."

"Shore. That's fine. Come in. But I'm going to ask you to do something for me, if you don't mind. I'm glad you come along. You call your friend, and then I'll tell you what it is I need."

Gary cleaned up his feet as best he could, and then he walked across the kitchen. Dennis stepped just barely inside and shut the door behind him. The kitchen was hot and smelled good, but the place was messy. A dog had been sleeping near the door on a threadbare rug. It got up now, and looked at Dennis, but showed little interest.

Dennis listened as Gary talked to Brother Stewart, who ran a dairy farm a few miles away. The conversation sounded encouraging until Gary said, "That's fine. I know you just can't drop everything. Come as soon as you can."

Gary turned around. "He says it might be twenty minutes or so before he can leave, and then it's going to be about that long again to get over here."

"That's not so bad," Dennis said. He glanced at his watch. The woman returned from another room. She was holding a rifle.

"Don't shoot," Gary said. "We didn't steal any chickens."

"Don't worry. I don't know which end of this thing the bullet comes out of. I don't like guns. But that's where I need some help. I got a cow down, dying, out there in the field." She pointed to the east. "I called a man who said he could come and finish her, and then haul her off. But he ain't come, and the poor thing has been bellowing all day. I just can't stand to listen anymore. I need someone to put her out of her pain."

Gary nodded. "Yeah, I guess we could do that." But he didn't sound very sure of himself.

"The only gun I've got around here is this little rifle, and I found this one shell that seems to fit it. That's all I got. My husband has a big hunting rifle in his truck, but he won't be home until late this afternoon. Will this one little bullet kill the poor old thing?"

"I don't know." He thought about it for a few seconds. "Maybe. If we do it right." Gary looked at Dennis. "It's only a twenty-two," he said.

"Well, if you think you can kill her, please do it. I'd shorely appreciate it."

Gary took the gun and the shell. He and Dennis walked out, crouched to get through the barbed wire fence and headed across the field. Dennis had shot rabbits, as a boy, back in Utah. But that had been a long time before, and he had lost interest in hunting. He would have preferred to stay back at the house and let Gary take care of this.

They found the cow near a little pond. She was a big animal, all white. She was down in the mud, where the snow was worn away. All four legs were under her. When Gary and Dennis approached, she tried to get up but only managed to swing her head and jerk in spasms. She had never stopped bellowing.

"Dennis, I've been thinking about this. The only way that bullet is going to get in deep enough is if we put the barrel right into her ear. Otherwise, we're just going to give her more pain." Gary was loading the rifle.

The thought sickened Dennis. He didn't plan to watch.

"One other thing. I'm gonna have to ask you to do it. I just don't think I can manage it right now."

"Oh, Gary, I don't know. I—"

"I'd really appreciate it, Dennis."

Dennis nodded, and Gary handed him the rifle. Dennis took a breath, tried to think how he could do it. He stayed well back, but slowly he reached out with the rifle. He saw the cow's big eye roll as he brought the barrel up to her ear. When the cold metal touched, the cow quivered and held still, as though she knew what was coming.

"You're going to have to get it right in there, Dennis."

Dennis moved a little closer, used the rifle to lift the ear, and then pushed the barrel inside. He felt his stomach turn. He took a long breath.

"That's okay. Just pull the trigger."

A second passed, and then two, three, four. Dennis took another breath. He tried to squeeze, but his finger seemed locked.

"Pull the trigger."

Dennis tried. He thought his brain had given the command to his finger, but nothing happened. His finger didn't move. And then he pulled the rifle back. "Gary, I can't do it. It makes me sick."

The two stood silent for a time. Dennis looked out across the cold landscape. He didn't want to look at the cow.

Gary was looking in the same direction, where the sun was managing nothing more than to turn the surface of everything into ice. Dennis could hear Gary taking long, deep breaths.

"Gary, maybe we better tell the woman that—"

"No, that's all right." He took the rifle. "I think I can do it. I've got myself talked into it." He stepped to the cow and began stroking her head, slowly, softly. He patted her neck, talked to her quietly. "You poor old thing, you've had a hard day," he said. The cow bellowed, plaintively, almost as though she understood. Gary kept rubbing her, patting her.

After a time he pulled the cow's head against his hip, and he brought the barrel up. He rubbed the cow's neck again, and then pulled her ear back. The cow quieted. Gary waited for just a moment, and Dennis saw him take a deep breath before he pushed the barrel into place. "This isn't so bad as it seems," he said, speaking gently—not to Dennis but to the cow.

And then his lips moved again. He said something, maybe to himself—something Dennis couldn't hear. At the same moment, a dull thud sounded, and then Gary lowered the cow's head.

Dennis couldn't move. He didn't even know that he was crying until he felt the tears on his face.

"That little rifle had a hair trigger," Gary said, still crouched by the cow. "It fired before I knew I'd pulled on it." He patted the cow's back, and then he said, "I'm glad I did it." When he stood up and looked at Dennis, he was crying, and not even bothering to wipe away the tears.

They started back toward the house. Dennis felt changed inside, and yet he didn't know exactly what it was he had experienced. He only knew that he felt something around him, caressing him. By now it had come to him what Gary had said, there at the end, when his lips had moved. "Accept this."

At the fence, Dennis stopped. "Gary, I hope you and Jenny will come over on Christmas Eve."

"Yeah. I'm sure we can. I think it would be good for us."

"Well, maybe. But I think I'm the one who needs it. I really need to . . . make some changes. I'd like to be a little closer to where you are."

Gary smiled. "I picked a hard way to get there," he said.

Dennis nodded. "Gary, by Easter everything ought to be a lot easier."

"Yeah, I think so. Just thinking about Easter helps me. But winter is all right too—if you think about it right. It has to come first." Gary ran his fingers through his hair, brushing it down. He looked back across the field, toward the pond.

Dennis looked too. He could barely see the big cow, part of the mud now. But the field of snow was dazzling under the sun, sparkling, flashing colors. It hardly seemed the same place.

"Accept this," Dennis whispered to himself. And he repeated the words over and over as he and Gary walked back to the house.

Leslie Norris is Humanities Professor of Creative Writing at Brigham Young University. A native of Wales, he was educated at the city of Coventry College and at the University of Southhampton. He has published fourteen books of poetry, two of them for children, and two collections of short stories. Among his prizes he includes The Karl G. Maeser Distinguished Lecturer Award and the John Hughes Prize for Literature, given to him at The Sunday Times Literature Festival in Wales earlier this year. He is married and lives in Orem.

THE WIND, THE COLD WIND

by Leslie Norris

I was almost at the top of Victoria Road, under the big maroon boarding advertising Camp Coffee, when I heard Jimmy James shouting.

"Hey Ginger!" he shouted. "Hold on a minute, Ginger!"

He couldn't wait to reach me. He ran across the road in front of the Cardiff bus as if it didn't exist. There he was, large, red-faced, rolling urgently along like a boy with huge, slow springs in his knees, like a boy heaving himself through heavy, invisible water. Jimmy couldn't read very well. Once I'd written a letter for him, to his sister who lived in Birmingham and worked in a chocolate factory; once he'd let me walk to school with him and other large, important boys. He stopped in front of me, weighty, impassable.

"I heard you were dead," he said. "The boys told me you were dead."

His large brown eyes looked down at me accusingly.

"Not me, Jim," I said, "Never felt fitter, Jim."

He thought that too sprightly by half. His fat cheeks reddened and he wagged a finger at me. It looked at thick as a club.

"Watch it, Ginge," he said.

He was fifteen years old, five years older than I, and big. He was a boy to be feared. I showed it.

"No, Jim," I said smiling soberly, "I'm not dead."

"The boys told me you were," he said.

107

He was looking at me with the utmost care, his whole attitude reproachful and disappointed. I was immediately guilty. I had let Jimmy James down, I could see that. And then, in an instant, I understood, for something very like this had happened to me before.

The previous winter, in January, a boy called Tony Plumley had drowned in a pond on the mountain. I'd spent a lot of time worrying about Tony Plumley. The unready ice had split beneath him and tumbled him into the darkness. For weeks afterwards, lying in my bed at night, I'd followed him down, hearing him choke, feeling the stiffening chill of the water. I had watched his skin turn blue as ice, I had felt his lungs fill to the throat with suffocating water, known the moment when at last his legs had gone limp and boneless. I had given Tony Plumley all the pity and fear I possessed. And later, in irresistible terror, I had gone with him into his very grave. Then, one day when I had forgotten all about him and was running carefree along a dappled path in the summer woods, there he was, in front of me, Tony Plumley, alive. I thought of all that sympathetic terror spent and wasted and I was wildly angry. I charged him with being drowned.

"It wasn't me," Tony Plumley said, backing off fast.

"It was you," I said. "Put up your fists."

But Tony Plumley stood still and cautious outside the range of my eager jabs. Taking the greatest care, speaking slowly, he explained that he was not drowned at all, that he had never been sliding on the pond, that his mother would not have let him. It was another boy, Tony Powell, who had dropped through the cheating ice and died. I had been confused by the similarity of their names. I stood there trying to reconcile myself to a world in which the firm certainty of death had proved unfaithful, a world in which Tony Powell, a boy unknown to me, was suddenly dead. Perplexed, I dropped my avenging hands.

"Get moving, Plumley," I said.

He slid tactfully past me and thumped away down the path.

So I knew exactly how Jimmy James felt. I'd used a lot of emotion on Plumley and Jim must have been imagining my death with much the same intensity. I understood his disappointment, deserved his reproach, stood resignedly under his just anger. I knew, too, how the confusion had come about.

"It's not me, Jim," I said, "it's Maldwyn Farraday. It's because we've both got red hair."

This completely baffled Jim. He looked at me in despair.

"What's red hair got to do with it?" he said loudly.

"We've both got red hair," I explained, "Maldwyn Farraday and I. And we live in the same street and we're friends. It's Maldwyn's dead. People mix us up."

Jim didn't say anything.

"I'm going to the funeral tomorrow," I said.

Jimmy James curled his lip in contempt and turned away, his heavy shoulders outraged, his scuffed shoes slapping the pavement. I waited until he had turned the corner by the delicatessen and then I ran. I ran past the shops still ablaze for the Christmas which was already gone, I ran past Davies' where unsold decorated cakes still held their blue and pink rosettes, their tiny edible skaters and Father Christmases, their stale, festive messages in scarlet piping; I ran past Mr. Roberts' shop without looking once at his sumptuous boxes of confectionery, at the cottonwool snowflakes falling in ranks regular as guardsmen down the glass of his window; past the symmetrical pyramids of fruit and vegetables in Mr. Leyshon's, the small, thin-skinned tangerines wrapped in silver foil, the boxes of dates from North Africa. I ran so that I did not have to think of Maldwyn.

Maldwyn had been my friend as long as I could remember. There was not a time when Maldwyn had not been around. He had great advantages as a friend. Not only could he laugh more loudly than anyone else, he was so awkward that with him the simplest exercise, just walking up the street, was hilarious chaos. And his house too, his house was big and gloriously untidy. In the basement was the workshop in which his father repaired all the machines in the neighborhood, all the lawn mowers, the electric kettles and irons, the clocks and watches. He also repaired them in the kitchen, in the garden, in the hall, wherever he happened to be. Our fathers' ancient cars were often in his yard, waiting for him to coax their tired pistons to another paroxysm of irregular combustion. Mr. Farraday's hands held always a bundle of incomprehensible metal parts he was patiently arranging into efficiency. He'd let us watch him tease into place the cogs and rivets of some damaged artifact, telling us in his quiet voice what he was doing. Sometimes, when we were watching Mr. Farraday, Maldwyn's two sisters, long, thin and malevolent, would come round and enrage us. Then Mr. Farraday would turn us out of doors and the sisters would giggle away to play the piano in another room. Maldwyn could roar like a bull. When he did this, his sisters would put their hands to their ears and run screaming, but Mr. Farraday just smiled gently.

Maldwyn's parents had come from a village many miles away, in the west of Wales. Their house was often full of cousins from this village, smiling, talking in their open country voices. They drank a lot of tea, these cousins, and then they all went off to visit Enoch Quinell. Everybody knew Enoch Quinell, because he was a policeman and enormously fat. My father said Enoch weighed more than two hundred and eighty pounds. But Maldwyn's family knew Enoch particularly well because he, too, had come from their village and always went back there for his holidays.

We knew a lot of jokes about Enoch, about how he'd cracked the weigh bridge where the coal trucks were weighed, how he was supposed to have broken both ankles trying to stand on tip-toe. I used to think they were pretty funny jokes, but Maldwyn would be very angry if he heard one of them and offer to fight the boy who said it. He was a hopeless fighter, anybody could have picked him off with one hand, but we all liked him. On Saturday mornings he went shopping for Enoch, for food, for shaving soap, cigarettes, things like that. Sometimes I went with him.

Enoch lived in rooms above the police station, and we'd climb there, past the fire engine on the ground floor, its brass glittering, its hoses white and spotless, past the billiard room, then up the stairs to Enoch's place. Once I saw Enoch eat. He cooked for himself a steak so huge that I could find no way to describe it to my mother. And then he covered it in fried onions. Maldwyn used to get sixpence for doing Enoch's shopping.

He had been working for Enoch on Christmas Eve. I hadn't known that. All afternoon I'd been searching for him, around the back of the garages where we had a den, in the market; I couldn't find him anywhere. Just as I thought of going home, I saw Maldwyn at the top of the street. He was singing, but when I called him he stopped and waved. The lights were coming on in the houses and shops. Some children were singing carols outside Benny Everson's door. I could have told them it was a waste of time.

"Look what Enoch gave me," Maldwyn said. Enoch had given him ten shillings. We had never known such wealth.

"What are you going to do with it?" I asked, touching the silver with an envious finger.

"I'm going to buy Enoch a cigar," he said, "for Christmas. Coming over?"

We walked towards the High Street. Mr. Turner, the tobacconist, was a tall, pale man, exquisitely dressed. He had a silver snuffbox and was immaculately polite to everyone who entered his shop. I knew that he and Maldwyn would be hours choosing a cigar for Enoch. I could already hear Mr. Turner asking Maldwyn's opinion.

"Perhaps something Cuban?" Mr. Turner would say. "No? Something a little smaller, perhaps, a little milder?"

"Ugh?" Maldwyn would say, smiling, not understanding any of it, enjoying it all.

I couldn't stand it. When we got to the Market I told Maldwyn that I'd wait for him there. I told him I'd wait outside Marlow's where I could look at the brilliant windows of the sporting world, the rows of fishing rods and the racks of guns, the beautiful feathery hooks of salmon-flies in their perspex boxes, the soccer balls, the marvelous boxing shorts, glittering and colored like the peacock, the blood-red boxing gloves. Each week I spent hours at these windows and I was a long time there on Christmas Eve. Maldwyn didn't come back. At last I went home. My mother was crying and everybody in our house was quiet. They told me that Maldwyn was dead. He had rushed out of Mr. Turner's shop, carrying in his hand two cigars in a paper bag, and run straight under a truck.

"I've been watching for him," I said. "Outside Marlow's. He went to buy a cigar for Enoch."

I went early to bed and slept well. It didn't feel as if Maldwyn was dead. I thought of him as if he were in his house a few doors down the street, but when I walked past on Christmas morning the blinds were drawn across all the Farraday's windows and in some of the other houses too. The whole street was silent. And all that day I was lost, alone. We didn't enjoy Christmas in our house. The next day Mr. Farraday came over to say that they were going to bury Maldwyn in their village, taking him away to the little church where his grandparents were buried. He asked me to walk with the funeral to the edge of town, with five other boys.

"You were his best friend," Mr. Farraday said.

Mr. Farraday looked exactly the same as he always did, his face pink and clean, his bony hands slow. I told him that I'd like to walk in Maldwyn's funeral. I had never been to a funeral.

The day they took Maldwyn away was cold. When I got up a hard frost covered the ground and the sky was grey. At ten o'clock I went down to Maldwyn's. The other boys were already there, standing around: Danny Simpson, Urias Ward, Reggie Evans, Georgie and Bobby Rowlands. We wore our best suits, our overcoats, our scarves, our gleaming shoes. The hearse and the black cars were waiting at the curb and little knots of men stood along the pavement, talking quietly. In a little while Maldwyn's door opened and three tall men carried out the coffin. I was astonished by its length; it looked long enough to hold a man, yet Maldwyn was shorter than I. He was younger too. I hadn't expected that there would be any noise, but there was. Gentle though the bearers were, the coffin bumped softly, with blunt wooden sounds, and grated when they slid it along the chromium tracks inside the hearse. I knew that little Georgie Rowlands was scared. His eyes were pale and large and he couldn't look away. The wreaths were carried from the house and placed in a careful pile on the coffin and inside the hearse. I could see mine, made of early daffodils and other flowers I couldn't name. My card was wired to it. I had written on it, "Goodbye Maldwyn, from all at Number 24."

"You boys will march at the side of the hearse," said Mr. Jewell, the undertaker, "three on each side, you understand?"

We nodded.

"And no playing about," Mr. Jewell said. "Just walk firmly along. And when we get to the park gates we'll stop for a second so that you can all get safely to the side of the road. We don't want accidents. Be careful, remember that."

"Yes," Reggie Evans said.

Danny Simpson and Georgie Rowlands were on my side of the hearse. As we walked up the street I could see my mother and brother, but I didn't even nod to them. They were with a gathering of other neighbors, all looking cold and sad. We turned and marched towards the edge of town, perhaps a mile away. The wind, gusting and hard, blew at our legs and the edges of our coats. There were few people to see us go. At the park gates the whole procession stopped and we stood in a line at the side of the road. We saw the car in which Mr. and Mrs. Farraday sat, with their daughters. I didn't recognize them in their unaccustomed black, but Urias Ward did. I saw Enoch Quinell in one of the following cars, and he saw me. He looked me full in the face and he was completely unsmiling and serious. Picking up speed, the hearse and the other cars sped up the road, over the river bridge, out of sight. Left without a purpose, we waited until we knew they were far away.

"Let's go home through the park," Danny Simpson said.

We walked in single file along the stone parapet of the lake, looking at the grey water. The wind, blowing without hindrance over its surface, had cut it into choppy waves, restless, without pattern. Everything was cold. Out in the middle, riding the water as indifferently as if it had been a smooth summer day, were the two mute swans which lived there all year round. They were indescribably sad and beautiful, like swans out of some cruel story from the far north, like birds in some cold elegy I had but dimly heard and understood only its sorrow. I remembered that these swans were said to sing only as they died, and I resented then their patient mastery of the water, their manifest living. And then there came unbidden into my mind the images of all the death I knew. I saw my grandfather in his bed, when I had been taken to see him, but that was all right because his nose was high and sharp and his teeth were too big and he hadn't looked like my grandfather. He hadn't looked like a person at all. I saw again the dead puppy I had found on the river bank, his skin peeling smoothly away from his poor flesh, and this was frightening, for he came often to terrify me in nightmares, and I also wept in pity for him when I was sick or tired. And I saw the dead butterfly I had found behind the bookshelves where it had hidden from the approach of winter. It had been a Red Admiral, my favorite butterfly, and it had died there, spread so that I could marvel at the red and white markings on its dusky wings, their powder still undisturbed. I held it on the palm of my hand and it was dry and light, so light that when I closed my eyes I could not tell that I held it, as light as dust. And thinking of the unbroken butterfly, I knew that I would never again see Maldwyn Farraday, nor hear his voice, nor wake in the morning to the certainty that we would spend the day together. He was gone forever. A great and painful emptiness was in my chest and my throat. I stopped walking and took from my overcoat pocket the last of my Christmas chocolate, a half-pound block. I called the boys around me and, breaking the chocolate into sections, I divided it among us. There were two sections over, and I gave them to little Georgie Rowlands because he was the youngest. Tears were pouring down Reggie Evans' cheeks and the winds blew them across his nose and onto the collar of his overcoat.

"It's the wind," he said. "The bloody wind makes your eyes water."

He could scarcely speak and we stood near him, patting his shoulders, our mouths filled with chocolate, saying yes yes, the wind, the cold wind. But we were all crying, we were all bitterly weeping, our cheeks were wet and stinging with the harsh salt of our tears, we were overwhelmed by the recognition of our unique and common knowledge, and we had nowhere to turn for comfort but to ourselves.

Douglas H. Thayer was born in Salt Lake City and grew up in Provo, Utah. Mr. Thayer joined the army at seventeen and served in Germany, where he returned to serve a mission. He graduated from BYU in English and later took an MA in English at Stanford and an MFA at the University of Iowa in fiction writing. Mr. Thayer is a professor of English at Brigham Young University, where he served as director of composition and associate dean in the College of Humanities. Previous publications include a novel, Summer Fire, *and two collections of short stories,* Under the Cottonwoods *and* Mr. Wahlquist in Yellowstone. *Mr. Thayer recently finished a collection of personal essays called "Provo Boy" and is working on a novel. Mr. Thayer is married to Donlu DeWitt and has six children. He currently serves as advisor to the Deacons quorum in his ward.*

THE RED-TAILED HAWK

by Douglas H. Thayer

I remember how icy the alarm clock was that morning when I jerked it under the covers and fumbled for the button. I didn't want my mother to hear it and get up too, because she would make me eat a cooked breakfast, fix me a big lunch. She would tell me again I shouldn't kill birds, insist how dangerous the river was for me alone, especially in winter, even if I was fifteen, and say that it was almost Christmas. I listened. Then, glad when I couldn't hear her door down the hall, I put the clock back and pulled my Levi's and shirt under the covers to warm. I was going after geese, ducks too, but mostly geese, Canada geese. Standing in the south field after chores, I had seen them twice that week coming up off the lake to feed in the fields. The great grey Canada birds were fantastic, huge almost, wild and free, with a clamorous gabbling that made me shiver. Yet I had never killed one.

"Let me go with you."

I turned to face Glade, the oldest of my three younger brothers, his head just raised off his pillow. How I hated to sleep with him, feel his warmth beside me in the bed, hear him breathe, wake in the night to find him touching me. "No, you can't go. I told you last night."

"I've got some shells. Please, it's Christmas."

115

"No. Shut up and go back to sleep."

His face pale in the dim light from the frosted windows, he stared at me, then lowered his head and turned to the wall. Glade followed me everywhere, swimming in the summer, fishing, hunting, on hikes. My mother made me let him go, said I should want him to go, that we were brothers. We fought at night. Straddling him I held my pillow over his face, him bucking and twisting, sucking for air; or I jabbed him savagely under the covers until he cried, when my two youngest brothers would holler from their bed that we were fighting. I could hear my father coming. He cuffed me, threatened to lick me, said, "You're not too big yet for a damned good licking." And I hated him for that, for grabbing me by the collar, for kicking me in the butt hard, for always shouting that I was a fool. But I never cried. He couldn't make me.

I wanted to be left alone, wanted that fiercely, didn't want anybody around me, touching me. I wanted to be alone like the birds. Birds were alone. I loved birds. I had taken a taxidermy course, two dollars for each mailed lesson, my haying money, and out in the barn I skinned the birds I killed and made their cotton bodies. I hung them from the barn rafters on long wires, suspended them in flight, meadowlarks, robins, magpies, crows, ducks, hawks, and hanging from the ceiling in my room on a wire, a large red-tailed hawk, wings spread, soaring. Birds could fly wherever they wanted, could be alone. Nothing touched them but the air.

At night, Glade asleep, I would sneak off my pajamas and curl tight under the blankets but not really feel them in the darkness because they were warm like my skin, like air. And that summer often I lay on top of the covers spread out, stared up at the hawk, lifted my naked arms. I fell asleep like that once, and Glade woke before I did. "You're going to go crazy with that stuff!" my father yelled at me. "What the hell's got into you lately anyway?"

But it wasn't sex, not that kind. I wasn't innocent, for no farm boy could be. But I didn't know girls then, not at fourteen and away from town, and my loins and heart did not burn as they would two years later, although even at fourteen I dreamed and woke in the darkness, my sleep having become frantic with a boy's passion. But mostly I dreamed other dreams, dreams of flying, soaring, lifting away from the earth, being an eagle or a hawk, vanishing into the yellow sun.

My Levi's and shirt got warm under the covers. Feet curled against the cold linoleum, I dressed. Kneeling to feel for my heavy wool boot socks, I looked up at the red-tail. "The Albatross—Six-Foot Wingspan," a sailplane I built, had hung there first. Proud of me for once, my father said I should enter it in the county fair. But I didn't. Carrying the five-foot detachable wings, Glade carrying the body because I couldn't carry both, I climbed into the hot summer cliffs, where I sailed it into the afternoon thermals, watched it soar to disappear into the sun. Then I stepped to the very edge, raised my arms. Glade screamed, and he told my father. "You trying to kill yourself, you little fool?" my father yelled at me that night, called me a fool again for losing the plane. Younger, I would let my kites go, hold them until the ten-cent ball of string ended, then let them go, watch the wind carry them.

Careful not to let my drawer squeak, I got my shotgun shells. More than anything else I wanted a room of my own where I could lock the door, be alone, sleep alone, not hear anybody at night, not be touched. And I would have my birds in my room, the soaring hawks and eagles, and the giant grey-white Canada geese. Hanging above my bed on wires, they would be flying, and I could lie there at night looking up at them in the moonlight from the windows or use my flashlight, and perhaps the summer breeze through the open windows would stir them. I would be in a flock of birds.

I remember how I crept down the dark hall, my hand flat against the wall. I closed the hall door and walked through the cold front room past the Christmas tree and into the kitchen. After I ate a bowl of cornflakes I fixed me a sandwich and got my shotgun and other gear. It was two days before Christmas. I hated that too, hated the glittering tree, the music, everybody laughing. But mostly I hated the presents, getting them, people handing me things, putting their arms around me, patting me on the back, wanting something in return. I cringed, wanted to jerk away, run. I wanted the tree down, the ornaments, lights, and Christmas music put away in the cupboard. I wanted the house silent.

I did not dress warm against the cold, although the evening paper had said a big snowstorm was due that afternoon. I wasn't afraid of the cold. I pulled on my hip boots, put my brown canvas hunting coat on over my sweater, fitted my scarf. I didn't build the kitchen fire or turn up the oil heater in the front room. My mother might wake up and, because of the storm, change her mind about me going, or make

me take Glade. Through my cotton gloves I felt the cold metal of my
shotgun, a double-barrel. I didn't care if they all woke up to a cold
house. My father was on graveyard shift at the dairy, but my mother
would be up long before he got home a little after eight o'clock.

Closing the back door, I walked down the porch steps, my breath
rising in plumes in the icy air. Over the west mountains the moon was
a yellow glow behind the clouds. To the east the sky grew white over
the mountains. I stopped at the fence at the end of the second field, the
crusted snow a foot deep where I stood. My father's small farm was on
a bench. Below me were the river bottoms, narrow, then wider where
the river neared the lake five miles to the west. Black against the
snow, a wide band of cottonwood trees lined the river, a high clump at
the swimming hole two miles below the mouth of Spring Creek. In the
summer the bottoms were all planted to wheat, oats, sugar beets, and
hay, the houses and barns all a mile or two back from the river
because of the spring high water. It would be another ten years before
they built the dam in the canyon.

I loved that belt of trees and willows, the river. The school, church,
my father's house were all alien to me, prisons. I lived my real life
there in the bottoms, fished, swam, climbed in the high trees,
embraced limbs, sometimes ran naked and alone through the green
willows, lay spread-eagle under the sun, soared on the great rope
swing, hunted the birds, killed them. I was always hiding from Glade
and the others, the sheriff when he came down to see if we wore
swimsuits; always driven, I reached out for something infinite, not
knowing what it was, but feeling myself drawn to it, some final feeling
beyond the earth in the yellow sun.

One set of car lights moved along the bottom road, but I knew I
would be the only hunter so late in the season. Those who still hunted
had boats and decoys and hunted the open holes on the lake. I climbed
between the frosted fence wires and started down the slope. The cattle
gathered into the feedlots near the road all day, I would see only the
few starved-out horses left in the fields to winter. Sometimes the
horses died, froze icy, the legs sticking straight out. When the snow
melted, the magpies flocked out of the willows to feed on them.

I would jump shoot Spring Creek to the river and then blind up on
a sandbar and wait for the storm to push the geese and big ducks off
the lake. Strung out for a mile in the new light, a flock of crows was
already coming off the roost. Cawing, black against the snow when

they dipped down, a thousand of them maybe, they headed for the cornfields on the bench. Already my hands were cold in the thin gloves, but I shoved only my right hand under my coat. I liked the cold. It was clean and kept people inside. In April and May I swam in the cold river. I liked storms. My mother wanted me home early to help get ready for Christmas, but I would stay late.

I climbed through the last fence and came around a clump of willows. A blue Ford pickup stood parked off the lane near the wooden tractor bridge over Spring Creek. I cursed, the words steady and half silent, like a hiss. A flat sneak boat with two men in it drifted into the first bend as I stepped on the bridge. I watched it vanish into the vapor, the creek just wide enough for it, the voices coming back to me on the water. I cursed them again, loud now, cursed them for the ducks, for being there, for not letting me have it alone, cursed them for their voices and their noise. Then I heard shooting, and I cursed them for that too, even as I loaded my own gun.

I hoped for stragglers out of the small flocks of ducks I saw rise over the willows just ahead of where the boat must have been. But none came. One or two would fall out of the flock; I would hear the dull boom of the shotgun, but no ducks flew close enough for me. I saw no geese. A mile below the tractor bridge, I stopped to warm my hands. Too high for a shot, a magpie flew over me and dropped into a field with a dozen others and some crows near the partially covered skeletons of three cows killed by lightning that summer. Because it was swampy the farmer hadn't been able to drag them out. We had walked the two miles up from the swimming hole to see them the day after. For a month, if the wind was right, you could smell the heavy, watery stink across the fields. What little flesh was left was frozen hard or covered with snow. The magpies and crows watched me pass.

I hunted on down the creek. Magpies were smart. I killed very few of them with my shotgun. I killed them in the early summer with my .22 rifle when, just out of the nest, the young birds couldn't fly far. Tired of swimming, naked, the extra shells brassy in my mouth, I sneaked from tree to tree, shot the young birds, watched them fall in puffs of feather from the high limbs, the screeching old birds too smart to light. Then, because I knew what my mother would say if I brought too many birds home, I tied them with pieces of wire to the fences or climbed to wedge them back in the trees.

The sneak boat was tied up where Spring Creek emptied into the river. The two men sat drinking coffee, the ducks piled on the bow. I crept closer through the willows.

"How about that triple, Fred? Three mallards dead before they hit the water."

I aimed first at him, centering the bead on his head. A little closer, I could have blown big holes in the boat the same way I blew holes in sheds and wooden fences.

"Best shooting I ever saw you do."

I clicked my safety back on, turned and started down the river. Later I heard their motor and knew they had gone back up Spring Creek, knew they had limited out, knew then, too, I was on the river alone.

There was no trail in the snow. I broke my own, cut in and out to the riverbank, but jumped nothing close enough for a shot. Nothing was flying. The wind hadn't really started, wasn't strong enough yet to force the ducks off the lake, keep them low. I stopped often to look for geese against the black mountains and dark clouds, watched until my eyes watered, listened, strained for a sound I could not hear. I knew the storm would bring geese. I'd hunted them since I was twelve and my father let me carry a gun, but I'd never shot one.

I saw small flocks of crows and solitary hawks. Sandbars fed out into the river from the steep banks, but the channel was still full. I had been first across the swimming hole that April, Glade shouting for me to come back, not to try it, that it was too cold, two swift. They'd had to lift me out, build a fire for me. I vomited, blacked out, but I had been first across. I told Glade what I would do to him if he said anything.

I shot a crow that flew over, and it fell into the river. It beat its water-heavy wings and kept lifting its head, but the slow current took it. I liked to touch the birds I killed. A marsh hawk flew by, but not close enough. I watched for the wind in the tops of the trees. Finally, stomping my feet against the numbness, I built a blind on a sandbar where a week earlier I had seen goose tracks and droppings on the edge ice. Warming one hand at a time in my crotch, I ate my lunch and watched the river. A few yellow willow leaves drifted slowing by.

In the summer, alone, my swimming suit hung in a tree, wearing only my Keds, I liked to stand in the willows and let the fluttering green leaves touch me. Rifle in hand, I hunted unseen, alone, sometimes naked except for my feet, shouts drifting to me from the swimming hole. When a thunderstorm came over the west mountains, and the farmers, afraid of being hit by lightning, left the fields, I sneaked out to stand in the belly-high green wheat, watch the great flashes of light, hear the roar and rumble of thunder, feel the wind, the wheat waving against me. Or I climbed high in the bending trees, wrapped my arms and legs around the limbs, squeezed until the rough bark hurt, rode the trees. I loved trees.

And if I tired of hunting birds, I shot the surfacing carp, watched them fade into the deep grey water, set my rifle against a tree, followed them, walked slowly into the river from the sandbars until the water was over my head and the slow summer current carried me. I spread my arms and legs to touch the flesh-warm water, became nothing, only part of the water. Eyes open, I sank down from the grey-blue to the green and then the black, the light disappearing above me, completely alone, touched the cold bottom mud, then rose back again into the light. And I kept doing that until the vomit stung in my throat and I got dizzy. Then I lay in the yellow sun, looked at it through the cracks between my fingers, tried to see what it was. When Glade hollered that he had my clothes, that it was time for chores, I wouldn't answer. Days later I saw the carp near the edge of the water, bleached yellow-white and pecked by magpies.

Small flocks of teal kept flying upriver, but I didn't shoot, didn't want the small ducks. A lone greenhead mallard came up. Watching it through the piled brush, I stood, shot, dropping it dead, ragged, where I could drag it out with a stick, glad it didn't float away out of reach. Sitting in my blind again, I arranged the feathers, stroked them, touched the velvet green head. It was a big northerner with bright orange feet. The winter before on Christmas afternoon I had killed a mallard banded in Alaska. I made a ring out of the aluminum band, which I touched in school, in church, took off, read. Ducks could fly wherever they wanted to, up above everything, just in the air with nothing else around them, never touched by anything except water and air.

It was colder. Blowing across the river from the northeast, the beginning wind scattered a few leaves out of the willows and onto the rippled water. I stomped my feet, rubbed my numb fingers, remembered the story of the hunter who tried to kill his dog, to put his hands in the warm guts to keep them from freezing; but the dog wouldn't come close enough, and the hunter had lost his rifle. Finally

I decided to move father downriver, run part of the way, get warm and blind up again. The wind hit me when I left the willows, and I heard shooting from toward the lake. A few ducks flew against the black clouds; the growing wind would force them down. I heard geese once, pushed back into the willows, saw them off to the south, big, black, five of them, high, their gabbling faint. I remember how I spoke to them: "Turn, turn," I said, but, heart slamming, had to watch them vanish, just stand there.

I already knew I would stay until dark, knew it before I left the house that morning. I didn't care about my father; maybe he would be asleep, because he had to go on shift at midnight, wouldn't be waiting for me. My mother would just worry, not cuff me, not shout, just look at me, shake her head, talk, her eyes maybe filling up with slow tears, tell me it was Christmastime. The geese would come if I waited long enough. In my mind I saw them, five or six maybe, coming up the river, the great moving wings, necks out, the gabbling louder and louder. And I would kill one, maybe two, bring them crashing down with perfect head shots, the great wings all ragged in the air.

I crossed Spring Creek where a wax sandwich paper from the sneak boat had blown up the creek and caught in the weeds. Three times I cut back in to check the river but jumped nothing, the last time walked through the little grove of six-foot blue spruce. Twice my father had asked me, "Can't you get us a Christmas tree down on the river this year, save me buying one?"

"No," I said, "there aren't any."

"You sure? There used to be a few in the willows if you kept your eyes open."

"No," I said, all the time staring at Glade.

I didn't want to cut a tree, drag it up to the house, hang it with tinsel and lights, didn't want the smell of it in the house away from the river, didn't want to watch it turn brown. A hundred yards back from the spruces, under the snow, were the bones of a little spike buck I had killed a year earlier in August. He had followed the river out of the canyon. I shot him through the eye with my .22, watched him until he was quiet, and then turned him over so he didn't look hurt. I went back three times that day, squatted down by him, brushed off the ants. The second day the magpies were on him.

Except for a few horse tracks, the snow was clean, and I broke my own trail. Way ahead where the river curved, I saw the high cottonwoods at the swimming hole. It took five boys just to reach around the biggest tree, the rope tree. It was an old rope, two inches thick and frayed. We had board platforms nailed in the trees to swing from, but I liked to climb higher, up into the green leaves. The others watched me, faces upturned, Glade shouting for me not to go any higher, maybe bawling. Sometimes, standing on a limb, I let go and stood on just one foot to have the feeling, then grabbed the overhead branch again when I tipped. I liked the feeling, the shiver.

Holding the rope, chest tight, I lifted up, and it was like in my dreams when I flew over houses and trees with just my arms outspread. The warm air rushing against me, the trees blurred, I waited until just before I hit the top of the sweep before I let go. And for that one moment I flew, saw everything below me, soared, hovered. Then I dropped, felt the tingling in my crotch, felt the air, the rushing, heavier water. And I stayed under until they all thought I had drowned. I was both bird and fish. If anybody climbed as high as I had, I would climb higher, swinging again and again, falling until my nose bled, and I let the blood fall on my naked chest and stomach so that I looked wounded. The letting go, the soaring, was the very best part. I wanted to feel like that forever.

I built another blind on a sandbar above the swimming hole. The wind made the cold worse. I couldn't see my breath anymore. I kept my hands under my armpits, stomped my feet on the packed snow. Walking home I would be facing into the wind all the way. I knew that it was nearly four o'clock, that I should have been at least back to the tractor bridge on Spring Creek. People would be turning on their outside Christmas lights. The steady shooting from toward the lake meant more birds were flying. Teal kept slipping up the river in easy range, but I didn't shoot. I dropped a hen mallard out of a flock of five on the second shot. She was easy to reach. She was big, an orange-footed northerner, and I decided I would mount her too, when I did the goose, put her near a big greenhead I had hanging in the barn, make a pair. I liked the wind. I liked to go out in the barn on windy days, leave the door open and watch the birds move.

Later I climbed the bank to look for geese. Under the low, heavy clouds everything was almost black, even the snow. Willows clicked. Lower now, the ducks came in against the wind in singles and doubles and small flocks. Dipping down, wings whistling when they flew over, they came on, the wind forcing them lower. I saw two small flocks of geese, strained to hear them above the wind, stared them out of sight, hoping all the time they would turn, come my way, talked to them. But they kept on, drawn to some other place, left me empty.

Below the geese white points of light burned in the houses along the bench, the outside Christmas lights not visible from that distance. My mother would be pushing back the curtain at the kitchen window to look out. But I didn't care. In front of me, black against the grey snow, stood a starved-out old horse, head down, tail to the wind. Beyond the horse, only a black dot, was the big haystack at the end of Miller's Lane. The horse was the only thing in the field I could see alive. Swaying the tops of the trees, the wind brought the first scattered flakes of snow.

Just after I got back in my blind, two big greenhead mallards flew by in easy range, but I didn't shoot. More big ducks came. But I was waiting for geese, only geese. They liked to rest in the shallows along the sandbars, leave their sign. But they came late, and I, afraid of my father, had never dared stay. They would come though, I knew, if only I waited long enough. I listened against the wind, strained my watery eyes to watch down the river, watched, stomped my feet only when I couldn't stand the numbness, pounded my gloved hands against my knees, sure the geese would come, absolutely sure.

The big haystack at the end of Miller's Lane was where we left our bicycles when we went down to swim. August had been very hot, and I remember one night how I got up, dressed and climbed out the bedroom window. I intended only to ride my bicycle up and down the road in front of the house to get cool, but I turned off on the bottom road and then onto Miller's Lane, parked my bicycle. At first I took off only my shirt, but then my Keds and socks, and then, carrying my clothes, I was running naked down the sandy path, leaping, watching my legs flash in the moonlight. I wanted to scream and yell, throw my clothes away, run through the fields of ripe August wheat, but I didn't because I knew a farmer might be out with a late water turn, or I might cut my feet. The cows and horses did not shy as I ran past them.

The cottonwood trees shaded the moonlight from the swimming hole. The dark air over me, I floated, tried not to move, the water fusing with the darkness. When I climbed the trees the dark leaves touched me. The second night, in a wind I rode the trees, the high limbs, heard a million leaves, screamed into the sound. And when I swung on the rope it was fantastic because I couldn't see where the water started. The tingling went from my crotch clear to my skull, and I reached out to a world I had never known, something inviting me, as in my dreams.

I left the house four times at night, until on the fourth morning at three o'clock, my father was waiting for me in the yard. "What the hell you doing out at this hour?" he said, spun me around, felt my damp hair. "You young fool, you trying to commit suicide down there swimming alone at night?" I didn't answer. He backhanded me, told me what it was like to drown, shouted, said he'd beat me next time. I had to stay on the place for a week. "Fool," he said. "I'll send the sheriff after you if you try it again." At breakfast Glade kept snickering.

More ducks flew up the river, flocks. I knew it would soon be dark. And then I heard them, that gabbling, the sound at first like the wind. I listened, already reaching for my shotgun, as if by instinct I knew the sound was geese. They were on the river. My breath caught. Heavy loads already chambered, I crouched on the snow, pushed the safety off, smothered the sound with my glove, tightened my legs. Low, gabbling, three great Canada geese flew out of the greyness below me, shadows, but then blacker, coming right at me in good range. Big, bigger than I had ever thought, beautiful, somebody pounding me over the heart. I watched through a hole in the blind. "Wait, wait," whispering, "not too soon, not too soon. Big. Wait, wait." The gabbling grew louder—marvelous the wings, the long necks, the rhythmic birds.

Just as they came abreast I stood up. Flaring, they lifted with the wind, moving away. I shot, missed, shot again, and the lead goose turned completely over and fell broken-winged, crashing into the water. Even as he hit I was out of the blind, mindless of the other geese, ready to dance and scream. Upright, trailing the wing, the goose swam toward the far side. Cramming in a shell, I aimed carefully at the head and fired. The long neck collapsed, and the head pushed forward into the water under the force of the shot. The pounding in my chest died. The wind and the slow current moved him. He was too far out.

I didn't hesitate. I set my gun on my coat. When I pulled off my Levi's the cold wind stung my bare legs. Puffs of mud rose around my feet when I stepped into the river past the edge ice, the water colder than the wind. I swam sidestroke, the goose bobbing ahead of me on the waves I made. I wasn't afraid, though I knew I could cramp, sink, fade down into the grey water and yellow leaves. It didn't seem strange, not unreal, not dangerous. I reached out and took the goose by the neck, glad, wanting to shout, the feathers warm. And then, not feeling my body under the water, frozen, I turned back. When I touched the mud under me, I stumbled out and dropped the goose. Yellow, the broken wingbone stuck out through the feathers. I picked up the goose again and hugged it to me, felt the still-warm body against my numb skin.

The wind had blown my shirt and left glove into the water. My body was white. My head buzzed. I kept gasping for breath, and acid vomit rose in my throat as I tried to dry myself with my undershirt. When I tried to pull on my Levi's, I stumbled, covering my feet with the white snow. Dressed, I put the stiffening wet glove, shirt, and undershirt into the rear game pocket with the ducks, picked up the heavy goose, my shotgun, and struggled up the bank. The wind hit me square, blew the snow hard into my eyes, took my breath.

After ten minutes, fumbling, I stopped to brush the snow off my coat and to wrap my scarf around my face. Still my face slowly stiffened, and it was hard to open my mouth. My forehead ached; the snow filled my eyes. I carried the goose over my shoulder; my bare left hand had become wood or stone. Everything was black, even the sky, the only light coming from the grey snow under me. I couldn't see Spring Creek or the river. At first when I stumbled, the snow was colder than the wind, but only at first. The cold was like pressing naked against ice. I kept trying to brush the snow off my coat so I wouldn't be white. A magpie rose screeching from a willow clump and was whipped away by the wind. My shotgun was gone.

I pushed on and on against the wind and driving snow until I could not feel myself walking. I kept stumbling and falling. I wasn't carrying the Canada goose over my shoulder. I didn't know where I was. I seemed not even to breathe. I floated, left the ground, rose, hovered, and it was a sensation I had never known before. I expected to see the fences, willows, and trees vanish under me. I was becoming something beyond myself. I felt no limits, nothing stopping, nothing touching me, as if I were rising alone into light, rising, never falling back, the sensation never ending.

I stumbled a last time, fell forward into the soft snow, where I lay on my side not caring, the snow not cold anymore. Relaxed, sleepy almost, I stared at the white snow falling on my coat, saw then the horn and half-head of one of the summer lighting-killed cows. I raised my head, saw behind me the mound I had stumbled over. I crawled. Mechanically with my lower arms and dead hands, I pushed back the snow from the horn, saw the black, empty eye socket, the bone skull. I looked down. Snow filled the wrinkles of my coat; I was turning white.

All summer the cows had been vanishing, the wirehung birds too, the carp, the little buck. And I had no name for it, only vanishing, knew only that it was not swimming, not running naked in the moonlight, not embracing trees, not soaring. It was not feeling. I grew whiter, saw myself vanishing into the snow. I watched, and then slowly, like beginning pain, the terror seeped into me, the knowing. I struggled up, fled.

But I could not run, could not feel the ground through my feet to balance myself. When I fell I got up, pushed with my elbows, feeling no pain, my hands and feet gone. I found low places in the fences and fell forward, the wire tearing my clothes. I thought the posts and bushes were people rushing up to help me.

I could only see, not smell, hear, even my tongue cold in my mouth. And I wanted to raise my arms around my head to keep it warm so I could go on seeing, for I was afraid my eyes would freeze and I would fall down and be covered by the snow. But I couldn't see my arms.

And then I stopped, stood.

A light flashed through the driving snow. It was red. It flashed again. I saw headlights, and I began to run. I stumbled and I got up. I climbed up a bank. I fell down on my hands and knees. I looked at tire tracks filling with snow. I was on the lane. Slowly I stood up. I waited.

The headlights turned and came dipping, vanishing, a spotlight sweeping ahead and to the sides through the driving snow. The spotlight hit me and didn't move. The car came ahead and stopped, the red light on top flashing. It was the sheriff's car. The sheriff got out. He pulled his broad-brimmed hat tight against the wind. He buttoned the collar of his heavy coat. He stopped in front of me. He asked me my name. I stared at him. "Hell, kid, you've got your mother all upset. Your old man's out searching the fields with half-a-dozen neighbors in this storm. He's mad too, I can tell you that. You could freeze to death in no time out here with the wind blowing this hard."

The sheriff blocked out the lights.

Again he asked me my name. "What's wrong with you, kid, can't you talk?" He played his flashlight up and down me. "Where's your gun?" He stepped closer. "Where's your glove?" He shined the light into my eyes, and I couldn't close them. "Good hell, kid, we better get you in where it's warm." I felt him take my arm, grip it tight, and I fell toward his hand.

I was in the hospital three weeks. The surgeon cut three fingers on my left hand off down to the first knuckle, and afterward my hand was a white ball raised on a wire frame. I had pneumonia. The oxygen tent was like being underwater. When I rose up out of the blackness, I saw my mother or my father, sometimes both. My father sat in a chair and slept with his forehead resting on my bed. Then I would sink back down into the blackness again, spiral down into the not-knowing, vanish.

I was terrified of sleep. When I was out of the oxygen tent and could talk again, I told the doctor my hand didn't hurt so he would stop the shots for pain. At first he said no, but later he told the nurse. The pain wouldn't let me sleep too long. I cried sometimes at night because of the pain, but it was better than sleep.

Across from me was an old man with yellow skin who slept all of the time. At night I listened to him breathe, his mouth a black hole in the dim light. They kept putting his thin yellow arms and legs back under the covers. The nurses hurried to put a screen around my bed the night he died, but through the cracks I saw what they did. Later, after the nurse took the screen away, I watched two women turn over the mattress and put on all fresh bedding. They whispered back and forth across the bed and looked at me. A nurse made me take a sleeping pill.

When the doctor released me my father wrapped me in a blanket and carried me from the hospital door to the car in his arms, the corner of the blanket over my face. It was late afternoon when we got home. The whole family came out as we pulled in. My brothers were dressed in their Sunday clothes; my mother wiped her eyes with the bottom edge of her blue apron. My father carried me into the warm house that smelled of roast turkey and put me on the couch in the front room. Blazing in the corner was the Christmas tree with everybody's presents under it. They had saved Christmas for me, which I hadn't known. I bit my lip and turned away. Glade wanted to know what was wrong. "Nothing," I said.

Several neighbors came by to bring me presents; then we had supper, and after that, Christmas. My little brothers brought me my presents, helped me with the ribbons, stacked my presents for me. Later my mother said that I'd had enough excitement and needed to rest, so my father carried me down the hall to the bedroom. The bedroom was warm from a new oil heater. Warm under the covers in my heavy flannel pajamas, I lay and listened to my brothers playing in the front room. Above me the red-tailed hawk still hovered, the tail fanned, the wings spread to hold the air, the beak wide for screaming. The yellow glass eyes looked down, the bird motionless, dusty, suspended from a wire. Out in the barn the hanging birds were dusty too, some of them splotched with pigeon droppings.

That night Glade was supposed to sleep on the couch in the front room, where I could be during the day, but I didn't want him to. I told my mother he wouldn't hurt my hand, so she let him sleep with me. Later, just before he went on graveyard shift, my father came and stood in the doorway, the hall light behind him. He could see I was still awake, everybody else asleep.

"You all right, son?" he asked, quietly.

"I guess so," I said.

That was all he said. He stood there for a moment; then, leaving the door half open, turned and walked down the hall. He didn't turn the hall light off.

My presents were stacked on the dresser in front of the mirror. Over the sound of the heater I heard the wind outside. It was snowing. I raised my arm to turn the white ball of my hand in the light from the hall. I hadn't seen my hand yet. When I did, I cried like a baby in the doctor's office. At school I kept my hand hidden in my pocket, wore the same sweater every day because it had front pockets, and I stopped going to gym. I couldn't stand being dressed in a gym uniform, my arms bare; couldn't stand it in the showers naked, without even a towel to cover my hand; couldn't stand the other boys seeing me. Clutching my hand I prayed at night, even out loud, promised God everything, then woke in the early morning afraid to look. But my father made me start gym again.

"You can't hide; you have to live with it," he said.

And he made me do my chores, no matter how hard, no matter how many things I broke or spilled; and although he shouted at me sometimes, swore, he never again hit me.

Green, blue, white, red—the colored Christmas boxes and wrappings glinted on the dresser in the shaft of light from the half-open door. I stared up at the hawk. It was indistinct now, black, a hovering silhouette, a dark, still shadow above me. I moved closer to Glade, touched him. The dresser mirror reflected the boxes and packages. I had received the most presents.

Jerry Johnston was born in 1948. He was raised in Brigham City—a storybook town in the then idyllic 50s. Jerry served a mission to Bolivia in 1968 and attended Utah State University upon return where he majored in English . . . then political science . . . then music . . . then psychology. Jerry finally used his returned-missionary Spanish to CLEP twenty credits, and he majored in Spanish. He later followed his nose to the University of New Mexico where he got an MA in Spanish. Upon his return to Utah, he "bluffed" his way into a sports writing job at the Deseret News, where he works today writing book reviews, theater reviews and a weekly column called "More or Less." Jerry is married to Carol Westenskow (the girl almost-next-door from his youth). Jerry and Carol have several children and live in Brigham City where Jerry is still . . . "Searching for that storybook town I remember from the idyllic 50s."

JOURNEY OF THE MAGI

by Jerry Johnston

In 1954 I turned eight. That was the year Gramps set up housekeeping full-time in the barn while Grandma took total control of the house. I grew up thinking that was how farm families lived. It made sense in some ways—then and now.

I'm told the rift wasn't ugly or violent—more evolution than revolution. Over the years Gramps simply found more and more to do in the barn while Grandma found less for him in the house. I'm sure his tendency to "nip" and "use language" played a part. I'm also sure my grandmother's tendency to point out such flaws had a hand in things.

So, the barn was where I found Gramps on Christmas Eve, 1954, living in exile and happier than I'd seen him.

But then he was already a bit tipsy with Christmas cheer.

I found him sprawled on his old couch, his clock and gas heater nearby. I noticed he'd been doing some interior decorating; a new calendar was nailed to the wall. It featured a bare and buxom young dancer. The sight of her startled me. I almost forgot the message I'd been sent to deliver.

131

"Papa Rogers is coming by at seven and Grandma says your presence is cordially requested in the house," I told him. Papa Rogers was my grandmother's own father, and I delivered the message about him word for word—with no feeling for the sarcasm it contained, proud as a puppy of my wonderful memory.

Later I would see that I'd kicked over the lantern that almost sent the family up in flames.

"You what now?" Gramps said, giving me a glazed gaze. He'd heard, but pretended he hadn't. It was an old trick he used to stall for time.

"I didn't do anything, Grandpa," I said. "It's just Grandma said Papa Rogers will be here at seven and you're cordially invited."

"I am, am I?" he puffed, getting to his feet. "And 'cordially' you say." The name of Papa Rogers must have bashed against the Jack Daniels whiskey inside him like lightning hitting metal. His eyes flashed and he shot a stream of spit onto the ground by his feet. But realizing I was just the messenger—dumb but blameless—he just swatted my behind and sent me on my way.

"Get outta here you little bugger!" he said.

"Bugger" was one of my grandfather's two terms of endearment.

I hurried back to the house where our family's annual Christmas script was playing itself out.

Christmas in rural Idaho has always been a hodge-podge of rut and ritual. Meaningful tradition gets wed to mindless habit, so Christmases have both a solemn and silly side to them. Over the years the celebrations begin to blend in the mind until separating one Christmas from another is almost impossible. It takes a traumatic event to set one year in high relief from the others.

Back at the house I found Grandma readying the living room for Papa Rogers, putting out the Bible, putting away the magazines. Mother was linking pairs of socks with safety pins. Later she'd droop them over the backs of chairs for Santa to fill. Dad was secretly hum-hawing around in the bedroom closet where "Santa stored some of his toys so he didn't have to haul so many around the world."

I took my post by the window to await the arrival of Uncle Matt, Aunt Jean and T.J. Aunt Jean was mother's little sister. Their son, T.J., was my favorite cousin.

After a few minutes Grandma looked around. "Helen? Where's that husband of yours? I need him to splice this cord." My mother was scowling at the back window where the cold, onyx pane scowled back.

"He went out back," she said. "I think he high-tailed it to the barn to play hookey."

"Now, Helen!"

"Well," Mother said, "it's the truth."

Grandma had just begun giving mother a little lecture on long-suffering when two headlights flashed into the lane, breaking the mood.

We all knew who it was.

"T.J.!" I screamed. And a moment later my cousin came tumbling into the house with Aunt Jean close behind. There were hugs and kisses, with me fighting off Aunt Jean's sloppy kiss in a ritual that probably pre-dated Christmas itself.

"Did you bring Matt this year?" my mother laughed, "or did he forget where he put the presents again?"

"Matt went to the barn to get Daddy's tire chains," Aunt Jean said. "The road over the canyon's atrocious. He'll be right in."

And so the stage was set for the little passion play that would follow. All we needed was for Papa Rogers to make his grand entry.

In the lofty tradition of Mormon patriarchs, Papa Rogers was from the stern and stoic Lorenzo Snow school, not the feisty Pratt brothers school. With his bushy white moustache and unruly hair, he was both Albert Schweitzer and Albert Einstein—with a touch of Mark Twain tossed in. He was a school teacher who felt his vocation deeply. He spoiled no rod, spared no child. For forty years he'd dressed in black shoes, black suit and black tie. He dressed in his Sunday best just to listen to LDS conference on the radio. When he drove down the road in his black '49, he could have been mistaken for an Amish ambassador sent out to strengthen ties with the Mormons.

Yet once in a while a gleam filled his eye; especially when the topic turned to English literature. And he turned the topic that way often. He loved Charles Dickens. If I'd had an education then, I might have nicknamed him Mr. Pickwik or some such thing.

I assume Papa Rogers did what he did every year on Christmas; I was so busy playing I didn't notice. But I'm sure he rolled up the lane at three miles an hour, slid from his car, pulled his brass-handled cane and a can of mixed nuts from the back seat and stuttered into the house.

T.J. and I did know when he came through the front door, however. The scent of reverence quickly replaced the scent of Christmas cookies throughout the house.

"T.J.! Billy!" my mother called. "Come greet Papa Rogers!"

I groaned. I hated such moments. Besides, I knew my mother only called me in because she hoped some of the wise and wizened old gentleman would rub off on me. I swore to myself it never would.

Just the same, T.J. and I went in, shook the old man's hand, and plopped down on our bellies to listen—for at least a minute or two—to all the old stories.

Talk had just turned to Christmas traditions when Grandma looked down at me.

"You did tell your grandfather to come in, didn't you?" she asked.

"I told him he was cordially invited at seven," I said proudly.

Grandma bit her lower lip.

Suddenly, everyone was looking down at T.J. and me.

"Boys," Papa Rogers finally said, "tell me your favorite Christmas songs."

"Rudolph the Red-nosed Reindeer," T.J. said quickly.

I thought a minute. "Joy to the World," I said.

Papa Rogers slowly drew the top side of his index finger along the underside of his moustache.

"When I was your age," he said, "I had a fondness for 'Little Town of Bethlehem.' You like that song?"

"I didn't know any Sandy Claus tunes—like your 'Rudolph' there—until I was twenty or twenty-five."

T.J. beamed, feeling that made him a musical prodigy in some way.

"I remember discovering the old English carols," Papa Rogers went on. "'God Rest Ye Merry, Gentlemen,' songs like that. And then I came upon Handel's *Messiah*."

Papa Rogers paused a moment for effect. You could tell he'd taught a little drama in his day.

"I figured the *Messiah* was the end of the line, as good as Christmas music got. But I was wrong. I'm ninety-one now, and you know what I think tops the *Messiah*?"

"What?" T.J. said.

"'Town of Bethlehem' again," he said. He held up his hands. "The hope and fears of all the years," he said, slowly, stubbornly lacing his bony fingers together, "are met in thee tonight."

There was a moment of silence. Then—as if Papa Rogers had planned it—the faint strains of a song came filtering into the house. It was distant and jolly. The song was "We Three Kings."

We all had the same notion at once and scrambled to the front door to greet the carolers.

But there were no carolers—only the deep, dreamless sleep of a small-town Christmas Eve.

The singing was coming from out behind the house.

By the time I got to the back window, my mother was already there staring into the yard. Her face was a blank—no joy, fear, love or anger—just the flat look of a woman in a trance.

I looked out.

A tiny procession was making its way toward the house from the barn—three men marching in single file. Gramps, in the lead, hoisted the picture of the pin-up girl over his head like the company's patron saint.

But this was no ordinary procession. What we had here were the Magi on a pilgrimage. In this garbled version, however, they were working their way back to the mansion from the lowly stable.

My father, in step behind Gramps, hoisted a gift in each hand—two empty whiskey bottles. Uncle Matt—bringing up the rear—had tire chains drooping from his shoulders like Marley's ghost.

"We three kings of Orient are," they sang, "tried to smoke a phony cigar . . ."

My grandmother put the fingers of her right hand to her mouth and held them there as the three men passed beneath the trembling yard light, stomped the snow from their shoes and clothes and came shuffling and laughing into the house. Grandma snatched the calendar girl from Grandpa's hands, wadded the thing up and chucked it toward the old coal stove. I thought she might strike him across the face.

My father pinched my mother's behind, sending sparks from her eyes.

"It was loaded and exploded," my father sang, "and blew us to yonder starrrrr!"

Uncle Matt, usually foggy-headed anyway, was so crocked he'd misplaced an entire week. "Happy New Year!" he called across the kitchen to me. And that sent Aunt Jean fleeing from the room in disgust.

But the pilgrimage was far from over. It was soon clear they'd come to honor our family's own Thomas à Becket. They'd come to see Papa Rogers.

On they pressed into the living room, with Gramps grabbing Grandma's apron en route and tying it to his bulky waist as he walked. He looked like a sissy—or the ugliest woman in the history of Idaho—I couldn't decide. I covered a laugh.

In the living room, Papa Rogers had stood—sensing something odd and rather untraditional was in the works. He stood with his old legs apart, his hands bearing down hard on the butt of his cane. His eyes burned brown as two thimbles of coffee. His stance was bent but strong, like an arthritic old Juniper tree.

"Merry Christmas, Eph, you old fart!" Gramps called to him.

That was my grandfather's other term of endearment.

Then, like a prospector who'd hit pay dirt, Gramps broke into a bizarre little dance. Soon he was wheeling around Papa Rogers, prancing like a trick pony and singing "Camptown Races" in full voice.

Dad, Mom and the rest of us stood all amazed, frozen in place. Gramps was doing a minstrel show buck and wing. And his song and dance was pretty good. None of us had seen him dance or heard him sing in our lives.

Grandma grabbed my father's arm.

"Len!" she said. "Len, you've got to stop him before he knocks Papa down. Stop him before someone gets hurt!"

I'm sure Dad could see things were turning ugly, but he couldn't see well enough to be much help. Alcohol, I was to learn, actually drained my father's courage. He didn't move a muscle. Uncle Matt—never much help—stood nearby, jiggling his chains in rhythm and joining in on the "doo-dahs."

Then something rather remarkable began to happen.

Slowly, like the first movements of a locomotive, Papa Rogers started to shuffle his feet. Using his cane for a hub, he rotated, keeping up as best he could while Gramps wheeled about him like a wild gypsy.

I see them with visionary clarity today: Gramps, prancing and kicking, Papa Rogers revolving. They formed a two-man merry-go-round; a two planet solar system—a spinning earth and stable sun.

And they were smiling. At each other, and at the mischief of it all, I suppose.

I was eight, but I knew the scene would be with me for life. I didn't know the big words—words like "reconciliation"—and I definitely didn't see a lesson in it all.

Now I do. In those rare moments when the part of me that's Gramps stops warring with the part of me that's Papa Rogers and the two pull together for a moment of unity—of wholeness—I think of the two of them that night. And I smile—just as they did. And for a little while I find that mustard seed of faith in humanity once again.

But that night I didn't think such things. I don't remember thinking anything at all. All I knew was our family's hopes and fears seemed far, far away; that the barn had disappeared and so had the house.

All I knew was Gramps and Papa Rogers were dancing to the "Camptown Races" on Christmas Eve.

Dancing with each other.

MICE IN THE HAY

out of the lamplight
    whispering worshipping
the mice in the hay

timid eyes pearl-bright
    whispering worshipping
whisking quick and away

they were there that night
    whispering worshipping
smaller than snowflakes are

quietly made their way
    whispering worshipping
close to the manger

yes, they were afraid
    whispering worshipping
as the journey was made

from a dark corner
    whispering worshipping
scuttling together

But He smiled to see them
    whispering worshipping
there in the lamplight

stretched out His hand to them
    they saw the baby King
hurried back out of sight
    whispering worshipping

Leslie Norris
(For information about the author see page 107.)

MARY

Even as I am a woman, as all other women,
And tonight I feel awkward and cold and afraid.
The hurt binds my breath, my body is heaving,
And the anguish wrings tears of pain.
But oh, this ecstasy . . . how this ecstasy?
This weakness I feel when I touch his face?
The softness, the wonder that he lies here breathing,
Warm and pulsing within my embrace?

So this is the beauty that lights my countenance,
This the knowledge that burns in my eyes,
This the joy that pulses my being,
Transforming my body and heart and brain.
There are people here, and noise and speaking—
But he and I lie apart and alone.
Joseph smiles and speaks to me silently;
I think he knows, I think he knows.

I perceive that this baby is different, special,
I know he belongs to his people, and God,
But he is my firstborn; exquisite, divine.
Tonight there is no one—prophets nor angels—
For I am his mother . . . and he is mine.

Susan Evans McCloud
(For information about the author see page 179.)

"A Pair of Shoes" is adapted from Marilyn Brown's Road to Covered Bridge, *the 1991 first prize novel of the Utah State Fine Arts literature contest.* The Earthkeepers, *her historical novel about Provo, Utah, won the first novel contest of the Association for Mormon Letters, and* Goodbye, Hello *was a winner in the LDS Novel Writing Contest in 1984. Now attending the University of Utah, Marilyn hopes to achieve her Ph.D. in creative writing. She lives in Springville's Hobble Creek Canyon with her husband, real estate broker, Bill Brown. They are the parents of six children and now have six grandchildren.*

A PAIR OF SHOES

by Marilyn Brown

Because my grandma was sick on the couch, we weren't allowed to come in and out of the house. We could stay in or we could stay out. But we could not open and shut the door.

"They never get it right!" my grandfather growled.

"Shut the door, Elaine," my mother said. "Not hard!"

"Let them go outside," my grandmother said.

"She can't handle it, I tell you . . ." my grandfather said.

I tiptoed behind Elaine and shut the door myself. Easy. Grandfather watched me. But he buried his head in the newspaper. Two grandmothers, my grandfather in the newspaper. My father was still drawing gunwales in Puget Sound. The nights were so dark, that the moon rolled up into the sky and disappeared in snowy clouds.

We didn't have a car. We sat around in the tiny front room and fed Grandmother Helena with a spoon while she lay very ill on the couch under the quilt spotted with pictures of old trains. Grandfather E.K. stayed behind the newspaper. He must have known everything by now—at least everything that appeared in newspapers or in books. Very early on Friday morning he walked in the dark to spend the day at the library. He did not let the snow stop him. When he returned, he peeled off his galoshes, turned them upside down and emptied them of murky brown water. Mother watched it dribble on the carpet and turned the other way. Grandmother Jessie sopped up the water and put towels down. Then Grandfather peeled off his socks and wrung

143

them out in the towels. If there were no clean socks in the laundry, he grumbled like he always did about three women who could never do enough housekeeping, and put the wet socks back on again.

"He'll miss Christmas if he don't hurry," Grandfather said.

"He'll be here in time for the Sunday School Christmas pageant," Mother said.

I knew they were talking about my father, but I couldn't picture him. I thought he wasn't as tall as my grandfather; his hair was a lighter color. But I couldn't see his eyes or his cheeks. I saw his letters. I knew he was still alive in Puget Sound.

Elaine and I were angels in the Sunday School Christmas pageant, "A Pair of Shoes." Sister Haggarty had put it together retelling something vaguely resembling "The Little Match Girl" and "The Other Wise Man." Lucinda took the part of the shepherd who could not walk to the baby Jesus because she did not have a pair of shoes. The poor shepherd sat down by the house of a rich farmer and looked into the window where she saw all of the cakes sagging under icing, the butter, the grapes and tangerines lying about on the table, and she sat down in the yard hungry and cold, holding her lamb in her arms. She sang a song that began "I am someone too." I thought the song sounded a little bit like a Raggedy Ann song we played on a record in Bremerton, Washington, but Sister Haggarty assured us it was original and that everyone in the pageant would be able to claim they were in a world premiere performance.

Tag entered as the sheep boy whose donkey had carried Jesus into Nazareth. He sang a song that sounded like "Jesus Wants Me for a Sunbeam," and while he walked into the room Sister Haggarty put on a classical tune on the victrola that blended in nicely with it. Elaine and I and Suzanne stood in the background draped in sheets and sang "Hark the Herald Angels" while the boys in the back shone their flashlights into our faces: mainly Jimmy Hurd and Cory McDonald. In the rehearsal they got carried away snapping the lights off and on. They giggled and counted "One, two, three," so they would turn the lights off at the same time. At first the brightness of the lights brought up tears into my eyes, and when they flashed off it was pitch black. Sister Haggarty took the flashlights away from the boys and gave them to Emily Munk who held them in both hands and looked serious over the dark rims of her glasses. At the end of the angel scene she slipped out of the back and into her bedspread robe to play the rich farmer's wife. She looked out the imaginary window and saw Lucinda holding her lamb.

"Why are you crying, little girl?" the rich farmer's wife said.

"I don't have shoes to go to the place where lies the baby Jesus," Lucinda said.

Rodney Munk was the rich farmer. He strode into the house with Benny Frazer, who played the part of King Herod.

"There is something afoot in the land," King Herod boomed. "The wise men say a child is born who will be king. There cannot be another king. We must see that all the babies are killed."

"I will ride out with you in the morning," Rodney Munk said. "But first let my wife feed you dinner."

King Herod sat down on the floor and took off his robe and his shoes. Emily presented all the dishes before him. While he ate and drank, Virginia Brown and the girls from the Mia Maid class, fully dressed, did a version of Egyptian belly dancing. Herod ate and drank until he was so tired that he leaned back against the cushions and began to fall asleep. At this moment Emily picked up his shoes and walked out into the cold night air. She took a couple of cakes with her and a bunch of grapes. When she gave the cakes and grapes to Lucinda, she reached from under her cloak and gave her Herod's shoes.

"Put these socks in them and you will be able to walk for a long time," Emily said. Then she paused for a moment. "There is not anything I would rather do than to go myself to see the baby." Then she took off her rich-looking chains and her gold ring. "Take these to the baby," she said. It was a dramatic moment. Lucinda put the jewels in the toes inside of the shoes, pulled on the socks, and began to walk forward with the lamb in her arms.

All of us in the background began to sing the other original song: "We Have a Gift to Give Jesus."

Sister Haggarty began to cry. "It's beautiful," she said. "You're doing beautiful."

At the end of the rehearsal she offered all of the children south of the chapel a ride home in the back of the Haggarty truck. We bunched up in the dark, trying to keep our feet and legs from touching. I could feel Jimmy Hurd's toes on the soles of my boots.

"Why don't your father ever come to church?" he said.

Suzanne said "Her father's in the Navy. Shut up."

We were sitting around the table in front of our plates on the morning of the pageant when my father came home. Grandma Jessie had fixed a stack of hot pancakes and corn fritters. Grandma Callister was sitting up at the table wrapped in the train quilt, drinking hot peppermint tea.

We heard someone stomping out on the front stoop and my mother got up so fast her fork flipped off the edge of the plate.

"It's Bill," Grandma Callister said.

"By cracky," Grandfather E.K. said. He was already in his galoshes ready to set out for the library as soon as breakfast was over. "By cracky," and he got up too and stood half up and half down at the table trying to peer out the front windows.

My mother ran into the front room, her napkin floating from her robe to the floor. We followed her. My father's face was blurred gray at the glass in the front door. I did not recognize him until he was in the room. He flipped the scarf off his neck, held out his arms. Sissy stood back with fingers in her mouth.

"Hi girls!" he said. He leaned down and put one arm around Elaine and one around Sissy. He patted their backs and laughed a small laugh. "Did I miss the Christmas pageant?" His hair fell in his eyes.

He put his arm around Mother, too. He patted her and laughed the same happy laugh. Then he walked into the kitchen. Grandma Callister tried to get up. He put a hand on her shoulder. Grandma Jessie took away a plate and put a new plate of corn fritters down in front of an empty chair.

"I was sorry to hear you weren't feeling well, Mother," my father said. "Do you think you can go to the Christmas party?"

"Who, her?" my grandfather said. "She's sick. Doesn't know if she's coming or going."

"I know, but don't you want to come with us to see the girls being angels?"

My grandfather began blowing his nose into his handkerchief. "She's not fit," he said. "Are you, Helena!"

"I'll hold you up," my dad said.

"Well, sure. All right," my grandmother Helena surprised us all.

My grandfather covered his face with the handkerchief.

When the bishop said he would drive us over to the church in his truck, Grandfather E.K. decided to go with us to the pageant. I couldn't believe it. Grandma got up from the couch without hanging onto her blanket. When we got out of the bishop's truck I noticed my grandfather still had his galoshes on. He slushed through the parking lot making a path for my grandmother's feet. After we got into the chapel and sat down, he took them off, tipped them up and emptied the water out of them. He leaned over, pulled off his socks, wrung them out and put them back on during the first part of the pageant. I turned the other way and tried not to notice all of this. But I heard Jimmy Hurd say "I can smell your grandfather's feet."

When Lucinda began her journey in her large treasure-packed shoes, the first thing she did was run into the baby, Harry McDonald. He was sitting down on the floor crying.

"I'm hungry," the baby said.

Lucinda leaned over with the lamb in her arms and gave the baby the last cake and the last few grapes.

As she continued her walk, she found Sarah Berryman rocking her sick baby doll in her arms. A few of the Sunbeam class stood around her hanging on her sheets.

"I have no food to eat. My children are hungry."

Lucinda took off Herod's shoes and emptied the treasure out of them. She gave the woman the necklace and the ring.

After she pulled her shoes back on to continue her journey, Lucinda ran into Bobby Murphy who was limping along on a crutch, his head bent under a mop.

For a moment Lucinda stood holding her lamb tight against her chest.

"My feet hurt," Bobby said. "I have no shoes."

Lucinda bent down and once more removed the shoes. As she handed them to the old man, she said in almost a whisper, "Can you tell me where I might find Jesus?"

"He is very near," Bobby Murphy said.

The music came up on the victrola and the members of the manger scene came out to the middle of the hall. Lucinda carried her lamb over to the manger. As the audience sang "Joy to the World," I noticed that my grandfather had hold of my grandmother's hand.

Most of the audience had seen the show's rehearsals a dozen times, but they still managed to clap when it was over. The Relief Society served heavy pieces of cake with real Oregon grape leaves and a cherry on top supposed to remind us of holly. Inside the paper dishes, the cakes swam in a syrupy gray sauce that looked a lot like dirty bath water. My mother baked some of the cakes using a recipe that Sister McDonald, the Relief Society President, handed out to all the ladies on the Sunday before the pageant. But all of the cakes still looked so different you would never have known they were baked from the same recipe. The dirty bath water sauce was the same, cooked by Sister Smith in one black pot. The amazing thing was that it all tasted very good if you didn't pay attention to how it looked. The ladies did not call it cake, but pudding.

That was the only time my grandfather came inside of the church building in all eight months we were there. I still remember that when he first sat down in the back with my father and my grandmother Helena, and would not move, my mother came up to the front row for a few moments to take flash pictures. That was when he took off his galoshes and I thought I was going to die. When he took his socks off and wrung them and put them back on just as he did at home I tried to hide behind Suzanne and Elaine. But I could not help hearing Jimmy Hurd say "Your grandfather's feet stink."

On the way home my father said "That was a lovely story. What do you think you learned?"

I wasn't sure what the story was about, but Elaine seemed very confident. "Shoes or no shoes," she said. "Jesus is very near."

Michael Fillerup lives in Flagstaff, Arizona with his wife, Rebecca, and their four children: Jessie, Carrie, Samantha, and Benjamin. They are Michael's most avid readers as well as his most candid critics. "That's pretty bad, Dad!" Or, on very rare occasions: "Now that's baaaaaaad, Dad." A collection of Michael's prize-winning short stories was recently published by Signature Books. A novel is in progress.

LOST AND FOUND

by Michael Fillerup

Over the years he had tried all kinds of tricks to outfox it. He had eaten humble pie by candlelight in the dark privacy of his hovel while reading the nativity story from Luke. He had tried to lose himself in anonymous acts of service in the village. Once, in a fit of self-spite, he had driven two hundred miles into Gallup and gotten roaring drunk. Another time he had gone all the way to Flagstaff to sit through midnight Mass at St. Mary's Church—as a novelty and a diversion more so than religious devotion: he had his own church. Sort of.

Tonight he was going to drive to the top of the mesa in a snowstorm to rescue a beautiful young woman in distress.

Actually, he did not know if she was beautiful. Nor did he know if she was truly in distress. Her foster mother in Phoenix seemed to think so. Her voice, scratched to obscurity by the crackling static, was controlled hysteria on the phone. "Well, we'd do just about anything to get her back." A telling pause. "Well, just about. I mean, we really want her back. Especially under the circumstances."

Her name was Loretta Yellowhair and she had been missing from the Indian Placement Program since August. It was a mystery. No one knew where she had gone, not even her natural parents, or if they did they weren't talking. But a week ago the caseworker had heard a rumor . . .

"I guess what happened is that last winter was really hard on the family. A lot of sheep didn't make it. Loretta's mother got real desperate and borrowed a thousand dollars from some old fellow with the promise he could marry Loretta in exchange."

149

Another voice, Brother Myers', interrupted on another line: "Yeah, if you could, we'd like you to intercept the old coot's pass, so to speak!"

Tom winced at the reference to old coot.

"The caseworker says Loretta can go back on Placement and finish up her senior year," Sister Myers explained, "but she's got to be in Phoenix by Tuesday morning for an interview, absolutely positively."

"Tuesday?" Tom said. "What's so sacred about Tuesday?"

Sister Myers chuckled, almost intimately. "Monday's Christmas, silly!"

"What's so sacred about Christmas?" Tom quipped. And he laughed. Once.

Sister Myers was silent.

"Sorry," Tom said, wondering who had given her his name and number. The missionaries maybe. Or the idiot caseworker. At moments like this he almost wished The Tribe hadn't put in phone lines a year ago. Electricity, yes. Running water, great. Telephones? They reduced his insularity. He could feel the outside world creeping in, tightening its noose.

Tom clasped his hand over the receiver and looked at his cat, an ornery old half-breed Siamese-and-something curled up on the rumpled bedspread that drooped to the warped floorboards beneath his metal frame bed. "What do you say, Nashdoi? You up for a little adventure tonight?" The animal didn't stir. Beside the bed was an old chest of drawers. A single light bulb burned in the cramped kitchen where a pine sprig in a glass jar served as Tom's token tribute to the holidays. Normally his quarters seemed warm and cozy, but tonight they felt dark and claustrophobic. Grim.

"I just hate to see it happen," Sister Myers said. "She's just such a wonderful girl—bright, gifted, a valiant testimony. I know it's Christmas Eve, but . . ."

Tom unclasped the receiver and whispered into it, tentatively, so as not to arouse false hope, "Sister Myers, I'll do my best!"

"Oh, thank you, Bishop! We really do appreciate this!"

Tom winced again. He wasn't really a bishop but a branch president by default: he was the only ordained Elder in the area. But he had retired from truly active duty years ago—he thought he'd made that clear.

He fed a couple sticks of juniper into the wood stove, turned the vents down low, and put on his Marlboro Country coat—suede with a sheepskin collar. He was tempted to bring Nashdoi along for company, but he didn't have the heart to awaken him from such a deep, exclusive sleep. He was a little jealous, really.

Snow was falling lightly but steadily as his battered blue pickup rumbled past the trading post, a big stone box locked up for the night. The village was abandoned—a ghost town. Winter had pronounced it dead and tossed a white sheet over it. A pregnant mutt, her swollen teats dragging along the snow, plodded towards the rock schoolhouse where Tom earned his daily bread. About the only joyful thing in sight was the play of the snow in the lone security light. The dainty flakes were twisting and tumbling like gleeful little gymnasts. But even here he saw a tragic element in that they could just as easily be butterflies trapped inside a jar of light, trying desperately to break out. He could almost hear their wings beating frantically against the glass. Or was that his heart, rap-tap-tapping, or his truck thumping across the cattle guard?

Or his heater? He flicked the switch and the little fan rattled like dice in a cup, spewing out lukewarm air. Up ahead he could see Hosteen's old hogan, a black face with a white helmet. Two years ago he would have asked Hosteen to join him. The old man had just the right touch of craziness for a wild goose chase like this—and it would be a wild goose chase, Mission Double-Impossible, Tom knew that. So why was he going? Well, boredom was a factor. (What else was on his agenda tonight besides huddling by his wood stove feeling sorry for himself?) And duty. (She was a lost sheep; it was his job to find her.) And, yes, there was curiosity, too: who was this young beauty who commanded a bride price of a thousand dollars, a phenomenal fifty sheep in Navajo currency? He wanted to know.

Tom smiled recalling the way the old man's eyes used to peer out from under the flat brim of his black felt hat, the dark little orbs floating behind his Coke bottle lenses like jellyfish in formaldehyde. A fringe of silvery whiskers dripped from his gaunt jaw like pieces of clipped fishing line, and calluses doubled the size of his gnarled little hands. Tom had first met him twenty years ago while making home visits with the missionaries. Hosteen was limping out of his outhouse on skinny bow legs, zipping up his fly. One look at the missionaries in their dark suits and white shirts and he had grinned: "What are you folks doing, selling life insurance?" Tom had liked him instantly. Later, when the missionaries asked the magic question—"Is there anything we can do for you?"—the wrinkled corners of the old man's mouth had twisted sardonically. He led the threesome back behind his hogan and pointed to a huge mound of piñon and juniper. "You folks can cut all that up for me. About this size," he said, spreading his hands shoulder width. "Better hurry, though. Sun's going fast." Hosteen used to say he didn't exactly believe in the old ways or in the new ways either. "I'm just a horse-teen of a different color," he would chuckle, punning on his Navajo name.

Tom tried not to think about Hosteen; it still saddened him. Somehow that, too, had been his fault. He turned his thoughts elsewhere—Sister Myers. He could still hear her voice crackling in his ear. "Well, they think she might be up to the mesa."

The mesa! Swell! Talk about a needle in a haystack!

"Or they say she might be staying with Louise Yazzie's brother-in-law. Do you know Louise?"

A needle in three haystacks.

Driving the desolate reservation roads on a winter night, Tom could go for miles, light years, without seeing anything but the infinite swirl of snowflakes. He was an astronaut hurtling solo through outer space, and the feeling could be terrifying or exhilarating, depending upon his particular state of mind. At that moment he felt neither terrified nor exhilarated, only a general desolation that always seemed to intensify about this time of year. The simple truth was, he really didn't much care what transpired tonight. He just wanted to get it over with, "it" being this night.

His front tire plunged into a pothole, rattling the truck and sending a shaft of pain into his lower back. Several years ago he had injured it falling off a horse, and now every little bounce or vibration was a voodoo pin in his fifth lumbar. Great, he thought. Swell. I'll be a pin cushion before the night's through.

The pickup crawled past the little trailer where for one hour every Sunday morning Tom went through the holy motions on behalf of old Sister Watchman and a few other faithfuls of the Bitterwater Branch of the Mormon Church. Sister Watchman, who had no eyes to see but could weave an intricate rug of many colors, could also read the desperate scribble on his heart: "I feel sad for you, Hastiin T'aa geed 'Asdzani. You feed all these others, who will feed you?"

"My Heavenly Father," he used to say, but each time with a little less conviction.

Straight ahead a giant boulder was sitting comically atop a skinny spire, like a giant head with a pencil-thin neck. Striped with snow, it looked like a weird giraffe-zebra hybrid straight out of Dr. Seuss. In the background, the mesa rose up like a great white wall. In the fuzzy snowfall it appeared to be wavering ethereally, as if any moment it might swell up and crumble down upon him like a tidal wave, or simply vanish altogether, like a mirage.

Tom wondered about Loretta Yellowhair. Who was this young Navajo woman in distress? "Yellowhair" would be a misnomer. Black hair, dark eyes. He tried to visualize her in his mind, but she remained as fuzzy and obscure as the falling snow.

"Distress" might be a misnomer as well. His personal feelings about the Indian Placement Program had always been ambivalent. The dark view held that Navajo children were being taken from their natural families so they could be transformed into white and delightsome little Mormons. The "inspired" view said it gave them a shot at a "real" education. Tom had seen both sides of the coin. Placement was a ticket out, but to where? Anything to spare them the boarding schools. Every year when his handful of little sixth graders graduated he felt an overwhelming sadness, as if he were sending them off to war. The girls would end up pregnant, the boys would come back little drunkards and dopers. Placement? Stealing their culture? There were six sides to that story. Ask Celeste Bighorse.

Tom had always been lenient on Placement interviews. If a kid had a shot, he wasn't going to nix it on a minor technicality.

"What church is this?"

A look of stupor. "Uh . . . Catholic?"

"Close enough."

The snow was falling so thickly now he seemed to be submerged in it. The pickup struggled along like a submarine in rough waters. His thoughts drifted back to the little church trailer he had passed a few miles back. A week ago Sunday, opening his official church mail, he was shocked to see his mug shot, albeit a very outdated one, on the MISSING PERSONS BULLETIN. By some computer glitch, perhaps the simple inversion of two digits in his Social Security number, Church Headquarters had failed to link one of their anointed local leaders with the black-and-white countenance on the bulletin. It had been sobering to see his face amidst the other Lost Sheep: teenage runaways with pimpled cheeks and hair in their eyes, a watermelon-shaped man who could have been his father, a jolly white-haired woman who reminded him of Mrs. Claus. Tom had always felt depressed when perusing these monthly alerts. Each face was a tragedy in miniature, a despairing tale of loss. He pictured heartbroken parents grieving for their prodigal sons, grown-up children searching desperately for crippled mothers and fathers on the run. Sometimes, studying the photographs, he would invent stories of his own—whole sagas and family histories. And sometimes, in the process, he would mentally rewrite his own. He sometimes wondered who, if anyone, might be grieving for him?

He had noticed a crucial difference between his mug shot and the others. They were accompanied by a brief physical description (height, weight, color eyes, color hair, distinguishing features), the location where the individual had last been seen, their hometown, and a contact person to call. His read, simply: THOMAS DAVID BARLOW 6/24/51. That was all. No contact person, no phone number.

Tom had recognized his high school graduation picture. The blond ponytail was gone now, and the cocky grin. His chiseled cheeks were padded, tanned and leathery, and his jaws were beginning to sag in the sad sack manner of Dick Nixon. Mentally he had updated his description: 5'10", 205 pounds, built like an over-the-hill linebacker. Hair (the surviving patches on top) like sun-singed grass. Hazel eyes—vacant. Twin flashlights with dead batteries.

His hands had trembled while handling the sheet of paper, as if ghosts or spirits had been captured on the page. On the one hand, it had been like reading his own obituary. On the other, it meant that someone, somewhere, was still looking for him. But who? His mother and father had gone AWOL before he could even walk; he had no brothers or sisters, no real family to speak of. . . . His father-in-law, maybe? Tom sneered. "You're a very intelligent young man, Tom; you're very smart. But you've got no heart. You're a taker, not a giver." That was the last thing Bishop Tyler (the *real* bishop) had said to him two days before Tom had eloped with his only daughter. She had liked him because he was a California oddball who was going to set the world on fire, although he wasn't quite sure how. She had liked him because her father hadn't. The Bishop had mapped out his daughter's life a little too perfectly: temple marriage, kids, grandkids, death. Sorry, that wasn't Kathy. Of course, Tom had had to be baptized and join the fold. Kathy was saucy and spicy and radical for her little Utah town, but she was still Mormon. "I want you forever," she had whispered during an erotic moment, "not just the here and now. Don't you want me forever too?" Sweet persuasion. Failing that: "Look, I'm not a one-life stand!" So he had played the game until it had become almost real to him.

He had promised her the sky but instead had given her Bitterwater, Arizona.

He switched on the radio; it spit and crackled. He should have had it fixed back in October. He fiddled with the knob, searching for a voice, any voice, but found nothing but fuzz and static, an audio version of the falling snow. He noted the permanent film of dust on the dash, and the ever-widening cracks across the faded blue vinyl: they were tragic mouths, gaping wounds, sarcastic smiles aimed at him.

He tried to keep his eyes and thoughts on the road, but they kept drifting to Christmases past. One year—he was six or seven, he forgot exactly—but he was living with Aunt Margie in Del Mar and decided to play a joke on his cousins. He made them all joke gifts. They were poems: 'Roses are red / Violets are blue / Christmas is dumb / And so are you!' Stupid little ditties. Christmas Eve he placed them under the tree. But when he got in bed, something funny happened. Maybe it was the carolers outside. Or maybe Uncle Max had spiked the egg nog again. Tom wasn't sure. He just felt weird about it. So he sneaked out and took back all the joke gifts, and he trashed them.

Except he didn't get them all. He thought he had, but he missed Sherry's. She wasn't retarded, exactly, but she was . . . well, she was slow. Her present was buried at the bottom of the pile, and before Tom could stop her, she'd unwrapped it. She started jumping up and down, shouting, 'A present from Tommy! A present from Tommy!' She gave it to her mother to read because she couldn't. Aunt Margie smiled at first, and then her face turned to melted mush. She gave Tom a dirty look but smiled at Sherry. And then she read: 'Roses are red / Violets are merry / Christmas is here / And I love Sherry!' Tom had never seen his cousin so happy. She threw her arms around him and danced and danced. He couldn't look at his aunt. He couldn't look at anyone after that. He just stood there feeling like absolute dirt.

It was the story of his life: big plans, big screw ups.

Tom put his hand over the heater vent: still lukewarm. He should have had *that* fixed, too. He could feel the cold creeping into his toes, slowly taking over. The steering wheel was turning to ice; his hands were stiffening. Why hadn't he brought his gloves? He always brought gloves—always! He gripped the steering wheel in anger and stamped the accelerator to the floor. The truck lurched forward and hit a slushy spot, shimmying several yards before the tires regripped the road. More Christmases came to mind. This time he was eight, living with his Aunt Winnie (they were never blood relations, but he liked to call them "aunt," "uncle," "cousin," if they allowed it). For Christmas she had given him a little pet hamster. He loved it because it was small and soft and furry and warm and absolutely his. Two days later he woke up and it was dead. He hadn't even named it yet. Charlie. Furry. Toby. He was still trying to decide. It was his fault. He wasn't sure why, but it was. It was the first thing he had ever really truly loved, and he'd killed it.

That night he had a dream. There was a noise, a rattling in the plastic bucket under the bathroom sink. He reached in, thinking it was Hamster. He grabbed—and screamed! Not Hamster, but a giant rat leaped onto his collarbone and bit into his neck. Like a vampire.

Tom clenched his eyes shut a painful moment, trying to clear the white fog in front of him. He tried to think of other things: the Missing Persons Bulletin. He had been tempted to call Church Headquarters to see if he could find out who had placed him on the bulletin, but— why borrow trouble? No news was good news.

A third of the way up the mesa, in the proverbial middle-of-nowhere, he saw off to his right a tiny nest of colored lights, like a multicolored constellation. You just can't escape it, he thought, not even out here. Then he felt ashamed of his feelings as he turned down a side road and made a silent confession: he didn't like Christmas. Every year, privately, he wished he could drop a black cloth over it. In his head he knew better: Christmas. The birth of Christ, Lord, Savior and Redeemer of the World. The Prince of Peace. But he couldn't feel the occasion, couldn't feel the music or the cheer. He wasn't a Scrooge about it; he always put on a good face and taught his students some carols and encouraged them to decorate their little classroom tree. But he was always glad when it was finally over, yet saddened too.

The pickup squirmed and squiggled down the mushy side road leading to Louise Yazzie's shack. The snow had graciously covered the splintered dwelling with a fresh white coat. Chicken wire covered the lone window. A slender little woman with beautiful almond eyes answered the door. A few threads of gray lined her shiny black hair, which was tied in a traditional Navajo bun.

"*Ya'at'eeh, shimayazhi*," Tom said, offering his hand. They touched palms, Navajo-style. "I'm looking for Loretta Yellowhair. Do you know where I can find her?"

Louise's lithe frame blocked the narrow doorway. Two little girls poked their black-braided heads around either side of her pleated skirt and giggled.

"No," she said. Short and bittersweet. Although Tom had visited Louise on several occasions, she always treated him like a total stranger. Why did he always have to play these stupid games? He wearied of them. He wearied of frantic foster parents. He wearied of everything. But he knew the rules. Fight fire with fire, ice with ice. He waited, stubbornly.

"She's up on the mesa, I think," Louise said. "I don't think you can get up there tonight."

"I need to talk to her about Placement," Tom said coolly.

Placement! It was like saying *abracadabra!* Suddenly Louise became cooperative. She knew the score.

"Yes, I think she wants to go on the Placement. I think she's at my brother's house. I'll tell him you came by."

"I need to talk to Loretta tonight," Tom said. "I need to interview her. She has to be in Phoenix by tomorrow."

"Tomorrow?"

"Yes, tomorrow."

"I can go up there and tell her, I guess."

"Maybe I could follow you over . . . since I need to interview her."

Louise didn't like that idea. Tom posed what he knew would be a more agreeable option. "Or I could just drive there myself—if you can tell me where to go."

"Okay," she said, "why don't you just drive over there yourself. It's Sam Bizaholoni. Just follow the road. You'll see a trailer. There's a camper shell out front."

"Okay, I'll try there. I'll drive to the top of the mesa if I have to."

"Well, she might be on the mesa. Or she might be in Sheep Springs, at her mother's. Last weekend she went to Sheep Springs. Her mother lives there."

A needle in six haystacks.

"Thank you," Tom said. "*Ahehee.*"

"*Aoo'.*" she said. And then she reminded him of what night it was. "*Ya'at'eeh Keshmish!*"

Tom flushed, embarrassed. Of course. "Merry Christmas to you, too."

He continued up the mesa, the pickup crawling stubbornly through the mud and snow mix. The sky continued falling, swiftly and steadily. The road before him was paved perfectly white; behind, it was a black and white smear, like a child's chocolate finger painting, or the tracks of a drunken skier. Scrub pines hunkered on the rock ledges like Cro-Magnon hunters in polar bear skins. Lying in wait, it seemed.

Again he tried to visualize Loretta Yellowhair. Instead he saw the ghost of Celeste Bighorse: small, slender, doe-eyed. A heart-breaking dimpled little smile. Glossy cheeks, glossy black hair in a ponytail that dropped past her waist like a long velvet cord. She must have had a crush on him from the very beginning because she would always stay after class, just sit there with her brown hands clasped on her wooden desk until he would finally ask, "Celeste, would you like to erase the blackboard?" And she would dip her chin shyly and smile—those sweet little dimples! Kathy's smile in miniature. And she had a gift—she could draw horses that leaped right off the paper. Every day after school he would help her with her sketches. She liked it; she liked him. Then one day he told her she had a great future if . . . No. Not that. Something terrible had been misconstrued, hopelessly lost in translation. He had never ever, ever . . . except for maybe an encouraging hand on her shoulder. No! No! Her *shoulder*, just her shoulder. Like this—see? Just like this.

But she was an early bloomer, a sixth grader with incipient little breasts, and he was—well, he was white, and he was alone. And no white man chose to live alone out there. No normal white man. There was talk. Celeste was having bad dreams, her mother said. And she was a big intimidating woman who wore sunglasses and stretch pants and had her hair permed in Albuquerque. "You *bilagaanas* think you can come out here and get away with anything!" She went to a crystal gazer who intimidated Tom, then took Celeste out of school for two weeks to have a *yeibichei* ceremony performed over her. Hosteen said Gladys Bighorse had a bug up her rear end, but it was only the protests of Sister Watchman that had saved Tom his job. After that he had always walked on eggshells, careful to avoid even the appearance of idiosyncrasy. He had kept a safe, professional distance from everyone—students, teachers, men, women, missionaries. It was a lonely life. Safe, but lonely.

Celeste graduated from the elementary school that June. She was supposed to go on Placement but after the incident her mother had withdrawn her application. So little Celeste had left for the boarding school in August, young, pretty, talented. A year later she had returned a mini mom.

Tom found the trailer with the camper shell in front. He left the truck running. No colored lights here: the power lines stopped at Louise Yazzie's place. A paunchy man with oily black hair met him at the door.

"Are you Sam Bizaholoni?"

He eyed Tom tentatively. "Why?"

"I'm looking for Loretta Yellowhair. She wants to go on Placement. Louise said you might know where she is."

His face scrunched up like a sponge. "Louise?"

"Your sister. Do you have a sister named Louise?"

He smiled. Tom counted three teeth in his impoverished mouth. "She's not here," he said, shaking his head. He was barefoot in baggy pajama-like pants. Tom relished the heat wafting out from the wood stove. He could hear little children laughing and a woman's voice. She was singing "Jingle Bells" in Navajo. Tom thought it should make him feel happy, but instead it was a rusty nail scratching more sad graffiti on his heart. He heard phantom voices, phantom laughter.

"She's not here," Sam said. "I think she's up on the mesa."

"Or in Sheep Springs, maybe?" Tom muttered under his breath.

"What?" He was clever, playing the dumb Indian. "Did you say Sheep Springs? No, I don't think she's in Sheep Springs." He chuckled indulgently. "No, she's up on the mesa." Sam poked his head outside. "Brrrr! Wouldn't go up there tonight. Nas-teee!"

"Can you tell me where to go? It's very important. I need to interview her for Placement."

The magic word again! Tonight it seemed to hold more hope, more promise even than the word "Christmas." "Sure!" he said, flashing his three-fanged smile. "Just follow the road. You go past the cattle guard, the third cattle guard I think. There's a great big rock, it looks like a whale kinda." Then he laughed in that inimitable way of the Navajo. "You can't miss it!"

"Thanks. *Ahehee.*"

"*Aoo'*," he said. "*Ya'at'eeh Keshmish!*"

Tom had to smile. Sam reminded him a little of Hosteen, that same wry humor. But then he was overcome by an old despair. It was not Christmas this time, but close enough. Winter. White. Cold. Snow. Icicles hanging like six-foot fangs. He had made a rare trip into Farmington to buy supplies. He still wondered what spirit had prompted him to check into a Motel 6, and for not just one night but two? When he returned late Saturday evening, they said the old man was *adin*—it didn't mean "dead" exactly, but gone, not existing. He had died in his sleep, and *chindi*, his ghost spirit, had claimed the hogan, forcing his brittle old wife and two daughters to vacate. The only white man in the village, Tom routinely prepared and buried their dead: the Navajo wanted no contact with *chindi*. In his absence, though, they might have simply burned the hogan down—they had done that before. Instead they had wisely waited three days for his return so he could remove his friend's body and prepare it for proper burial, meaning a "proper Christian burial." They had known that he, too, had lines that couldn't be crossed, although Tom had always tried to respect their beliefs and traditions. "We know you don't believe," Hosteen had once said, "but at least you try and understand. You don't laugh behind your sleeve like the others." He had wondered what Hosteen had really meant by that, "the others?"

Although in his head Tom knew better, something still whispered that it had been partly his fault; that if he had not gone to town that day and stayed so long, Hosteen would still be alive. He also knew his logic made as little sense as their childlike fear of Hosteen's ghost, but . . . one man's superstitions were another man's religion. He had learned that much.

Tom was glad to get out of the blowing cold and back into the lukewarm cab. His feet were numb from just that short stint outside. Ice has crusted on the windshield, infringing on the easy sweep of the wiper blades and cataracting all but two hemispheres of glass. He glared at the eternal snow. This is crazy, this is stupid. Why am I doing it?

For Loretta, he thought, or tried to convince himself. For God. Inasmuch as ye have done it unto the least of these . . . Okay, for me, then. Me. And how so me?

The tires spun and the rear-end wriggled as the truck struggled up the slick road. Although he couldn't see beyond the hood, he could feel the road growing steeper and narrower. The snowfall thickened; it was pouring down like sugar through a giant sifter. Far to the right he saw a tiny light shining in the white commotion. It was a dark horse chance, but he decided to take it: anything beat driving to the top tonight. He left his truck parked in the road, the emergency flashers spitting blood onto the snow, and plodded several hundred yards until arriving at a homestead: a couple of shacks, a hogan, a corral, an outhouse. Padded with snow, they looked artificial, like stage props or pieces in a diorama. He wondered what he must look like, laden with snow—a ghost maybe, or the Abominable Snowman.

As he headed for the lighted hogan, three mutts sprang out from under a plywood lean-to, snarling and barking. He cooled them off with a couple of snowballs. A big, stocky woman answered the door, remarkably indifferent, Tom thought, as if this were nothing out of the ordinary, a *bilagaana* appearing at her door in a blizzard on Christmas Eve. She looked about forty-five. A green velveteen blouse covered her broad shoulders and torso, and a pleated skirt dropped to the middle of her pillar-like calves. She had big, bulgy cheeks, as if she were hoarding walnuts in them, and the part down the middle of her gray-streaked hair appeared to be widening, as if from some peculiar erosion. She appeared understandably suspicious.

"*Woshdee*," she said at length, and he stepped inside, ducking his head a bit.

It was a large hogan, with a dirt floor. The smell of fried potatoes and mutton tortured Tom's empty belly. Instinctively he gravitated towards the makeshift wood stove, an old oil drum whose sweet heat seemed to reach out and grip his frostbitten parts, pinching them painfully, wonderfully. The stovepipe soared through the square smokehole top-center like a fat periscope. He noted the coats and cowboy hats hanging on nails along the north wall, most noticeably a red Pendleton jacket that appeared brand new. A Mexican felt painting, wild stallions on the run, and family photographs and certificates of school achievement covered the rest of the wallspace. Three youngsters were cuddled together like bear cubs on sheepskins beside a small piñon tree, laced with strings of popcorn and dripping with tinsel. Little wrapped gifts were loosely stacked around the wooden stand, and the ochre hand of one sleeping boy rested upon a cube-shaped gift as if he were prematurely claiming it. The tin foil star on top of the tree reflected the stingy light from the kerosene lamp on a wooden table where a skinny old woman with arms as dark and tough as greasewood was kneading a mound of dough. An old fellow with a gray mustache that drooped below his chin and a face as deeply seamed as a casaba melon was sitting cross-legged nearby the children, keeping vigil. He wore a black felt hat with a flat brim and a silver band, reminiscent of Hosteen's. There were two other women, young mothers growing fat in T-shirts and blue jeans. One was casually feeding her brown breast to her baby. Nearby a young man with a thick mop of black hair eyed Tom like a deer smelling trouble. On the other side of the hogan were two middle-aged men, one innocuously big and round, the other austerely cut, with the high, chiseled cheekbones of a warrior. He was wearing a red headband around his silver hair, and his dark eyes were fixed on Tom like bullets waiting to be fired. Tom wondered if this were not the old coot to whom Loretta had been promised. If so, he looked quite formidable: a Navajo Clint Eastwood.

The heat was suffocating. Tom quickly regained the feeling in his hands and feet, and his armpits grew soggy with sweat. He wanted to doff his suede coat, but chose not to: he didn't want to sent the wrong signal. This would be a short visit.

The matron spoke first, surprising him. "She's out there," she said, motioning towards the door. Tom was confused. She? Loretta? "Last night," she explained, "in my sleep, a man in white came and took her away. He said don't worry. She'll be all right. He said she's coming with me. That's how come I knew you were coming."

Tom felt a tingling warmth. He looked at his sleeve: most of the snow coating him had either melted or dropped to the floor, but it had made the point. This was going to be easier than he had thought.

"I need to see Loretta," he said. "Loretta Yellowhair."

"Loretta?" Now the matron looked confused. Tom wasn't sure how to interpret her colossal disappointment.

"Are you her aunt?"

She shook her head. "No," she nodded solemnly. "Loretta's not here. She's on the mesa."

"On the mesa?"

"Aoo'."

Tom gazed up through the smokehole at the wild flurry of snowflakes. They were insects flying too close to a fire, or falling stars melting by myriads. They wanted in, it seemed, but the instant they came too close to the invisible heat—poof! Oblivion. They were the opposite of those white butterflies caught inside the cone of light. Or were they brothers? Cousins maybe? Tom looked at the sleeping children by the tree and thought that maybe he wanted to sit down. Maybe he wanted to stay awhile. He did not want to leave, he knew that.

"*Ahehee*," he said, and he could feel their eyes upon him as he trudged back into the snow.

An hour later he curved around the great whale-shaped rock only to find himself facing a meadow of knee-deep snow. He pushed in the clutch and jerked the stick into reverse. The gears whined as the truck struggled backwards fifty feet. He shoved the stock forward and bore down on the accelerator, gathering speed down the plowed stretch until the headlights slammed into the snowbank. It was like ramming into a tackling dummy: the snow gave a bit but then held firm. Steam rose from the extinguished headlights. He backed up and took another running start. Again the snowbank relented a few feet and then held fast. He tried again, gunning the engine full throttle. The snow gave a little more, but not much. This time he did not back up. He pressed the accelerator to the floor. Huge pinwheels of mud and ice flew past the side windows, black and white blurs, as the headlights burrowed deeper and deeper into the snow. He could smell the transmission cooking.

"Damn!" He slammed the cab door and checked in back: no shovel. He must have forgotten to put it back after clearing his walkway. "Dammit to hell!" He knew he shouldn't swear, but right now he didn't care. He didn't care about anything except getting his damn truck out of the damn muck. He glared at the falling snow as if some invisible nemesis were hiding behind it, or within it. He felt like yelling at it, challenging: Come out and show yourself! Come out and fight me face to face! He threw himself on his knees, by the front tires, and began scooping out the snow with his bare hands, madly, angrily. The cold nibbled piranha-like through his fingers and his legs from the knees down. At first he was too angry to feel any pain, but after awhile, each time he plunged his hands into the mud it was like sticking them in a fire, or into the jaws of a wolf to be briefly masticated. He buried them over and over, until they were gone, and it was just his arms, sticks with floppy pads on the ends, which he kept stabbing into the muck, muttering and cursing until tears leaked from his eyes—tears of anger and frustration and a pain that cut much deeper than this simple calculable cold; an anger and frustration that had nothing to do with his impossible quest to find Loretta Yellowhair.

He dug, he scooped, he swore, angrily, fanatically. Insanely.

The snow kept falling, relentlessly, invidiously, like a great white plague; like locusts attacking his precious crops. He stood up and waved his arms wildly to chase them away. He felt utterly helpless, like a blindfolded kid trying to break the piñata but his older brother keeps yanking it impossibly out of reach. He turned a circle and saw nothing but white madness. Distress? Who was in distress? That seventeen-year-old kid? Distress! He could tell you all about it! He wondered bitterly if anyone was braving the storm to visit *him* tonight? He whirled around and roared at the omnipresent snow: "Where the hell's *my* home teacher? Who the hell's going to rescue *me?*" So this was his reward! This was his fate, his destiny! His stinking rotten lousy miserable thanks! "Your vessel, your lonely solitary vessel, and what do I get? Shat on, spat on! Well, to hell with them! To hell with You!"

Then he repented. Sort of. He thought the real Jesus would understand his momentary craziness under duress. The real Jesus would accept his intentional lack of Christmas fanfare. The real Jesus wouldn't be dumb enough to be born in the dead of winter, either. In a stable, yes. In rags, sure. Winter? Never. The real Jesus would know better. He'd understand about Hosteen and Kathy and Celeste Bighorse and the Missing Persons Bulletin and Loretta Yellowhair and all the rest. Didn't care about colored lights and tinsel. Wasn't sitting by a fireplace opening gifts and getting fat on rice pudding. The real Jesus was probably walking some dirty ghetto street waiting (wondering? hoping?) for some true blue disciple to invite him in, out of the cold. To heat him up a can of soup and make him a ham on rye. Wherein saw ye me a stranger? Naked and clothed me? Hungry and fed me? Wherein? Whereout? Where?

He tried to reassure himself. The time his appendix ruptured and Hosteen drove him to the hospital in Farmington and sat by his bed all night in ICU singing ceremonial healing chants. (The nurse had told him this, after he came out of anesthesia.) Later Hosteen had brought him a Louis L'Amour paperback—Tom hated Louis L'Amour, but the thought—the thought! When he asked about the healing chants, the corners of the old man's mouth curled in his familiar way: "Hell, I was just singing a bunch of old squaw dance songs—just a lot of Indian mumbo jumbo. It was the only way they'd let me stay in that crazy place with you all night." Hosteen! Five years later he was dead. *Adin.* Removing his body from the hogan, Tom had been startled by its lightness. Hosteen was tiny anyway, but minus his spirit it was like lifting a large piece of balsa wood. Carefully, lovingly, Tom had prepared the corpse for burial, wrestling the purple tunic of velveteen over his stiff little doll-like body, the silver concho belt around his narrow waist. At one point Tom's fingers had searched the old man's face, reading the deep corrugations there. Each wrinkle was a lifeline, an arroyo, a timeless impression in the land Hosteen and his forefathers had claimed by blood and birthright. At that moment, Tom had never felt so lonely and displaced, so totally outside the pale. He had wept, and through his tears he had watched the old man's face grow smooth and soft, youthful, but thin as air; like a full-color shadow or a reflection on water. Tom thought if he had pressed down, his hand would have punched right through it. Instead, he held up his own palm like a hand mirror only to see his face in similar form: soft, smooth, youthful—a shadow. He made a fist and it had all disappeared. Later, as he was delivering the eulogy, a small miracle had happened. Halfway through, several hands went up. Heads were nodding, shaking. He looked at his interpreter, Sister Watchman's son. What? What? Had he said something, done something *bahadzid*? No, Herbert's expression said. And his gritty little smile formed beneath his black mustache. Just keep talking. You don't need me.

Tom had gazed down at the crowd of wrinkled faces, headbanded and cowboy-hatted men, silver-haired women, packed in rows of folding chairs beneath the red and white-striped revival tent, all nodding, nodding, nodding. And later he would not recall a word of what he had said, only that it was like a beautiful gold scroll rolling out of his head, and all he had to do was read it. He couldn't recall any of the symbols—they were runes, Chinese cuneiform, hapless kid scribble—yet at the time they had made perfect sense to him, to them.

Tom glared at the falling sky as if it were attacking him personally. His teeth were chattering and his shoulders shaking. What was he trying to prove? What was he doing here? Boredom, duty, curiosity. No no no! He clenched his teeth and plunged his frozen paws deeper into the muck.

Then a thought: Sticks! Branches! He got up and staggered through the knee-deep snow, flailing his arms like a drunkard or a blind man on the run, until he smacked into a dead piñon tree whose brittle branches he began attacking with Kung Fu kicks and karate chops. Using his numb arms like giant tweezers, he carried the broken branches to his truck and laid them in two narrow trails behind his rear tires. But when he looked back he saw the snow was smothering the sticks faster than he could spread them.

He crawled back into the cab. Most of the interior heat had dissipated, but it was a relief just to get out of the blowing cold. He could feel the voodoo pins everywhere: back, chest, neck, legs. He closed his eyes and groaned mournfully: Dear God, please get me unstuck. But then he felt guilty. It had been so long since he had prayed sincerely, beyond the banal Sunday rote to appease his little congregation. He felt ashamed for waiting until his moment of despair to finally cry out. Or was he admitting something else? Confessing even more: I don't just don't like; I hate. Who? What? Wherein? Whereout?

He tried to turn on the ignition, but his hands were gone. It was like trying to thread a needle wearing boxing gloves. He swore, he laughed, and then he stuffed his hands down his pants, between his legs, and waited as his body warmth slowly carved out of the two cold clods fingers, knuckles, creases, hair.

He tried again. The starter whirred, the engine grabbed, the wheels churned, and he went nowhere.

"Dammit all!" He slammed the door again. His whole frame was shaking now, and for the first time he thought he might be in authentic danger. He thought he ought to start a fire, but he had no matches, no lighter. And even if he did—how, with these worthless hands? Idiot! Stooge! Moron! Had he set himself up for this or what? He knew better—he knew! Suppose he couldn't get out now and the snow kept falling? He looked around to get his bearings and saw nothing but a white blur. His truck was gone, its tracks were covered. He was next. He imagined the snow building, rising like flood waters: it was at his knees, his waist, his chest, his neck. He was under. Buried. Gone. *Adin.* He imagined his body stiff at attention, like an arctic sentry, frozen on duty. Who would know, until the spring thaw? And who would care? Nashdoi maybe? Would his cat notice the difference, as long as someone—anyone—filled his plastic bowl with table scraps? And who would feed old Nashdoi? Who would come looking? Sister Watchman perhaps?

He wondered about his spirit passing through the veil. His mother and father had disclaimed him in life, would they do likewise in death? How would Kathy receive him? With open, loving arms? Had he fought the good fight? Or would she turn her head in shame, embarrassed by the way he had squandered his life, his whole damn life, among this people? Oh, he had married them and buried them; had taught their children to read and write, had wiped their runny little noses on cold winter mornings. But would she embrace him for that, or merely out of marital duty? Or deny him altogether? Would she, too, condemn him for Celeste Bighorse? Or had she died for his sins? Then where was the real man in white? Where was the real Jesus? Or was he the white veil with a zillion fluttering parts, waiting to smack or lovingly smother you?

Then another possibility came to mind: suppose the Mormons were wrong, the Navajos right? Suppose the hereafter was a nebulous netherworld, an eternity of falling snow.

Tom calmly sat down and waited as the cold consumed him cell by cell. It had taken his legs and belly, and was moving into his chest now. Soon it was a blanket covering him with motherly warmth. He lay back, closed his eyes, and succumbed at last to the Christmas memory he had been trying to evade all night: their first Christmas Eve together as man and wife, their first on the rez. They were still strangers in the village. She was eight months pregnant, very vulnerable, atypically weepy. Sitting in their dark little kitchen staring glumly at the little scrub pine he had cut down and which she had dressed with her construction paper decorations, he did something very stupid. He made a little joke: "How about some egg nog?" And right there her spirit snapped. He thought he could actually hear it. "Egg nog? *Egg nog*? Very funny! What egg nog? What anything in this lousy rotten hell-hole? Drunks and dead dogs, that's all you ever see. Egg nog? All anyone ever wants around here is a big fat handout! They come to church for handouts, they come to the school for handouts! If they're so broke, how come everyone's driving a new pickup? *We* can't even afford a tuneup for our lousy rotten VW Rabbit! And these people act like you owe it to them. They look at you with their hatchet faces: gimme gimme gimme gimme. I'm sick of it, Tom! I'm fed up! Every time it rains or snows this place turns into a chocolate swamp. And if it's not the rain, it's the damn wind blowing so thick you can't see your nose in front of your face. I hate it, Tom!

The water's orange. God knows what creepy critters inhabit that stuff. And this lousy rotten trailer. This stupid tin can. We freeze all winter, fry all summer. I'm sick of it. There's no one—absolutely no one here for me to talk to. You go to work, sure, to your little rock schoolhouse where you're treated like the Great White God, but I'm stuck here in this tin can. Stuck! No telephone, no TV. I carry water in a bucket. I practically cook over an open fire. I hate it! I'm not a damned pioneer. I said whither thou goest, but this is the end of the road for me! I mean it, Tom. This is it! My father was right: you're a loser and you'll always be a loser! Misery's your middle name!"

Later she apologized: "This volleyball in my belly. It does weird things to you. It really messes up your mind." But when he told her to forget it, he understood, she unleashed again: "How could *you* understand? You had nothing to lose, I had everything!" And then fled into the bedroom and slammed the door: "Merry Christmas!"

It was close to midnight when he was awakened by a knock. He had fallen asleep on their ragged little sofa. It was Rose Tsinijinnie, the secretary at the elementary school. A tall, slender cowgirl, she was out of breath. "Come to the school," she panted. "Hurry!" And ran off.

Tom put on his snow boots and coat and trudged over to the rock schoolhouse. Rose met him at the door. "Where's your wife?"

"My wife? You didn't say anything about—"

"Go get your wife!" she ordered. Then laughed in that delightfully free manner of Navajo women. "Go get your wife or we'll have to find one for you!"

He trudged back to the trailer and asked—begged, really—her to come.

"I was almost asleep."

"We can't say no. You know how they are."

Grumbling, she threw on a maternity smock, boots, and a coat. "I feel like an Eskimo," she muttered.

"A very beautiful one," he said.

"Don't placate me."

"Okay, ugly as an Eskimo. Fat as an Eskimo. Ornery as an Eskimo. Snotty as an—"

"All right, all right. I get the picture."

When they arrived at the schoolhouse, the lights were out and Rose was gone.

"Swell," Kathy muttered.

They were wet, cold, and the snow was falling. As they turned back towards the trailer, Rose appeared around the corner, waving them to the side door. "Hey! Psst! Come on!" As they stepped inside, the lights came on. And the most incredible thing: the whole community was there—parents, students, babies in cradleboards, grandpas in cowboy hats, grandmas in pleated skirts. Two hundred plus crammed into that little room, and they were all smiling while the children sang "We Wish You a Merry Christmas," which Tom had taught them the week before in school. There was a pine tree in the corner with presents piled up underneath—baby clothes, boxes of disposable diapers, Navajo rugs, turquoise jewelry, a cradleboard of varnished cedarwood. He and Kathy stood there, stunned, silent, and wept.

Afterwards they trudged through the mud and snow back to their dingy little trailer with the wood stove and the foot-long cockroaches and the scrawny little Christmas tree, and they made the wildest wickedest love they ever had. Tom remembered lying in bed afterwards, listening to the snow like gentle fingers tapping on the glass. Her head was on his shoulder and she was curling his chest hairs around her finger as she whispered, "I'm so happy!" And at that moment so was he. It was the first time she had ever really said that. She had said "I Love You" often enough, but never that. And for the first time he really honestly truly thought they were going to make it.

A week later as they were driving home from a New Year's Day shopping spree in Farmington, he fell asleep at the wheel. When the VW Rabbit veered onto the shoulder, jerking him awake, he overcompensated and the little car hit the gravelly shoulder and became a flying missile. And that was it: two in one blow. Why he had survived and not her still angered and puzzled him. Maybe God leaves behind the one with the most rough edges. (But he could hear her counter from the other side: "Don't placate me!") Besides, he knew better: he was doing penance.

Hosteen used to tell him it was bad luck to speak about dying or the dead: to even think the act would increase its likelihood of happening. Tom always wondered if there wasn't some truth to that, or if Kathy had just had a premonition. A month or so before, she had instructed him—no, ordered him, was more accurate: "If anything ever happens to me, I want you to remarry!"

"But who would ever be stupid enough to marry the likes of me?" he protested.

"I don't know. But look hard. You'll find some sweet little sucker. But just make sure you do! I don't want a horny husband meeting me on the other side of the veil! Understand rubber band?"

He had had no intention of staying. In fact, his plan was to leave immediately. Just go. But where? To whom? One year ran into two, two to three and before he knew it he was stuck there, stuck up to his axles. He was like the snowflakes swirling around in the cone of light: white butterflies trapped in glass.

He jackknifed to attention, brushing the snow from his body as if it were some kind of white vermin. The snow had stopped and the skies had cleared except for a small patch where the moon was peering through a crack like an eavesdropping eye. Stars appeared like tiny ornaments. Moonlit, the snow-covered expanse looked like a weird florescent icing: cold, clean, beautifully barren. A glittering wasteland. Radioactive. Out of this world. Tom closed his eyes and took a deep, cleansing breath. He saw a light shining at the foot of this white cliff far ahead. As he trudged towards it, the snow started up again. The sky was perfectly clear but flakes were falling, as if the whole Milky Way were fluttering down. Soon he was the man in white again. Hands, feet, legs, head. His body was numb but his heart was on fire. He trudged: left foot, right foot, left foot.

It was a homestead almost identical to the one he had stopped at down the road—the corral, the outhouse, the shacks, the hogan. Three pair of eyes glowed orange underneath a plywood lean-to. The same matron answered the door. Clint Eastwood was there too, glaring at him but sadly this time, as if his bullet eyes had prematurely misfired. The old woman with the greasewood arms was kneading her dough, and her black-hatted old mate was keeping vigil over the sleeping children by the tree. The young mothers and the young man with the black bangs watched.

This time the matron spoke sternly to him. "She's in *there!*" she said, and her finger steered his eye across the corral towards a little hogan on a hill. "This morning, we dug a hole for you. There's a pick and a shovel too. Last night, in my sleep, a man in white came . . ."

And then he understood.

She belonged to the Salt Clan and was born in the year the cottonwoods greened early, which made her a little over ninety but under one hundred, and that was all he would know, all they would tell him. But as he trekked across the white field towards the hogan on the hill, all the rest would become clear to him. He would wonder, since the year the cottonwoods greened early, how many hundreds of sheep had she shorn, how many thousands of pieces of fry bread had she made, how many rugs had she woven, how many winters, snows, how many Christmases had passed? He tried to picture her in his mind. Instead he saw the dimpled smile of Celeste Bighorse. He looked back only once, and saw the others watching on the far side of the corral: the bell-shaped matron, a young woman in a screaming yellow windbreaker, and the sketchy silhouette of the old man as he touched his forefinger to the brim of his black felt hat, and with that simple gesture thanked him across the white eternities of the omnipresent snow.

*Susan Dean Smallwood was born in Chincoteaque, Virginia and raised an Army brat, living in Kansas, California, Hawaii, and Germany. She was baptized on her eighteenth birthday through the efforts of her next-door neighbor who was on a mission. She also married him a year later, exactly two weeks after he returned from his mission. She's been involved in raising their seven children since that time. Their oldest daughter Dawn has cerebral palsy. She returned to Averett College in Danville, Virginia last year and will graduate in the spring with a major in English and Journalism. She has published two novels—*You're a Rock, Sister Lewis *with Hatrack River Publications and* True Rings the Heart *with Deseret Book.*

GIFTS

by Susan Dean Smallwood

Lois put down her needlepoint and pulled her reading glasses down to the end of her nose to peer out the frosty living room window. "There she is out getting her mail," she said. "That's about the only time you see her."

Her husband Joe grunted but didn't put his paper down. "Shouldn't be so nosy," Joe chuckled from behind the sports section.

"I'm not nosy. I just wish I knew more about her and that boy who lives with her. He looks like he's . . ." She struggled to remember the more modern word for what used to be called mongoloid.

"Down's Syndrome," Joe finished. He put his paper down finally and looked at her. "You know you could go visit her sometime. Take her some of your cookies."

She looked up and caught his stare. "Well, if you're so full of the Christmas spirit, why don't YOU take them some cookies? You certainly know where they are." She stuffed her needlepoint down in her bag impatiently.

After that, she didn't think much more about their conversation until the next morning as she dragged her garbage cans out to the curb. She saw her neighbor bringing out a big bag to add to the pile at her curb. Lois turned quickly to start back in the house, but she hit one of her garbage cans and sent the lid clattering into the street. She

173

went after it, stopping it with her foot, and glanced up to see her neighbor smiling.

"They make enough noise, don't they?" her neighbor called.

"They sure do," Lois answered. She slammed the lid back down on the can and hurried into the house.

By the time she looked out the kitchen window, her neighbor had disappeared into her house again. Staring out the window, she thought, "I really don't have any reason not to go over. And won't Joe be surprised when he comes home to find out I took them some cookies and had a nice conversation? Maybe that boy won't even come out."

"Okay, I'll do it," she said to herself. "I don't have to stay long." She got out some plastic Christmas plates she used for cookie deliveries and began to fill one up.

A few minutes later she stood in front of her neighbor's door and checked the plate once more. The red bow she had stuck on top was slipping.

The door opened as the bow fell to the porch. "Hello," her neighbor said.

"Hi," Lois answered, standing back up from picking up the bow. "This bow doesn't want to stick."

"Sort of like garbage can lids," her neighbor laughed. "Won't you come in?"

Lois walked in and held the plate out self-consciously. "I'm Lois Gillespie. I thought you might like some Christmas cookies."

"We'd love some," her neighbor said. "Freddie, come see what we have."

"Oh, I don't want to bother you," Lois said.

"No bother." She called again into the back of the house and Freddie came out.

He was shorter than Lois and chubby with the thick lips and slanted eyes of Down's Syndrome. Lois was relieved to see that he was immaculately dressed in corduroy slacks and a knit shirt.

"This is my brother Freddie," Lois' neighbor said. Then she laughed. "Oh, I'm Catherine Ellington." She put her arm around Freddie. "Freddie, this is Lois and she brought us some cookies."

Freddie stuck out his hand for Lois to shake. She shook it and surprised herself by smiling at him.

"Thank you," he said. It was a little slurred, but she was relieved he could talk because she didn't know any sign language.

"You're welcome," she answered.

"Freddie," Catherine said. "Why don't you take the cookies into the kitchen and pour yourself a glass of milk? You can have a snack with your TV shows."

"I will do that," he said. He took the plate carefully with both hands and left the room.

"Please, come sit down," Catherine said, pointing to the living room.

As she walked in the room, the beauty of it struck Lois. Not only was it tastefully decorated in mauve and blue, but on every wall were beautiful watercolor and oil paintings. Paintings of colorful spring gardens, luscious meadows of wild flowers, and elegant birds in golden bird cages were everywhere.

"These paintings are lovely," Lois exclaimed. She walked over to look more closely, realizing as she did that the name painted in the right-hand corner was Catherine's. "You did these?" she asked.

"Yes," Catherine answered with pride. "I painted a lot more, though, before our mother died a couple of months ago and we moved here."

Lois sat down at her invitation but couldn't keep her eyes off the paintings, especially the birds. "You must love birds. And what beautiful cages," she said, noticing offhand that she had forgotten to paint doorways on the cages.

"I do," Catherine said. She picked up one of the smaller bird paintings and looked at it wistfully. "Birds have such freedom."

For some reason she couldn't even explain to herself, Lois turned to Catherine and said, if you'd like me to come and stay with Freddie while you do some Christmas shopping, I'd love to."

"Oh, I would really appreciate that," Catherine said. Lois could tell by the way she said it that she really meant it.

"How about tomorrow morning then?" Lois said. "I'm free."

"That sounds wonderful," Catherine said. "Freddie really isn't much trouble at all."

"I'm sure I can handle it," Lois said, not sure at all that she could.

The next morning, with needlepoint bag in hand, Lois walked over to Catherine's house in plenty of time for her to be at the mall when it opened. She was a little nervous, though she didn't exactly know why. After all, she delivered mail at the hospital once a week.

After Catherine drove away, Lois settled into a comfortable chair and began her needlepoint, listening closely to the sounds in the back room where Freddie was watching TV.

Before she could finish even a row, however, Freddie was standing silently before her, holding a checker board and box of checkers carefully out in front of him. "Do you like checkers?" he asked.

"I'll play a game with you," Lois said. She was going to let him win, but he beat her handily anyway. They played two more games before she finally won. Then she followed him into the den where they sat and watched a couple of game shows. Freddie seriously shook her hand and congratulated her each time she knew a correct answer. Soon it was noon and he told her that it was his lunch time, so she got out the sandwich and fruit that Catherine had left and poured him a glass of milk.

As he ate she wandered back into the living room and over to one of the larger bird paintings, remembering what Catherine had said about the freedom of the birds. As she contemplated that, it seemed even more odd that the bird cages had no doors.

Freddie came in from the kitchen. "It's time for my exercises," he announced. Putting on his hat and coat that hung near the back door he waited while she went and got her coat. She followed him out to the porch swing in the backyard.

Freddie was still swinging when Catherine came through the gate with an armful of packages. "I had the best time," she said. "I hope Freddie wasn't too much trouble."

"Not at all," Lois said. "I enjoyed my morning, too. In fact . . ." She had thought about this, so she was sure this time. "I would love to come over one morning a week and sit with him while you go out and do whatever you want. I really would."

After that, Lois didn't see either one of them for a couple of days. The day before Christmas as she was finishing up the gift-wrapping the doorbell rang. "Oh no," she said aloud. "I'm in no mood for company." She untangled herself from the ribbons and gift wrap to hurry to the door.

Freddie stood before her with a brightly wrapped package in his hands. Behind him she saw Catherine across the street watching closely.

"Merry Christmas," he said. "I came over by myself." He handed her the flat square gift.

"Why, thank you, Freddie. Can you come in?"

"No. It's time to eat. Good-bye." He turned around and held tightly to the handrail as he walked down the steps.

Lois waved to Catherine and yelled thank you before going back into the house.

Sitting down at the kitchen table, she fingered the gift and tried to resist the temptation to open it. It felt like a plaque or something, like those at the drugstore with sayings on them.

Giving in to her curiosity, she turned the gift over and quickly unwrapped it. It was one of Catherine's paintings. Lois was thrilled; it was beautiful. Then her heart sank. How could she ever find something this late to give them that was as nice as their gift to her?

She held the picture in front of her, trying to remember where in Catherine's house this painting had been. Suddenly, as she traced the elegant bird with her finger she realized that this was a new painting she had not seen before. The colors, the bird, and the cage all seemed much the same as the others, but this bird sat perched before a tiny door opened wide to the beautiful garden beyond.

Suddenly she knew that her gift to them had already been given. And as she sat in her kitchen with the dim winter twilight deepening around her, she hugged the picture to her heart and knew she would give it many times more.

Susan Evans McCloud has been a published writer since the age of thirteen. As a young woman she wrote feature articles with her own byline for the Telegraph in Dixon, Illinois. She has to her credit award-winning screenplays, filmstrips, a stage adaptation, and many published lyrics, including two hymns for the new LDS hymnbook. Her twenty books are mainly historical fiction, though she has one volume of poetry, Songs of Life, *a biography,* Not In Vain, *and two books for children. She is the mother of six children, is a docent in Brigham Young's Beehive House, and teaches English and writing at a small private school. She enjoys music, poetry, gardening, and being with her family which is very involved in Scottish activities; her daughters dance the highland dances and her son, Jared, plays the bagpipes.*

BE STILL

by Susan Evans McCloud

1.

City sidewalks, busy sidewalks,
Dressed in holiday style,
In the air there's the feeling
Of Christmas . . .

The cheerful strains blared over the store's loud speaker. Anne heard them and scowled. She was angry that she had so much shopping still left to do. If they hadn't all had the flu the week after Thanksgiving, and Brad's piano recital to get through, and then Richard going off on a business trip, something he seldom did. Now, suddenly, they were more than halfway into December and the stores were crowded and some of the best things picked over.

She checked her list; it seemed to grow longer and longer each year. And these small, annoying gifts for people she felt she had to buy for, although inexpensive when considered one by one, ate into her precious funds.

She looked at the long line ahead of her, shifted her weight and sighed out loud. Each year she determined: next year I'll have more money and I'll organize early. I'll find clever, unique gifts and I'll do

179

more baking and read more to the children—and here she was. Standing in a line of late shoppers, her feet on fire, a dull ache in the small of her back, an hour behind schedule, and looking for bargains because her wallet was getting too thin.

She wished Richard had come with her, but he was home watching the children. Richard made shopping fun. He liked picking and choosing, a window-shopper, you might say. But not her. With Anne shopping was a task, something to get through. Especially this year. It seemed a dull, lifeless market: few new toys, no new dolls or teddy bears. At least it was fun to buy things that pulled at your heartstrings. The doll Alicia had asked for didn't do anything for Anne. But that's how it was. Even the clothes styles were awful this year.

She reached the counter at last. Even paying cash for her purchases took her nearly ten minutes. She timed it, not bothering to conceal her anxious glances at her watch. Ridiculous the incompetence of young people they hire these days!

She hurried from the store, weaving in and out among dozens of people who seemed stupid and slow. My, it was cold. No snow yet. She was grateful for that, though the children longed for it. But they didn't do the shoveling or clean up the floors or scrape off the cars.

She drove with the same tense annoyance she'd shopped with. Things seemed to get in her way: a back-up of cars at the stop light, a rude driver who pulled out in front of her and then putted along like a grandmother. Whoever said people were kinder at Christmastime? Anne didn't think that was true. They were more preoccupied with themselves and more determined to get precisely what they wanted, and heaven help anyone who should get in their way. It was the commercialism, of course. Sometimes she found herself longing for the old-fashioned Christmases her grandparents had: a tree cut down in the woods just behind their farm, homemade dolls and hand-whittled toys, sleigh rides, homemade cakes and donuts, carols sung round the fire. So elemental. So uncomplicated. So inexpensive.

She took the freeway exit and headed toward the Avenues. She was glad she lived here. Old Salt Lake. It seemed like a town, not an impersonal suburb. There were some problems, of course; there were problems wherever you lived. But the houses here were old and the streets were quiet, and Anne liked the feeling that gave her.

She turned onto C Street. She saw the ambulance. It registered, barely. Enough for her mind to think fleetingly: Sister Ross. Has she suffered another stroke, poor thing? As her car took her closer, she saw that the ambulance was parked beside her house, near the end of the drive which Richard's jeep blocked. Still no sense of warning. She slowed the car. What could be going on? That's all she thought.

Then she saw Richard emerge from the house with a stranger. She saw Richard's face. She inched the car forward. Beyond the ambulance sat a police car, and another small red car that she didn't recognize. The ambulance pulled away, turning on its red lights. Richard saw her, and began running toward her. She saw the policeman now, standing in their yard talking to the stranger.

She turned off the car's engine and sat trembling. "What is it, Richard?" She said the words before he had opened the door and could hear her.

"Thank heaven you're here."

His voice, for some reason, sent shudders through her.

"Alicia's been hit."

"What do you mean, she's been hit?" What a stupid question! Her own voice sounded strange in her ears.

"By a car, Anne. Move over. I'll explain on the way to the hospital."

"Is she all right?" Of course, of course, she's all right!

"No, she isn't. She's unconscious. She hit her head hard—"

"Richard, how did this happen?" Her words had a shrill note to them.

He had turned the car around. He was driving with care and speed.

"Richard, who's with the children?" The panic inside her was building.

"Beth came. They're okay."

She thought illogically of the clothes that were still in the dryer and the roast she needed to thaw.

"Was it that little red car?"

Richard glanced at her. "Yes. Can you take this, Anne?" He reached for her hand. She pressed it and nodded.

"Alicia was in the yard playing with the dog and that old yellow ball—"

"I don't believe it! Why wasn't Brad with her?"

"He was. I called him in to answer the phone. It was only a minute. She ran into the street right in front of the car—"

"Well, why did he hit her? Why wasn't he watching?" Anne knew she was screaming, but her voice was a current of feeling she couldn't control. "He was speeding, wasn't he? Wasn't he! Who is this man?"

That stranger I saw in the yard, in my yard!

"I don't know, Anne. I don't remember his name. The police have all that."

"He's young. He's young and selfish and ignorant." She tore her hand away. "Tell me. Was he speeding?"

"Maybe a little."

"I knew it!" She bit out the words between clenched teeth. "How dare he? How dare he?"

"Annie, everyone speeds. We speed sometimes—"

"Not on neighborhood streets, not on streets like ours!" She leaned forward, her hands clasped together. She could feel herself trembling. A sharp pain was building inside. There was panic now.

"She was watching the ball. She ran out right in front of him," Richard explained. "That's always been one of my fears when I'm driving. I don't think he could have avoided—"

"How far are we from the hospital?" Anne interrupted.

"Just a few more blocks now."

"She'll be all right, won't she? Won't she, Richard?"

He didn't answer. She needed to hear him say: yes dear, she'll be all right. Richard was afraid. She could feel his fear. She couldn't remember ever seeing Richard like this before. It struck terror through her, and irrational panic she could scarcely control.

He was parking the car now. They were here. She had the door open before he'd turned off the engine. A sudden need to see Alicia washed over her. She bent to the wind that drew icy lines on her cheeks and forehead. My head aches, she thought. My head and my feet and my throat. Oh, I can't get sick.

Here was the door. Richard opened it for her. The warmth drew her in. She shuddered gratefully, but hung back from the desk, let Richard do the explaining. She came at his nod and followed him down one of the passageways sided by doors, numbered emergency rooms. Where is Alicia?

I've never been in a hospital except to have a baby, Anne realized. I've never been here. Beth and Sylvia have both had their kids in emergency for cuts and fevers, and even a broken arm once. But never me. I don't know anything about all this!

Richard pushed at a door. Anne hung behind with a sudden reluctance. Richard reached for her hand. Then she was standing beside Alicia who lay on a board stretched across an examining table. She was still, more still than in sleep. But her face was a blank, there was no pain on her face, no expression, nothing at all.

Someone was talking. She looked up. "Dr. Grant," she sputtered, with a rush of relief as she recognized him. "How did you know—"

He put his hand on her arm. "Richard called me."

Of course. Richard would. Thank heaven for Richard's thoroughness, Richard's calm.

"We've ordered a lateral neck X-ray," Dr. Grant told them, "and a CT scan."

This means nothing! Anne thought. "Why?" she asked.

"To determine the extent of her injuries." Dr. Grant's voice was soft, with a patience in it that calmed Anne a little. "I suspect a subdural hematoma."

"What then?" Richard asked.

"We operate as soon as possible." He turned back to Anne. "This will require time, my dear. Let Richard take you for something to eat."

She shook her head.

"Something warm to drink then. You need it." His words had the force of authority.

"I want to be there." She touched the small hand that lay white on the sheet. Will she be all right? She couldn't make the words form in her mouth, though she longed to speak them, over and over again until they told her!

The men let her wait until they had taken her child on the stretcher into the small X-ray room. The dark room swallowed her. Anne turned away. The panic had dulled now into a pain that sat hard in her stomach.

"Richard, how can I wait? I can never bear waiting, you know that. He said two hours, at least two hours!"

"Well, we've got to eat something. That will fill up some time."

She shook her head.

"It will make you feel better. Then you can call home."

He had her arm and was leading her forward. Dear Richard. Will your persistence overpower my stubbornness? I hope so.

She walked, both eyes forward, through the ill-smelling halls. It was too bright here. Bright and efficient and antiseptic. And cold. She let Richard lead her. She didn't care where she was going or how long it took her to walk woodenly there.

2.

Anne had eaten the food set before her somehow, and the time had crawled by. She stood at a phone booth and dialed "1" for Provo, then her mother's number. This isn't happening to me! The thought played across her mind like a broken record.

"Hello, mother, it's Anne."

When she heard her mother's voice she gave the receiver to Richard. He did much better than she would have. She could tell that her mother was becoming slightly hysterical. Richard handled her well. But when he hung up the phone he grimaced.

"Thank heaven that's done. She said she'd call your sister and anyone else she can think of." He managed a smile.

"This isn't a party!" Anne's voice betrayed anger. "No one's had a baby. Why does she have to tell everyone?"

"She meant people who ought to know, Anne. Besides, sorrow seems lighter sometimes when it's shared."

Anne moved back to the wall lined with chairs and sat down. The last time I called from a hospital was when I did have a baby. How wonderful that was! I could have kept calling people all night, just to talk about it. I was sleepy and dreamily happy . . .

When Alicia was born! My first daughter, my only daughter. How pretty she was. Delicate, not like the boys. Richard was so proud, and a little afraid of her, handling her gently, as if she might break. Everything was pink and lace. Mother bought a small locket Alicia wore the morning we blessed her—

Richard, don't let her die! Heavenly Father, don't take her away from me!

"Anne, Dr. Grant's here."

She looked up. She hadn't noticed, hadn't heard him approach. The two men had been talking. "They've decided to operate, Anne."

George Grant sat down by her side. He was a friend of the family. She had known George for years, but that didn't seem to make any difference, that didn't help.

"A subdural hematoma, Anne, is a blood tumor beneath the dura mater. We will simply go in and make small burr holes so we can suction off that fluid."

Anne closed her eyes. She couldn't bear to think, couldn't bear to picture what he was saying.

Operate on the brain of a five-year old! Cut that small head, that pale, perfect skin!

"This procedure will allow the brain to re-expand—"

"And it will?"

"It ought to."

"If it doesn't?"

Dr. Grant shook his head. "Various things could develop. It's senseless to explore any of them unless we are forced to. It will take a few days—two, three, maybe four—"

"Take a few days to what?"

"To tell how the brain will react, to see what it does. Alicia will most probably remain comatose."

Anne shook her head. I don't want to hear any of this! She felt her bottom lip start to quiver. She couldn't control it, couldn't stop it. She rose. "Do whatever you'd like. Whatever you think you have to."

She took a few steps away. George Grant rose, too. He and Richard moved off a short distance. She knew they were talking. She didn't care what they said, what they thought. It took what strength she had left to hold back the tears that were threatening, to control her face which wanted to crumple into a horrible, shapeless mass and leave her no place to hide.

Hospitals are not made for restless, impatient people. Time has a whole different meaning in this little world. Time is suspended and life becomes waiting. And waiting and pain can unravel the impatient sufferer . . .

"Anne, dear, sit down."

"I'm all right, mother."

Anne came back slowly to the brightly-lit room and the faces and eyes that surrounded her. Her parents were here. Her mother fidgeting, wound up, too loud; her father silent; her sister Lynda and her husband Doug, whispering in the corner, uncomfortable and showing it. That was all. Her two brothers lived in the East and Richard's family, all non-Mormons, were in the Mid-West. He had called them, of course. They had been quietly shocked and sympathetic. But what could they do? They were too far away, too removed.

Anne looked at her father. He and Richard had blessed Alicia before she went into surgery. Did you hear them, my dear? Did you feel your Daddy, know he was there by you, loving you? Not once in her life had her own father given her a blessing. The ward was going to fast. That's what the bishop had said. Anne had never fasted in her life, not really. Fast Sunday fasting, missing one meal or two, but not something like this. Not real agonized, serious fasting!

How pathetic I am! Like a new convert without any moorings. And I'm afraid. Afraid Heavenly Father won't listen, or won't really care, won't understand that he can't let her die!

"Annie, here, sit by me."

It was her sister. Anne tried to smile, to control her face.

"Would it help to talk some?"

Anne shook her head. Talk, talk about what? What we should wear to the family party next Friday? What gifts we've found for those difficult children of Lewis's?

This isn't real! This isn't happening to me!

When Dr. Grant came into the room he walked directly to Anne. "The operation went well, my dear. We're lucky to have such an excellent neurosurgeon as Dr. Marks here and available." He took her hands. "Don't worry, Anne, her condition is promising."

"She's in God's hands."

Who said that? Anne turned. Of course, Mother. I should have known. What does she mean when she says such a thing? Does it make her feel better? I suppose we are all in God's hands. I know I am. But what will he do, what will he do with me now that he has me at his mercy?

The quiet group slowly broke up. It was late. There was still tomorrow that had to be faced.

"I want you to go home with your folks, Anne, take a hot bath, get some rest."

She knew Richard meant it. It was his no-nonsense tone that he seldom used with her. She did as he said. She felt relief to walk out of the hospital into the night. The cold air made her feel alive again. But she felt so alone. She insisted on crawling into the back seat where she sat, small and huddled, listening to her father's car radio:

Joy to the world—

Carols. Christmas carols, of course.

The Lord is come,
Let earth receive her king—

This is better than talking. Much better.

Let every heart prepare him room,
And Saints and angels sing,
And Saints and angels sing—

Anne felt the words move inside her head. Saints and angels sing. Maybe the angels sang at Christmastime, but did anyone else? Did all the people out there buying presents and planning parties, worrying over budgets and schedules, ever stop to rejoice? To rejoice at the birth of a Savior.

A Savior. Dear God, don't let her die. Nobody dies at Christmastime.

Her father pulled into the drive. There was no sign of the little red car. There were lights in her house. She hated the thought of facing the children. She walked up to the door. Her parents followed, subdued and quiet. Before she could get out her keys Beth had the door open wide and was pulling her in. Thank heaven for Beth's straightforward normalcy!

"Richard called, Anne, so you don't have to tell me anything. The kids are all in bed. Brad was determined to stay awake until you came, but he finally fell off. Just as well, for your sake."

She smiled at Anne's folks, hesitating briefly, then folded her friend in a warm, close hug, brief as possible. Anne's chin trembled. Beth kissed her cheek.

"I'll be off. Get some sleep if you can, Anne. I'll see you tomorrow."

She shut the door gently. Anne looked at her mother. The silence was deep.

"Things will be fine, Anne, now don't you worry. Get some sleep like Beth said. Everything looks better after a good night's rest. Dad and I will handle things here. You just take care of yourself."

She meant well. Anne nodded. "I think I'll just check on the boys."

She leaned on the railing as she climbed the long stairs. She wasn't just tired, but weary. She opened the door to the room Brad and Mark shared. They lay snuggled together. She couldn't bear to think of them worrying here alone, falling asleep at last out of exhaustion. The room was neat, toys and clothes picked up. Beth's doing.

She paused at the door of the empty, pink-papered room. I won't cry, I won't cry.

She peeked into the nursery. Jon, curled up on his side, looked like a slumbering cherub. She went closer, bent and kissed his cheek. He didn't stir. She closed her eyes tight to shut out the vision of the pale face on the hospital sheets. She walked into her room, her dark, cheerless room, and shut the door tight behind her.

3.

Anne forgot it was Sunday. Back in the hospital time stood still. There were no days of the week, no seasons, no identities. She walked the long hall. There was nothing to do but wait. Wait and pray and be patient. Wait upon the Lord.

"It's a lovely morning again."

She turned at the sound of the voice.

"Look at those mountains. The way the clouds hug their flanks and the snow on their peaks. Have you ever seen anything like it?"

Anne glared at the woman. Her face was fair, only lined slightly by the age her white hair betrayed.

"You're the mother of the little girl in Room 5, aren't you? I peeked in there this morning before you arrived. What a beautiful child."

Yes, Room 5. Fitting, don't you think, for a little girl who is just five years old?

The woman reached for Anne's hand and patted it gently. "How hard for you, dear. I do hope all will go well for you."

Anne took a step back. The woman felt her reluctance and let go of her hand. She smiled sweetly. "I'll be here in Room 12 if you need someone to talk to." She pulled the heavy door open and slipped inside. Anne stood blinking, fighting her reactions. What could this woman know? Does she think a little grandmotherly comfort can help me now?

She stumbled ahead. At the end of the hall a nurse was pushing a wheelchair. In the chair sat a little girl perhaps ten years old. Her long blonde hair fell in wide curls about her pale cheeks.

"Doesn't Nancy look like something this morning?"

The nurse was addressing the question to Anne. Anne stopped and looked at the child. She really was very lovely.

"My mother's coming today. She'll be here for Christmas." The girl's voice was as gentle and sweet as her face.

"That's nice," Anne replied. She had to say something. She felt uncomfortable here with this child.

"Are you going home then for Christmas?"

The merest shadow moved across the child's face.

"No, I mean my mother is *coming*. From California. That's where she lives."

Anne raised an eyebrow. "I see." She added as she turned away from them, "Well, I'm glad she's coming. Goodbye now."

She hurried off, back to Alicia's room. She disappeared inside gratefully. Richard was there. He was sitting at the bedside, bent over their child, pushing her dark hair away from her forehead with gentle fingers. He was bent low, crooning something Anne couldn't hear. She came up behind him and rubbed his neck and shoulders for a moment. He looked back with a smile. But there were tears in his eyes.

"You look tired, Annie." He took her hand and held it in both of his. "You run along home. Your mother has a meal ready."

"What about you?"

"She fed me—three helpings and apple pie. The kids are anxious to see you."

She was suddenly anxious to see them, too. She kissed Richard, then leaned over Alicia—the marble form, as flawless, as fair as Snow White. A cold chill ran through her body. She felt an impulse to shake her daughter, to make her wake up, make her stir, make her seem alive—even a little bit so! She kissed the pale cheek and turned away.

It was snowing outside. A fine layer clung to the windshield that Richard had cleaned. She drove with care. She felt calm in a drugged way, going through the regular motions of living by rote, not really seeing or feeling anything.

When she walked in the front door she heard it instantly, one of the songs Alicia loved from the Primary Let's Sing album.

> *Give, said the little stream,*
> *Give, oh give, give, oh give,*
> *Give, said the little stream*
> *As it hurried down the hill.*
> *I'm small I know,*
> *But wherever I go,*
> *The grass grows greener still—*

Brad came up to her. He seemed almost shy. "We thought you'd like it. You know how Alicia was, Mom, always making us play this dumb record. But it helps hearing it now."

Anne drew him close, blinking away the images and feelings the song brought to mind.

No tears, no tears! What of the children?

Mark was here, dragging Jon. Jon was only two. This was not hurting him much, except for missing his mother. How good he smelled, how soft he still was. She held him so tight that he squirmed. With reluctance she let him go. They sat down to the table and after a few minutes the boys seemed all right. Anne knew her parents as well as Richard had been explaining things to them. But she still marveled at the almost heartless resilience young children had.

"You missed the Christmas program," Brad said.

"I know. I'm sorry," Anne answered.

"It was boring," Mark assured her. Anne stifled a smile.

"Didn't you primary children sing?"

"Well, that part was good. But there were a lot of boring talks."

"Except for the bishop," Brad disagreed. "Mom, do you know what he said?"

Anne looked up and gave her son her attention.

"He said that Jesus' birth was the first step in his sacrifice for us, and if we want to know joy, we must be willing to go through sorrow and sacrifice the way Jesus did."

Anne leaned forward. Her mother was watching her with moist eyes.

"I'm glad you told me that, Brad," she said carefully.

"Do you think he was talking about us?"

"What do you mean?" Anne cleared her throat. Brad knit his brow, thinking hard. He dropped his eyes.

"With Alicia. You know." He took a deep breath. "It's pretty scary."

"Yes, it's pretty scary," Anne repeated softly.

"But isn't it growing through sorrow like the bishop said? We can understand Jesus just a little now, don't you think, Mom?"

Anne's mother reached over and hugged Brad. Anne didn't think she could speak. She met Brad's eyes, and what passed between them was enough.

After the dishes were done they gathered around the tree. Brad plugged in the lights and a hundred white stars sparkled in the green branches. It was a good tree, so beautifully formed and so fragrant. Alicia had been the first to discover it. She had danced all around.

"Let's take this one, Mother. It wants us, I know it does."

The lights blurred and Anne blinked her eyes. Her mother was at the piano, her father ready to lead them in singing hymns. He would go back to his office tomorrow, but her mother would stay for a few days. She looked at her father. How kind my father's eyes are. He is a good man, my father. But I never know what he is thinking. What is he thinking right now? He's never said what he feels. He just goes through life quiet and patient, trying to do his best. How hard is this for him? I've never wondered about what my father might suffer.

Her mother played well. The children were singing with all their hearts.

Full of adages, my mother; safe, simple homilies life can be lived by. Even as a child when I'd come to her crying she'd quote something to me: waste not want not—all's well that ends well—there can't be blossoms without any rain—things like that. What was it you said at the hospital, mother? Trust in the Lord, his love never faileth. Is that your way to keep down the pain, to make sense out of life? Well, it won't work for me. I want to know why this thing had to happen. Why did it happen to me? And to my beautiful, innocent daughter, the only daughter I have. There could be no reason for him to take her. I need her! He knows I can't go on if he takes her from me!

"You aren't singing, Mother."

Brad's too observant. He always has been.

"Your mother's tired, dear." That was her father. "Just let her sit there in peace."

In peace! What peace? I'm consumed with pain. I used to think peace was having all the bills paid, dinner ready on time, family home evening every week, the kids off to Church on Sunday mornings without fighting and tears.

> Peace on earth, good will to men,
> Peace on earth, good will to men.

The children's eyes were as bright as the lights on the tree.

I don't know what peace is. This is the season of love and peace and I'm hurt and afraid. I'm a stranger to peace. Will I ever know peace again?

4.

There were still presents Anne had left to buy. They must go on living. The world wasn't calling off Christmas on their account. It doesn't matter, Anne thought. All the things I've worked my life around simply don't matter. If I get all the candies and cookies baked that I want, if I lose five pounds, if I find a new dress for the party, if I come up with more clever and beautiful gifts than my friends do—how does it really matter? It all seems so empty, so pointless.

Richard took a few hours off to spend at the office, then came back to spell her. He sent her off to the mall. It would be good for her, he insisted. Anne didn't think so. She found herself watching the other people, resenting the fact that they were going merrily about their business, unaware of her pain, unaware that life set her apart from them by this monstrous mistake, this thing called an accident that was destroying the child she loved.

She thought of the man she had met this morning. The man who drove the red car. He wasn't really so young. He was an ordinary, decent young man, and he hadn't been speeding. He had a wife and baby, a college degree, he had served a mission. He was consumed with remorse and concern at what had happened.

Richard had made her come out, made her meet him and talk with him. She would always think that was cruel.

"There is nothing to forgive, Annie," Richard kept saying. "He didn't do anything wrong. It was an *accident*. In fact, the officer at the scene said that a less skillful driver would not have braked so quickly and the impact might have been far worse."

She shook her head, shutting out images again. He was there, wasn't he? Why did he have to be there on my street at that very moment? Why wasn't he somewhere else doing something, anything? I can blame him for that.

She wandered a little aimlessly, having difficulty making her mind come to any decision. She picked things up and put them back down again. Just outside the toy store she saw a woman hurry past with a child. It made Anne draw in her breath. She stared after them. The wave of the dark hair, the way the girl walked, the curve of her cheek as she looked up at her mother. It might have been Alicia she watched!

She leaned against the wall, shaken, and stood there, just staring as the people walked past, feeling a darkness around and within her—a loneliness more engulfing than pain. She noticed a young, tired woman stop and scowl at her two year old, shake her roughly, then yank the child's hand and hurry on, dragging the little one after her. It made Anne feel sick. She thought of the times she'd been cross with Alicia.

What a short temper I have! How many times have I thoughtlessly hurt her? Why didn't I know? Why did I forget how precious she is to me?

She remembered last year when she had promised Alicia she would read her the Nutcracker book. It was a thick book, too mature for a four year old, and Anne had purposefully stalled. There was so much else to do, and her days seemed to melt away from her. Every night when she tucked Alicia in and helped with her prayers the child would ask her, "Will you read the Nutcracker story tomorrow?" And Anne, feeling guilty, promised she would. But Christmas day came and went with the story unread. And now?

Anne drove back to the hospital. It was beginning to snow. Large, thick flakes that swirled helter skelter, obscuring the sky, even the trees and the cars in front of her. When she was a child she used to sit and just watch the snow fall. Alicia did that. The boys wanted to be out in it, running and playing. But Alicia would sit, with her little feet tucked beneath her, and look out at the snow, humming melodies to herself.

Anne sent Richard home. It was his turn, and he had things to do. Dr. Grant had been in. He assured Richard that all the vital signs still looked good. Any time now she should snap out of it, come around. Any time now.

Anne had been fasting all day. She felt a little lightheaded and irritable; she wasn't accustomed to this. She knew the ward members were fasting with them. But when you fast you should pray. What were the ward members praying for? Comfort the Hunters. Bless them in their hour of need. Bless them how? Bless me by helping my daughter to live! That was the sum of her prayer. She had no room for any other.

It was hot in this room. Hot and airless. At the window the snow drove relentlessly on, without sound, like the snow on a stage, something false and outside Anne's world. On the narrow bed lay her daughter, as still as the snow against her backdrop of white. I can't see you, Anne agonized. Where is your mind? Are you resting somewhere and oblivious, or are you in pain? Are you straining to come back to me, darling?

Anne went out into the hall. She couldn't bear the quiet confinement. She spotted the stranger right away, in time to slip back into the room, but for some reason she stayed. The woman was young, perhaps twenty-five, but her face was gray, drained of color, but not expression. When Anne looked on her pain she knew instinctively that this woman had gone where she never had been.

Anne moved a step forward. The woman saw her, looked into her eyes.

"Did you lose a child, too?" she asked.

A great shudder moved through Anne's frame. "Not yet," she heard herself whisper.

"My baby is gone." The words struck Anne with the force of a shock. "It was only a fever. A cough and a little fever. How was I to know?"

She took both Anne's hands in hers and hung on with a power that frightened Anne.

"Finally I took her to the doctor, and he sent her here. Imagine that. They put her in the oxygen tent and told me—" she shook her head, unwilling to re-live the details. "What does all that matter now? She's gone."

The girl looked into Anne's face. "She was only a baby. Eight months old—her first Christmas—" There were tears coming now. "And do you want to know the worst of it?"

No, I do not. No, I can't bear even this much.

Anne pressed the cold hands and nodded.

"When she was born I took a month off work to be with her, but then I went back. I had to. So many bills. Bob expected me to. Besides, I have a good job. You don't let go of a good job when you've got one."

"No, of course not," Anne said.

The young woman made a strange sound. "I wasn't with her. The first word she said—I didn't hear it. The first time she crawled—"

She pulled her hands away and wrung them in front of her. "How could I know? How could I know I was going to lose her before she was mine? I meant to quit work—I would have quit someday, but now she's gone—" Her voice broke—"and I don't even know her. I don't even know my own child."

Somehow Anne found herself holding the woman. Her frame shook with sobs. Anne looked on, with terrible clarity, out of eyes that were dry.

She went home in the early evening to put the children to bed and eat the warmed-up supper her mother had ready. The sidewalks were shoveled clear. Who could have done that? With a rushing sense of relief she walked into her house. Here was warmth, here was beauty, here was a sense of herself. And here was love. She clung to her children as long as she could when they hugged her, trying to close her eyes to the image of that young woman going home to an empty apartment, an empty crib, and an incriminating silence she could not escape.

"Who shoveled the walks?" she asked her mother.

"A young man from your ward. Seemed a nice boy. His name was Jeff something."

"Not Jeff Madsen?"

"Yes, I think it was that."

"Did he say who sent him?"

"Actually, he behaved a bit sheepishly when I asked him his name." Anne's mother seemed about to smile. "I'm not sure he wanted you to know. Said he just thought you might need a little help and he's been shoveling snow since before he was twelve."

Jeff Madsen. Anne shook her head. Last year when I caught him ditching Priesthood with three younger boys I read him the riot act. Told him he was the oldest and ought to know better. I'm sure I embarrassed him. He's been pretty cold with me. I thought he disliked me. What made him come? He's the last one I would have expected . . .

That wasn't Anne's only surprise. Sylvia Thomas had brought over a casserole and some hot rolls. And Edith Williams had taken her children to an afternoon movie, to get them out of their grandmother's hair, as she put it.

"I don't understand," Anne confided to her mother. "Some of the people who've helped are my best friends and neighbors. But three in one day—three people I didn't think cared if I lived or died. Sister Thomas doesn't even talk to me when we pass in the foyer. And Edith—sometimes I wish Edith wouldn't take notice of me. She's so critical, mother. She points out everything I do wrong or fail to do right. She can be downright obnoxious—"

Anne's mother looked at her thoughtfully. "Perhaps Edith doesn't realize how critical she is, perhaps she really means well. And perhaps Sister Williams is more shy than she appears. 'Forbear to judge, for we are sinners all,'" she happily quoted, adding "Shakespeare said that."

Anne smiled, and the smile was sincere. "Thank you, mother." She kissed her cheek lightly and hurried from the room.

They had a short home night. Anne couldn't have done it on her own, but her father conducted. The children were good and responded to the questions he asked them.

"When Jesus was born why did the shepherds come to worship him?"

"Because they saw the new star," Mark beamed.

"Very good, and what else? Brad?"

"Didn't the angels tell them? Didn't they hear the angels singing?"

Anne held Jon on her lap. He was all ready for bed and sleepy. He relaxed in her arms. She stroked his hair and his soft little cheek.

When the Savior was born it wasn't a cold, snow-laden night. There was spring in the air. Mary must have felt something like I felt when Brad was born. My son born in April, my first-born child. There was such joy in my heart, and such reverence. I wish I knew how she felt, what she thought about. She didn't know what his work would be, all the great things he had been sent for, or how he would die—

Anne's thoughts hit the wall of that word and bounced off it with crushing pain.

The Savior was born to die for our sins, to make that sacrifice for us which we never could make for ourselves—the pure child born to die—

Brad was tugging at her sleeve. "See the list Grandma made?"

The story was over. They had gone on to other things. "Tell me again."

"We decided we want to help. Grandma made up the list."

Anne took it and scanned it quickly: clear table, dry dishes | make beds | clean up rooms | don't argue | feed dog | take out garbage. The boys had written their names by the chores.

"We'll take turns every day. It will be fun," Mark said.

"These are all things you don't like to do." Anne had said the words without thinking, they had simply slipped out.

Brad made a face. "We know. But it's different now. You need us, and we want to help. Really."

The tears were close, closer than she'd ever felt them.

"Thank you so much," she said. "This means more to me than you know. It's the kind of present Jesus would want you to make at Christmastime."

The boys grinned at her praise. She took the hand her mother extended and held on tight, fighting the softness which seemed to hurt more than her hard core of pain.

*   *   *

Later in the night when she tucked Mark into bed he asked with wide, solemn eyes, "Will Santa Claus still come on Christmas?"

"Of course, he'll still come, Mark. Why wouldn't he?"

Mark squirmed a little. "I don't know. He might get mixed up. Where will he take Alicia's presents? What if she doesn't come back? Does Santa have time to go all through the hospital looking for her?"

She held her son close to her. "Don't worry, Mark, Santa will know what to do."

She fought a sudden vision of herself, her arms loaded with presents, going from store to store: Will you take these back please? Yes, this doll, yes these little dishes. You see, we don't need them now. They were bought for our daughter for Christmas, but now she's dead—

The word froze and her mind went black and the images died. She tucked the covers around Mark and Brad and turned off the light.

Two days until Christmas. It can't be that close. I'm not ready, I'm not ready to face it.

That night by her bed she knelt for a long time in silence, afraid to pray, knowing her prayer could not be acceptable. Give me my child! I'm sorry for people like the young mother at the hospital, truly I am. I don't know why children have to die ever. But don't take mine. Maybe some women can bear it, Father, but I know I can't. I'll do anything, be anything you want for the rest of my life. But please don't take Alicia from me! Forgive me for being so weak, but please let my child live.

She knelt there pleading until cold and exhaustion drove her into her bed.

5.

Day Three since the operation, still no signs of change. Dr. Grant seemed a little concerned. The steroids should be taking effect. They should be seeing some change. They would monitor her closely. Anne walked slowly down the long corridor. What will I do? What will I do if she doesn't come out of it?

"Hello, my dear."

Anne looked up to see the older woman she'd met Sunday morning. The cheerful smile was still there, but her face had deep, tired lines in it and her kind eyes were dull.

"You look as if you've had a hard night," Anne said.

"Well, yes dear, I have. It was my Mary who had the hard night, so I didn't sleep much."

Anne was suddenly curious. "Your daughter? Is that why you're here?"

"My youngest daughter. She's dying of cancer."

"Oh, I didn't know."

A slight tremor misshaped the sweet mouth, then the old smile returned. "She's twenty-eight and has three small children. It's been a hard blow."

Anne couldn't answer, Anne couldn't say anything.

"Yes dear, it's hard. Hard for me to watch her suffering. She's my baby, you know. I wish my Johnny were here to help me. He went last year." She touched Anne's arm and leaned a bit closer. "But that's a comfort, you know. He'll be there, she'll be going to him."

Anne swallowed and managed a nod.

"It's the children who tear our hearts apart. What about them? Mary can't be reconciled to leaving them." She shook her white head.

"Are you reconciled? How do you look at it?" Anne suddenly needed to know. She could tell that her voice sounded strained, even desperate, but she no longer cared.

"It's taken hours of prayer and pain, but I know in my heart that what the Lord does is just and good. It is her time to go—"

"How do you know that? How can you accept that?"

"Through faith, my dear. Faith I have built up over the years, gaining bits here and there—most often from what I have suffered."

"I don't think it's fair. How could anyone need her as much as they do—those little children?"

Anne's voice broke on a hoarse note. The woman's hand on her arm tightened with a reassuring pressure.

"It's not that way, you know. We can't see the needs of eternity, nor even the needs of ourselves. We can make blessings out of the worst sufferings, even this. Think of the strengths and sensitivities her children may glean from the things they are asked to suffer. Think of the things they might do in their lives which they might not otherwise have done."

Anne shook her head. "I don't like it."

The woman drew closer. "When I was a girl my mother used to repeat this verse to me. Whenever I feared, or questioned, or began to rebel. She would say it gently, so gently, with her hands on my face: Be still and know that I am God.

The words moved like light through Anne's being.

"There are times when we simply must do that and give him our hearts. He is all-knowing and all-loving. If we truly believe that he is, then we can trust him without reservation."

"But I don't want to grow. I don't want what's best for me. I just want to be happy," Anne cried out. "I want my child."

The woman's arm had crept round her shoulders. "I know that, my dear. But you do not yet understand how he loves you; you do not know in your heart that nothing matters as much as that love which will hopefully lead you to someday loving as he loves, and knowing his joy."

"But there is so much pain in the process!" It was the protest of a child. Anne knew it, but she couldn't help herself. The kind eyes grew warm, warm and deep and loving.

"All things come at a price. He honors you when he molds you. It's his way of saying that he knows you're made of the right materials. He can purify the dross within you and find gold shining there."

Anne had to smile, though the smile was a faint one.

"Besides," the woman went on, "all people walk around with their secret burdens, dear. Don't you know that?"

I've never thought about it, I guess I've never cared. An image of the man who had driven the red car came into her mind.

"Feeling sorry for yourself isn't good. You're not the only one suffering. There's a man in my ward who is dying of cancer. He's frightened to death. He finds escape in entertainment and frenzied activity. He goes to at least three movies a week, even if he has to watch some over and over. But you'd never know. To see him just sitting in the theatre, how could you tell?"

Anne was relaxing some. She took a deep breath.

"I've another neighbor who is a single mother, divorced. Her oldest son is hopelessly entangled with drugs. Do you think she suffers? When I've been up taking care of Mary I've seen her lights on into the wee hours of the morning. And where can she turn? Who can help her?"

Anne shook her head. No one. No one can help!

"Only One. And he *can* help—this woman, my Mary and me, you and your little daughter. You must believe he will help, and not let you senselessly suffer."

The woman squeezed Anne's shoulders and withdrew her arm very gently. "I must get back."

"What's your name?"

"Sally Simpson."

"It sounds like you."

Sally laughed. "And your name, my dear? Isn't it Anne?"

"Yes, Anne Hunter."

"Well, Anne, I will see you again. Have a good day." She turned and walked on. Anne called after her.

"Excuse me, but what of the little girl? The little girl I saw in the wheelchair. I think the nurse called her Nancy."

Sally took a step or two back toward Anne.

"Do you know anything, Sally?"

"Oh yes, yes. As I understand it she's been here on and off for months. Diabetes, with complications I'm not sure about."

"But won't she go home for Christmas?"

"I don't think so, my dear. She has no home really. Foster home after foster home."

"But she said her mother was coming."

"It was wishful thinking. She said the same thing last year. And on her birthday." Sally lowered her eyes. "It's a horrible shame. She's such a pretty, sweet thing."

Sally turned and walked on. Anne stood rooted. Grant me a grateful heart, Lord, and eyes to see. Isn't it Mother who used to say that? Oh, how can I bear to even think of such lonely unhappiness?

At last she moved slowly away. When she reached the door to Room 5 she opened it softly, still wrapped in a spell that had something of warmth in it, the amazing warmth of Sally's kind smile.

It took a moment for her eyes to adjust, and her thoughts to merge with them. She had moved silently; he had not heard her. He knelt at the bed with his hands folded over the covers.

Richard, Richard, don't cry.

She had only seen Richard cry twice before: on the day they were married—but those had been tears of happiness—and when he heard that the cousin he had grown up with and loved like a brother, who had even served in the same mission with him, had left the Church and married a woman who was not a member.

Anne stood very still. What shall I do? Richard, please don't cry. Richard was the strong one, who could make all the right decisions, who could think and stay calm, who always knew how to help her when life seemed too hard.

I haven't thought about what you are suffering, Richard. I've only thought of myself. I've let you face this alone. How selfish I am! And I've taken all the help you could give me, while you went without help yourself.

She moved across the room slowly, with care, until she stood by his side. The porcelain-faced child beside him looked more like a life-sized doll than a flesh and blood child. Anne fought a panic in her throat which she knew was a scream. She moved to kneel. Richard stirred. He looked up at her, eyes wet with tears. Anne felt for his hand.

"It's all right, Richard. Go ahead, cry." You poor thing, how you must have suffered. "I'm here with you now. I'm here, Richard."

She pillowed his head against her shoulder. For the very first time she felt a small strain of strength, a mere trickle that seemed to run through her veins, as life-sustaining as blood. And this new strength, to Anne's amazement, brought comfort with it.

6.

Day Four. Dr. Grant explained again what was happening now. Right after the accident the brain cavity had been filled with blood and gathered fluid. Once that had been drained the suppressed cerebral cortex of the brain, or white matter, had re-expanded too far, had swelled past its size. They administered steroids to correct this. When these got into her system the brain should spring back, and Alicia spring back into life. Like a miracle. Like Sleeping Beauty at the kiss of the prince.

But it wasn't happening yet as it ought to, and no one knew why. If it didn't happen soon that might mean permanent brain damage. Anne recoiled from that thought. There was no way her mind could accept that as a possibility.

"Hang in there," Dr. Grant said. "Let's hang in there a day or two longer."

Easy enough to say when it isn't your child lying at death's door!

Anne watched the nurse deftly change the bed sheets and re-position her child in the hope of avoiding bed sores. This was foreign to Anne. She had scant knowledge of medical practice, and as little curiosity concerning it. Even now. She didn't need to know all the workings, all the technical names. All she needed was to see Alicia's eyes open and gaze into her own.

There were other, smaller dangers to watch for, muscle atrophy being the prime one. The word frightened Anne. She pictured a child with no control lolling helpless as a rag doll. The first time she saw Alicia's arm jerk and then bend grotesquely Anne screamed out loud, bringing a worried nurse to her elbow. It was little comfort to know that what they called posturing was a natural muscle reaction. Anne stared at the unconscious child until her eyes ached in their sockets. She could close them and see in clear technicolor Alicia in an old tied-up prom dress twirling across the room, moving her arms and her legs with such supple grace. She could see those small hands cutting cookies while she squealed with delight at the shapes she was making, or taking Anne's big wooden spoon to help stir at the stove, with her apron tied just like mother's.

"Look what I have," she would say, digging in the apron's large pocket. "A scrunched-up Kleenex just like yours, Mommy, to use when I sneeze."

So intent, yet so filled with laughter and music. So filled with *life*.

Anne wanted to scream until she had no voice left—no brain to think—no heart to burn up in her chest. She felt sick and exhausted, and as though something within her was shriveling up and would die.

Day Four. And tomorrow was Christmas Eve. Christmas Eve in some world they'd forgotten. Anne and Richard sent their gifts to the company party along with their regrets. Anne folded up her sewing machine and put the partially-cut materials in the back of the drawer. Next Christmas perhaps. And what her mother could manage to bake would just have to do. Though the ward had not yet forgotten them, and the offerings kept pouring in. It made Anne feel vaguely guilty. At this busy time, when every cent and every spare minute was budgeted, how could so many people manage to find room for them?

"Giving blesses the giver more than it does the receiver," her mother would chide when Anne got to fretting about all this attention. And the fasting went on, with various families fasting intermittently, herself and Richard as well. And the idea no longer offended Anne. Actually now when she prayed it helped to think of those others whose hearts prayed with hers, who somehow loved her enough to do this.

Love. Can their love and faith make a difference? Perhaps even compensate in some measure for what is lacking in mine?

Anne went home on the fourth day and gathered the children about her.

"There's a little girl I have seen," she told them, "who needs our help." Then she explained to them about Nancy. She saw them eye the gifts under the tree, nicely wrapped and waiting for Christmas, the gifts they knew were for them. The tags all said "from Mommy and Daddy." The gifts Santa brought would be set out in all their splendor on Christmas Eve.

"What can we give her?" There was no hesitation. "I know the long green box is that game I wanted. I shook it a few times," Brad admitted. "Do you think she'd like it?"

"She's a girl, Mom, that makes it harder."

But they came up with enough. A cuddly teddy bear, the game, a book. Mark even insisted that she take the new model he'd built. "Lots of girls like cars," he argued. "She can look at it and pretend it can take her wherever she most wants to go."

Anne nodded. The car was an excellent gift for Nancy.

"I'll take you to the hospital Christmas morning," she promised, "and you can visit Alicia and give all these presents to Nancy yourselves."

Anne's mother cried at the idea, of course, and fixed up a big plate of goodies, not only for Nancy, but for Sally's Mary as well. "I think I'll have your father bring up that quilt I just finished," she said, almost shyly. "The sick woman would like that. And I've embroidered pillow cases for Nancy."

Anne knew how hard her mother's arthritic fingers had worked on that quilt. She hugged her tightly. Her own mind was swimming. This felt so right. Though she couldn't picture this Christmas morning, she knew it would come. And the prospect had less of nightmare in it than Anne could have hoped for a few days ago.

Beth came over for just a few minutes: a kind word and a hug, and a favorite book she thought Anne might like to read during her hospital hours. Anne's sister Lynda came, too. She'd been calling daily. She had done some of Anne's ironing and mending and brought it back with an almost embarrassed air.

"It's nothing, Anne, really. I feel so helpless. I've done so little—"

They talked of small things. Anne felt tired, but looking into her sister's eyes she saw her own need and fear reflected.

"I don't know how you're doing it, Anne. You're handling everything so beautifully."

That's all you know! I'm not handling anything at all. Just because I'm not screaming or dissolving in tears . . . I'd gladly give up. I'd lie down and die if I only knew how.

I've been lucky, Lynda's eyes said. Anne read the thought there. Nothing like this has ever happened to me.

Maybe you have been lucky, but I have been blessed. The thought came into Anne's mind from nowhere. It wasn't her thought. She strove to reject it, but the impression was made. Without her agreement, the thought left its mark.

Jon chose this night to be fussy. Perhaps he sensed after all much more than his two-year-old mind could express. Anne rocked him to sleep singing songs she had sung to Alicia.

> *Lullaby and good night,*
> *In the soft evening light,*
> *Like a rose in its bed*
> *Lay down your sweet head . . .*

The sound of the words had a lulling effect on Anne's tired mind. She sang on and on.

> *When at night I go to sleep*
> *Fourteen angels watch do keep . . .*

Fourteen angels . . . I hope you are watching my little girl now!

Earlier Mark had asked, "Will Alicia die?"

How could she answer him? She knew what her mother and Richard would say, what they had said half a dozen times over. She's in God's hands. If it is meant for Alicia to live, she'll be with us again. If she is supposed to go back to heaven—

The child in her arms had grown heavy with the relaxation of sleep. Anne shifted his weight wondering if he would awaken if she tried to place him in his crib.

So much begins with the birth of a child. If we only knew—would we have courage enough to face it?

She could see by the glow of the street light the winter trees: black branches outlined in snow like a pattern of lace; delicate, intricate beauty.

All this, she mused, he created to give us pleasure, to ease our hearts when the pain of life grows past bearing. A simple tree, with its branches etched over the sky . . .

It was a mystery to her. Love and beauty, that's what life is. Why do we always forget? And get caught up in things that don't matter, that aren't real?

Love and beauty and pain. The sacrifice of God's only begotten son began with his birth on earth. So does our sacrifice for our children begin at that moment when they first draw breath and are placed in our arms . . .

I will sacrifice. I'll sacrifice sleep and money and pleasure, I'll even sacrifice health and selfishness to raise up my children. But don't ask me this! Don't ask me this ultimate sacrifice—

The moon through the trees was as bright as the street light, but mellow and gently diffused, like fine silver mist sifting downward. Anne stared until the trees became blurred and the light hurt her eyes. Then she rose heavily and laid her young child in his bed, and covered him carefully, then walked quietly out of the room.

7.

Day Five. Christmas Eve. Day Five. Which was it? Could both be the same? Anne felt exhausted. Can I face the hours that lie ahead? I wish Christmas was over and done with. I've no heart for all this.

They ate an early Christmas dinner with the children, hung stockings, sang favorite carols, read the story of Jesus's birth from Luke, knelt in family prayer, tucked the boys into bed. It was too much for Anne. She felt stifled, or overwhelmed, she wasn't sure what she was feeling.

"Can I go back?"

Richard looked up at her question. All this was good for him. He was a man, and men's minds need action. He could work on the toys, keep his hands busy.

"I want to go back to the hospital. Please."

Richard looked at her closely. "Will you be all right, Annie?"

"Yes, it's what I want. I need to be alone, Richard." Away from all of you. Is that all right? Does it even make sense?

She got her coat and her purse. She kissed Richard goodbye. "I'll be home later," she said. "Don't come for me. When it's all right I'll come back."

"And tomorrow morning we'll give Alicia a blessing." He kissed her again. A Christmas blessing. Day Six, when the nightmare should already be over. When the Sleeping Beauty should have already awakened.

At the last minute Anne grabbed the book from the shelf. *The Nutcracker*, the original story by E. T. A. Hoffmann.

She drove through the snow, through the sleepy, muffled streets. All the houses were lighted. Santa was busy tonight, she thought wryly. She hoped each house she drove by was a happy house, filled with kindness. She couldn't bear to think of unhappy or mistreated children. Only kindness tonight.

The hospital hallways had become so familiar she could walk through them with her eyes closed. They were quiet tonight. No one stirring, not even a mouse. She should find Sally and go check in on Nancy. But later, not yet. Right now she had something to do.

Room 5 was too bright. Anne turned all the lights off except one for reading. The little tree on the table blinked its colored eyes at her in a bright, friendly manner. The ornaments gracing its boughs were Alicia's favorites. Perhaps the first time she opens her eyes she will see this tree . . . or her baby doll, silent and waiting, or this little bear, the fat brown teddy bear she was given the day she was born.

Anne pushed the damp hair away from the pale cheek, then she kissed its cool surface, the small forehead, the rounded chin—

"Where are you?" she whispered. "Come back to me, my darling, I'm waiting."

She sat down in the chair. She opened the book and began to read.

> On the twenty-fourth of December Dr. Stahlbaum's children were not allowed to set foot in the small family parlor, much less the adjoining company parlor—not at any time during the day—

She didn't notice the sound at the door. She was concentrating, listening to her own voice.

> An eerie feeling came over them when dusk fell and, as usual on Christmas Eve, no light was brought in.

She did hear the door close. She looked up to see Nancy standing there, thin as a reed, her face wary and guarded.

"I didn't mean to disturb you." Her voice was no more than a whisper. "Sally said—you might—"

"It's all right, Nancy." Anne was uncomfortable, too. She shrugged her shoulders. "It's a story Alicia always wanted to hear. Would you like to listen?"

The child hesitated. "That's okay. I'll just—"

"No, please stay. She's still sleeping, she can't really hear, but you'd like it, I know. It's *The Nutcracker.*"

Nancy's eyes brightened. "I saw parts of it once. The ballet, on television. It was like some kind of a dream."

"Did you walk here yourself?" Anne asked, seating her comfortably with a quilt round her knees.

Nancy nodded. "I'm getting better."

Anne swallowed. Where does this lead? Getting better so you can go—where, little Nancy, where?

She moved her chair so that it rested close beside Nancy's. "Now we can both see the pictures."

She began again at the beginning. The magic was there. The magic of wonder and make-believe, dancing and song, and the dreams of a little girl's heart.

> It was getting late—almost midnight. Godfather Drosselmeier had left long ago, and still the children couldn't tear themselves away from the glass-fronted cabinet, though their mother had several times urged them to turn in for the night—

The Nutcracker story was long. They read page after page, not wanting to break the magic. The army of mice had appeared now, grotesque, loud with squeaking, and the music box with the sweet voice of tinkling bells, had awakened the dolls, all the inhabitants of the glass cabinet.

> *Awake, awake*
> *On to the fight, this very night,*
> *Awake, awake!*

Anne looked up. Nancy's eyes were drooping. The door swung wide and a crisp nurse pushing a wheelchair shattered the spell.

"Time for bed, young lady. In fact, it's way past your bedtime." She winked kindly at Anne. "Up so late—and on Christmas Eve."

For a moment Nancy's eyes, with mild panic, met Anne's.

"I'll finish the story tomorrow." She touched the thin hand. "I promise." She leaned close. "And besides, you'll have presents and surprises tomorrow."

"I will?"

"Yes, you will."

"Well, that's something to go to sleep for. Good night, Mrs. Hunter." In one swift, efficient sweep they were gone. The small room seemed lifeless, drained. With a little shudder Anne turned to the form on the bed. She looked down at the page, marking her place in the book. The words, urgent, rhyming, repeated themselves in her mind:

> *Awake, awake*
> *On to the fight, this very night,*
> *Awake, awake!*

She bent over the beautiful form. The words moved on her lips now.

> *Awake, my beloved, awake!*

She sank back into the chair. I am worn out with suffering, Father. She dropped down onto her knees. But no words of entreaty would come. Instead, from somewhere inside, came a story she had known as a child of a pioneer mother who had buried her little girl on the lonely trail, in a shallow, frozen grave, and had left her there, her small resting place unmarked and untended.

My own great grandmother buried four daughters—I've seen their pictures—fair girls with grave, beautiful faces. All died within three weeks from typhus. Anne heard herself moan . . . Whom the Lord loveth . . .

"Who am I," she said out loud to the silent room, "to pit myself against God?" If by suffering, by bending my will to his, I can come to know him, I will certainly be in good company.

I question him, yet I claim to believe in him. I have made vows, sacred promises. Now when it's hard for me—

Anne rose to her feet. She walked to the table and, with shaking hands, took up the book that was lying there. She turned the pages until she found what she wanted: Section 122. She knew the words nearly by heart, but she read them out loud, wondering suddenly: Why have I loved these words all my life? I never knew what they really meant. They were not in my heart.

The word of the Lord to his servant, Joseph, in Liberty Jail. Anne read the section through once, then again, until the wild pounding inside her head softened and she could breathe, and the words became more than mere words.

> *If thou art called to pass through tribulation . . .*
> *If thou art called to pass through tribulation . . .*

What of Mary, the mother of Jesus? She bore the pain, the exquisite anguish of her role, and where is she now? It is not death, but love that I see here. It is power, not pain.

> *If thou be cast into the deep, if the billowing*
> *surge conspire against thee; if fierce winds*
> *become thine enemy; if the heavens gather*
> *blackness, and all the elements combine to hedge*
> *up the way; and above all, if the very jaws of*
> *hell shall gape open the mouth wide after thee,*
> *know thou, my son, that all these things shall*
> *give thee experience and shall be for thy good—*

Give thee experience and be for thy good. Anne moved to the window. The words brought a strange calm she could not understand. It was the German writer Nietzsche, she was sure, who had said, "What doesn't destroy me makes me stronger." So truth is truth. And who am I to set myself against it and hope to stand?

She moved shakily to the bed and reached out to her daughter, smiling gently at the beauty before her and the love that it stirred.

"Whose little girl is Alicia?" she whispered. This was their favorite game. They played it over and over again.

"Mommy's little girl."

She could hear the small voice, edged with laughter, feel the hand on her cheek.

"Whose little girl is Alicia?"

"Daddy's girl," she would cry. "Grandma's girl—Spotty's girl. (Spotty was their old dog.)

"Whose little girl is Alicia?"

"Jesus's girl," with that shine in her eyes.

Jesus's girl, Jesus's girl—so you are, sweetheart. When you came to me, I thought you were mine, like some beautiful doll I could show off and play with. But mine to keep.

How perfect you are still, Alicia! Father, help me, I cannot see! Help me to have faith in the midst of this darkness!

She fell to her knees. Christmas morning. She heard somewhere, dimly, the chime of a clock. In a few hours Richard would join her, would take sacred oil, place his hands on the head of their daughter, and with power God-given bless her. And how would he bless her? To rise up and be well? They had given her a blessing to help through the operation, and another to help through recovery.

My fear stood in the way. Father, forgive me my weakness and selfishness. Faith is power. How many hundreds of times have I heard those words and not understood? Faith is power and love is power. And Jesus came not to die, but to conquer death and bring life everlasting. Life everlasting through love.

Anne's eyes were no longer dry. At last the cleansing tears came. She knelt and cried them all out. Then she touched the small hand on the covers; so small, so still.

"Whose little girl is Alicia?" She murmured the words. I must let go! Help me, Father.

In the cold dawn of a Christmas morning Anne said in her heart: Do what you will, Father. She is in your hands, and so am I. I will accept whatever might happen and see in it your love.

After long, quiet minutes she rose. She walked back to the window. On the distant horizon a pale light was starting to show. She could make out the shapes of the mountains. She drew a deep breath. The fear is gone, that terrible darkness inside me.

She heard him come through the door. She recognized his walk and the feel of him.

"Annie, I know you told me not to come after you, but—"

"It's all right, Richard." She turned to face him. He looked into her eyes.

"Yes, it is," he said softly. "It is, I can see that it is."

He moved to the window where she was standing and took her into his arms. When he kissed her a deep sensation moved through her.

What is this I feel? Richard seems part of me, in some kind of harmony I've never felt until now. With Richard beside me like this there is nothing I cannot endure.

They stood together looking out at the pale sky that heralded dawn. Christmas morning coming gently and quietly into a world muddled with sorrow and fear and confusion, but tinged like the pale sky with hope—hope born of faith and made bold by love.

8.

They went home together and watched the children exclaim over what Santa had brought. There was a sense of muted timelessness which seemed to surround them, the first such feeling Anne had experienced, the first such feeling they had shared. Peace built not of resignation, but of knowledge and strength. Strength enough to go through the interview with Dr. Grant.

"We'll have to take other measures in the morning," he told them, "do additional tests, try to determine what's happening and why she hasn't come round." He put his arm around Anne. "I'm so sorry," he said. "I had hoped so much that by Christmas—"

"It's all right," she assured him. "It isn't your fault." There was real pain in his eyes. "You've been wonderful." She squeezed his big hand.

The children were in the hall waiting; Richard brought them all in. Jon wanted to kiss "Lishie," so they held him up while he placed a moist kiss on her cheek. Strength enough to do that, to watch the boys overcome their shyness and perch on her bed, talking to Alicia as though she were listening, showing their toys, overcoming their initial awkwardness enough to reveal their deep love. How close children are to heaven, how pure they remain for much longer than we choose to notice.

Anne stood watching the scene, drawn in by the sweetness of it, untroubled by pain, holding Richard's hand and feeling, through that small touch, his love.

The children were anxious to meet Nancy. Anne had cleared the visit before, but she found herself nervous about it. How would Nancy react? Would the boys do something to make things awkward?

In one of the small reception rooms they gathered together, waiting. Nancy came through the door and stood poised, her long golden hair shining, her eyes warm, but confused. Anne's mother stepped out from the background.

"Merry Christmas, my dear. Look what the children have for you."

On that signal they moved, rushing up to her, talking and laughing, thrusting presents into her arms.

"Sit down, Nancy," Brad begged, "and let us watch you open them."

The boys crowded next to her and she seemed to love it. They shared her excitement as each gift was opened, but when it came to the car, the model Mark had built, then wrapped all by himself, Anne saw her son hesitate.

"It's nothing," he said, reaching out for it. "You don't have to open it now."

"Is it from you?" Nancy asked.

"Mark made it himself," Brad bragged for him. "And he did a good job. He did better than I could have."

Mark couldn't help the pride that for a brief moment lit up his brown eyes.

Nancy undid the ribbon and paper with care. Long, delicate fingers, Anne thought. She has a very feminine way about her.

When she drew out the car she held it up, balanced on the palm of one hand. She was silent still. She ran a finger along the sleek hood. "You really made this?" she breathed. Mark nodded. He was watching her carefully.

"Oh, please, don't cry." His young voice was tight with concern.

"It's the most lovely gift—" She paused and looked at him, tears on her cheeks now, "the most lovely gift any person has ever given me."

Mark looked at his feet and shuffled them back and forth along the ribbed carpet.

"I wish you were mine. My little brother." She said the words softly, almost too softly to hear.

"Don't you have any brothers?" Mark looked up, forgetting himself in this new, unlooked-for concern.

Nancy shook her head and shrugged her thin shoulders. "It's all right," she said.

"It's not all right!" Mark rose to his feet. "I'll be back. You wait here."

He walked over to where his parents stood watching. "Did you hear her?" he asked, lowering his voice as much as he was able.

"We heard her," Richard replied.

"Daddy, would you two mind? Well, couldn't we be her brothers— sort of?" He paused. He wasn't sure how to go on.

"I think that's a wonderful idea," Richard answered. "Do you mean it?"

Mark looked up, somewhat taken aback.

"You have to mean it for more than just these few minutes when her tears have moved you. What about when we go home? Will you remember her still? Will you still want to help her, want to do things for her?"

Mark cocked his head. He was thinking about this.

He's pretty young. Anne was watching him carefully. *I wonder if he'll understand.*

"Like Alicia. Love her like Alicia?"

Richard nodded. "That's right. Go on, go back. Tell her whatever you'd like, tell her you'll be her brother."

Mark turned away with a grin. Anne looked at Richard. "I think the social worker is still somewhere about."

"I was thinking the same thing," he said. "I believe I'll go look for her, talk to her anyway, see what she says."

Anne nodded.

Richard, Richard, I love you.

There was something inside Anne which she had never felt before, and it pierced through her heart with a power that seemed to nourish her spiritually and tinge all the long hours of this Christmas day with a joy unlike anything she had experienced on any Christmas before.

It wasn't an easy day. There were rough moments, there were sharp stabs of pain, even whispers of the fear she had faced down. But Anne wasn't the same. What had happened to her by Alicia's bedside was real. She could still feel the strength of it, the sweetness, the gratitude. That was the word. She had never understood that scripture: *receive all things with gratitude. All things.* Her heart was beginning to glean some meaning from it which she was afraid to explore. But she hugged the new feeling to her along with all she had felt, all she had seen and understood on this exceptional day.

At last the hours wound down, the children were safe in their beds. *The Nutcracker* story was even finished to Nancy's satisfaction. Anne stood at the window with Richard beside her, this strange new peace in her heart. The dull stretch of red in the far sky was fading as the curtain of night settled down. Christmas night in their world where, past injustice and pain, God's love reigned supreme, and he enclosed all these things in his hands, and he knew their ways, and he upheld those who leaned upon him.

It was Richard who turned, who first sensed a movement. Anne felt and turned with him in time to see the blue eyes blink open, in time to be there when the slow blinking steadied and focused on Anne's glowing smile.

I let go. I gave her into your keeping, Father, with all my heart. Only then did you give her back to me.

"Alicia."

A faint blush of expression touched the lines of her face.

Anne bent to kiss her. She knows me. There is so much I see in her eyes.

She took Richard's hand. His joy enveloped her, coursing through her being with wonderful light.

"Welcome home, Alicia. It's Christmas. Merry Christmas, my dear."

Jack Weyland is the classic case of a dual personality—physics professor by day, hopeless romantic by early morning (6:00 to 8:00 a.m.). He has considered receiving counseling for these two-hour lapses, but because they're so much fun, it's doubtful if he'll ever get the help he so desperately needs. Jack has had published eleven novels, three books of short stories, two stage plays, over two dozen stories for the New Era, *one screenplay, and an upcoming science book for youth called* Mega Powers. *He loves his wife Sherry and his five outrageously wonderful children.*

THE THREE WISE GUYS

by Jack Weyland

It was a simple plan. Bring the youth of the ward together, have them fill boxes with food and presents, then send them out to deliver the boxes to needy families in the ward. "This will help our youth experience the true spirit of Christmas," a member of the bishopric explained.

At eight thirty at night two days before Christmas, Dan Turner, Jonathan Garcia and Chad Nadig, were given the assignment to deliver one of the Christmas boxes. Their teacher's quorum adviser offered to drive them but Chad thought they'd get done faster if they didn't have to ride around in a car with others who also needed to deliver boxes.

"I'm getting bored with Christmas," Chad said as they started to walk the four blocks to the address they'd been given. "It's the same thing year after year. I mean every Christmas Eve my dad reads the Christmas story to us. I've heard it so many times. I complained about it once and my mom goes, 'But Chad, the Christmas story changes from year to year.' Yeah, right. Like some years he's born in a Holiday Inn, and other years instead of shepherds coming to see him it's a group of Girl Scouts from Toledo. Just once I'd like the innkeeper to say, 'Hey, no problem, we've got a vacancy.'"

"What'd your mom mean about the Christmas story changing every year?" Jonathan asked.

215

"I don't know. I think she started to explain but the phone rang or something."

A few minutes later the three boys stood in front of a small house on the edge of town.

"Are you sure this is the right place?" Jonathan asked.

"Yeah, sure. Where else could it be?" Dan said.

They walked to the house. Dan knocked on the door.

A woman came to the door. She looked tired. Two children clung to her skirts and peered out at the strangers at the door.

"Hi there . . . we're from the Church . . . this is for you." Dan handed her the box. "Merry Christmas."

Her face lit up. She let out a stream of words in a language the boys couldn't understand.

As they left her house they felt good. "Well, that wasn't so bad, was it?" Dan said.

"No, not really," Chad said.

"Hey, Jonathan, was she talking Spanish?" Chad asked.

"I don't know. I haven't taken it yet."

"But your name is Garcia. You're supposed to know things like that."

"Where do your ancestors come from?"

"Germany."

"Then why don't you speak German?"

Chad paused. "It's not the same thing."

"Hey, look," Jonathan said, pointing to the house next door. They could see inside because the woman had the drapes down; she was washing the windows from the inside. "That's the family that moved into the ward last week. I can't remember their name but she talked to my dad about getting her membership transferred. They look like they could use a Christmas box too. I wonder why . . ." He stopped talking. "Hey, wait a minute. Let me see the paper with the name on it."

Dan gave him the list. "Way to go, Dan," Jonathan said. "We gave the box to the wrong address. It was supposed to go to 2440 Haskins Street and we gave it to 2436."

The other two boys glared at Dan.

"Anybody can make a mistake," Dan said. "Look, we'll just go back and get it."

"How long is this going to take?" Chad complained. "I didn't want to do this project anyway. I'm going home. I've got a lot to do tonight."

"Like what?"

"My brother's home from college. He and I rented a bunch of movies for tonight," Chad said.

"I need to go home too," Jonathan said. "I haven't practiced yet."

"Look, you guys, you're not going anywhere—we're in this together," Dan said. "Besides it's not going to take that long. The woman probably knows it was a mistake so all we got to do is knock on her door, ask for the box, and then walk over and give it to the people next door."

They approached the house again. Dan knocked on the door. The woman came to the door.

"Hi, it's us again. Look, we made a mistake," Dan said. "Wrong address. The box should go next door."

The woman said something they couldn't understand and moved aside so they could come in. In the living room, in front of a small black and white TV set, two small children were eating green beans from the box that had just been delivered.

"Oh no," Dan muttered. "They're already eating the food we brought."

"They were supposed to wait until Christmas," Chad said.

"What do we do now?" Jonathan asked. "She's looking at us funny, like she expects us to do something."

"Let's sing 'Silent Night,'" Dan said.

"Are you crazy? I'm not singing," Chad said.

"Sing or else I'll pound your head into the ground," Dan threatened.

"Some choir leader you'd make," Chad muttered.

They sang "Silent Night." By the time they finished, the woman had tears in her eyes.

"We've got to find a way to tell her she's not supposed to have the box," Dan said privately to his friends.

"I think she *is* speaking Spanish. My brother took it in high school," Jonathan said. "I know where his Spanish dictionary is."

"Let's go get it," Dan said.

Dan addressed the woman. "Look, whatever you do, don't cook the turkey yet." It was obvious she didn't understand.

"Get down and gobble like a turkey, Jonathan," Dan said.

"What?"

"You heard me. Gobble like a turkey."

Jonathan hunkered down and gobbled like a turkey and flapped his arms. The woman laughed, the children laughed and started following Jonathan around the room gobbling too.

"No cook turkey, no cook turkey," Dan shouted.

The woman repeated solemnly, "No . . . cook . . . turkey."

"She's got it," Jonathan said.

"Yeah, except she doesn't have a clue what it means," Chad said.

"We're going to go get a dictionary, okay?" Dan said to the woman. "And then we'll be back."

A minute later they walked down the middle of the seldom-used street.

"I can't believe her kids are eating just green beans with nothing else," Dan said. "I hate green beans."

"I think people from some countries really like green beans," Chad said. "Every year they have these green bean festivals. I think I read that somewhere."

"Since when did you ever read a book?" Jonathan said.

"Hey, I do a lot of things people don't know about. I went to a symphony concert once."

"Did you like it?" Jonathan asked.

"No, not really, too many violins."

"I play the violin."

"I know, but it's okay. We'll still be friends. Look, if you ever want to burn it, call me up, I'll bring the marshmallows."

"That woman was so glad about the box we gave her," Jonathan said.

"Yeah, but she must know it wasn't for her," Dan said. "I mean why would we give her food? We don't know her. And she's not even a member of the Church."

"Chad, does your sister ever talk about me?" Dan asked.

"No. Why should she?"

"I don't know . . . no reason I guess . . . I kind of like the way she looks."

"You're talking about my sister?" Chad asked. "You like her? You must be crazy."

"Look, if you ever get a chance, say something nice about me, okay?"

"Like what?"

"I don't know. Just something nice."

"Gosh, I'd really have to think about that before I'd be able to come up with something."

Jonathan's parents weren't home. They went to his brother's room and found the dictionary.

"What are we going to say?" Chad asked.

"I don't know. We'd better write it out first," Dan said.

"How about, 'We want our food back,'" Chad said. It sounded like a threat.

"Okay, let's see, the Spanish word for *we*. . . ." Dan said.

"She might want to know why we're taking it back," Jonathan said. "How about this? 'Excuse us, but we're from the Church and we were out delivering boxes of food to needy members. We made a mistake in giving you the food. We should have given it to the house next door. So now we'd like it back. You don't have to give back the green beans. They can be our special Christmas gift to you, but we do want everything else back and right away because it's late and some of us need to get home and practice."

"Great idea, Jonathan!" Dan said as he banged the dictionary on the table. "What you said would only take me about ten weeks to translate."

"C'mon you guys, let's get this over with," Chad said. "I'm missing my first movie."

"Quit complaining," Dan said. "The bishop sent us out to do a job and we're not quitting until we've done it. Let's start back now. We'll decide what to say on the way back."

They paused at each street light to discuss what they were going to say.

"How about this? 'Food not for you. Give it back,'" Jonathan suggested.

"Why don't we just let her have it?" Chad said. "It's just a few cans of green beans, some potatoes, some bread, a turkey, and a few presents."

"She's taking advantage of us; you know that, don't you?" Dan said.

"How do you figure that?" Jonathan said. "She opens the door, we give her a box of food, she takes it. You think she lies in wait for people to come to her door and give her a box of food by mistake?"

"Yeah, that's the way it is," Chad joined in. "In fact I saw a thing about it on the news. It's this big crime ring, you know? And every year they rip off as many as a hundred and fifty cans of green beans. My gosh, do you guys have any idea what the street value of that is?"

Jonathan burst out laughing.

"Very funny," Dan muttered.

"We thought so," Chad said. "Man, I wonder if the Three Wise Men ever had problems like this. I can see it now. 'Hey you, we want our frankincense and myrrh back!'"

"What exactly is a myrrh anyway?" Jonathan asked.

"Hey Mister Library Appreciation Days, I bet you could look that up," Chad said, referring to an honor bestowed on Jonathan for his frequent use of the school library.

"You guys shut up and let me think." Dan said.

"Ladies and Gentlemen, the first time ever in this century! Dan the Man is now going to think."

"How about this—'Food goes next door . . . give it back,'" Dan said.

"Forget what I said about Dan thinking," Chad said.

"Chad, if you'd put as much energy into helping us instead of complaining all the time, we'd be done by now."

"What about the green beans? Are we going to snatch them out of her kids' mouths?" Chad asked.

"She can have the green beans but she has to give back the turkey."

"And that's our final offer, right?" Chad said.

"What are we going to do if she won't give it back?" Jonathan asked.

"I know," Chad said. "We'll make her listen to Jonathan give a report on the history of a myrrh," Chad said. "That'll bring her around soon enough." He faked a woman's voice. "No, no, not footnotes, anything but footnotes!"

They worked out a message in Spanish. Dan practiced it by the light of a street light. Finally they stood in front of the house.

"Let's go," Dan said.

"Not me," Chad said, shaking his head. "I say, let her have the box. She and her kids need it bad."

"I agree with Chad," Jonathan said.

"All right then, fine, I'll do it," Dan grumbled. "I don't need you guys anyway."

Dan went up and knocked on the door. The woman, with a big smile, let him in like he was a friend of the family. As he stepped inside, he could detect the unmistakable smell of a turkey baking in the oven.

He looked down at the message in Spanish and cleared his throat.

A few minutes later he returned to his friends.

"Where's the food?" Chad asked.

"She was cooking the turkey."

"So she can have everything, right?" Chad said.

"Yes. I'll call the bishop and tell him what happened."

They walked for half a block before Jonathan noticed. "Hey, wait a minute, weren't you wearing a jacket when you went in the house?"

"I must've left it there by mistake," Dan said.

"And a sweater too, you were definitely wearing a sweater," Jonathan said.

"I'll go back and get it tomorrow."

"Why not get it now?" Chad asked.

"I said I'll get it tomorrow, okay?" Dan snapped.

Silence.

"You gave away your sweater and your jacket?" Chad asked.

"Look, I don't want to hear another word from you guys about it, okay?"

"Why'd you give away your stuff?" Chad asked.

"The two kids can use it as pajamas. Sometimes it gets so cold at night."

Nobody said anything for a while, but then Dan began. "When I went in, the kids were eating bread, no peanut butter on it or anything—just plain store-bought bread."

"My mother made some really good home-made bread today," Chad said.

"My mother makes this terrific strawberry jam," Jonathan said.

"There's nothing like homemade bread, jam, and milk," Dan said.

"And another present for the kids," Chad said. "What do you say we all chip in some money for a ball or something? I can get it at the Mini-Mart by my home."

"We'll meet back here in fifteen minutes, okay?" Dan said.

An hour later, after presenting their gifts to the woman, they started home.

"Maybe my mother's right, maybe the Christmas story does change from year to year," Chad said.

"How can it? The story always stays the same," Dan said.

"Maybe what happens is the Christmas story changes us," Jonathan said.

"Thank you, Mister Library Appreciation Days," Chad said. "Well anyway, I've got a lot of movies to see tonight. You guys are welcome to come if you want. If not, I'll see you later." He started walking off toward his home as did Jonathan too.

"Merry Christmas," Dan called out, standing in the middle of the empty intersection.

Much to his surprise they each stopped and turned around and wished him a Merry Christmas too.

On his way home Dan sang "Silent Night." It had never sounded so good.

Herbert Harker was born in Cardston, Alberta and grew up on a farm near Glenwood, Alberta. With his first wife, Beryl, he lived in Calgary, Vancouver, Santa Barbara, and Guadalajara, Mexico, satisfying, his mother said, a restless urge passed on to him by his maternal grandfather, Danny Greene. Beryl died in 1972, and he later married Myrna Ellison. For the past twenty years, he and Myrna have lived in Santa Barbara, where they attempt to monitor the lives of their seven children, their spouses, and fourteen grandchildren. The author's first novel, Goldenrod, *was a Book of the Month Club alternate selection, and was filmed as a CBS Movie of the Week. Since then he has had three other novels published as well as numerous articles and essays for magazines.*

MR. GREGORY

by Herbert Harker

The Primary Christmas party ended early that year. The lady who was playing the piano for our dance fainted and fell off the piano stool. I didn't care. I would have died rather than ask a girl to dance with me. Besides, I thought I could get home in time to do my chores before dark. But mother met me at the door. "Frankie, you're a big boy now. You're old enough to take this over to Mr. Gregory for me." She handed me a brown grocery bag, folded over; I could feel the weight of something heavy in the bottom of it.

Immediately I felt sick. "What is it? A Christmas present?" I opened the bag and saw in the bottom a package wrapped in a red ribbon with a big bow on top. "How come he gets a Christmas present? Dad says Santa Claus had a bad year. Nobody's getting much for Christmas this year, Dad says."

"But everybody should get something. And contrary to popular belief, Mr. Gregory won't hurt you."

"I'm not scared of him," I lied.

"Then what's the problem?"

"He's just funny, that's all. He eats gopher meat."

She laughed. "He doesn't eat gopher meat."

"He's got a shotgun behind his door. Loaded with salt."

"Where do you get these stories?"

223

"Everybody knows it. He shot some kids one Halloween."

"They were probably trying to tip over his outhouse."

"He can't even talk anymore. He's been up there alone for so long he's forgotten how to talk."

She sighed. "I think it's time you paid Mr. Gregory a visit; clear up some of these, shall I say 'misconceptions?'"

"Yeah, and he'll lock me up in his chest. He does that, you know. He thinks it's teasing, but one kid died."

"Don't be ridiculous."

"He's mean as a sow-pig, Dad says. He'd eat his own babies."

"Well, we don't have to worry about that, do we? Mr. Gregory doesn't have any babies. And even if he is mean, we want to give him a present, don't we?"

"I don't."

She frowned at me. "All right. I'll give it to him myself. But I need you to take it over to his house."

"Do I have to?"

"Yes. You have to."

"Gee whiz. This is a free country, Dad says."

"You're completely free to do whatever I tell you," Mother said. "Now, off you go before it gets dark."

Just the thought of it made my stomach hurt. "I don't feel very well," I said. "Maybe Dad could drive over there when he gets home."

"Your father will have plenty to do when he gets home. Christmas is a busy time, you know, and this is something you can do to help."

Still I argued. "He's just an old drunk, anyway."

"He's more than a drunk, Frankie. You didn't know him when he was young. He was the finest teacher this town ever had."

I was surprised. "He what?"

"He taught me in the sixth grade."

"So, if he was such a great teacher, what happened?"

"Nobody knows. One summer he made a trip to Utah to get married, but he came back all alone. He never told us whether his girl died or changed her mind, or what. It was all very mysterious. First he started drinking, then he quit teaching, then he wouldn't even leave his house. Well, he didn't have a house of his own. He moved into that shack on McGillan's place, and old man McGillan let him stay. Forty years, he's been there. He doesn't want to see anybody, he doesn't want to talk to anybody. He just wants to be left alone."

"I'm all for that."

"Once a year's not going to hurt. A lot can happen in a man's heart from one Christmas to the next. Anyway, he was good to me when I was a little girl. I want him to know that I haven't forgotten."

I took the paper bag and walked out to the gate. At the end of the snowy street and half-way up the hill, I could see Mr. Gregory's shack. It looked a long ways away, but almost before I knew it I was past the town limits and beginning to climb the twisty little road.

A feeling of desolation came over me. It seemed that nobody cared about small boys—not their mother, not their Heavenly Father. I had been praying all the way that something would save me, but it looked like I was all alone. Then why would it matter what I did? If nobody cared about anything else, who would care if I disobeyed my mother? Suppose I went and threw the paper bag in the river; she would never know. She never saw Mr. Gregory; all she did was send him a Christmas present every year.

Well, there I was, standing in the middle of the road in front of Mr. Gregory's gate. The little two-roomed house looked almost black, the boards were so dry and old. The mortar had all fallen out from between the chimney bricks, the window screens were half ripped off, the shingles on the roof all worn and curled. The barbed wire fence was falling down, the garden patch a rustling forest of dry sunflower stalks lightly dusted with snow. And through the window, I got a glimpse of Mr. Gregory looking out at me.

I wanted to run; I tried to make myself run. But I'd thought about it all the way coming, and now I knew I never could. Something my dad told me kept getting in the way.

Just a week before he'd taken me skating on the river, and by the time we started to walk back home it was almost dark. A cold wind had begun to blow, and there I was walking along behind my dad, half frozen. Suddenly he stopped. There was a newborn calf lying in the snow by the side of the road. "Now, how'd he get here?" Dad asked.

"Beats me."

It was clear the calf had been born right there. The ground was trampled, and there was blood all over the snow. "Where's his mother?" Dad asked. "She wouldn't leave him."

"But she did."

"Who'd be calving at this time of year, anyway? Somebody must have driven the cow off—didn't notice the calf and drove her home with the other cattle. Those Taggart boys! Their bull is always getting loose, and they're about the only ones crazy and blind enough to do a thing like this."

"We better go and tell them," I said.

"If we do, this little fella will never last till we get back."

"So? What can we do?" I was cold, and in a hurry to get home by the fire.

"We'll have to carry him," Dad said.

"Carry him?" I asked. "He's all wet."

Dad unbuckled his belt and slipped it out of the belt loops. "Take your belt off."

"It's no use," I said. "He'll die, anyway."

"How do you know that?"

"Well, I guess I don't," I admitted.

"Then take your belt off."

Dad slipped our belts under the calf's stomach, one just behind the front legs, and the other in front of the back legs. Then he took a belt in each hand on one side, and I took them on the other, and we lifted and carried him down the road. It was awkward walking half-turned sideways, with the weight of the calf pulling me down, but for a while I shuffled along as best I could. The calf was slimy and cold and kept bumping against me so my clothes got all wet and then they started to freeze. My hands were so cold I could hardly hang onto the belts. We'd stop to rest, but Dad made us hurry on—he said the "little fella" was getting weak. Finally I couldn't hang on any longer; I let go of the belt and dropped to my knees in the snow. Dad hardly paused. He undid his coat, and picking up the calf in his arms he held it against his chest half wrapped up in the coat and hurried on down the road. I could hardly run fast enough to keep up.

"It won't do any good," I cried. It felt like the tears were freezing on my cheeks. "The stupid calf is going to die, anyway." I wanted him to take me up inside his coat and carry me in his arms.

"Come on," was all he said.

"I can't go any further," I bawled, and stopped dead, and sat kerplunk in the snow.

Dad turned and knelt on one knee, so he could rest the calf on the other one for a moment. "Frankie. There's something you need to know, and I'm in a hurry so I'll only tell you once. 'Never stop in the middle.' Do you understand?"

"It's going to die anyway," I said.

"Right now it's still alive. I can feel its heart. This is what I want to tell you, Frankie. Be careful when you make up your mind about something, because everything else that happens afterward depends on that. But once you decide what to do, do it. Don't stop in the middle and wonder if you've made a mistake." Before I could say more he was off again, carrying the calf up the hill, and I was huffing along behind.

When we got to Taggart's they took the calf in the house to warm it up, and gave it a shot of brandy, but it didn't do any good. It died anyway, and I glared at my dad. He just shook his shoulders and zipped his jacket and started off home. And I thought he'd been foolish. But now, standing in front of Mr. Gregory's, I remembered what he said: "Never stop in the middle."

So, finally in a fit of rage and fake bravado I marched up the path and pounded on the door.

No sound.

I knocked again. Maybe I hadn't really seen him.

A voice came from inside the shack. "Go away." It was a high-pitched voice, cracked and slightly shivery, but forceful enough. My inclination was to do what it told me. I could just leave the package on the step. But I was too worked up; I was absolutely seething that on Christmas Eve I should be thus humiliated. I knocked again.

The door sprang open so suddenly I almost jumped off the porch. There stood Mr. Gregory, half hunched over so his face was about level with mine. His lips drew back over his teeth in somewhat the shape of a smile, but there was nothing pleasant in his whole countenance— even his eyes glinted with fierce agitation. "Well?" he snapped.

There came to me a sudden joyful rush. My ordeal was almost over; in another minute I'd be out the gate and down the road. And I'd never have to face Mr. Gregory again; surely he'd die before another Christmas. I handed him the paper bag. "My mother sent you a Christmas present," I said.

He snatched the bag out of my hand and looked inside. Then he looked at me. "You the Deering kid?"

"Yes, sir."

He looked back inside the bag. "Another pair of socks, huh? Doesn't your mother think I have any socks of my own?"

"They're not socks," I said.

"Then what?"

"I don't know. It's too heavy for socks."

He lifted the package out of the paper bag—it was almost too big and heavy for him to lift with one hand. "Now, what do you think it is? It's not socks. Too heavy. It's not mitts, it's not a scarf. The only thing your mother ever gave me was something she knitted herself." He hefted the package. "She didn't knit that."

"I have to go." I edged back down the step.

He came out and sat on the step beside me, shivering without his coat on. He looked at the package in his hand. "Think I should open it?"

"Go ahead." I was curious myself.

Mr. Gregory's thin and knobby hands moved awkwardly as he began to untie the ribbon and tear back the paper. Inside the wrapping was a fancy gold box. Mr. Gregory sucked in his breath when he saw it. Reaching into the gold box he pulled out a bottle—a carved and glistening bottle full of something that looked like brown vinegar. "Oooh," whispered Mr. Gregory. His eyes were as round as the cap on the bottle, and every line in his filigreed face curled up. "Hot damn!"

The label on the bottle said, JIM BEAM. "What is it?" I asked.

"This?" Mr. Gregory held the bottle up so it sparkled in the dying sunlight. "This is dragon milk." He looked at me. "What's your name, sonny?"

"Frankie."

"Frankie Deering. This . . ." He raised the bottle higher still. "This is the Cadillac of juices. This is all the shade and the shine of Mother Ocean captured in one golden cupful. I know I'm never going to get to heaven, Frankie Deering, but it doesn't matter. I'll build my own heaven right here on earth, and a bottle of Jim Beam is all I need to do it." He slapped his knee. "Ya-hoo! Frankie Deering, this is going to be a Christmas to remember."

I didn't know what to say.

He began to twist off the bottle cap, but suddenly he stopped and his face turned flat.

"Don't you like it?" I asked.

He cursed. "I almost forgot. I quit drinking yesterday." The smile passed quickly from his face. "Now what am I going to do? Doesn't your mother think I've got enough trouble? She's just making fun of me, that's all."

"She wouldn't do that," I said. But I was as puzzled as Mr. Gregory. Why would my mother do such a thing?

Mr. Gregory sat for a long time looking at the bottle. "I'll just have a sniff," he said at last. "There's no harm in that, is there?" He unscrewed the cap and reached to hold the open bottle under my nose. I sniffed, and jerked away. It was awful. He laughed. Then, holding his head up high, he passed the bottle under his nose, and an expression of pure rapture moved across his battered old face. "Hey, it's Christmastime, isn't it? No time to be unhappy, that's for sure—not when you've got medicine like this on hand. I'm just going to take a little bite." He put the bottle to his lips.

But he didn't tip it. As I watched, a tear ran down his cheek. He lowered the bottle from his mouth. "It's your mom, Frankie. Don't you see? She wasn't laughing at me; she was spitting on me. 'Here, have yourself a fling,' she says. 'You old drunk, you're no good for anything else.' That's what she's saying."

"I don't think so."

"So I might as well drink it up and have done with it, right? I can always stop drinking again; I've done it plenty of times before. It's hell to be sober, anyhow." He paused. "Oh, Frankie! What a night I'm going to have. You ever got drunk?"

"No, sir."

"It's like starting all over again. You're happy as a little kid, but you're seven feet tall. You got the energy of a steam locomotive, and you're wise as Solomon and kind as Mother Teresa. Everybody loves you. It's warm and sunny and the whole world is beautiful. And nobody can hurt you. It doesn't matter if they cuss at you, if they laugh at you. Even if they quit loving you it wouldn't matter. You'd just laugh, and it wouldn't make any difference. Do you want a drink?" He reached the bottled toward me.

"No, sir."

"Of course you don't. Your mother taught you never to touch the stuff, didn't she? You better do what your mother says." He shook his head. "I don't want to drink anymore. I stopped, just yesterday, and I don't ever want to start again. I can't drink this stuff. You'll just have to take it back to your mother."

"She won't drink it," I said.

He nodded. "Of course she won't." For a while he just sat while the tears dried on his cheeks. Presently he screwed the cap back on the bottle. "Do you know what your mother was really saying to me? 'Don't spend your money on that ten-cent whiskey.' That's what she's saying. 'I'm giving you this bottle of Jim Beam.' That's what she's saying. 'But don't drink it,' that's what she's saying. 'If you can leave this Jim Beam alone, white lightning'll never tempt you again.' That's what she's saying, Frankie. But she didn't say it in words. She knew if she told me a thing like that I'd never pay any attention. She wanted me to figure it out myself, so now I have to pay attention. When a man talks to himself he better listen to what he's saying, or he's doomed; I mean forever—doomed. Frankie, she did the meanest thing to me that any soul could ever have done. What am I going to do now?"

"I don't know," I said.

After a while he said, "I'll tell you what I'm going to do. Come on inside."

I followed him into the shack; it was freezing cold out there on the step.

The place was decorated in early American squalor. Books were what I noticed mostly—books scattered everywhere, on the table, the chairs, the floor. He shoved some magazines off a shelf, and set the bottle of Jim Beam in their place. The room seemed dark to begin with, and at this time of day it was doubly so. Still that bottle gathered what light there was and shone it out through the intricately scrolled glass, and the restless amber liquid inside. "Doesn't it look fine?" Mr. Gregory said. "I'll just set it there for a reminder."

"A reminder?"

"So I don't forget I've quit drinking, you see."

I could hardly see anything, it was so dark in there. "I better go home," I said.

"Tell you mother I figured it out." Since we came into the house he hadn't taken his eyes off the bottle of Jim Beam. It seemed to sit there dancing in the darkness with a light all its own. "Tell her I got the damn message."

I was getting vexed with Mr. Gregory. "You shouldn't swear like that, you know."

"One thing at a time, Frankie." I could see his face in the half-dark, his eyes fastened on that bottle almost without blinking. "I didn't used to swear; drink either. I say one thing at a time. First, the Jim Beam, then the whole world."

"I'll tell her."

"Tell her this is the cock-eyed craziest idea I ever saw, but it works. That's the thing, you know—it works. I can feel it working. Tell her that. Tell her . . . I'll just stare at that bottle all year long, but I won't even touch it; not one time. You'll see." Suddenly he looked at me. "Oh, Frankie. Don't ever take a drink, you hear me? If I ever hear of you taking a drink, I'll tan your britches clean off your backside. You listening to me?"

"Yes, sir."

"You tell your mother . . . I guess that means I have to quit smoking, too. And cussing. Lying and cheating; and ever other damn thing. Frankie, I have to tell you—I'm not a liar, and I'm not a cheat. Does this mean I have to start going to church?"

"One thing at a time," I said.

"That's right. One thing at a time." Mr. Gregory couldn't sit still. First he was up, then sitting down; pacing the floor, stretching his neck, shifting his shoulder. "That's right. One thing at a time. One damn hellbent godforsaken piece of misery after another." Abruptly he turned, and yelled at me. "You tell your mother . . ." He grabbed the sacred vial of Jim Beam off the shelf and threw it against the stove. The bottle shattered; tiny crystal slivers mixed with the liquid shower that sprayed across the room. "Tell her I don't need her damn present! Tell her I've got no use for it. Tell her she's too late—I've already quit drinking." He sank onto a chair and bent over, and I thought I could see him growing smaller and smaller.

At last I said, "Are you okay, Mr. Gregory?"

He raised his head, and switched on the light. "You still here?"

"It's me. Frankie."

"I thought you'd gone. I'm not used to having anybody around."

"Are you okay?"

Suddenly he twitched his shoulders in a gesture of dismissal. "Get out of here! You and your damn Christmas presents . . ."

I think my mouth fell open. I just sat there staring.

"Anything I hate it's a mother hen, clucking around the farmyard puttin' everything right; puttin' all the pins in order and dryin' out the drunks. Maybe she thought she was tryin' to help—that's the whole damn trouble. What does she know?"

"No!" I cried. I couldn't stand for him to talk about my mother that way. "You don't understand. She really likes you."

"Sure she does. Hah! She can brighten up her whole Christmas just buyin' a bottle of hooch for an old sot."

"There's more to it than that."

"Yeah. Tell me about it. What more?"

He'd stopped me cold. What had I gotten myself into? I groped for something plausible to say. "She says you're the best teacher this town ever had."

"Get out of here, kid."

"You taught her in sixth grade. She still remembers."

"Well, now I'll teach her one more time. You tell her for me to just leave it alone, okay? Leave me alone. I don't want her; I don't need her. Just stay out of it, okay? I'm doing fine. Tell her that!"

I felt terrible. This was the worst Christmas I could ever imagine. In my anguish and confusion a wild idea occurred to me, and I didn't even pause to consider it. I said, "She wonders can you come to dinner tomorrow?"

He stopped; everything about him held steady. He quit shifting, moving, turning; even his eyes held absolutely still, fastened on me.

"It's true," I said. "She'd like you to come and have Christmas dinner with us." I was half-petrified myself. I'd never told a deliberate lie before, and besides, what was my mother going to say? Or worse, my father?

Slowly he shifted in his seat, taking a minute or two before he was settled again. "You think I'm crazy, kid?"

I was in it now. There was no way I could back out. "No. I mean it."

"Me sit down with your mom and dad?" He looked down at himself. "Just look at me."

"You could shave," I said. "You could change your clothes."

"I don't have any other clothes."

I had made the suggestion on an impulse, and then regretted it. But now I felt passionately that he must eat with us. "You're okay," I said. "You're just fine, the way you are."

He grinned. "Remember that old Australian proverb, 'One thing at a time?'"

"Of course I do."

"I think it applies here. Maybe next Christmas."

He might not even be alive next Christmas. I said, "But my dad has another proverb. 'Don't stop in the middle.'" He looked a little puzzled. I explained, "It means if you start something, don't stop until you finish."

"That's good advice."

"Well, we're almost friends, you and I. I mean, don't you think so? Halfway friends, anyway. And if we stop now, we're finished. Maybe we'll never be friends. Maybe . . ." I couldn't think of how to say it—I just sat there like a dummy.

"Of course, I might be able to find something else to wear," he said.

"Then you're coming?"

He groaned. "I don't know if I dare, Frankie. You scare the daylights out of me."

"Does it make your stomach hurt?" I asked.

"My stomach hurts all the time."

"That's 'cause you're sick of canned peas. You need a good turkey dinner."

"Oooh," he sighed. "Yes I do . . ."

"Mom always asks me to set the table for her. So I'm going to set a place for you."

"An empty chair? They say that's what the Jews do, you know, in case Elijah comes."

"Okay, you be Elijah, and I'll see that your chair is ready."

He laughed out loud. "I'm no prophet, Frankie. There's only one thing about me that's like Elijah: I'm coming. Now you get home and tell your mother."

"Yeah, sure." But I reflected a moment. What was I supposed to tell her? Was he just talking about the dinner invitation? There were all those other things he'd mentioned. "I'm not sure what it is you want me to tell her."

"Just tell her Merry Christmas."

"Is that all?"

"There's nothing better than that."

Linda Sillitoe is a writer, editor, and filmmaker living in Salt Lake City, Utah, along with her husband and their three children. She has published two books of fiction, Sideways to the Sun *and* Windows on the Sea *with Signature Books, and co-authored* Salamander: The Story of the Mormon Forgery Murders *with Allen D. Roberts. Currently she is co-author of an ethnobiography,* One Voice Rising, *with Clifford Duncan, a Ute tribal leader and healer, for the University of Utah Press.*

KIDNAPPING GRANDMA

by Linda Sillitoe

The snow flickering outside the window as they talked lay in cuffs along the sills, Julie noticed, by the time they compromised. For a few minutes the three of them sat quiet, each watching winter's confetti drift and mount relentlessly, beautiful but indifferent.

The compromise between parents and daughter? Late that evening Lindsay could take the Tempo, pick up her friends, attend midnight Mass, take her friends home, and then drive home herself. She would be very careful although, inevitably, she would be very late. She would beware of Christmas Eve party goers, the snow, icy roads, black ice, and deputy sheriffs eager to enforce curfew.

What loomed in the center of the conversation like a bulky ghost was the family Mercury, wrecked now for two months. More than that, thought Julie, Lindsay's mother, like any abandoned wreck this ghost-car had collected minor inhabitants, small vapors that oozed now from the shattered windows. She closed her eyes momentarily not wanting to acknowledge their presence—the spooks you don't believe in can't hurt you. With a glance, she and Len had already congratulated themselves and each other for their restraint in not mentioning the wrecked Mercury to Lindsay. Her confidence had been shaken enough by her accident. Besides she could see the ghost.

The snow that should have bolstered their case against Lindsay's plan, instead had whispered like something holy at the windows as Lindsay spoke. She had wanted to attend Christmas Mass for a long time; it was a beautiful, moving ritual. Julie suppressed a smile

235

remembering the younger, beribboned Lindsay who had pulled her little siblings out of Primary one morning when the chorister suggested that anyone who didn't want to sing could leave. Later, ribbon replaced by a beret, Lindsay had informed her MIA teacher of the Church's sexism and racism. Now she sat before them, twisting the inexpensive gold cross around her neck and mentioning the First Amendment. Tactfully, she then explained that her friends' parents were too parochial to comprehend such an urgent but subtle need as Christmas Mass—nor would any of them provide a car.

And Lindsay's parents, Julie amended silently, had been high school debaters themselves and could appreciate Lindsay's eloquence even as she racked up points.

Occasionally as they talked, a gust flipped snow like a handful of salt against the glass and Julie saw Len wince. She knew he didn't relish waiting until two or three a.m. for Lindsay's return. He couldn't even consider the consequences of another car accident. However he had jolted his own parents by converting to Mormonism when not much older than Lindsay. And together, years later, they'd disturbed both the Mormon and Masonic sides of the family by gradually finding peace outside any chapel walls.

Seated at what seemed the center corner of a triangle, Julie observed frustration rise in Len and in Lindsay, and saw both father and daughter wrestle it down. Neither would allow a raised voice nor an unjust word. Lindsay is growing up, Julie thought. Not honoring this effort would be a crime.

Snow burdened the pines outside the large window that overlooked the back yard. Julie imagined herself a bird nestled against the trunk behind the snow. While her Christmas Eve list was shorter than it had been when the children were small, it still demanded her attention. When her turn in the discussion came, she saluted both the First Amendment and Len's safety concerns, then revealed her own cause. Her family would arrive by the half-dozens late Christmas morning for brunch. "Yes," Lindsay broke in, forgetting herself for a moment. "If Christmas doesn't fall on Sunday, Mormons don't go to church."

The point was, Julie said, that Lindsay would be missed and the First Amendment would hardly seem sufficient reason. While their little family might wander the edges of the fold, the rest liked the coziness of the center and saw no attractions elsewhere. Besides Grandma would be here.

The vapors around the ghostly Mercury grayed, gaining substance. Grandma was actually Lindsay's great-grandmother, Len's grandmother, but despite the presence of other grandmothers in the family, "Grandma" without further reference meant her. All three sighed and looked away. Mentally each had just entered the nearby nursing home where Raelynn sat twisted in her wheelchair, head tipped so she could monitor visitors through her badly crossed eyes. From down the hall, Cleo screamed, "Help me! Help me!" And Grandma—Grandma who had lined up giggling with the kids in the hall every Christmas morning between Lindsay's first steps and Grandma's last—sat hunched in her wheelchair, almost unseeing, almost unhearing, almost unable to speak. But knowing she was someplace she hated, knowing she couldn't go home. Len shook his head at the flakes rounding the corners of the windows. "How will we manage her wheelchair in all this snow?" he said.

"The parking lot will be shoveled," Julie hoped aloud, but the weight of tomorrow settled behind her eyes.

Lindsay took an audible breath and agreed to miss morning Mass if she could attend midnight Mass. She wouldn't even wear her cross to Christmas brunch. And she would drive with extreme caution.

Later from the kitchen windows, Julie watched the street while she prepared salads and cookies and applesauce cake for brunch. Next year she would try to remember to plan the menu around the foods Len fixed. The ache in the back of her legs and the scratchiness growing in her throat indicated Christmas Eve familiarly enough. But little else seemed the same. Years before they had moved to this house and Grandma had moved to the nursing home, Julie had sent the children next door on Christmas Eve to Grandma. As they grew older, they would decorate her tree, choose bows for the presents she wrapped. Still, their excitement would be such that the hard candy, cookies, and soda pop Grandma gave them soon shot them on a sugar-high out her door and home again.

Both at Grandma's and at home, Lindsay, as a child, had always put Santa to the test on Christmas Eve—both through her behavior and the written requests left beside cookies and milk: "Please have Mrs. Santa sign on the line below. I would also like Blitzen's hoofprint." By the time Tom was born, they had learned to let her exchange a present or two to ease the anticipation. Then Tom's anxiety over whatever he wanted most became agony as Christmas approached. They had learned to let him know he wouldn't be disappointed. And later Sarah had bounced like a tiny dynamo from one moment to the next, updating them on every thought in her nimble mind.

Now, of course, Lindsay and even Tom were sophisticated beyond acknowledging the childhood traditions their parents had arranged; rather they delighted in detailing their own early exploits to find Santa out. Nevertheless, Sarah likely would convince them to exchange presents this afternoon. Mainly Lindsay was preoccupied with her gifts for friends. And Tom faced a dilemma, having received a too-expensive present from his seventh-grade girlfriend.

They weren't the only people debating the success of certain gifts. Julie hoped this Christmas Tom would not return most of what they bought him. Rather than try to fathom his quirky adolescent tastes, they had simply purchased fewer items but all bearing the insignia of his preferred brands. Still, only broken sleep could be patched around Lindsay's wee-hours return and Sarah's early rising, and tomorrow would bring the arrival of between twenty and thirty kin. Julie made a mental note to have someone wipe off the telephones, which became remarkably grimy, and clean the bathrooms—again.

The cars speeding blithely along the wet, sanded street facing the house seemed to carry passengers whose trees were lit, presents were gilded and stacked, and children were cheerfully pulling taffy. These people were probably out doing good works for the less fortunate without a care for their car insurance payment in January. Not even the snow daunted them, for they were equipped, no doubt, with chains, two-way radios, repair kits, flares, and thirsty credit cards.

Here, no one had bothered to plug in the Christmas tree lights or check the mailbox for last minute cards—or bills. Instead six bare feet (despite scratchy throats) pounded when the telephone rang. No one had tried to spot an elf-informant peeking through a window, nor would the three of them, outfitted in new, rubber-footed pajamas, consider Santa's snack. Kids' stuff, Tom would say; manipulative parents' stuff, Sarah would accuse, an eye out for Lindsay's approval.

Julie belatedly turned on the oven, for the batter curved now in the Bundt pan. She knew that more than feet dashing for the phone trembled the dishes in the china closet. The house silently reverberated with the continual thrust of Lindsay's heels as she tried to launch herself into her own true life. Maybe it wasn't fair for them to keep shifting, avoiding one hard place from which she could shove off. And Tom, Julie suspected, was studying Lindsay to improve on her methods for his own getaway.

"You've done it," her therapist friend Susanna had told her over lunch last month. "They're independent, eager to grow up. That's good—that means you've succeeded. You need to worry when teens don't want to leave home."

Words to remember on Christmas Eve, Julie thought, and smiled at Len, who burst through the side door, shaking off snowy sleeves, stomping his boots. He gave her a cold hug from behind. "Where's Tom? He can finish the driveway."

"Maybe Santa Claus should have bought him a snow blower."

"I don't think Polo makes them" Len replied, and they laughed.

"Did I tell you the house looks very festive?" he asked a bit formally. "Believe me, none of this would happen if it were up to me." Len had the capacity to ignore Christmas all but two weeks of the year and then be alternately bewildered, overwhelmed, and pleased when it came. Julie had learned to take vacation time the week before Christmas and then let Len cope with the week between Christmas and New Year's.

"You think anyone would notice it if didn't happen?" she asked, wrinkling her nose to avoid sounding pathetic.

"They'd notice," he said, brushing her hair up to kiss the back of her neck. "Everyone would notice."

"Dad!" Sarah's voice admonished. "Mom's busy. Don't get mooey."

They smiled at her as she expected, but Sarah's smile vanished. "Lindsay says she's going to midnight Mass."

"That's what we hear."

"But that's not fair. When she comes in, she'll see everything hours before we do. Maybe you trust Lindsay not to peek, but I don't."

"Don't tell me again how she taught you to find the presents in our closet," Julie sighed. "Maybe Santa just won't come until Lindsay gets home."

Sarah presented her most skeptical look. "You two really think you can stay awake that late?"

Julie tickled her. "Who said anything about us? You were talking about Santa."

"Mom. Be serious. I'm not a child."

"No? What are you?"

"I'm a pre-teen." And Sarah was serious. In fact, Sarah was nearly upset.

"Don't worry, honey. Instead of listening for Santa's sleigh bells, you can listen for the Tempo's squeaky brakes and its sigh of relief when Lindsay climbs out."

Sarah laughed, her brown eyes sparkling again.

"Don't quote me on that," Julie warned, as Sarah bounded down the stairs. After four bumps she was back. "What about Grandma?"

"We're kidnapping Grandma," Len said. "What did you think?"

"Just checking." She was gone again.

They called it kidnapping because the first time their venture from the nursing home had been so unplanned it felt surreptitious. After Grandma broke her hip while recuperating at Len's parents' home from her stroke, no one had dared take her anywhere. For a while she practiced walking with a walker, therapists at either side, but she did less and less well. They fed her too much, she complained. She was gaining weight. She feared falling again. Julie and Len, with or without the children, visited her at least every other day. Grandma kept up on the details of their lives even though names escaped her and they needed to fill in the blanks in her side of the conversation.

Yet that first Thanksgiving she spent in the nursing home, when Len and Julie had visited her it had seemed impossible to leave her with the few patients who had nowhere to go and the few staff members who'd had to work. Also, although Grandma's few comments were pleasant enough, she seemed to expect an invitation.

They exchanged despairing looks above her head, and then Len had said, "Well, we've got to go, Grandma. We're taking the kids to Julie's folks' house for dinner."

"Oh, that will be fine," Grandma said.

A moment passed while silent questions and cautions flew over her newly-permed hair, and then Julie asked, "Well, do you think you could manage riding in the car and everything?"

"Sure," Grandma said, as if that were a foregone conclusion.

"What about your folks?" Len murmured to Julie.

"They'll make room," Julie grinned, her spirits lifting.

The aides were equally unconcerned. One helped Grandma into the bathroom while another got an extra pad for her wheelchair and her familiar raincoat from the closet. Len wheeled her out to the car. They maneuvered her into the front seat, and Julie lifted Grandma's legs in and settled the afghan while Len folded the wheelchair and placed it in the trunk. They were off—yet almost expected to hear sirens wailing behind them.

The November day's muted colors hummed below a hazy sky. Grandma marveled at everything, staring out her window. How much could she really see? Julie wondered. Light, at least, light that wasn't artificial; mountains, trees, shops, sky—all that miraculous world. Her home sat empty. They didn't dare take her there. Thankfully they no longer lived across the driveway.

When they wheeled her up the walk to collect the children—who had still been children—six startled eyes met them. "Hi, Grandma," "Hi, Grandma." Lindsay pulled Julie to one side. "Is it all right to take her out?" They shut the front door behind Grandma and there she was, in their house with the triumvirate she had fished out from under the beds, scolded for throwing crab apples, and read to before her vision faded and Sarah read to her. "Would you like to hear me play the piano, Grandma," volunteered Lindsay, who used to resist Grandma's importuning to practice and perform.

"Ooh," Grandma said, and fluttered her hands to show her appreciation.

Sarah played after Lindsay. Grandma listened closely to every note, grasping their faces between her twisted hands afterward for a kiss.

"Grandma!" Tom called suddenly, and they turned to see him scale the door frame with hands and feet akimbo, then hang from one corner. Grandma laughed and threw up her hands in concern and delight when Tom thumped down.

After that they had kidnapped Grandma every year for holidays and the children's birthdays, even for summer parties. Her presence on those occasions became a poignant gift no one dared articulate.

Kidnapping Grandma continued even after something happened to her at the nursing home—not a stroke exactly—some disturbance no one explained, and she almost died, twisting and shouting at the air. A nursing home van took her to the hospital and she was revived but only part way. Her speech and comprehension diminished. Her hands and feet and knees, so long damaged by arthritis, now pained unceasingly. Her stomach hurt. On visits they had to call her back from wherever it was she went. They didn't go to see her so often, and each time it took greater resolve. Then one Sunday they couldn't be sure she knew the children were there, talking into her ears, holding her hands, pushing the chair. After that, Len and Julie didn't urge the children to go to the nursing home but still kidnapped Grandma on holidays.

When they visited they sometimes brought her favorite homemade chocolate chip cookies and broke off bits to feed her as they talked. "Tom's playing basketball," they told her one afternoon. "He's gotten so tall."

"Yes," she answered, her first clear word the whole visit. "I see him sometimes." Her hand motioned dribbling the ball down the court.

They smiled at each other in surprise. "Lindsay's started high school, Grandma, can you believe that?"

"Yes," she would say and shake her head.

"Sarah wants another Cabbage Patch doll but she still loves the one you gave her the best."

"Oh, that girl," she would say fondly, and pat their hands with her gnarled, translucent fingers. She didn't ask why the children no longer came.

"They're good kids," Julie told her once when she seemed lucid. "You did a good job with those kids, you know that?"

"I know," Grandma said, and all the minor and a few major disagreements about how those children should be disciplined, medicated, or schooled fell away. Grandma had insisted on being their primary babysitter, although sometimes they came home to find her exasperated or exhausted or both. Lindsay resisted authority, Tom bedeviled his sisters, Sarah had cried. Yet within twenty-four hours Grandma would call to exclaim over what a wonderful time they'd had and ask when they would need her again.

They invited her for impromptu suppers and Sunday dinners when she could visit without tending. "Here's your starving boarder again," she would apologize, pulling up her chair. Still, whenever she found out the children were scheduled to visit other grandparents or had a babysitter coming, she'd turn huffy.

"Grandma, we're going to wear you out," they'd explain. "Oh, no," she'd say, "they're always good when I'm there."

Gradually, almost imperceptibly, the roles shifted and they realized that Grandma was not so much tending the children as they were tending her. Tom, for instance, not only mowed her lawns but matched his swift feet to her cautious gait and they walked to the store.

Grandma's neighbor told them how he located products on the shelves, read her the prices, figured the best deals, and pushed the shopping cart. Often Julie or Len would call and say, "I have to run to the store, Grandma. Can I pick up anything for you?" First they must complete a ritual of assuring her it was no trouble, and then she would give them a detailed list.

Nevertheless, the little she'd let them do couldn't keep up with her needs. She wouldn't let them take home her dirty laundry even though she had replaced their washing machine when it wore out, but not her own. She wouldn't consider moving close to them again or sharing her home with a companion even after someone climbed in her bedroom window. Nothing was stolen, but from then on Grandma slept on the couch. She always found a ride with friends or relatives to stand in line for free cheese and butter the government gave away, then pressed most of it on Len or his brothers so it wouldn't go to waste.

"It's the Depression mentality," Len would say, putting the cheese in the refrigerator. "She won't pass up her share even though she doesn't need it and it would be easier to buy it at the store." Finally Sarah (who spent croupy days with Grandma) reported that Grandma only ate wieners, jello, cottage cheese, and toast unless adult company came. And one day after Grandma washed her curtains and wiped up the kitchen floor, she had a stroke. Afterward she scolded them for taking her to the hospital that night instead of leaving her alone. She would never move home again.

Snow was falling when Lindsay left for Mass at 10:30 p.m., and continued while Julie polished up the kitchen. She startled from sleep on the couch at 2 a.m., looked out at the driveway to find no car yet, only a downy white carpet. For a moment ice, accidents, and teenagers spun in her brain and she decided that if Lindsay returned home safe—and her friends were safe—Christmas would be fine no matter how weary. Fifteen minutes later, Lindsay woke her gently. "Thanks, Mom," she said, and went quickly to bed.

Len and Tom shoveled the driveway the next morning, the drifts along the sides now shoulder-high. Julie had the girls gather the wrapping paper, save the bows, arrange the presents, and begin dipping the bottoms of candles in honey so they would stand straight in the nativity carousel.

Leaving the nursing home, Grandma cried out when they bent her knees enough to get her into the front seat, even though they slid the seat all the way back. Len crept along the slick roads, his caution opposing Julie's eagerness to have Grandma safely indoors.

The children worked at showing Grandma their favorite gifts while Len and Julie carried out bagels and buns, turkey and ham, and salads. Julie's back ached. Something had slipped when she helped Grandma out of her chair in the bathroom. This could be the last year they could kidnap Grandma, she thought, no matter how long she eluded death. Twice in the last nine months Grandma had come close, crying with her hands extended, "Come get me! I want to go home!" How many more times could they wish her godspeed? How long could they bear to see her linger? How could they give up on her? Tom, for one, would be furious if Grandma didn't come for Christmas next year. Again the image of that rowdy crew lined up in the hall on Christmas morning stung Julie's eyes.

And then cars began pulling in the driveway and lining the street, slushy boots and smiling faces came in the side doors, everyone had a story of a near-miss in the snow. Grandma, silent and vague in her wheelchair, faded as the conversations rose, children scouted the sweets, dishes were uncovered and set out, coats hung up, toys found, fixed, and displayed, babies and ornaments rescued.

A pause for a quick blessing on the food. Then the cousins lined up, their parents lagging behind, their grandparents still admiring this new sweater or that stuffed animal. Len hustled back and forth, refilling the vegetable plate and the punchbowl. Ladling punch for a never-ending line of small hands, Julie caught sight of Lindsay, across the room, feeding Grandma the soft foods she had captured before the line formed. The next time Julie stopped chatting and ladling long enough to check, Tom had taken over, opening his mouth each time Grandma opened hers. Seated on the floor, Sarah guarded Grandma's sore and slippered feet, an eye out for toddling cousins.

The moment crystallized in Julie's mind, erasing time in a sudden round of knowing. Not that she foresaw the night when Tom, grown taller still and muscular, would jog at midnight over to meet them at the nursing home. He'd make it home by curfew to find Sarah alone, crying into the cat's fur. He'd be difficult to dislodge from the chair by the bed that swallowed Grandma. He'd clutch Grandma's hand, weeping (though he hadn't let them see him cry for years) as her desperate face and shrunken form gurgled and gasped with the fluid in her lungs.

Nor did Julie foresee how Lindsay, the day after that midnight drowning, would march into Grandma's room and say through her tears to the bent hush curling sightless, toothless, motionless: "You don't have to fight any more, Grandma. I'm grown up now. I have a job and an apartment, and I'm going to the university. Tom and Sarah are growing up, too. We love you and we'll miss you, but we understand you have to go."

Or maybe Julie did know. For watching her children hover around Grandma without suggestion or reward, as Grandma had once fussed over them, she knew they were going to be fine. Thank you, she told Grandma silently, for giving us this time.

Children covered the living room floor now, heaped plates before them; their parents lined the sofa, her parents praised the buffet, honeymooners curled in the papa-san, and babies watched from high chairs, pensively smoothing salad through their hair. The snow facing every window beamed light around the room. Abundance rang through the house like bells. In this noisy dance, Grandma would tire quickly and need to go back early. Never mind. For the moment, conversation frolicked, the lit tree sparkled, and particles flickered in the air, as small and fast as thoughts, as white as angel down.

Donald R. Marshall's popular collection of short stories, The Rummage Sale, *opened the doors for the current renaissance of Mormon literature when it appeared in 1972. It was followed by another collection,* Frost in the Orchard *(1977), and two novels,* Zinnie Stokes, Zinnie Stokes *(1984) and* Enchantress of Crumbledown *(1990).*

Marshall has won numerous awards for his writing, including first place in the 1988 Utah Arts Council Writing Contest and first place in the 1989 Deseret Book Children's Book Contest—both for Enchantress of Crumbledown. *The musical version of* The Rummage Sale *(for which he wrote book, lyrics, and music) won nine awards in 1986 from the Utah Valley Drama Guild. And when his short story "Christmas Snows, Christmas Winds" (from* Frost in the Orchard*) was adapted for film and TV in 1981, it won three regional Emmys.*

Marshall has also won many awards for his composing, painting, and photography. He is currently at work on two novels, a book of interviews with the world's greatest living film directors, a play, a musical set in the 30s, and another children's book.

Born and raised in Panguitch, Utah, he earned his B.A. in art and his M.A. in English literature, both from Brigham Young University, and he later earned his Ph.D in American literature from the University of Connecticut. Having taught for some years at the University of Hawaii, he is currently a professor of Humanities at Brigham Young University.

He and his wife, the former Jean Stockseth (arts editor of Provo's Daily Herald*) reside in Provo with their three children, Robin, Jordan, and Reagan.*

FRIENDS AND LOVED ONES FAR AND NEAR/ MERRY XMAS FROM OUR HOUSE TO YOURS

by Donald R. Marshall

Maccine and all:

XMAS GREETINGS FROM OUR HOUSE TO YOURS: 1971

Thank heavens for such things as ditto machines, when card-sending time rolls around it may not make it quite so personal but it sure beats cramped fingers plus all the expense of store-bought cards that don't hardly give you room enough to say boo. Now if we could just think of a way to get rid of licking all those stamps, etc., etc.

Our biggest news this year is that I finally got my trip up to Oregon to see Glorene and Norland and their girls. They've been wanting me to come up ever since they moved up there last May. Wiley wouldn't go, he said somebody had to tend to things here at home, so I took the first bus I could get last August and stayed up there over two weeks. Everything was just grand, Norland's fast becoming one of the big wigs there at the plant and sure to be boss of the whole shebang one of these days, they've got them a nice new home just outside Portland, all electric and everything. Of course, they treated me like a queen every step of the way and wouldn't let me pay for a thing. They wined me and dined me day and night and saw to it I got the grand tour of everything there was to see and then some. I wish I could of brought little Janiece and Patsy Ann home with me, they're just so grown-up and ladylike, just like Glorene, but I guess they'll have to wait until next year to see their Grandma.

Roy Dell and Vergean are still in Frankfurt, Germany, with the army. From the last reports all are doing fine. Roy Dell Jr. is going to the American school there and smart as a whip, just like his dad. I sure wish they'd come home or else I could get over there, but Wiley says he's not going and I guess that's that, although I'd sure like to.

RoZann, our baby, is a senior in high school and involved in so many different activities we hardly ever get to see her, I don't know how she keeps it up, playing in the pep band and all.

Come and see us, our doors are always open.

The Lowders of Eureka, Dolpha, Wiley, and RoZann

P. S. Forgot to put in here that Willey was in the hospital for a week last fall. It was his stomach again but he is almost back to normal. merry Xmas. Dolpha

FRIENDS AND LOVED ONES FAR AND NEAR: 1971

As the Christmas season draws closer, our thoughts turn once again toward our many dear friends and relatives scattered upon this great land of ours.

We feel indeed blessed this year, grateful for the health and strength that have been ours and ever thankful for the abundance of God's bounty that we have enjoyed throughout the past months.

Our children continue to grow and amaze us all with their many activities and accomplishments. KaeLynn is almost sixteen now, lovely and feminine, delightful to be around, a pure joy to have in the home. Among her many talents are sewing, singing, playing the piano, giving dramatic readings, tutoring the neighbors' children in reading . . . and many, many other things too numerous to tell.

Jolene is thirteen and our little homemaker, winning a blue ribbon for her wool suit in the Orange County Fair last fall. She loves cooking, drawing, music, gymnastics, science, typing, reading, volleyball . . . and, of course, sewing. She is also our newest babysitter, so conscientious about this new responsibility and therefore always in demand.

Kevin is our eight-year old . . . all boy, but such a priceless little spirit. Cars, guns, math, softball, riding a skateboard, and, of course, helping his daddy are among his many interests. He is a regular little scholar as well, winning first prize over all the third graders in the whole school district this last September for his composition on reptiles.

LeMoine is currently engaged in the ambitious task of enlarging the family room and redoing our food storage area. He was number one in sales at work again this year and thus both he and Maccine are anticipating another wonderful trip to either Disney World or Houston, Texas.

Maccine is busy with church and civic activities as usual and finding motherhood more and more fulfilling with each passing day. She is presently enjoying the conveniences of a new dishwasher and water softener and looking forward to an enlarged dining room and extension to the kitchen and laundry room in the not-too-distant future.

Our hearts are full this year as we pause to contemplate our many blessings and to ponder as well the priceless value of friendships and family ties. May this find you all as joyous and blessed as *we* feel this holiday season.

The Shelman Family

P.S. Dolpha and Family: Holiday Greetings and sincere Best Wishes that the New Year may bring many cherished moments of Great Joy. Warmly, Maxine

XMAS GREETINGS FROM OUR HOUSE TO YOURS: 1972

Once again here I am with the news from the Lowders in Eureka.

Well, our biggest news is Glorene's divorce. We feel good to have it all over with as it was sure a mess the way it was. The break-up was hard on the girls, Janeice is still just seven and Patsy Ann four and a half, but it's like I told Glorene, it's a darn good thing she got out while the getting was good. Everything was just going from bad to worse. I sometimes think if I could of got up there more often it might not of happened, but I think we're all realizing more and more that it's good riddance to bad rubbage. I could tell things weren't right when I was up there last February, and then when Glorene had to have her cyst operated on in March, I went up again to be chief cook and bottle washer and I told her right then and there I wouldn't of been able to live with him five minutes if it was me. Norland's been a poor loser about the whole thing, fighting every step of the way, but Glorene's got charge of the girls and is determined to keep them—and just as far away from him as she possibly can if any of us have anything to say about it. I think all that power (he was almost top dog) just went to his head, and, it's like I told Glorene, she just had to put her foot down somewhere. He was neglecting her and the girls and gone a whole lot more than he was ever to home. Poor Glorene's had her hands full, being in and out of court all year, and an operation on top of that, but I tried to get up there as much as I could, and I guess it's finally over and we're all glad of that. For the time being her address is still the same, but I'm trying to get her back down here where we can look after her.

Roy Dell and Vergean are doing just swell, last we heard. They don't write as much as we'd like but I know they all send their love to all of you. You'd think they'd of had enough of Germany by now, but I guess sometimes you have to do what Uncle Sam wants and not what you want.

RoZann, too, probably wishes she was back home here instead of being stuck way up there in Fairbanks, Alaska, where the radio says it's forty degrees below zero, but she and one of her girlfriends got them a chance to work up there for awhile and she claims she's having a good time.

Well, come and see us when you can.

Dolpha and Family

FRIENDS AND LOVED ONES FAR AND NEAR: 1972

Once again, as we approach the Christmas season, we are prompted to recount our multitudinous blessings and to contemplate once more the wealth of friendships and precious family bonds which mean so very very much to us in our daily lives.

Our cup continues to run over. How fortunate we are to have three beautiful healthy children, our lovely home here in Fullerton, another new car . . . now that KaeLynn is of driving age! . . . and so many other blessings too numerous to count.

KaeLynn is a lovely and feminine sixteen, popular and pleasant to be with, a pure delight to have around the home. Not the least among her many interests is music, both instrumental and vocal, followed closely by sewing and reading, not to mention drama, debate, and choral reading.

Jolene is fourteen now and such a joy. In addition to the numerous awards she wins for her sewing, she continues to amaze us with her many other interests and abilities, among which are cooking, typing, reading, music, science, tumbling, swimming, jumping on the trampoline . . . and, of course, babysitting, as she is becoming the most sought-after sitter in the whole neighborhood.

Kevin is our nine-year-old, every inch a boy, but such a help to his daddy and such a pleasant little soul. Among his many interests this year are science, math, machines of any sort, . . . and, of course, softball, wrestling, and sports of any kind.

Besides being honored at work for the fifth straight year, LeMoine keeps busy around the house with his present project being a new carport. We're hoping his company will send us either to Atlanta or Spokane for this year's convention!

Maccine is enjoying working in the home and trying to hold numerous church positions as well. She loves her new kitchen . . . especially the new microwave oven . . . and is hoping Santa will bring her a humidifier this year.

We count your friendship among our most cherished possessions and hope that this new year will bring you great joy and blessings in abundance.

    The Shelman Family

FRIENDS AND LOVED ONES FAR AND NEAR: 1973

As we welcome once more the spirit of Christmas into our hearts, we recall the many wonderful blessings that have been ours this year and count ourselves lucky to have among our many cherished friendships such dear close friends as each of you.

Our three lovely children continue to be the source of our inspiration and joy. KaeLynn is almost eighteen, growing more feminine and lovely by the day, it seems. What joy her music brings to us, not to mention her many other talents, among which are such varied things as needlework and the dramatic arts, all of which continue to bring her numerous awards and recognition untold.

Jolene is our little seamstress. When she is not being sought after as the number-one babysitter in the neighborhood, she is busy sewing on countless projects, many of which bring her state-wide acclaim.

Kevin is our ten-year-old this year, such a little man and such a helper to his daddy. He dearly loves school, especially such subjects as math and science and physical education.

LeMoine keeps busy as usual at work and at home, still number one in sales but finding time around the house to do the carpenter work and plumbing. If all goes well, the company will send him . . . and Maccine, of course . . . to either Hawaii or the Bahamas. Wish us luck!

Maccine is still busily working in church affairs and thoroughly enjoying her new living room carpet and drapes.

We want you all to know as the Christmas season approaches how much we think of you and how very important we feel your

acquaintance is in our lives. Our wish for the New Year is that you may be even partially as happy and blessed as are
     The Shelman Family

XMAS GREETINGS FROM OUR HOUSE TO YOURS: 1974
     Here I am a year late. I'm sorry to have disappointed you last year but I was in too much of a dither to even get the ditto typed up, let alone have it run off and stamped, etc., etc.
     Well, I was in and out of the hospital a whole lot last year and only got up to see Glorene's family twice. I have a lump that just wouldn't go away and the doctor wanted me to have it taken care of so I did. It turned out to be a hernia and if that wasn't an ordeal! My bathroom was exactly 103 steps down the hall from my room and when you got there the door was so heavy it would just about kill you to try to swing it open. After a week of that, I ended up getting a new hernia and I had to wait another three months for the first one to heal so they could cut me open and start on the other one.
     Anyway, I did get up to Idaho a couple of times to help Glorene out, but most of the time I just had to talk to her on the phone. She and her new husband Harlow are still acting like a couple of newlyweds although it has been almost a year now. She is happier than I've seen her in a long time and of course she's expecting again after all these years which adds to it all. Her finding Harlow was the luckiest thing that ever was as he is everything that Norland was supposed to be and wasn't. And of course I don't mind saying that Harlow's darn lucky to have him a good little wife like Glorene. I went up to be with them this Thanksgiving and left poor Wiley to do for himself (I gave him his choice). They have a nice new home in Boise as Harlow is from there and has him a real good job with a big dried foods company where he's right up there at the top doing most of the hiring and firing. They sent us a whole case of dried okra that's sure come in handy a time or two. He treats Glorene just grand, a real change for her after what she had to go through with Norland. But Harlow is just as good as gold and I sure wish she had run onto him about ten years ago before she ever got mixed up with you-know-who. Harlow has two children, one of each, which they try to get as often as possible. Those little kids of his were just about a nervous wreck when they first got them last summer, but after two weeks you wouldn't of believed the difference, that's how Glorene is, she had them giggling

and acting like normal kids in no time. Janeice and Patsy Ann are growing cuter (and more and more like Glorene) every day. Patsy Ann still has a tendency to talk a little baby talk, Harlow thinks they ought to take her to a speech therapist, but I tell him they're only young once and she'll probably outgrow it soon enough. I usually call them up two or three times a week and just love to hear that little voice recite "Twinto, Twinto, Witto Staow" over the telephone, she says it so cute, I just can't imagine her any other way.

Roy Dell and Vergean have been home from Germany for four and a half months now. He is stationed at Fort Devens, Massachusetts, so they don't get to see us much oftener than when they were over there. I want Wiley and me to take one of those tours back there but if I can't talk him into it, I'm going to catch a bus one of these first days and go back there anyway. Vergean says that Roy Dell Jr. is taller than she is now (which isn't saying too much, I guess, as she is practically a midget), but I'm sure anxious to see them and I'd imagine they could use all the help they can get trying to get situated into a whole new place.

RoZann flew back and visited with them in November instead of coming here for Thanksgiving like we hoped. But I was glad they each had family for Thanksgiving anyway. RoZann liked it so well up in that neck of the woods, though, she got her a job in Nova Scotia and now who knows when she'll get to come home. Seems like we're scattered halfway around the world. Thank heavens Glorene's close. I don't know what she'd of done if I hadn't been able to get up there and help her through some of those bad times. Let's just hope Wiley's stomach doesn't act up and I don't get another hernia so I can be up there to help her out in February when the baby comes.

Our doors are always open.
Dolpha

FRIENDS AND LOVED ONES FAR AND NEAR: 1974
As the year draws to a close and the spirit of Christmas fills our hearts to overflowing, we once again take time from our busy schedules to remember those who are so near and dear to us, and to enumerate the infinite blessings showered upon us this past year.

Not the least among them are, of course, our three dear children—KaeLynn, Jolene, and Kevin. KaeLynn, such a pleasant, lovely, feminine young lady, is going on nineteen, attending college, and continuing to astound us . . . and everyone who knows her . . .

with her spectrum of talents, ranging from music to drama to sewing skills.

At sixteen our Jolene is personality plus. Still everyone's favorite babysitter, she somehow manages to find time to win a number of sewing awards. Interested primarily in home economics, she also delights in sports of all kinds, to say nothing of the liberal arts.

Our eleven-year-old Kevin is quite a little grown-up man these days, pleasing everyone with his never-ending wit and knowledge. He loves everything, not the least of which is being with and learning from LeMoine, who continues to be a model father . . . and salesman, of course . . . at work and at play.

Maccine is still happily involved with church duties as well as domestic ones, thoroughly enjoying many new additions in the home this year.

Many family excursions and events highlighted the year.

What joy your friendship brings! Again we feel unduly blessed to have, as such an integral and priceless part of our lives, friendship such as *yours*.

        The Shelman Family

XMAS GREETINGS FROM OUR HOUSE TO YOURS: 1975

Well, 1975 sure has been a big one. Wiley had to have two-thirds of his stomach taken out and now he has to practically live on baby food. Trying to fix three meals a day that he can manage and still be what help I can to Glorene is a full-time job I wouldn't wish off on anybody. Thank heavens for dried okra, I just boil it down, toss it in the blender, and there you have it.

Glorene and Harlow stopped in just long enough to say hello goodbye last summer on their way home from Disneyland and I got them to take me back up with them to Boise to help out for awhile and still had to go up again three weeks ago when her new baby was born a month early. Kimberly will be a year next month and the baby is just barely three weeks. They couldn't decide on a name, Harlow wanted it Ralph and Glorene had her heart set on Jared. I was a little partial to Jared myself but I finally told them why didn't they name it Jared Ralph and so they did and now Glorene calls it Jared and Harlow calls it Ralph. They're trying to work out a way so that Harlow can adopt Janeice and Patsy Ann, but I don't know what's going to happen because every time Norland gets hold of them he poisons their minds so much they don't think they want to come back.

While I was up there during most of August they had Harlow's two with them for awhile so it was your kids, my kids, and our kids for three or four weeks. I was glad I could be there to help out. Harlow tried to talk me into going back to see Roy Dell and Vergean in Main and RoZann up in Nova Scotia as long as I was up there, offered to pay my way on the bus and everything, and I guess I should of done it while I had the chance but Wiley thought I ought to get back home here and anyway RoZann was talking about maybe going off to Europe with some friends and when I called Roy Dell he said it had been so hot back there all month he couldn't see how I'd enjoy coming back right then, so I still haven't got my trip out there yet.

Roy Dell says they're doing just fine and RoZann says she's still planning to see Europe one of these first days. I'm going to try to get up to Glorene's again after New Year's. She's going to need all the help she can get with those two little babies both in diapers and trying to teach a class every week on fascinating womanhood to boot.

Come and see us if you can, our doors are always open, and in the meantime I'll try to keep you posted on all that's new with the Lowders.

Dolpha

FRIENDS AND LOVED ONES FAR AND NEAR   1975
Christmas 1975 finds us blessed beyond measure, ever mindful of the countless advantages and opportunities which are ours. And once again our thoughts drift toward each of *you* and the friendship . . . so rich, so choice, so meaningful . . . which we continue to share.

Our little ones, it seems, are ever growing. Our sweet KaeLynn will soon be twenty; she is presently debating between pursuing her career in music or accepting one of numerous proposals . . . ranging from a dashing young law student at Stanford to a handsome executive she met last summer in the northwest.

Jolene is seventeen, so lovely and feminine these days, winning awards galore and being chosen, it seems, for almost every honor imaginable.

Kevin, almost a teenager now, is such a reliable and dependable young man, whose knowledge and abilities never cease to amaze.

Numerous diversions made the year a rich and full one for the Shelmans, LeMoine ever the conscientious breadwinner and Maccine continuing to relish the eternal challenge of managing the home.

If our busy schedules do not permit time for personal notes or if this letter seems shorter than usual, know that our hearts are with *each and every one of you,* as always. May your blessings be even a tenth of those showered in such abundance on
> The Shelmans of Fullerton

MERRY XMAS FROM OUR HOUSE TO YOURS: 1976

Thank heavens for these letters once a year, otherwise it wouldn't be possible to keep you all informed on all the activities of the Lowders in Eureka. We're still plugging along here, only I've had trouble with my nose and Wiley seems to be keeping the road hot going up north to see one specialist after another and having his stomach treated.

Glorene, I'm happy to say, finally got out of that mess up there in Boise. She and the girls were here with us for awhile, but she finally got them a little house in Mapleton. Of course I wish they would of stayed here with us but Wiley seems to be showing his age a whole lot more than I am and I guess having the kiddies around twenty-four hours a day would get on his nerves, etc., etc. I try to get over there three or four times a week, though, as the kids need to see their Grandma and Glorene of course needs all the help and moral support she can get. Thank heavens she doesn't have to put up with those two of Harlow's any more. I wish all of you could see Glorene's four though, every one of them just as pretty as a picture. The oldest two put me in mind so much of Glorene herself when she was their age. Of course, she hasn't changed a whole lot herself. Janeice is the babysitter now, already thirteen and going to be just like her mother. And little Patsy Ann, such a doll, is becoming quite the little lady. Now it's little Kimberly who's the thumbsucker, Patsy Ann's just about given it up, and little bitty Jared has got the cutest set of curls you've ever seen. I hope she never has to cut his hair, he puts me in mind less of Harlow (thank heavens) than of how little Roy Dell Jr. used to look before they cut off all his hair and he started traipsing off to the ends of the earth so we hardly ever see them at all. RoZann seems to be taking after them, she's got her a job as a stewardess and seems to fly everywhere you can think of but Eureka.

Well, hope your year has been a little cheerier than ours, although things are looking a whole lot brighter now that I've got Glorene close to us here. Harlow still gives her a lot of trouble, he's worse than Norland for that, but if I have my way, he won't get within a mile of her or those kids. Glorene still feels kind of blue once in a while, but

I tell her, looking as young and cute as she still does, it won't be long before someone falls for her, I just know it. She's had a couple of raw deals but we're still in there rooting for her.

Until next year,
The Lowders of Eureka
Dolpha,
Glorene,
and Wiley

FRIENDS AND LOVED ONES FAR AND NEAR: 1976

As we stand on the brink of this promising new year, we look back with thanksgiving in our hearts for the multitude of blessings that have been ours, not the least of which is the wonderful kinship and friendship we share with so many dear friends and loved ones so frequent in our thoughts and so close to our hearts though, in most cases, so very far away.

The blessings and responsibilities of the Shelmans continue to increase as our family begins to branch out and grow, for KaeLynn is now Mrs. N. J. Marchant (pronounced Mar-*shawnt*) of Seattle, Washington, where her husband is vice-president of Miller-Marchant Associates. Maccine is looking forward to visiting the Marchants in their lovely new home in the very near future.

Jolene, as busy as ever, is faced with the dilemma of going on to college to become a fashion design expert or choosing one of several other . . . equally attractive . . . alternatives.

Kevin is all teenager, a real thinker, with a mind of his own, forever a joy whenever he is present.

Our lives continue to be rich and full, always a challenge. This has been such an eventful year in the Shelman household, LeMoine forever seeking new opportunities and Maccine busier than ever at home and working on various projects.

May we impress upon you our sincere best wishes for the coming year. Our lives would be so empty without the many dear and cherished friendships which so enrich our daily lives despite the miles that separate us. Season's greeting to one and all from
The Shelmans

Dorothy M. Keddington is the author of four best-selling romantic-suspense novels: Jayhawk, Return to Red Castle, Shadow Song, *and* Flower of the Winds. *A fifth novel,* The Mermaid's Purse, *is currently in progress. The novels are equally popular with teens and adults and have received praise for their lifelike characterization, vivid, sensory descriptions and meticulous research. In addition to her novels, Mrs. Keddington has written a screenplay of* Shadow Song, *and a full-length musical play,* The Twelve Dancing Princesses, *which she co-authored with daughters Laura and Stephanie. Mrs. Keddington has taught creative writing and novel writing both privately and in community schools. She is also a popular lecturer for civic, religious, cultural and educational groups. Dorothy attended the University of Utah where she majored in English and minored in music. She and her scholar-teacher husband, Michael, are parents of six children; two daughters and four sons. The characters that appear in this story are taken from* Flower of the Winds.

SERGEI'S FIRST CHRISTMAS

by Dorothy M. Keddington

Sergei Alexandrov sat in his living room at one in the morning, frowning at the Christmas tree. Strings of multi-colored lights wove a shining path through the needled branches, lending a magical glow to the otherwise dark room. Festive symbols of the season surrounded him on every side—bayberry candles and garlands of holly, mistletoe, whimsical elves and a ceramic Santa with a sack of toys.

Sergei's fingers tapped a frustrated rhythm on the arm of the sofa. He felt as if he were waiting for something to happen, but he wasn't sure what. A feeling maybe. Or some kind of realization. Surely there ought to be something inside to let him know this holiday had meaning.

Although he would never admit it to Cassandra, his wife, Sergei was a little confused and disappointed in the holiday Americans made so much of. He found no fault with its pleasant traditions. Purchasing and decorating the Christmas tree had proved to be very enjoyable. Seeing the sparkle in Cassandra's green eyes, the radiance of her smile and the new roundness of her shape where their child was growing, filled him with contentment and awe. But the source of these feelings was the overwhelming love he felt for her, rather than the season.

The past thirty years of Sergei's life had been spent in the Soviet Union, so sleigh bells and snow were no novelty to him. Neither were candles in the window. Even Santa Claus seemed vaguely familiar, a chubbier version of the Russian "Father Frost," who also brought gifts.

Sergei's dark eyes shifted to the base of the Christmas tree where a small avalanche of gaily-wrapped packages awaited the coming of morning. A rueful smile played about his mouth when he considered the staggering sum of money he had spent on gifts for his wife. Those clever capitalists made it quite painless. A small plastic card and his signature were the only requirements. The real difficulty lay in deciding what to buy.

He and Cassandra had done most of the shopping together, but he'd wanted her gifts to be a surprise. Like a lost child looking for its mother, Sergei had wandered through the stores of a large shopping mall, wondering how on earth he would ever make his choice from such an endless selection. Then he discovered the art store and some fine camel hair brushes for her painting. In a small shop carrying import goods, he was amazed to find a set of Russian nesting dolls. Next, he'd seen a pair of jade earrings that matched the color of Cassandra's eyes. Sergei was so delighted, he hadn't bothered looking at the price. As the clerk rang up the purchase, he experienced a sick moment of panic, but the feeling dissipated when he imagined how beautiful his *Kasenya* would look wearing the earrings. Picking out maternity clothes had given him some unsettling moments until a smiling, gray-haired woman with the name badge "Peggy" offered to assist him. Peggy called Sergei "honey" and "dear," and seemed to know exactly what his wife would need and want. He left the store an hour later, loaded with packages and maternal advice. By that time, Sergei was so proud of his excellent choices, he couldn't resist buying a gigantic toy dolphin, even though the baby wasn't due for another three months. Other children might have teddy bears, but the son of an oceanographer deserved a dolphin. Sergei was on his way out of the toy store when the thought struck him their baby might be a girl. To allow for that possibility, he went back and bought a furry pink kitten with china blue eyes.

Weary but satisfied, Sergei sat on a mall bench observing the long line of parents and children waiting for a brief interview with Santa.

He listened with interest to various requests for dolls, bicycles, video games, and a multitude of other toys. Beads of perspiration gleamed on the forehead of the white-bearded man, yet he continued to chuckle and smile as child after child took a turn. It was a harmless enough ritual, Sergei decided, yet he couldn't dismiss the feeling that some element was missing from this holiday scene. His glance passed over a store window lavishly decorated with gold ornaments, red velvet bows and poinsettias. In another, mechanical elves grinned at him from a forest of plastic snow and artificial Christmas trees.

A strange sadness washed over Sergei as he stared at the animated scene. Was Christmas nothing more than a fairy-tale? he wondered.

The same thought troubled him now. If Christmas were truly a religious holiday, why couldn't he find any evidence of religion in the way it was celebrated? It seemed inconceivable to him, and sadly ironic. Especially, in a country which took such pride in granting its citizens religious freedom.

A childhood memory suddenly stirred his thoughts, and Sergei saw his mother in her one good dress, pulling on sweater and coat, fur-lined gloves, a woollen scarf and ugly black boots in preparation for the solitary walk to attend church services on Christmas morning. The distance from their apartment to the old onion-domed church was more than two miles, yet his mother never uttered a word of complaint. And always, when she returned, cheeks and nose red from the bitter cold, there was a certain look in her eyes. Sergei was curious and eager to experience whatever it might be that gave his mother *that look*. One year Sergei had asked if he could go, too, but his father had denied him permission. "It wouldn't look right, Seriozha," he'd been told, the affectionate nickname failing to soften his father's stern words. "I am *partinii*—a party member. If someone should see you, there could be trouble—for all of us."

His mother remained silent, but there had been sadness in her eyes. He hadn't asked again.

Sergei leaned against the sofa cushions with a sigh, trying to ignore the familiar ache inside which came whenever he allowed himself to think of home. Most of the time, he had only to remind himself how good his new life was for the ache to go away. He adored his wife. He had the security of employment and a comfortable home. And no matter how strange some of its customs might be, Sergei felt a deep, abiding gratitude toward his newly-adopted country.

But tonight, the ache persisted. He wished he could talk with his mother. There was so much he wanted to ask and understand. About Christmas . . . about God. In spite of an atheistic education in a communist society, Sergei had come to the private conclusion that he believed in a power higher than himself. For years, necessity dictated this belief should remain unspoken. Now, he longed to give voice to the feelings of his soul. But his mother, along with the rest of his family, was thousands of miles away, part of the old life and old ways he would never see again.

Sergei wiped a frustrated hand over his eyes, weary of the conflict within him. Was Christmas only a pleasant tradition—a yearly excuse to give gifts and visit family and friends? Probably, he was expecting too much.

Sergei determined that when dawn came, he would somehow conceal his disappointment from his wife. She had worked so hard to please him, knowing this would be his first Christmas. It wasn't her fault he felt so empty.

"Seriozha?"

Cassandra's voice rescued him from his thoughts, and he turned to see her standing in the doorway of the living room. She was dressed in a soft flannel nightgown, with her long hair falling about her shoulders. Sergei was silently amazed at his wife's beauty. The glow of the Christmas lights seemed to cast an unearthly aura about her face.

"Are you coming to bed?" she asked. "It's awfully late . . ."

"I thought you were asleep," he said, not answering her question.

"The baby got me up," she replied with a sleepy smile, padding barefoot across the floor to join him in front of the fireplace. "Are you all right, *dushenka*?"

"Fine. Just my nightly visit to the bathroom."

Instead of sitting beside him, Cassandra curled up at Sergei's feet and laid her head across his knee. His hand sought and found the softness of her hair.

"Mmm. The tree looks so pretty." Contentment purred in her voice.

He only nodded, not trusting himself to speak for fear his earlier thoughts might somehow be communicated to her.

"What time is it?" she asked, after a moment.

"A little after one."

She lifted her head to give him a warm smile. "It's Christmas . . . our first Christmas!"

The love and wonder in her eyes made him feel ashamed.

"I want you to open one of your presents," she went on, getting to her feet and going to the tree.

"Now? But I thought you told me it is imperative we should wait until morning."

Cassandra laughed and impulsively searched through the presents until she found what she was looking for . . . a squarish box with a gold bow. She presented it to him with a kiss and soft, "Merry Christmas, Seriozha."

Feeling foolish, Sergei struggled with the ribbon and the wrappings, then lifted the lid of the box. Words failed him as he stared at the black, leather-bound book inside. He removed it carefully, then ran his fingers across the smooth cover.

"I've thought and thought about what to give you," his wife said. "And then I realized what I really wanted to give you for Christmas was . . . Christmas . . . the first Christmas."

"I have never owned a Bible," Sergei admitted, his voice stunned. "A real English Bible . . ."

"I couldn't find one in Russian. I hope you don't mind . . . I mean, I hope it's all right."

Sergei stopped staring at the book to kiss his wife. "*Spaceba, dushenka.* Such a gift . . ." He shook his head, struggling to find the words. "It puts to shame those things I purchased for you."

Her smile held a large portion of relief. "I'm so glad you're pleased. I wasn't sure what you'd think . . ."

"My grandmother owned a Bible," Sergei told her. "It was one of her most valued possessions—as this shall be for me."

Cassandra moved the wrapping paper and ribbons aside, then snuggled close to her husband. "Would you do something for me? . . ." she asked, then went on before he could answer. "Would you read the Christmas story?"

Sergei shrugged, feeling hesitant and unsure, yet knowing he could deny her nothing. "If it pleases you."

She smiled and nodded.

"Where do I find it?"

"In Luke . . ." Cassandra opened the Bible and searched through its thin pages. "Here it is."

Sergei glanced down at the black print. His throat was dry and his heart was hammering inside his chest. The habit of years suddenly seized him and he felt as if he were about to partake of something forbidden.

"The main story begins in chapter two," she said, giving his hand an encouraging squeeze.

"It seems an odd thing to start in the second chapter of the book," Sergei mumbled and turned back a page. "I will begin with the first."

He had thought the English words would sound strange and lose their meaning, but their beauty pierced his heart. *Fear not . . . for thou hast found favor with God . . . . for he that is mighty has done to me great things . . . and his mercy is on them that fear him from generation to generation . . . . to give light to them that sit in darkness . . . to guide our feet into the way of peace. . . .*

Understanding flooded his soul. That's why she'd walked those miles. God was guiding his mother's feet . . . giving her His light. His peace. That's what he'd seen in her eyes . . . .

Sergei stopped reading to gaze at his wife. Something was happening inside that was totally new to him, yet strangely familiar. Cassandra's shining, tear-filled eyes said she understood.

His voice trembled as he began to read once more. The emptiness inside his soul was gone, filled by the words of the ancient physician: *. . . For unto you is born this day in the city of David a Saviour, which is Christ the Lord.*

Phyllis Barber has published five books, the most recent of which are And The Desert Shall Blossom *(a novel) and* Legs: The Story of a Giraffe *(a juvenile book). In 1991, she received the Associated Writing Program Award Series Prize in Creative Nonfiction for* How I Got Cultured: A Nevada Memoir, *which is forthcoming from the University of Georgia Press in 1992. She is one of the founders of the Writers at Work Conference held in Park City, Utah, every June; a faculty member of the Vermont College MFA in Writing Program (a low-residency program); and she currently lives with her husband and three sons in Colorado. (This story will be published in a different form in* How I Got Cultured: A Nevada Memoir, *by The University of Georgia Press.)*

CHRISTMAS STORIES

by Phyllis Barber

Zip and Vernon's Famous Story

When relatives gathered on Christmas night at our two-story house facing hills of sand instead of drifts of snow, my father and his brother, Zip, never failed us.

Ritual was the first order of business, however. We had to pray over the food on our buffet table before we scooped and plucked and mathematically figured how to fill a plate to capacity. The children found places to sit cross-legged on the floor, the adults on the sofa or a kitchen chair brought into the living room. Everyone balanced clear-glass hostess plates on their laps, careful not to spill the raspberry punch or topple quivering jello salad and stacks of sliced ham, roast beef, and cheese arranged between halves of Mother's feather-light rolls.

"Vernon, you lucky dog," Zip said. "How did you ever find this woman who could produce such beautiful food!"

"Vernon's not a dog," my mother said from across the room, her literal mind offended.

"This food is good," Aunt Mindy agreed and pressed her lips together as if she hadn't put enough lipstick on the upper lip and was making last-minute repairs. "That's the one thing Zenna sure knows how to do."

Mother looked half pleased, then half hurt. She was constantly wary of Mindy's tongue, and at the moment seemed busy interpreting her words. Had she said my mother only knew how to do one thing, nothing else?

"True enough," said Uncle Jackson, whose only entree into Christmas night conversations was to express his appreciation for Mother's cooking. The rest of the time, he stayed tight by his wife Roma's side.

At the back of this small talk was a sense the evening would soon light up. After the dirty plates were collected and Mother's candy was set out in cut-glass dishes, the uncles loosened their belt buckles one notch, and everyone waited for Zip and Vernon to begin.

"Well, you know," Uncle Zip began, "we weren't always perfect." Everyone laughed, no matter how many times they'd heard him use that line for openers, and everyone settled back in their seats, comforted that the Christmas night story was coming and that things never changed.

Sitting on the floor with my cousins, I leaned against the sofa's seat cushions between Uncle Zip and Aunt Mindy's legs, also content to know I was about to hear the famous tale of my father and Uncle Zip almost blowing up the side of a mountain in Ruth, Nevada.

"We'd fallen in with a ring of thieves," Zip said, "something like Ali Baba. You know that story, don't you?"

"They were the same boys we played with every day, actually," my father, an honest man, said. "I was the smallest one," he continued. "Those big boys lifted me up and pushed me through the window of the munitions shed on the side of the mountain. 'It's in the box with three Xs,' they said as they pushed me into that dark, spider-infested shed. 'Don't throw it out, though, just hand it to us.'

"I fumbled around until my eyes adjusted to the dusky light and then saw those three big Xs staring back at me like a poison label on a pharmacy bottle. I pulled the screwdriver out of my back pocket and wedged the lid open. The dynamite looked like cardboard-covered candles with wicks—a thousand of them, it seemed. 'Hurry up,' I heard them whispering like hoarse coyotes.

"I stood on my tiptoes to pass the dynamite over the ledge, then realized I was too short to pull myself up and over the window. 'Get me outta here,' I yelled. They told me to shut up quick, then yanked on my arms and dragged me over that ledge. If I think about it much,

I can still feel the pains in my stomach where those splinters scraped my skin."

"And then," Uncle Zip, the relay runner standing ready with an open mouth, lifted the baton from my father's hand. "We crawled up over rocks, almost losing our footing, almost sliding back down the hill on that loose gravel, but we were like lizards, our bellies scraping over boulders and brambles. Sweat running down our faces, mixing with the dust so close to our noses."

"It was Don Belknap who set the cap and blew the fuse," my father retrieved the telling. "He was the biggest one of all of us, eighteen, which meant he got sent to prison, to reform school. You should have seen the people burst out of those houses below us when they were suddenly besieged with those rolling rocks and clouds of dust."

"Boulders," Zip said, lifting his arms to recapture the story again. "Gigantic boulders rolling down toward Ruth, gaining speed. I never in my life wanted so much to be an eagle so I could fly to some crevice to hide deep down inside where no one could see me. Boy, were those people mad. One man even ran outside with a gun."

"A gun?" Aunt Mindy said, slapping her knees so heartily I felt a breeze on my neck. "That's a new twist. But then, you two have to have at least one new twist every year. Right, Zip?"

Zip ignored Mindy. "Damn rights," he said. "I just never mentioned it before."

"I don't remember that part either." My father folded his arms and looked sideways at Zip.

"Well," Zip said, sliding to the front of the sofa cushions, leaning further into the story, not looking at my father, "I do. You must not have noticed it in all the excitement. The sheriff and some men of the town came roaring up that hill like bulls in a fury. They picked us up by the back of the pants and carried us under their arms like we were Christmas hams."

"You're Christmas hams all right," Aunt Mindy said, and I turned to watch her throw her brightly painted face back to laugh. I laughed, too, always happy for an opportunity to laugh with the irreverent Aunt Mindy who opened forbidden doors. So did my cousins and Uncle Jackson.

"My stomach was still hurting from the window ledge," my father said, interrupting our laughter too soon. "When I got picked up and carried by my belt, I thought I might die right then and there."

"And you should have seen our dad when we arrived home," Zip said. "Grandpa to you nieces and nephews. He was a picture of the Black Death—black in the face, unbuckling his belt to take us out to the chicken yard where we stacked wood. He must have lashed me with that belt over fifty times. He was one mad José."

"You sure about that?" Mindy asked. "Your numbers seem different every year."

"Well, maybe not quite that many." Zip frowned.

"Maybe two or three?" My father smiled a cat-got-a-mouse smile.

"They were going to send me up," Zip slid away from any answers, "but Mother pleaded with the judge. She told him she'd make us do dishes for a year and feed those stupid chickens who smothered each other when they got too cold and tried to keep warm. She never let us forget our crime, kept telling us how lucky we were to be at home and not in some wild animal cage with iron bars on the windows."

"They didn't consider me a candidate," my father said, snatching a piece of peanut brittle from the bowl on the coffee table. "Lucky for me, I was too young."

"Well, I was sure in big trouble there for a while," Zip said. "Lucky Mother had such a convincing way with the law."

For a moment, I thought I heard some unlikely emotion in Zip's voice, but then, both my father and Zip grabbed handfuls of Mother's fruitcake, toffee, and peanut brittle. I stretched forward to the same plate and pinched a slab of fruitcake with the most gumdrops visible—yellow, orange, green, and red all together in the same piece. My lucky night. Everyone else followed suit, and we sat in a momentary lull, listening to the sound of teeth crunching candy.

Sitting quietly between Aunt Mindy and Uncle Zip's legs, I was wishing we could go back inside the story and that the story would go on and on and never end because when it ended, we were all the same people sitting in the same squared-off, tiny living room with the tall metal gas heater crowding the space. We were something different inside a story; we had possibilities other than the ones in this yellow plastered room. And I wondered if some of the other relatives were wishing the story would end, just for once, with as big a bang as it started.

Every year I kept hoping everyone except Zip would be quiet. Then the story could really become a story, and something more awful or miraculous could happen to Zip and my father in Ruth, Nevada, just once. Maybe they'd have to go to reform school where they'd be forced to eat thin gruel for breakfast and dig up old highways with pickaxes. Or maybe a gigantic boulder would be rolling perilously close to a house in Ruth, Nevada, and an angel with wings would appear out of nowhere and lift the boulder into the air in the nick of time.

But even with the same, anticlimactic ending, there was something soothing about the story, maybe because it was always the same with a few minor variations. Maybe everyone was relieved the story wasn't worse and the law had been merciful to two men we loved.

"Wouldn't be Christmas without your candy," Uncle Zip told my mother when he stood up to pass the caramels to the cousins who couldn't reach the coffee table without social embarrassment. "Wouldn't be Christmas at all."

"Wouldn't be Christmas without your stories," my mother told him as he leaned down to buss her on the cheek.

Aunt Roma's Story, Almost

Next on the Christmas night program, Aunt Roma took her turn to tell her favorite story—the one about the flatcar. Once on a Christmas Eve, it was pulled by a hissing steam engine into the town of Ruth on frost-covered tracks.

Aunt Roma always looked sad, as if she lived in a bleached seashell with only the echo of the living ocean. Something about her had crawled away and left her to fend for herself. She seemed permanently faded except for the vivid moisture in her hazel eyes when a tender memory was evoked. Even her laughter on Christmas night was often muddied by what sounded like tears in her throat. The relatives said she was just like her mother.

"The flatcar was piled with burlap sacks filled with oranges," she said, patting her husband Jackson on the knee as if his presence made the world a safe place. "Kennecott brought them in for the children of the miners, accountants, truck drivers, secretaries, and foremen who worked for the copper mine. Riding beside these bulging bags of oranges that year was the biggest, fattest, roundest Santa Claus I ever saw. Not like your department store Santas today." She paused to swallow and pull her handkerchief out of her small purse. "He tossed those oranges through the air, and we all caught them. There was a shower of oranges like we were standing under a giant tree dropping everything in its branches on our heads."

"We rarely saw oranges in those days," my father said, his pale blue eyes looking as if they could see the fruit at that very moment. "Catching an orange was almost as good as the silver dollar I got once. Do you have any idea how much a silver dollar could buy in those days?"

"Vernon," my mother whispered behind the shield of her hand. "It's Roma's turn."

"And, I'll never forget," Roma said, looking at the ceiling as if it were a movie screen reflecting the past. "That Santa Claus pulled me up to the top of the flatcar. I reached out to him, and he grabbed my hands and pulled me up beside him. He said I was the prettiest little girl he'd ever seen." She dabbed at a sliding tear on her nose. "And he slipped a quarter into my hand and whispered for me not to tell anyone. I never felt richer in my whole life."

Roma's voice broke. The tears came. No one knew what to do or how much attention Roma needed or didn't need at that moment.

"Well," my father said carefully, "do you remember that time I came home with a silver dollar?"

Roma shook her head yes and blew her nose. I watched Mother bump her knee against my father's. "Not now," she whispered.

"Roma won't be able to talk for a few minutes," I heard him whisper back. "Maybe you kids don't know this," he said to the children seated on the floor, "but I used to deliver papers when I was your age." He focused his eyes intently on one particular cousin to avoid his wife, who was still Roma's champion.

"One year I delivered up in Ely's Red Light District." His face turned bright with the words. "The Red Light District," he said confidentially, "is the place where ladies of the night live and conduct their business." He smiled out of one side of his mouth so Mother could see he was aware of the children's sensibilities.

"What are ladies of the night?" a cousin asked.

"Ah," he said, "they were dancers and entertainers who painted their faces, poked feathers in their hair, and dazzled the eye. They were the most generous customers I ever had."

"They're down and out whores," Aunt Mindy whispered loudly enough to Zip that I could hear. "Why does Vernon always tell this story? Poor Zenna. Look at her over there wishing she could change the subject."

I heard the emotion creeping into my father's voice, the emotion so easy to touch, so close to the surface in both Roma and him. I could feel it rising, feelings as much a part of the Moore heredity as our noses, pale eyes, or bone structure.

"She was probably trying to drum up future business," Uncle Zip guffawed. "Was she successful?" Zip winked. The adults laughed, except for my mother. I looked down at Aunt Mindy's red-patent shoes with red-patent bows clipped to the toes. Her feet were squirming inside the shoes as if she were preparing another Aunt Mindy comment which was usually a cross between a pygmy's poison arrow and a court jester's quip. For once, I hoped she'd keep her own counsel.

"Don't ruin this for me, brother," my father said without looking at Zip or my mother, or any of us, really.

"Around Christmas, these ladies seemed to know it wasn't too easy being a newspaper boy 365 days of the year in the mud, rain, and snow when you're only eight years old. One of the older women, her name was Francy, drew moles on her cheek and extended her eyebrows with a pencil; she slipped me a silver dollar one snowy day when I was collecting. Do you have any idea how much money that was then? A silver dollar? And she told me I was the nicest newsboy she ever had, stroked my chin with the feather in her hand, and said why didn't I buy a present for my mother and myself, but mostly for myself? She wore a softly woven shawl over a violet satin dress. She had the prettiest eyes. Heavy dark eyebrows. Violet eyes like her dress. Never saw any like them before or since."

My father suddenly looked like a small boy sitting by himself in this crowd of relatives. He was shivering in the icy wind of a high mountain mining town, trying to gather the courage to call out to passersby, "Paper?" The small boy was unnoticed because he was uncertain, not knowing whether or not to apologize for standing there in the cold asking for pennies to take home to his mother.

"Those women were angels," he said, still holding his finger in the air, which meant he had a bit more story to tell. But he paused, unable to overcome the feelings playing havoc with his narrative.

I felt the sympathy rising in me, the quick water in my eyes, for the sense of a powerful gift given my father. I only knew my school teachers, Dr. Jones's nurse, the sisters in the Relief Society. They didn't paint their faces much; they wore simple clothes and no feathers. They helped when a woman in the ward had a new baby or there was death or illness in the family.

Ladies of the night: "whores," Aunt Mindy called them; "angels," my father called them. Whoever they were, they seemed to nurture during the hours their sisters rested from the cares of the day. They looked after my father, who'd moved from town to town every year of his life, and sold papers to buy shoes because his father kept stumbling home at night, asking for someone to help him find his bed and the money he'd meant to bring his wife. But those were stories from other occasions, not Christmas night.

"Whenever kindness is present," my father finally said as he wiped his eyelashes with one finger and uttered the last sentence of his story, "God is there, too."

Al Jolson Saves the Day Story

"Just how many schools did you attend?" Aunt Mindy asked my father as she passed him the caramels my mother had boiled to soft-ball stage, cooled, and wrapped in plastic. "I never can get that straight because it seems like you Moores were forever moving around."

When Aunt Mindy wasn't talking about her daughters, she was subtly scratching the paint on the Moore family image. She always did it with charm, adept at hiding her frustration with her in-laws and her husband, Zip. She both loved and loathed this man she couldn't shape into the right mold, the same one who happened to be a part of this Moore clan, no proud clan as far as Mindy could tell.

"Well, I think," my father said, "let me see. One, two, three . . . maybe eight elementary schools and five high schools."

"No wonder you Moores are such a crazy bunch," Aunt Mindy said, charming most of the children with her laughter, her smile, the things she could get away with.

"Dad believed the next bend in the road was the perfect place to stop," Aunt Roma said with charity in her voice. She was sitting even closer to Uncle Jackson, her hand laced into his even though he seemed to be counting the minutes until he could say good-night gracefully.

"We saw a lot of living," Zip said, leaning back on the legs of the kitchen chair, patting his stomach with both hands. "We met lots of people from San Diego to Salt Lake City to Brigham City, Utah, where we returned four different times; then there was Nevada—Ely and Ruth, and then Idaho."

"We lived in a warehouse once." Roma looked up at the ceiling again, and I saw Jackson squeezing her hand and patting her wrist.

"Just for a short time," my father defended as he sat up straight in his chair. "In Ely. We were waiting for a company house to become available."

"We always had lots of friends," Zip said. "Hundreds of friends everywhere we moved. And our family was close. We loved each other. Poor little Mother had a hard time of it, but she loved us more than her own skin. We'd do anything for each other, I swear we would. And we always had a good time laughing, making up jokes, playing pranks on each other. Anybody want some gum?" he asked, pulling the tab on the package and taking a piece for himself. "I brought a giant pack tonight for anyone who wants some. You pass it around, Ed," he told my brother, "and everyone give him your wrappers so Aunt Zenna won't have a big mess to clean up."

"Remember Birgette?" Roma's eyes brightened for the first time that evening while the package of gum made the rounds. "The way she'd go out in the streets and do impromptu music theater on the sidewalks? Remember how she sang 'Swanee' better than Al Jolson? Remember how she'd tap dance through a crowd of miners until one of them handed her a nickel or a dime? She never asked for money, but they gave it to her. Birge. I wish she were here now. Little Birge. Why won't she come spend Christmas with us?"

Sometimes I thought Roma's tears waited just under her eyelids, waiting only for the next tender moment to show themselves. I never ceased to be fascinated by her eyes—pale, hazel, almost faded as if the sun had stolen the color from them. Roma's eyes were full of some unnameable sorrow, some regret that could never be satisfied, some hole in the middle of her somewhere.

My father and Roma had inherited their mother's eyes. I'd seen pictures of Grandma. Pale, pale eyes. Too much flooding, too many tears. Zip's eyes weren't pale, though. They were snapping brown, swarthy, desert eyes like his father's. He seemed tougher than Vernon or Roma. Maybe his eyes made him stronger and more vital.

"Will somebody sing 'Swanee'?" Aunt Roma asked. "Does anybody know it? Julia, can you play it on the piano?"

I shrugged my shoulders. None of my piano teachers had taught me "Swanee," although all of us children except for Kathy could sing, "Swanee, Swanee, *how* I love you, *how* I love you," in the Al Jolson way, emphasizing the "how," shaking our palms every time we sang it. Our father taught us that much one evening after we finished dinner and he had no appointments to keep.

"My dad can sing 'Swanee,'" I said, curling one strand of hair on my finger mischievously.

"Yeah, Vernon," everyone clapped. "Let's hear it from Vernon," Zip shouted, chewing his fresh piece of Wrigley's rapidly on one side of his mouth.

My father didn't need much encouragement. He and Zip could be talked into performing any place, any time. "A family disease," Aunt Mindy called it. "You'd think they were good or something."

My father sank to his knees and walked on them to the middle of the room. "I hate to make Al Jolson look bad," he said, "but all idols have clay feet. Right?" Then he clasped his hands in the middle of his chest and put pleading into his arms and face. "Swa-nee. Swa-nee," he talked rather than sang, changing his clasped hands from one side to the other, convincing his audience he loved dear old Swanee. "*How* I love you, *how* I love you . . ."

I looked up at Aunt Roma, mouthing the words with my father, her face shining with wetness. Then she covered her mouth with her handkerchief and placed her other hand over her neck to disguise the sobs pulsing against her throat and chest.

Then Zip stood up and fanned his hands out wide. "If only I had those white gloves Jolson wore," he said. Then the two brothers sang the words, "My dear old Swa-nee," together. All the children jumped up from their places on the floor and mashed into the two uncles, jumping, hopping, skipping, singing, "Swa-nee, Swa-nee," until everything got rowdy and one of the cousins knocked over a chair, and my mother said, "Oh no, you've put a hole in the plaster," and everybody began talking all at once until it seemed as if it was time to go.

The King of Stories

The doorbell rang. Everyone was surprised because the Christmas night party at Vernon and Zenna's was almost over. The clock said nine-thirty. Consensus had been growing that it was time for everyone to be getting home and let the curtain drop on Christmas for yet another year.

When the doorbell rang, my father opened the door, and the king of stories came into the living room like a prince, a duke, a man of royal blood: my grandfather in a rare appearance.

He hadn't brought his new wife, Marian. She'd been waiting a long time for him, pursuing Grandpa when Grandma was still in place. Marian was convinced Grandpa needed her and only her, and she'd finally captured him. But Roma, Vernon, and Zip weren't ready to forget the woman who'd mothered them, changed their diapers, taught them to tie shoes. They wanted Christmas to resurrect their mother's laughter, even if it had been bittersweet. They wanted the memory of their mother's eyes even if they had to look at Roma's eyes to be reminded—those uncertain windows unable to hide her hesitation or her apology for taking up space on earth.

So Grandpa came alone.

"We were wrapping things up," my father said, "but there's still some of Zenna's candy left."

"Just as well," Grandpa said. "I can't stay for long. I left Marian alone."

He was a little man, squat in some ways, not in others. Sometimes he seemed imperious, as if he'd been crowned king once upon a time. At other times he seemed to be running after the crown that had rolled off his head one day. Without his crown, he was a commoner. But even though he never found it, he didn't shed his courtly ways or forget he was king of stories. He could shine the inside of a story into pure gold.

"Always a story," my mother said in disgust because of the way Grandpa didn't pay much mind to his first wife, who'd been sick with melancholia, the way he'd stay out late at night drinking, telling stories to people too drunk to care. "Always a story," about where he'd been and what he'd been doing when he explained to his wife at 2:00 a.m. One story built upon another, a house of stories upon stories, floor after floor, stacks of stories, and who could ever tell where the truth was in all that flurry of stories?

Aunt Roma and Uncle Jackson scooted over from their places on the sofa. "Sit here, Dad," Roma said, patting the cushion. "How's my little daddy?" She squeezed his bicep as he sat down and then rested her head on his shoulder for a brief second.

"Fine as things will allow," he said, straightening the knees of his trousers, but then he was back up again, center floor. "Children," he said. "Do you want me to tell you about the time I was selling eggs and had to balance my way across a railroad trestle? Or do you want me to tell you about my favorite chicken who fell down the outhouse hole and squawked like a mighty condor until . . ."

"What about the one about the cow that showed up out of nowhere?" my mother said.

"Well, all right," Grandpa said. "If you insist." He cleared his throat and held up his hands as if he were preparing to conduct his audience. Then he closed his eyes for a minute to concentrate before he began with words.

All of us children were looking up at the man standing in the middle of the floor on the beige sculptured carpet. He seemed to have a glow on him, almost as if emanating from a portable spotlight he carried with him for occasions such as this. He was a man who'd seen the world and lived to tell about it; he was a mystery man we'd heard about in whispers—a man who bought a new car when he hadn't paid for the one he had, a man who had enemies because they owed him money, a man who came home late at night and made our grandmother cry. We'd heard the whispers.

"He acts like he's been drinking again," Mindy whispered to Zip as she tapped her right foot close to my knee. They forgot me sitting at their feet, privy to their clandestine commentary. "He never shows up on Christmas night. What's he doing here now?"

"Shhh," Zip said. "He's ready."

Grandpa stood in the middle of our living room as if he were a treasure to be revered and appreciated, a wild turkey spreading its tail, a man alive because he had an audience to validate him, say "Yes, yes, you are the king." Still looking for his crown.

"As you children know," he began, his eyes still closed, "we never had much money when I was a little boy. There were eleven of us, not counting Mom and Dad."

"You sure you don't want to sit down, Fred?" my mother asked.

"No, no. I like to stand when I tell stories." His eyes were opening. "My mother was a real stickler for the church, you know. She followed every admonition given her by the authorities, one of them being tithing. My dad wasn't quite so attached to the principle, but he could see how upset she was when he told her they'd better not pay their tithing this one particular month. They didn't have it to pay.

"Well, as you might imagine, Mother went into a tailspin, crying like a reed pipe in the wind, wailing how the Lord would take care of them if only they had enough faith. Where was his faith? She was going to take their last money to the bishop then and there. Right that minute.

"My father could see she had her mind made up, so he said he'd walk with her over to the bishop's. They had nothing to lose, he guessed, except they wouldn't be able to feed their children now. He hadn't done well by them, he confessed as they walked.

"When they handed the bishop an envelope with the last of their money in it, they didn't say it was all they had. They paid as if this was the smallest pittance possible in their vast fortune raining down from heaven above. The bishop smiled and said, 'The windows of heaven shall open onto you. The sun will shine so bright you'll wish you had a windowshade to pull down. Bless you, my faithful brother and sister.'"

"Wasn't that just before his dad did himself in?" Mindy whispered more quietly than I'd ever heard anyone whisper and still hear it.

Grandpa pulled at his jaw, stopped to think about something, his mind stretching further out of the room than before. Roma's eyes were moist, as well as my father's. My mother looked at all the children, pleased we were all tuned in, rapt witnesses to this finer moment of our grandfather.

"Well, for two days we didn't have anything to eat. Mother was afraid to borrow from the neighbor again, so we chewed on the last of the wheat we'd stored in the basement. Chewed it like chewing gum. Speaking of gum, Zip, why do you chew it the way you do? It doesn't become you."

Zip was startled. I could feel his body react because I was leaning against the side of his leg. "Sorry, Dad." He pulled the gum out of his mouth and wrapped it in a corner of scratch paper he had in his shirt pocket.

"Just about the time our stomachs were gnawing like rats in an empty loft, this brown and white cow wanders up to our door. I mean up to our door, not into the yard. She walks up and talks to us with a long moo. No rope was hanging on her. She didn't look like any of the neighbors' cows. She was new to our eyes. We'd never seen her in anyone's pasture. And she was ready to milk. Full and tight, her teats spread out like swollen fingers.

"'Whose cow is that?' my mother asked.

"'Nobody's I know of,' my father said. 'Fred, you run around to all the neighbors in this part and ask if any of them are missing a cow.'

"Well, I ran as fast as wind around the neighborhood, then ran back to the house with the good news. And nobody came looking for that cow, either. Not one person. That cow was probably brought to our door by one of the Three Nephites. Led right to our door by the Lord's anointed."

He held his hand in the air with his last word. No one spoke while his hand stayed in the air, the fingers pointing upward in praise of God. He held us as if we were an orchestra whose strings he didn't want to stop vibrating. Then he closed his hand and thumped his heart once with his fist.

"And with that," he said after a slight pause, "I must go back home. I wish you all a happy new year. I wish you all faith. I wish you all peace. May one of the Nephites help you if you're in need and the angels smile upon you."

I hated the end of his story. He knew how to weave the words and his hands and his eyes together into the magic requisite for a tale. His story was the only one being told on earth while he told it. His was the last word.

Everyone broke into clusters, shaking hands, kissing cheeks, wishing "Merry Christmas" one last time before it was too late. I watched my mother put her arm around Grandpa. "Thank you for that beautiful story, Fred. You touch my heart every time you tell it. Thank you, and please tell Marian we missed her."

"Hypocrites," I heard Mindy whispering as she gathered her skirt to stand up and while her red patent shoes squeaked. I still sat on the floor with my back resting on the sofa's seat cushions. "Both Zenna and your dad. Can you believe she can say she missed Marian or that he can tell a story like that and not tell the whole story. Then he walks out of here and lives the way he does."

"Be quiet," Zip said. "Have a little respect for the man."

"Respect! Him?"

"He's my father."

"But he's so full of bull, even you say so."

"He's my father."

And Grandpa walked the full circle of relatives, saying good night to his children, then looking each of us grandchildren straight in the eyes and telling us to have faith like his mother had faith, then we'd be able to find the way.

"The windows of heaven will open for you," he said to me as he held my hand in his, not letting me act on the impulse to escape. "Everything will be given to you; all will be understood. You are a good girl, aren't you Julia? Obedient to God's and your parents' word, aren't you?"

I shook my head yes, trying not to show the shame I was feeling in this act of supposed affection between a grandfather everyone whispered about behind his back and his granddaughter who heard all the whispers. The words of his story, the whisperings I heard, Mindy's words, all were liquid in my head. What manner of man was standing before me? Whose hand did I hold? Which stories were the true stories?

Standing outside the stories, I could feel them colliding with each other. They tumbled from everyone's mouth and filled my ears until I was confused by them. But every time I was inside a story, there was no confusion, only the clarity of a tale spun and the sound of the spinning wheel.

So as I held my grandfather's hand, the only thing I could think to say was, "Will you come back sometime and tell us another story?"

"You like my stories?" he said.

"I do."

It was Christmas. All was calm, all was bright. The cardboard story of peace on earth was arranged on top of our Baldwin spinet—an awed Joseph, a round yon Virgin kneeling over the glow of her heavenly child.

Filled with this serenity, I smiled at my grandfather. I held his hand until we became another story, he and I. He was the king of stories, and now I was the queen at his side. My grandfather could be anything I wanted him to be. He was safe with his hand in mine.

Nancy Black is a relative newcomer to the LDS writing scene. Her first novel, entitled Gert Fram, *was published recently by Hatrack River Publications. "A Marshmallow Santa For the Newborn King" will be her second published work. Nancy lives in Garland, Texas with her husband, Mike, and their three daughters.*

A MARSHMALLOW SANTA FOR THE NEWBORN KING

by Nancy Black

Three Sundays before Christmas my husband, Ted, called a "family council meeting" to discuss finances. I told him there really wasn't anything to discuss since we didn't have any finances. He wasn't amused.

Christmas was coming fast and every year we went through the same routine. We'd shop a little, buy a little, charge a little. Then, as the big day got closer, we'd change our pace somewhat: shop a lot, buy a lot, charge a lot. It just didn't seem right though, that it took practically a whole year to pay for the toys, but only a week to break them.

"This year is going to be different," Ted lectured. "Money has been pretty tight these days, with the dog's retina surgery, Paula's pierced ear infection, Jeff's softball encounter with the Johnson's windows, not to mention just plain, old, ordinary overspending! I think it's time we all learned to be a little more thrifty."

He was doing great until he used the word "thrifty." The mere mention of the word drummed up images of desperate women fighting over blue-light specials and lugging around three-pound files of coupons in a broken-handled tote bag from the "as-is" department at D.I. I'd be wise and I'd be frugal, but never thrifty.

He went on to say that we could cut expenses everywhere possible, starting with the grocery bill, and explained how the neighbors would probably survive if the Wilson family stopped feeding them. It was one thing feeding our own four children, but we hardly needed to feed their friends and their friends' friends and their friends' friends' friends. He

281

also stressed how, during the holiday season, we needed to put less emphasis on acquiring things, and more emphasis on giving to others and being more thankful for the things we already have. The kids had their own version of that concept. They figured the more presents they had sitting under the tree, the more humbled and thankful they could be that they had been sent to a father with a good job.

Ted had a good point about the food, though. I had always wanted my children to be popular, but it was beginning to backfire on me. The kids had even given me my own joke: How many people does it take to feed a neighborhood? One, if she's as big a sucker as Sister Wilson. Oh well, I guess it could be worse. I could have the reputation of old Sister Hickenlooper, who was known to chase kids with a broom if they went anywhere near her begonias, and even refused to buy Girl Scout Cookies from sweet little Sally Jones. Now that's low.

After an hour and a half of lectures, questions, answers, more lectures, more questions and more answers, the family finally agreed on a battle plan. And, after a little negotiating, a lot of pleading, and one or two dramatic begs, it was decided that for Family Home Evening on Monday, the family would have one last fling at Albertson's before bravely subjecting ourselves to the Storehouse Market experience. The kids really deserved to win that one, considering how they had already made the supreme sacrifice of missing "T.V.'s Funniest Home Video's" (without complaint, even) due to the family council meeting.

On Monday night we all loaded into the van for our final visit to Albertson's before launching our "Tightwad Campaign" as we affectionately called it. The purpose for the outing was for each person to pick out one favorite, expensive food item that would never in a million years be found at Storehouse Market. For me the decision was easy: Grandma Tilley's Marshmallow Santas. Only the better grocery stores carried them, and I knew Storehouse Market didn't stand a chance. They were the most incredible things I had ever eaten in my life, and as they say, you get what you pay for. A box of eight cost around ten dollars, but they were worth every penny, not to mention every inch on the hips. I looked forward to the holidays all year round, just to stock up on them. My favorite time of the year used to be the Girls Scout Cookie drive, but after tasting Grandma Tilley's Marshmallow Santas, Thin Mints just didn't make the grade.

I know it sounds obsessive (and it probably was), but I normally bought them by the case. It took a little pondering, not to mention all my self control, but I finally decided that if everyone else in the family had to sacrifice, I needed to be the prime example. So I reached for one single, solitary box and clutched it to my bosom in fervent passion. Oh, the pain of being a parent.

Saving money is not one of my favorite things. In fact, up until the time Ted dropped the Tightwad Campaign on us, I had never given it much of a try. Who would have thought my emotional energy would be exhausted on such matters as which brand of peanut butter was cheaper per ounce, or which toilet paper had more sheets on a roll, or if Storehouse Market offered double coupons or not.

Ted could squeeze a quarter so hard the eagle belched, but I always thought that if I bought the most expensive brand of everything, I'd be doing what was best for my family. That's why I shuddered with each generic product I threw into my shopping cart. And threw them I did. In fact, I threw them hard. In my opinion, third-rate groceries shouldn't be regarded in any significant manner whatsoever. I couldn't look upon a no-name label with the same respect fitting Del Monte; it just wasn't in me.

Another big challenge was fixing low-budget meals that were also exciting. At the end of the first week of our war on spending, I went to serve dinner and suddenly realized everything was beige. How could six days of leftovers all turn out to be the same color? After only a week I was already losing my spark. I felt like a still-life painting; "Dinner in Beige," by Maggie Wilson. So I randomly tossed some cherry tomatoes around, just for color, and presented "Dinner in Beige Embellished With Red" to my family, who looked up at me in unison with all the enthusiasm of a pine cone.

By the time dinner was over and I had everything cleaned up and put away, I realized it was almost 8:30. That was the standard time of night my sweet tooth kicked in and I'd ransack the entire house in search of just the right snack to appease my insatiable urge to pig-out on junk. I stood helplessly at the door of the pantry, realizing how the sub-standard selection of munchies was almost as depressing as dinner itself. I stared blankly for a moment, and finally reached for a plain-label bag of gingersnaps.

As I munched away, I thought in disgust how generic cookies clearly didn't deserve the name "junk food." I longed for a Marshmallow Santa. The last precious box I bought earlier in the week hadn't lasted three days. So how was I supposed to get through the rest of the holiday season without them? I wasn't handling it well at all. The more I thought about Grandma Tilley's Marshmallow Santas, the more obsessed I became until I couldn't stand it any longer. So I made a decision. I used my free agency and made a deceitful, wicked decision that shocked even myself. I couldn't survive the holidays without Grandma Tilley's Marshmallow Santas; it just wasn't possible. It tore my soul from every angle until I finally had to clench my fists and grit my teeth. It was settled. On the morrow I would sneak off to Albertson's and fulfill my inner need.

The next morning I awoke with mixed feelings. Those of great anticipation, along with those of immense guilt. I tried to block out the latter by making myself busy doing piddly jobs around the house, but by lunchtime I couldn't stand it any longer. So I threw together some peanut butter and jelly sandwiches for the kids, put the twins, Patti and Paula, in charge of baking Christmas cookies all afternoon, and went on my way.

I was a basket case walking through Albertson's, hoping I wouldn't see anyone I knew. I was so nervous that I ran into an old man's cart, practically knocking him over, and scattering Bran Flakes all over the floor. I quickly apologized, then breathed a sigh of relief as I rounded the corner to the candy aisle. "My aisle" as I liked to call it.

I stifled a squeal of delight as I reached for a box of Grandma Tilley's Marshmallow Santas. As I turned to leave, the thought struck me that since I'd already committed the sin, I might as well get the most out of it so I grabbed three more boxes.

As I stood in the express line I couldn't help but watch my surroundings in paranoia as I waited my turn. I don't know what I expected to find. Possibly a private detective hiding behind the Alpo display? A doubtful probability, but still I was overwrought with anxiety as the clerk rang up my purchase. Thus, my unstable reaction when asked the inevitable question, "Paper or plastic?"

"I don't care!" I found myself screaming. "Just put it somewhere!"

Acne-scarred face and all, the bag-boy seemed sincerely concerned when he answered, "Is plastic okay?"

"Well I don't know," I said. "Why don't you ask it? Hello, plastic, are you okay?"

When I realized I was actually speaking to a plastic grocery bag, I knew I was over the edge. My composure was shot; an archival scrap. I gave the poor boy an apologetic gaze, grabbed my merchandise and hastily made my exit.

I stood outside for a moment with the nip in the air relieving my flushed cheeks. Then I shamefully looked down at my bag. I felt like a low-life; like dirt; like my next move should have been to knock over a fruit stand or something. There I was, standing in front of Albertson's, holding my plastic bag of iniquity and feeling like a low-down, filthy, rotten scum-raker. That is, until I got to the car and tore open one of Grandma Tilley's Marshmallow Santas. I consumed it in seconds flat, and then tore open another, then another, until I suddenly looked up and noticed the short, burly man pounding on my window and yelling at the top of his lungs. He wanted to know if my car was broken down or did I just want him to park clear at the back, walk across the icy parking lot, inevitably slip on his wingtip shoes, and die, leaving behind a pregnant wife and six children. It took a moment of thought, but I decided another Marshmallow Santa wasn't really worth the man's life, even if he did have on the ugliest, green paisley tie I'd ever laid eyes on.

I quickly pulled out, allowing him my front-row space, and sped off toward home pondering the critical nature of how those sweet, innocent Marshmallow Santas were obtained, but more importantly, trying to determine a place to hide them.

The last couple of weeks leading up to Christmas seemed to drag on forever. Maybe it had something to do with the secret I was harboring deep in my soul. I was keeping the proverbial Marshmallow Santas on the top shelf of my closet behind a stack of sweatshirts, thinking that would give me the freedom to escape into my room and sneak one or two at will. Boy, was I wrong. It seemed the harder I tried to make excuses to "go to my room for something and be out in a minute," the more reasons my children had for needing to talk to me right that second and following me wherever I went.

"Gee, Mom," Jeff remarked one afternoon. "You sure need to go to your room a lot these days."

"He's right," replied Paula. "What's the deal with you?"

As I stood there, dumbfounded, trying to think up a legitimate reason without actually lying to my children, I realized that that wasn't possible. The children noticed my dismay and suddenly my little Abby started jumping up and down, clapping her hands and squealing, "It's a surprise! A surprise for Christmas!"

"I'm afraid it isn't, Abby-buns," I humbly replied. (The nickname that she was stuck with dated back to her infancy when she had to wear size large diapers at three months old.)

"Yes it is! I know it is! Yippee!"

Once again, I felt like dirt. You'd think I'd have been used to it by then.

Even Ted was starting to notice a change in me. An "agitation," he said, which seemed to surpass my standard neurotic behavior. I'd fly off the handle at the most ridiculous things. Like the sock lint left on the carpet when Ted changed his shoes. You'd think it was the end of the world.

"Do you think Mr. Rogers leaves sock lint lying around the house," I said. "No! He wouldn't dream of if! And he changes his shoes twice in each show!"

Another time we were going over some family records on our personal computer. I was having some trouble remembering certain dates and Ted was trying to encourage me by saying, "Just think Maggie. Think!"

"I don't have to think!" I said. "That's why I have a computer!"

"It's no big deal, Maggie." He was doing his best to calm me down. "I didn't mean anything by it."

"Oh yeah? Well, maybe we'll just have to drill a hole in my head and insert a disk drive!"

Still another time, as I went to my room for a "quick fix" and found Ted on the bed reading a book, I found myself desperately trying to get rid of him.

"I hate to bug you honey, but could you please take out the garbage? You know how the smell of it makes me dizzy."

"Garbage pick-up isn't for two days," he mumbled.

"Well, why wait until the last minute?"

He gave me a strange look, then continued on with his reading.

"You know," I persisted, "Bob Eubanks says it'll be below freezing all week long. Maybe you need to chop some wood for a fire and we can roast marshmallows and cut the heating bill all at the same time.

Sound fun?" I was trying not to be too obvious in my attempts to kick him out.

"I think that's my cue to leave," he said, pretending to be understanding when it was obvious he was annoyed. "The kids and I are going to the store to get some Duraflame logs so that you can have your 'space,' which you obviously need, and we can all enjoy a fire with minimal effort."

He left, and as I stood there by myself it was plain to see that Grandma Tilley's Marshmallow Santas were not only becoming my downfall, they were becoming a crutch. The more frustrated I became, the more I'd crave them. I pondered that thought for a moment as I sat down on my closet floor. I started looking around at that tiny bit of space that had become my haven.

"This isn't normal," I said out loud. "I'm becoming too intimate with the inside of my closet . . . and now I'm talking to myself . . . and now I'm answering myself!"

It was ridiculous. I thought about Ted, out running around in the freezing cold with all the kids so I could be left to wallow in my eccentric mood. Then I suddenly realized that through his eyes there was no obvious reason for my disposition and I had been ranting and raving over absolutely nothing. The poor man; he must have thought I was loosing my mind. He may have been right.

I reflected on my squeaky-clean, goody-two-shoes past. It should have been a relief to me that the absolute worst thing I ever did in my life was to sneak out and buy some expensive candy I didn't need, while everyone else in the family went without, and then suffered through tacky meals so I could justify spending the extra money on my foolish obsession. I should have been proud that I never did anything really horrible and the only "skeleton in my closet" was a simple wad of marshmallow, shaped like a Santa Claus, and covered with chocolate. Nevertheless, I didn't feel proud. A lie was a lie, and deception was deception, and even though I was the only one in the world who knew about it, I still felt guilty. But not quite guilty enough to stop me from buying five more boxes before Christmas even got there.

Sister Walenheimer brought new meaning to the term "organist." It was evident she actually believed that she would become one with the organ as she fervently accompanied each hymn. Christmas Eve was no different.

Our Bishop had started his own tradition of meeting in the chapel on Christmas Eve for a short program about the true meaning of Christmas. I had to admit, I wasn't feeling very spiritual at the time. The Marshmallow Santa saga I created had basically overshadowed the aspects of Christmas that I should have been concentrating on in the first place. Not only that, but I actually had one of the culprits in my coat pocket. Before we left, I had gone to the closet for my coat and "needed" to eat one, so as not to waste the moment of already being in the closet for a legitimate reason. However, when Ted came in to change his shoes (adding even more sock lint to the already lint-laden carpet), I quickly shoved the Marshmallow Santa in my pocket so as not to get caught.

Upon entering the church, I was sure everyone there was staring abhorrently at the bulge in my pocket, knowing full well the whole, ugly truth. Needless to say, it was not a comfortable situation. I wasn't worthy of being in the chapel.

I tried to make a discreet exit, but as I hastily walked down the aisle, Ted came in from the men's room and asked why I was leaving.

"What is this, an inquisition?" I forcefully whispered, letting Ted know there was a definite yell under my breath.

"I'm just worried about you, Maggie. You're not being normal."

By that time the entire congregation was watching intently, so I put on my best "I'm angry but people are watching" smile and said, "I'm never normal, Teddy dear. You should know that by now. And if you're going to worry about something, worry about what Abby's bubble gum is doing to the hymn book. I'll be fine."

As I continued down the aisle, once again I felt every eye in the chapel probing into my pocket as well as my soul. I felt like my face was a giant billboard with flashing lights that read, "I'M A MARSHMALLOW SANTA SINNER!"

I was saved by dear Sister Waldenheimer who must have noticed she was no longer the focal point, for as she threw herself into another round of "Hark, The Herald Angels Sing," the crowd soon forgot my little drama and I managed to sneak out.

I wandered back to the cultural hall and stared at the nativity scene the Primary had assembled earlier in the program. Tears flooded my eyes as I realized what an imbecile I was turning out to be. Here it was, Christmas Eve, and it seemed I had missed out on all of the joy, the seasons greetings, and the whole "decking the halls" bit. I felt like a bystander in my own life.

I reached into my pocket and curled my fingers around the Marshmallow Santa that was destroying my existence. All at once I hated it. I hated what it had done to me, and I immediately started squeezing it and squishing it and digging my fingernails into it. The thought of eating another of Grandma Tilley's Marshmallow Santas made me dry heave. As I pulled the mangled confection out of my pocket and stared at it, I found myself saying, "Go ahead, make my day."

Then, in what seemed like a moment of slow-motion, a wave of peace fell over me. I felt like the world had been lifted off my shoulders. It wasn't too late to make it a great holiday after all. I could enjoy it without money or chocolate, and so could my family. Then I thought about my sweet husband and children sitting in the chapel without me. They had endured so much because of my childish stupidity. How could I ever explain that their enemy was a wicked little Marshmallow Santa Claus that tried to take over my life? I decided they never had to know; they'd never understand. It was time for a new beginning, free from Grandma Tilley's Marshmallow Santas. I couldn't wait to get home and flush what was left of them down the toilet. And with the help of a glass of Metamucil, I'd be officially cleansed from every last trace of the candy from hell.

I was jolted back to the situation at hand when I heard Sister Waldenheimer's aggressive introduction to "Joy To The World" and I realized that the congregation would be letting out any minute. I had to get rid of the evidence, so I leaned over to Baby Jesus, who bore a striking resemblance to a Cabbage Patch Kid, and stashed the disfigured Marshmallow Santa underneath the manger. At that moment I could have sworn the Wise Men gave me disapproving looks. There they were, kneeling at the feet of the Christ child with their precious gifts, and all I had to offer was a stupid piece of candy obtained in deceit. I shuddered at the symbolism.

I met Ted in the hallway, put my arm through his and said, "I'm ready to be normal now."

"I'm not sure if that's good or bad," he said with a wary look.

"I guess you'll just have to trust me."

We gathered up the kids and headed out to the van. For the first time during the holiday season I felt totally relaxed. I didn't even care that Abby's bubble gum had not only destroyed a hymn book, but did a good job on her hair as well. I didn't care that Patti and Paula had switched clothes again to confuse the rest of the family. I didn't care that Jeff had broken his glasses for the third time since school started and it would cost me fifty dollars to replace them. And I almost didn't care that Ted's parents would have arrived, let themselves in, and be in the kitchen waiting to eat when we got home. "Almost" is about as good as it gets when it comes to them.

I threw together a quick Christmas Eve snack, and when no one was looking, made my last sneaky escape to my room. I reached up and retrieved the remaining boxes of Grandma Tilley's Marshmallow Santas from my closet. Just looking at them made me nauseous. Then I locked myself in the bathroom, turned on the fan so no ruffling of wrappers could be heard, and triumphantly flushed every last one down the toilet. When I came out, Ted was standing by the door ready to knock. At least he looked like he was ready to knock. For all I knew, he could have been standing there the whole time.

"You okay, Maggie?" He was genuinely concerned.

"I am now," I said. "Merry Christmas!"

As I turned to leave the room, Ted held back a little.

"Maggie," he said. "We have to talk."

That worried me somewhat, seeing that whenever Ted has to talk, it's either about his parents or money, both of which were my least favorite subjects to talk about. Then I had a stark realization. Ted had probably noticed a money shortage and was more than likely going to confront me with it. I broke out into a cold sweat as I sat down beside him on the bed.

"I have a confession to make," he said. "I didn't keep our agreement. I've been spending money like a mad-man, buying presents for everybody over and over and over again. I've been sneaking them up to the attic for weeks, and you never noticed because you were always in here brooding."

My eyes grew as big as saucers. "It's okay, Ted. It's not that big of a deal."

"Not that big of a deal? You don't seem to understand, Maggie. I've got every Barbie accessory ever made, not to mention the entire collection of Fisher Price Fun With Food, and—don't kill me—our children will soon become complete Nintendo zombies. Not only that, but you've got a whole new wardrobe. I took the VISA to the limit, I took MasterCard to the limit, and American Express doesn't even have a limit, but I think I invented one."

I couldn't stand it any longer. My eyes welled up with tears and my head felt like it was going to explode.

"Oh, Ted!" I blurted out. "All you did was unselfishly buy presents for the people you love! I've done something much worse! I couldn't handle having no decent holiday munchies, and you know that candy canes just don't do it for me. So I've been sneaking around behind everyone's back and buying Grandma Tilley's Marshmallow Santas. I hid them in the closet and I've been eating them on the sly so no one would find out. I'm unfit to be your wife!"

"Don't be ridiculous. I'm the one that's committed the more expensive sin here."

"But it's not the amount that counts," I said. "It's what you did it FOR. Your reasons were of love and generosity. Mine were unscrupulously low and selfish and ugly and . . ."

"Okay, Maggie, I get the point. Besides, you couldn't have gone over budget more than a hundred dollars or so. We'll be paying for MY sins for the next two years."

"Well, I'll be paying for MY sins in HELL! I'm mean and rotten and hateful and I deserve to die a slow, miserable death and have my last meal be health food!"

At that we both laughed because we realized that even if it was my last meal, I'd never resort to such drastic action.

All in all, I guess you could say the whole thing turned out to be a good experience. It brought Ted and me closer together and we both vowed then and there to never keep secrets from each other again. How we were going to pay for Ted's little discrepancy was another story, but we decided we'd worry about that later. Besides, Ed McMahon was announcing the American Family Ten Million Dollar Sweepstakes winner in a few weeks and I sent my card in months ago. Maybe miracles did come true. I didn't hold my breath.

Christmas morning was the same as always. Four hyper children beating our door down, blinding us with the light switch, dragging us out of bed, and throwing robes in our faces. Of course, Ted's parents had been up for quite some time watching CNN and doing calisthenics, and were waiting for us when we made it to the family room.

After attacking the Christmas stockings, dumping them all over the floor, and "oo-ing" and "ah-ing" over what Santa brought, it was time to get everyone situated so the present-opening could begin.

Grandpa Wilson sat in the middle of the couch and when nobody sat by him he called out to Jeff.

"Jefferson!" He wasn't even content with calling him Jeffrey. He had to use the longest possible version of each person's name whether it was their given name or not, because that was "the proper thing to do." While Ted and I had accepted being Theodore and Margaret, the children were still a little confused.

"Jefferson," he repeated. "Come sit by Grandpa and bring little Abigail with you."

With that, I retorted, "Do as he says, Abby-buns," and smiled inwardly as I felt his critical glare at my terminology. There's just nothing like the satisfaction of being disapproved of by someone you can't stand.

The kids had been overwhelmed with Santa's generosity. It cancelled out the fact that they weren't going to get the usual number of presents under the tree. As part of our Tightwad Campaign, instead of everybody buying presents for everybody else, we were supposed to think of one special gift for each person and go in together on it. It was quite obvious the children were eager to give me my present first, so Abby brought it over to me, delirious with excitement, and returned to her spot on the couch, bouncing up and down, clapping her hands, and squealing her head off. It was amazing how a noise so loud could come from an opening so small.

I was familiar enough with the shape and feel of the package that I knew what it was before I even pulled the bow off. I glanced up at Ted who was doing his best to keep from laughing. Then tears came to my eyes as I tried to sincerely embrace the box of Grandma Tilley's Marshmallow Santas without vomiting all over the room.

"I don't know what to say." I choked down the sobs. "It's the best present I've ever received."

"Eat one! Eat one!" The kids were screaming in unison.

"Come on, Mom," Jeff added. "We want to see you eat one. I know it's been a long wait."

My hand shook as I reached into the box and pulled one out. I tore open the cellophane wrapper and the all-too-familiar smell of chocolate almost knocked me over. I slowly bit the feet off and with each chew, tried to pretend it was something else. As I carefully swallowed, my children beamed with satisfaction.

"You've no idea what this means to me," I said. And they didn't.

Then I insisted on sharing my precious gift with the rest of the family. They certainly deserved it.

"No, Mom, they're for you!"

"Eat 'em all up!"

"Yeah, pig out!"

Then Ted said, "Now kids, if your mother feels the need to share, it's not fair to deprive her of those blessings, is it?"

The box went around the room and, with Grandma declining, there ended up being one left. I nervously looked up at Ted as he said, "That one's for Philbert!"

"You're right, honey," I said. "We wouldn't want to leave the dog out of all the festivities."

We continued on with the rest of the present-opening before making our way to the kitchen for our traditional Christmas breakfast of star-shaped pancakes tinted with red and green. Within all the chaos, Ted managed to sneak me off in the corner to give me a hug.

"You know," he whispered, "someday you and I and the kids will look back and laugh at all this."

"If you tell the kids about my Marshmallow Santa escapade, you'll never laugh again."

"Oh, come on. Someday you'll need to tell them a story to teach them some kind of a lesson and this will be the perfect example so you'll tell them yourself."

I laughed. He was probably right.

I looked around the table at the greatest husband, the greatest kids, and the worst in-laws anyone could hope for. It was definitely the best Christmas ever.

Jay A. Parry is a professional writer who has published short stories in the Ensign *and* New Era, *as well as in a number of national magazines. His book-length fiction includes the illustrated* The Santa Claus Book *(published under the pseudonym Alden Perkes) and an LDS novel,* The Burning. *His nonfiction books include* The Mormon Book of Lists *(co-authored with Larry E. Morris);* The One Minute Secret: A Key to Greater Spirituality; Joy; *and* Soldiers, Statesmen, and Heroes: America's Founding Presidents.

WHEN SANTA SCRATCHED HIS BEARD

by Jay A. Parry

1.

Santa was nearly finished with his North American rounds when the trouble began. "Scratch your beard and lose a friend," the proverb says. Santa learned the hard way.

He hit a chimney with several inches of black soot and ashes on the bottom, so light and thick it felt like he was jumping into water. Everything puffed up into his face, getting into his eyes and filling his nose. "Stuff and tarnation," he muttered, coughing and sneezing. He rubbed his eyes and scratched his beard.

That's when his little Gnuf fell out of his beard and landed on the floor, bouncing on the carpet.

"Hey!" the Gnuf yelled in his tiny voice. "Help!"

Santa didn't notice. He rubbed his eyes again and pulled at his ears. He brushed his red suit off and quietly stomped his feet on the hearth.

"Santa! I've fallen out! Help!"

Santa couldn't hear—the Gnuf was too far away. Santa set his huge leather bag on the floor and reached far inside. Let's see, he thought. What did I have for this place? A little boy, huh. He grabbed a high-tech construction set and leaned it against the lower boughs of the tree. Then he turned and filled the stockings that hung almost haphazardly by the fireplace. "Ought to give them lumps of coal for having such a dirty chimney," he said. "Don't you think so, Gnuf?"

"Help me, Santa! I'm going to be lost."

Santa rummaged through the bag, making sure he wasn't forgetting anything. "You're not asleep already, are you, little Gnuf? Wore you out a mite early this year, didn't I."

He closed his bag, cinching up the drawstring, and stepped toward the fireplace.

"Wait! Why can't you hear me?" The Gnuf was shrieking at the top of his lungs.

It took only a moment for Santa to make himself small, then he stepped under the chimney and began to put his finger alongside his nose.

"Santa!" The Gnuf was crying now, calling out in a shrill voice. "Santa, if you leave me I'll never see you again. You'll never find me again. The world is too big."

Santa touched his finger to the side of his nose and rose up the chimney without a sound. The reindeer were waiting on the roof, their tiny feet dancing impatiently against the shingles. "Let's go, fellows," Santa called. "Finish this town, then we'll do the west coast, then off across the Pacific. Bet you're ready to get home."

They waggled their horns at him, sending the signal for *yes*, then lifted off and coasted to the housetop across the street.

Across the way, in the house with the sooty chimney, the Gnuf sat in the dark and sobbed. "He's gone. The best friend a creature ever had. I'm lost forever."

2.

Nearly everyone knows that Santa talks to himself on his long Christmas trips—and answers back, laughing at his own jokes. What they don't know is that he's really talking to his Gnuf.

Santa and the Gnuf first met in Louisiana's bayou country in the mid-1700s. Santa was already long famous. The Gnuf was unknown, the last of a race of tiny, intelligent creatures that date back millions of years. He was about a half-inch tall, a dull orange color, and thin as a pencil. He spoke seventeen languages and knew how to ask directions in two dozen more.

Santa agreed to let the Gnuf live in his beard—a cozy place for anyone his size. In exchange, the Gnuf kept it clean from the scattering of crumbs, drops, and scraps that seemed to be drawn like a magnet every mealtime.

It was the ultimate relationship. The Gnuf got to travel the world, free and secure, and Santa had a built-in traveling companion. From the moment they met they were never separated—not in the bath, not in the privy, not in bed, not anywhere. They got to know each other better than any other two beings on earth.

Then Santa scratched his beard.

3.

When he got home, Santa was so tired he could barely stand. He hung his coat on the hook by the door, leaned over and gave Mrs. Santa a light kiss on the lips, then sat wearily on the side of the bed.

"You look awful," Mrs. Santa said. "No offense."

"Thank you," he answered. "It's nice to come home to compliments."

"How long do you think you can keep this up? You're not as young as you used to be, you know."

"Yeah," he said, yawning. "Seems like you said that a century or two ago."

"I did," she said. She leaned over, unbuckled his left boot, and began to tug on it. It came off with a jerk. "And it's still true." She pulled off his other boot, and he lay back on the bed with a sigh.

"I don't remember when I was so tired before."

"Let's see, it must have been last year about this time," she said. "And the year before."

He loosened the top button on his shirt and closed his eyes. "Wake me up in June," he murmured. He let his body relax into the softness of the bed. "Good night, dear. And good night, little Gnuf."

The Gnuf didn't answer.

How long's he been sleeping? Santa tried to think through the fog of his fatigue. It seems like forever since I heard from him.

He couldn't think. But what did it matter? Let him sleep.

He tried to let himself drift off. But his mind wouldn't let it go. What if the Gnuf were sick? What if something had happened to him?

Santa opened his eyes a slit and looked over at Mrs. Santa. "I'm a little worried about the Gnuf, dear. I haven't heard from him for several thousand miles. Could you comb out my beard and see if he's all right?"

Mrs. Santa got the comb and began to gently stroke its teeth through the thick white strands of Santa's beard.

"I couldn't bear it if something happened to him, Mama," he said. His voice was unsteady. "You know what I mean?"

"Now don't you worry," she said. "Gnufs live forever." She stroked the brush down his beard, moving it slowly and as lightly as she could. "Never you worry. We'll find him any moment now."

But nothing was there.

Santa closed his eyes, rubbing them with his fingers. "What could have happened? What would have caused him to fall out of my beard?"

At first he couldn't figure it out. Then he remembered the sooty chimney, the sneezing, the deep scratching. Now where was that? Somewhere in southern Idaho, it seemed, or maybe Nevada. Or was it in California? He couldn't remember for sure. It was hard enough to keep track of all the cities and towns and villages and burgs in the world, along with every house and hut and cave. How could he be expected to remember where he scratched his beard?

Fatigue was swelling through his mind like a dark cloud. If I don't get some sleep soon I'll die, he thought. But all he could think of was the Gnuf, and he couldn't relax. What if he's in danger? What if there's a dog or cat in the house, or what if someone steps on him?

Mrs. Santa took off her square-toed black shoes and lay beside him with a sigh. As her head hit the soft pillow, he sat up with a jerk. "I've got to go," he said. "Got to find him."

"But you're too exhausted. And the reindeer will never make it."

"Doesn't matter. He needs me."

He pulled on his boots, buttoned up his shirt, put on his coat, and rushed out the door. Mrs. Santa blustered after him, fussing that he was foolish, he was going to die an early death, and didn't he want to take something to eat?

He only shook his head. "No, Mama. I'll be fine, Mama. No, Mama, I'll worry about food later."

The reindeer were already asleep. Santa had a few of the elves, bleary eyed themselves, harness them up. The deer stumbled slightly as they moved to their places, and when they lifted up their flight was sluggish. "Come on, boys," Santa called. "One more trip and we're done."

4.

The reindeer were so tired and flew so slowly the sun was nearly up before they touched down in Idaho. My memory's getting old, Santa told himself. But I think it was a little town here in the southwest corner. He checked Weiser and Payette, Fruitland and New Plymouth, Parma and Wilder and Marsing, stopping only at houses that seemed likely.

No luck anywhere. At most of the houses the people were still asleep, though he did surprise one little girl unwrapping presents while her family dreamed unsuspectingly in the adjoining rooms. At many of the houses he merely peered through the windows—that was enough to tell him not to waste his time there. Between Wilder and Marsing the reindeer nearly crashed twice, something Santa had never seen before.

"You've reached your limit, haven't you fellows. Well, one more town, and then I'll let you rest." He had the reindeer glide across the snow to a huge gray barn on the outskirts of Kuna. It was cold and empty inside, but leaning against it was a three-sided loafing shed, in which about a dozen cows stood placidly chewing on hay. The warm corners held plenty of room for a few reindeer. Santa released them from their harnesses and herded them in. "You all rest in here," he whispered. "Sleep, eat, drink, try to regain your strength. I'll reimburse the farmer later."

The wind was blowing hard when he went back out into the farmer's yard, whipping snow across his face and obstructing his view. Where to start? What should I do without my deer?

He had no choice. Simply go from house to house until a light of recognition went on. If there was no light—he stopped and brushed the back of his hand across his cheek. There had to be a light. He didn't have time or energy to go much farther.

He canvassed the town in only a couple of hours, walking as fast as he could through the snow, ignoring the houses and streets he remembered so well he knew they weren't his destination. No luck. It was the wrong town. He was sure of it.

He sat on a wooden fence on the road leading out of town, trying to think. The night before, he'd gone from Kuna to Melba. Could that be the place? He didn't know. There was only one way to find out.

He walked over to the side of the road, waited for a car to come by, and stuck out his thumb.

The first people to come by stopped and laughed at the fat man in the red suit trying to hitch a ride. "What's the matter, Santa? Ha ha ha! Get a flat on your sleigh?"

It was nearly a half hour before another car came by. A quiet Christmas morning. The driver waved but didn't stop. Santa was starting to get cold, despite his heavy suit. It must be the exhaustion, he told himself. Must be getting to me.

No other cars came by for a long time. Finally he sat down next to the fence, leaning back against it, and closed his eyes. I knew it was a fruitless search, he told himself. I was stupid to try it. The Gnuf is gone forever and I should be home in bed. I'm not helping anyone by killing myself and my reindeer.

He took a deep breath and let himself relax in the cold. The wind pierced the skin on his face; it felt like thousands of tiny needles stabbing into him, until his skin gradually grew numb.

I guess I'll just rest here for a bit. I can look some more later. If he's lost outside he's already dead, and there's nothing I can do about it. If he's inside he can wait a while.

A warm darkness began to close over him. It felt good just to sit down, not worrying about anything, not thinking, not feeling, just drifting away.

Maybe I'll just stay here forever. Maybe they can find another Santa Claus. I'm just too tired.

5.

He began to dream. He saw himself walking through a long and narrow corridor of pure white snow. The passageway was cold but he could see a blazing fire far away at the other end. Get to that and you'll be fine, he thought. Just get to the fire.

But a large and gawky black bird swung by overhead, his wings spreading a shadow over Santa's eyes. The bird opened his mouth wide and bellowed out a warning: "Harnk, harnk!"

Santa waved it away with his hands. "Get away," he shouted. "Don't get in my way."

The bird passed by again. "Harrrnnk, harrrnnk!" This time the sound was louder and longer.

Santa slowly opened his eyes. There was a pickup stopped in front of him on the road, a boy leaning out the window. "Hey, you all right, Santa? Got a problem?"

Santa shook himself, trying to come back to reality. He cleared his throat. "I need a ride to Melba," he said.

"Nobody goes to Melba. Besides, you should have been there hours ago. Know what I mean? Should have already made your rounds and all."

"I know," Santa said wearily. "But I've got an emergency and need to go back. Can you give me a ride?"

"Well . . . " The boy hesitated. "I'm supposed to get my uncle and take him back to my place for Christmas morning." He frowned, looking off down the road. Then, abruptly, he opened his door and jumped out onto the snow-packed road. "Hop on in, Santa. Passenger door's broke."

Santa heaved himself up and slid across the vinyl seat. He leaned his head against the side of the cab and closed his eyes. It will never work. I'll never find him. He'll be dead and it will be all my fault.

The boy interrupted the silence. "So how long you been one of Santa's helpers?"

"What?"

"How long you had that suit? Worked as a Santa Claus."

"Well." It wasn't the first time he'd been asked that question, of course. Nobody really believed there was an actual Santa. Every Santa they'd ever met was a fake. A nice fake, but a fake. He wasn't sure how they explained the extra gifts under the tree on Christmas morning.

His stock answer to such nonbelievers was simply to say, "Needed to make a little extra cash to buy presents this year."

Or: "You think I *like* dressing up like this and walking around like a stuffed tomato?"

But this kid was saving his life, and maybe the Gnuf too. He deserved a little more of the truth.

"I've been Santa for as long as I can remember," he said.

"You do look like you've got a few years on you," the boy said pleasantly. He was driving in a relaxed way, with only one hand on the wheel. The snowy road didn't seem to bother him much. "Been a Santa most of your adult life then, huh?"

"I've been *the* Santa *all* of my adult life," Santa said. He stared evenly at the boy, waiting for his reaction.

The boy snorted through his nose, then laughed. "Yeah, yeah. I get it. Got to keep up the image."

It took only twenty minutes to make the drive. The boy pulled up on the crest of a hill and stopped right in the road. "Here's Melba," he said. "Any particular house I can drop you off at?"

"Thanks," Santa answered. "But I don't remember which one it was. I must have been in a billion homes last night, you know."

"Yeah, I get it," the boy said, laughing loudly. "Well, merry Christmas."

"You've been a wonderful help. Merry Christmas."

The pickup did a U-turn and drove back up the road, leaving Santa gazing down at the quiet town. It looked like it had only a few dozen homes. What if this is it? he thought. Could I be so lucky?

He walked down the hill and around a curve, passing Poindexter's Pub and a granary, Leavitt's Blacksmith Shop and the grange hall. Then he came to where most of the houses were. Which way to turn? Where could the Gnuf be?

He stood at the crossroads for several long moments, trying to decide. Finally he turned left and walked by some of the houses across from the grade school. He went around the block and down a slope, then turned right. There, next to a grocery store, stood a little house with a broad porch. He looked up at the chimney, and a glimmer of recognition came into his mind. He held back a moment, uncertain, then walked up to the doorstep and knocked.

6.

At first there was no answer. He knocked louder.

"Grandma's here!" he heard a boy shout from inside. "Grandma and Grandpa's here!" The door swung open and a little boy in red pajamas looked up at him. His eyes grew wide. "You're not Grandpa," he said.

Santa chuckled. "No, I'm not." He stuck out his right hand and shook the boy's hand. "My name is Santa Claus and I'm happy to meet you, Mikey Balford."

The boy's eyes grew even wider. "Ho do you know my name?"

"I know everybody's name," Santa said. "At least I do when they stay at home. Would you mind if I came in and talked to your parents for a minute?"

A man's voice came from inside. "Who's there, Mikey?"

"Santa Claus!"

"Santa *Who*?" Mikey's dad laughed. "Well, tell him to come on in."

The living room was small, and the furniture was old and worn. But the family had a thick green tree in one corner, brightly decorated, and from the piles of colored wrappings strewn across the carpet, Santa figured they'd had a nice enough Christmas.

"Sorry to bother you on Christmas morning," Santa began. "But I lost something important while I was making my rounds last night, and I'm trying to find it."

Mr. Balford furrowed his brow. "Gosh, we'd like to help you, *Santa*," he said. "But we didn't find anything extra this morning. Did we, Mama?" He turned to his wife.

"Sorry," She shook her head, looking perplexed. She glanced at her husband, as though she were unsure how she should answer.

He stood and walked over to Santa. "Well, it sure was nice of you to visit this morning. Say good-bye to Santa, Mikey."

Mikey waved. "Thanks for the great Christmas, Santa."

"You're welcome, Mikey." He'd barely gotten the words out before Mr. Balford was propelling him to the door.

"I don't know who you are, Mister," Mr. Balford was saying under his breath, "but you have a lot of nerve coming in here on Christmas morning asking for a handout. I thought I'd heard of everything, but this just about takes the cake."

"Wait a minute," Santa said, trying to interrupt. He put his hand against the door jamb and refused to be pushed out. Inside the room he saw Mrs. Balford take Mikey by the hand and lead him through the door into the kitchen. She glanced uneasily back at Santa as she left.

Mr. Balford continued with hardly another breath, his voice getting louder and louder with each word. "Mikey still believes in Santa Claus, even if you don't, and here you're trying to destroy his innocent feelings. Trying to ruin Christmas for him."

"You think I'm an imposter, don't you. Just some guy dressed up in a Santa suit."

"If I didn't I'd be some kind of babbling idiot. Which I'm not. Now get out of here and let us have our Christmas."

"I've lost a little pet of mine," Santa said, trying to keep his voice even. "A very intelligent, very tiny creature called the Gnuf. He's lived with me for two or three hundred years, but I lost him on my trip last night. If I don't find him he might die." Then he thought, but didn't say, And I'll have a broken heart.

The man raised his index finger into the air and shook it. His jaw muscles were working vigorously, like twin pumps on the back part of his cheeks. "I'll give you the count of three. Then I'm calling the cops. One!"

Santa stared into his eyes, refusing to back down. This man doesn't care. Even if I were starving—which I could be, for all he knows—he wouldn't care. He just wants his peaceful, quiet home and let the rest of the world be hanged.

"Two!"

"He's about a half-inch high and kind of orange-brown," Santa said. "Actually, more orangish. His race is as old as the dinosaurs."

"Three! All right, that's it." The man strode over to the phone, picked up the receiver, and began to dial.

Santa raised both hands above his head. "All right, all right. I'm going." He backed out of the door. Mr. Balford slammed it behind him.

"And a very merry Christmas to you, too," Santa muttered.

So this was it. He could keep trying, but it was futile. The Gnuf was too small, the world too big. Like finding a needle in a haystack. No—like finding a grain of sand on an endless beach.

Might as well walk back to Kuna—or hitch a ride if he could—sleep with the reindeer in the barn, and fly back as soon as they all had strength.

His heart hurt to give up the search. But what else could he do? How much longer could he push?

He began to walk slowly back up the slope, heading toward the road that led out of town. But what if that *was* the house? he thought. What if the Gnuf were there and they didn't know?

He stopped, wondering if he should go back, when he heard the Balford front door bang open and a boy's voice call after him. "Santa, wait! Wait a minute!" Mikey came running up the sidewalk in his stocking feet. His mother came out after him, standing on the porch, the hem of her housedress blowing around her knees. "Michael, you get back here right now!"

"I just want to see Santa for a minute," he called back.

"He's not safe, honey!" she yelled.

"Santa's always nice," Mikey said. "He loves me."

He wrapped his arms around Santa's leg. "This was the most wonderful Christmas I ever had!" he said. "And thanks for the secret little guy you gave me."

Santa's heart began to speed up, and he put his hand on the boy's shoulder to steady himself. "What little guy?"

"You know, the little guy you hid under the construction set. Even Mommy and Daddy don't know about him. But what do I feed him?"

Mrs. Balford left the porch and began to step gingerly through the snow. She was wearing pink house slippers with a puffy ball on each toe. "Michael," she said firmly. "You get over here."

"Where is your little guy?" Santa said, trying to keep his voice calm.

"Right here in my pocket," Mikey said. He reached into the pocket of his pajamas' shirt and pulled out the Gnuf. "What is it, anyway?"

Santa held his hand out and the boy gently transferred the Gnuf. He was asleep and wasn't disturbed by the movement.

"He's a Gnuf," Santa said, "and he's my very best friend. He wasn't a gift, Mikey. He got lost at your house."

Mrs. Balford stopped beside Mikey and glared at Santa. "You'll be happy to know that the sheriff's coming right now. My husband called him and he's on the way."

Santa showed her the tiny creature in his palm. "I've got what I came for."

She stared down at the Gnuf, back up at Santa, then at the Gnuf. "It looks alive."

"It is alive. And he has as much intelligence as a human."

"Can he talk?" she asked.

Mikey looked up at her, his face glowing. "You ought to hear him. When I found him he kept whispering in my ear and never would stop. He kept jabbering away, telling me everything about everything until he got tired and went to sleep."

He turned back to Santa. "But don't I get to keep him?"

Santa shook his head. "I'm very sorry. I can't give him away because I don't own him. He's free, like us. He stays with me because we're friends."

Mikey looked like he was going to cry, but he shrugged and said, "I guess I thought it was a mistake anyway. No one gets a pet that can talk. And he *said* he wanted to go home." Mikey's face brightened. But wouldn't he have been something at show-and-tell!"

Santa laughed, feeling good again despite his fatigue. "I'll send you something, Mikey. I'll send you something no one else in the whole state has. No one else in the whole world!"

Mikey's eyes went wide. "No one in the whole world?"

"No one."

"Wow. For keeps?"

Santa nodded. "But now I'd better go. Before the sheriff comes." He winked at Mikey, patted him on the shoulder, and began to walk back up the hill.

He heard Mr. Balford join his wife and ask, "So who was that old kook anyway? And how did you get rid of him?"

She didn't answer for a moment. Then she said, slowly, "I can't be sure, Russell. But I think it's Santa Claus. Wonder where he keeps his deer?"

"Of course it's Santa," Mikey said, almost shouting. "You'll see when he sends me the greatest thing in the world all the way from the North Pole."

Santa smiled to himself and kept walking.

7.

He had trudged through the snow for almost a mile when the Gnuf began to wake up in his beard.

"Hey!" the Gnuf yelled. "I'm home again!"

"Yeah," Santa said dryly. "Now I just wish I were."

"Who needs to be home when they have me with them?"

"So says the little creature that's caused all the trouble," Santa answered. "You have any idea what you've put me through?"

"And worth every minute of it," the tiny voice answered. "Where else you going to find a beard cleaner like me?"

"Nowhere. At least on this planet."

The Gnuf grumbled something unintelligible, then said, "Admit it, old man. You missed me a lot."

Santa didn't answer, just trudged through the snow along the side of the road.

"Your heart was broken. You didn't know what you were going to do when you found I was gone after all those years we've been together."

"It has been a few years."

"You probably got all the way home to the North Pole before you missed me. Now that's gratitude. If you'd talk to me once in awhile you'd know if I was here or not."

Santa just shook his head.

"You think you can just take me for granted. Sure, you want a beard cleaner, but what about a companion? What about being your best friend? You don't even care, do you." The Gnuf's tone had been teasing at first, but now it was serious, and he began to snuffle.

Santa sighed. "You were a grain of sand on the beach, little Gnuf. And I didn't even know which beach. You want to know what love is? I found you."

The Gnuf started to respond, but stopped. Tears were dropping from Santa's eyes, rolling down the crevasses of his cheeks, and disappearing into his beard. "Oh, I'm sorry," the Gnuf whispered. "I really did know. I did. It's just that I was so afraid." He drank the tears to dry Santa's beard, then found a soft spot and lay down in it.

8.

Santa had walked for nearly a half hour when a pasty green pickup approached, seemingly oblivious to the slick road. It was the same young man who'd given him a ride before. Santa waved, but the pickup was already stopping. He did a U-turn and called out: "Glad I found you again. Need a lift back to Kuna?"

"Sure do. Left my reindeer in a big gray barn not far from where you picked me up." He settled down into the seat, hoping to find a way to relax. "You came by none to soon. I feel like I'm about ready to fall on my face."

"Well, climb aboard." He let Santa in the driver's side and waited while he slid over. "My name's Tom—never told you before, I think. Guess I already know yours." He laughed.

"Thanks for coming, Tom," Santa said. "But I thought you had to get your uncle."

"He had a sick cow, real sick, and couldn't come. Had to stay and keep an eye on her. Said the cow might not know the difference, but he would."

"Sounds like a good man," Santa Said, yawning.

"That's what the real Santa does, isn't it. He helps others even if it's not always easy."

Santa's head was nodding and his eyes wouldn't stay open. He tried to answer, but his lips just wouldn't move.

"That's why I decided to come back and look for you," Tom was saying, but his voice sounded like it was off in the distance. "You looked so cold and forlorn. And making sacrifices for others isn't just for Santa Claus, is it?"

Santa didn't answer. He was just too tired. But the Gnuf spoke up. "Only sometimes people don't recognize it."

"What's that? I can't hear you."

It seemed Santa had just fallen asleep when the boy shook him awake. "Hey, Mister Santa. This the barn you were looking for?"

Santa nodded. "You've been a great help." He began to get out, but Tom stopped him.

"I know this is none of my business," Tom said. He hesitated, then continued, "I'm sorry, sir, but I don't for a minute believe you have any flying reindeer in that barn. I'm a little worried you're getting out here with nowhere to go. Here it is Christmas day. Least I can do is take you on home to our place. We don't have much, but we've got enough. Will you come stay with us a bit?"

Santa reached over and clasped the boy's hand, squeezing firmly. "That's one of the nicest things anyone's said to me all day. But I'll be just fine. Now you go home and have a merry Christmas."

"Well, thanks," Tom said. "But you sure about this?"

"You're most kind," Santa said, waving as he turned his back and walked toward the barn.

The reindeer were asleep in a corner of the loafing shed. "Guess I'll join them," Santa said. "At least for a bit." He stretched and yawned. "Don't know when I've ever been so utterly and thoroughly exhausted." He settled back against a pile of hay and relaxed, stroking his hand down his beard to make sure he felt a tiny lump under the hair. "Little friend, I'll never scratch my beard like that again," he murmured.

"If you do, I'll grab your finger and hang on for dear life," the Gnuf answered.

Santa smiled and let his eyes droop shut. Never scratch your beard, he thought. Or you lose a friend. And it sure costs a lot to get them back. Then the Gnuf began a quiet lullaby and Santa drifted off to sleep.

Emma Lou Thayne holds a graduate degree in creative writing from the University of Utah, where she has taught English. She is recipient of the Distinguished Alumna Award from the University of Utah, the David O. McKay Humanities Award from Brigham Young University, and Salt Lake City Chamber of Commerce Honors in the Arts award. She is currently listed in Contemporary Authors *and* A Director of American Poets. *Emma Lou has served on the boards of the Utah Arts Council, the Utah Endowment for the Humanities, the Young Women's Mutual Improvement Association, and the Deseret News. She is the author of eleven books, including most recently* Things Happen: Poems of Survival *from Signature Books. She and her husband Mel have five daughters and sixteen (soon to be seventeen) grandchildren. And . . . she is a very formidable tennis player.*

CHRISTMAS VIGIL OF MOTHERS AT THE GATES OF THE PERSHING MISSILE SITE, MUTLANGEN, GERMANY

On Christmas Eve they come with trees
To let the trees do vigil, tempt fate
In front of the alien gates. Barbed wire
Is their only decoration; the mothers' declaration—the trees.
The women plant them in the wire of thorns,
These mothers among their priests
And their tall crosses
Made of wood.

They step out of time and place,
Cradle their missing, their unforgettable children,
Hoping to fill the day with lullabies of silence.
Hoping the metallic trucks—
With their loads of other people's missiles
To be aimed at still other people's missiles
Only borders away—
Will not try to deliver themselves on Christmas.

Beyond the gates, enough confused mechanisms,
Enough already profaning the dead leaves
And the scent of storm
And the bird cries gone off in search of trees
Not hung with fear.
The mothers in their scarfs and cloth coats,
Their wearable placards,
Their values warm inside their ribs,
Will lay their peace in front of the gates.
There its echo will be an unassailable target
Until the missiles are taken away
And trees take their place
To speak in the falling stillness of snow
Of the glittering that will come to their arms
With the sun.

Emma Lou Thayne

A former director of the BYU honors program, Thomas F. Rogers is a professor of Russian language and literature at Brigham Young University and author of a dozen or more plays, many on Mormon subjects. Four of these have been published in God's Fools *(Signature Books, 1983). His play,* Huebener, *will be re-staged at BYU next spring. He anticipates a second anthology of new plays at that time, including a reprint of the Huebener script. His latest published story, "Heart of the Fathers," appeared in the Summer 1991 issue of* Dialogue. *Rogers is the editor of* Encyclia, *journal of the Utah Academy, and author of a forthcoming critical monograph,* Myth and Symbol In Soviet Fiction *(Mellen Research University Press). Rogers and his wife Merriam are the parents of seven children.*

PAX VOBISCUM

by Thomas F. Rogers

Berlin, West Germany. A Christmas eve before the dismantling of the Berlin Wall. The cramped kitchen of a missionary apartment. Two young men in their early twenties face each other across a linoleum covered table. They wear white long-sleeved dress shirts and suit pants. The taller, blond and curly headed, also wears a conservative tie. He queries the other, a red head, in hushed tones.

"So how long has he been in there—in the bedroom?"

"Since P-day last week. After we took in that French film he insisted we go see. He'd studied French last year in college. That's where he wanted them to send him. France, not Germany."

"And he hasn't eaten since then either?"

"That's right."

"What's it called. The film?"

"*Gigi.*"

"Sure. I know it. It was an American musical."

"You're kidding me. You saw it?"

"The American version. It was really good. It had Leslie Caron and Charles Boyer. Old timers."

"Did you confess it to your bishop—before you came on your mission?"

"What?"

313

"That you saw this *Gigi*?"

"Why?"

"It's all about prostitutes. Or didn't you notice?"

"It wasn't even an 'R' film—the American one."

"Are you sure? You should have seen what those Frenchmen did with it. That's why I walked out on him."

"He stayed to the end?"

"Yeah, while I waited in the lobby. A good hour. I wasn't going to corrupt myself."

"Was there nudity?"

"Just as bad."

"Like what?"

"This innocent young girl—and very beautiful of course—is being raised, no *trained* by—get this! her mother and grandmother, who are both *whores!*—to follow in their profession."

"I know."

"And that doesn't shock you??"

"It has a very moral ending. The guy they have in mind for her—to become her permanent suitor . . ."

"And she's to become his mistress!"

"I know. He falls in love with her. And she falls in love with him."

"I caught that much before I walked out. But sincerity never justified fornication."

"What you missed out on was that the young girl—"

"Madame!"

"—won't let it go further until he marries her. Which he does. Much to her mother's and grandmother's disappointment."

"How decadent can you get? . . ."

"So, he hasn't talked to you since?"

"He said I was narrow-minded. And if that's what Mormon missionaries are like, he wants to go home. . . ."

"You think he'd talk to me?"

"I don't know, Elder Jensen. It's your job, isn't it? To solve our 'personnel' problems? He likes you a lot. You're the first person who took him tracting. He said it was the best day he's had here. Said he even enjoyed it. You can be sure he hasn't enjoyed anything since then—not with me anyway."

"I'll give it a try. Where will you be?"

"In the living room. With your companion. Where else?"

Elder Jensen goes to the bedroom door and knocks.

"Tony?"

"What?"

"It's me. Elder Jensen."

The door opens a crack.

"Hi."

"Elder Jensen. Where's *mein Fuehrer?*"

"Elder Nichols?"

"Yeah, Elder Nichols."

"In the living room. I'd like to talk with you."

"Just you?"

"Just me. . . ."

"Nobody else?"

"I promise. . . ."

"Okay."

Tony is clearly a year younger than Nichols and Jensen. He comes out and the two sit on the couch.

"I want to go home."

"That's what he told me. . . ."

"Well, what are you going to say to that?"

"I don't know. I can't think of anything to say just now."

"You know what made me come out, don't you?"

"No. I can't say."

"You called me by my first name. Isn't that against mission rules?"

"I suppose it is."

"So what kind of an example are you, Z.L.?"

"Not a very good one."

"Well, that's why I came out."

"I was hoping it would have that effect."

"So it was just a ploy."

"Yes."

"Well, it worked."

"I'm glad. . . ."

"So you want to know why I want to go home?"

"It's because we're too narrow."

"That's right. Maybe you're not. But the others. All my other companions."

"I'm sorry."

"You just don't know, Elder Jensen."

"Call me Larry."

"You mean it?"

"Sure. Papal dispensation."

"Who's the pope?"

"I am. Right now."

"Can I kiss your ring?"

"Later. If I manage to bless you . . . ."

"'Bless me'?"

"Be of some help. . . ."

"Okay. Where do I begin?"

"Tell me about your family."

"Well, my folks are divorced. My dad's an anthropologist. He's not a Mormon. Not anymore. By his choice."

"Are you close. You and your father?"

"Yes. We've been lots of places together. India last summer."

"I'd heard. What's India like?"

"It's tolerant."

"Tolerant?"

"You were expecting me to say it's 'hot,' weren't you? And 'crowded'—which it is—and describe all the poverty and filth, the starving *achuti*. The pariahs. The untouchables?"

"That's what you usually hear about India."

"Well, It—the people—are also mighty tolerant. And very intelligent. At least as keen as you and I. Does that amaze you?"

"No."

"Maybe you're just pretending it doesn't, to appease me."

"Maybe."

"Anyway, my dad and I had some wonderful discussions with the people there. The woman who was my dad's tutor—he was studying Sanskrit—had a Ph.D from Benares Hindu University in Vedic Sanskrit. That's the language's oldest form and very difficult. She also taught local Methodist seminarians. They often went to her instead of their own minister when they couldn't get along."

"Like you and Nichols?"

"Yeah. Like me and Nichols. But, you know, she was an orthodox Hindu. Ganesh hung on her wall."

"Ganesh?"

"The elephant-headed deity, if you can believe it—intelligent as she was, Ph.D and all. And she was ascetic—didn't wear jewelry or make-up or go to the movies. Not because anyone said she couldn't. She just wanted to be self-denying and vowed to 'detach' herself from something else each year until she died. But every morning before she went to the seminary or came to my father she'd visit the nearby Shiva temple and anoint his lingam with fresh milk."

"Your father's lingam."

Tony stares at Jensen, then breaks up. "You know what a lingam is, don't you?"

"Yes."

"How come?"

"I read a lot."

"And you'd dare think that?"

"It was just a joke. You didn't give me the correct antecedent."

"Hey, Larry, you're all right. . . . Well, she anointed *Shiva's* lingam."

"But she was also tolerant."

"Yes, very tolerant. Like the Pope here."

"Thanks. . . ."

"And unlike some of the Christians. At first—until we went to Benares—we were hosted by Methodists. We took meals for a time with an elderly couple from Great Britain. Evangelists. They'd already spent twenty years or so in Africa. The wife insisted that only Christianity could save India."

"Well?"

"Do you really think that India will ever be anything but fundamentally Hindu? Or that it ought to be?" Besides, this English woman was so narrow that she never asked about us. She acted like we didn't even exist—as a Church I mean. Because she didn't consider us Bible-based."

"But we are."

"I know that. And they also didn't think we were Christians because we don't interpret the Godhead the way the Council of Nicaea and Augustine and Aquinas have made all the other Christians think we should—even though their mystical view of it is totally irrational."

"Like Ganesh?"

"Ganesh? You remembered the name."

"Maybe I'd already heard of him. . . ."

"Well, yes, like Ganesh. But we still got the best of them."

"How?"

"There was this old man, a native Indian. He was the first Christian minister in the town where we were and he was revered by them. Considered a saint by the people. Netram was his surname—a Muslim Indian name. He'd stowed away on a ship to America as a young boy, and before returning he'd earned a degree in linguistics and theology at Princeton. When he came back he converted his entire clan. The local Muslims almost lynched him. Well, it was Good Friday. I'd gone to visit him. He knew about us, and respected us. By an amazing coincidence, his daughter and her husband had lived in Samoa and been employed there as translators, at the Mormon Church College. They were very impressed with the Church. Many Samoans are Mormons, you know."

"So I've heard."

"Or read?"

"Just heard."

"You've got sharp ears."

"No sharper than yours."

"So here I was in the middle of India, visiting this lame old man, now widowed, who was so impressed with the Mormons. Probably the only Indian, besides his daughter and son-in-law, who'd even heard about us for a thousand miles. He even showed me pictures his daughter had given him of our temples. And he kept them right there in his living room in a fat album. We spent the afternoon together. Then suddenly he asked if I was planning to attend the Good Friday service at the Methodist chapel. It was already early evening. He was going there, so I said I'd accompany him. My father was somewhere else at the time. So off we went, both of us in white cotton pajamas—this venerable Indian leaning on a hip young Mormon American—past the cows and goats and bicycle riders and naked children playing in the dust and bangled women in saris carrying tall jugs of water. We blended right in. But you should have seen those Christians—mainly the faculty from the seminary, some British, some Americans—when we went in the chapel. Their old minister had his arm crooked inside mine, and we sat together in his special pew."

"Sweet vengeance, huh?"

"Well, something like that."

"Tell me Tony, why did your father leave the Church?"

"I think it was because of my brother."

"Your brother?"

"He came to this same mission."

"Berlin?"

"Five years ago. That's why, when I got my call, he became so bitter."

"Your father? Why?"

"Bruce—my brother—never came home."

"From his mission?"

"He completed it, but then he went to Switzerland—to hike the Alps. He went there alone."

"Without a companion?"

"Got caught in a blizzard. And never came down."

"They never found him?"

"My father did. He flew over—requisitioned a helicopter and a crew of mountaineers. But it was my father who found his skeleton. Just a mile away and a little off the trail from his lodge. Pecked clean by the birds. He must have fallen—not hurt himself too badly, just broken his ankle so that all he could do was crawl. And maybe lost his way. So that before anyone could find him it was night and he froze to death. At least, that's what they made of it."

"So then your father renounced the Church."

"Yes."

"There's always an explanation."

"Is there?"

"I think so. We just don't always know what it is at the time. Particularly where others are concerned."

"What do you intend to be, a psychiatrist?"

"No, Tony. But I hope to go into medicine."

"A surgeon maybe? I've noticed your fingers. You could be a concert pianist, too. I heard you playing after Church last Sunday. You're talented."

"Thanks."

"What were you playing?"

"It was just the accompaniment to an art song by Schubert. For Sister Fredricks. She's singing at the service next week."

"What's it called?"

"*Pax Vobiscum.*"

"'Peace unto You.'"

"Yes."

"But that doesn't change anything, Larry, not right now."

"No?"

"We ran into an old man last week when we went tracting. It was on a really poor street in Spandau."

"Yes?"

"Well, he invited us in. The shabbiest apartment I've ever seen. Nothing on the walls. And the man looked like he'd never had enough to eat. But on the table in front of him was a large family Bible. He listened to our spiel and I thought to myself—maybe this is our golden one. After we got through we waited for some response. He hadn't said anything 'till then."

"What did he say?"

"First he reached for that Bible. Then he held it to his breast like it was his mistress and gave us to understand that this one book contained the sunshine and the substance of his entire being. By the look on his face and the spirit of his words he showed us—showed me anyway—the most intense and uncontainable joy I've ever witnessed. Then, in the kindest way possible and without the slightest reproach he told us that we had nothing for him, nothing he needed beyond what he already knew. Instead, he gave *us* something—a sense I'd never had before, the profoundest vision of what it means to love God and live at all times by his Spirit. It had been raining that morning. The sky was dark and ugly. But just as we stepped out of his door the sun broke through. It was like a heavenly benediction, and it warmed me for the rest of the day."

"And your companion?"

"I doubt it warmed him. In fact he seemed angry. I didn't dare talk about the old man. You're the first person I've mentioned it to."

"I'm glad you did."

"And another thing. We like to think that others—even a lot of Christians—aren't as high-principled as we are."

"We do?"

"You know we do. Well, when we were in India my father engaged a tutor for Hindi. He was a young Kshatriya—that's their second highest cast. They even wear a sacred white thread like the Brahmans. Well, one day I heard him telling my father about an incident the year before—with another of his students, a divorced American woman. She apparently made a play for him—tried to get him drunk first. But he refused to go along. Instead, he went home and told his wife. This will amaze you, but his wife asked him why he hadn't gone along. 'I wanted to,' he told his wife. 'But I knew that if I let it happen, I'd want to another time. And then another. And another.' So he didn't. How's that for honesty? He already knew better. Instinctively. You and I didn't have to show up in white shirts and ties to tell him."

"That's good."

"Good? Then what are we here for?"

"Let me tell you about an experience I had just the other night in the mission office."

"Sure. I've said too much."

"No, you haven't. I'll just relieve you for a spell. It was after eleven, and I was the last one up. I had just a few more orders to pack and address—the latest *Ensign,* Books of Mormon and various tracts—for some of you guys in the field. Then the phone rang. I answered. As soon as I announced the name of the Church, the man at the other end asked for my name, then said he'd be coming over to see me and hung up. I had no choice. I had to wait up another half hour. When he got there the first thing he wanted to know was, was I an American. Then he gave me *his* long spiel. He said he was from the East Zone. He'd managed to pass through the checkpoint at Brandenburg Gate on a non-renewable pass. The reason he'd come over was to purchase some medicine for his wife that he couldn't get in the Zone. Without it, he said, his wife would pass into a coma and die. When he'd tried to return with it the East German guards had confiscated it but said he could stay in West Berlin until midnight. That's when, in desperation, he said, he'd phoned me. There was an all night apothecary nearby. But he didn't have any more money, he said. Well, you know the mission rules and how often we've been taken by con artists. So I had my guard up. In fact I told him I couldn't help him."

"How much did he want?"

"Fifty marks."

"That's too much. What did he expect?"

"He even started to leave. Then something hit me, and, against all my better judgment, I stopped him. A little angry even, I took fifty marks out of my billfold and pressed it in his hand."

"No kidding?"

"Do you know what happened next?"

"He didn't thank you?"

"That's true. He didn't really thank me; he threw himself on my neck. His head fell on my shoulder, and he wept."

"No kidding? He was sincere?"

"So I misread someone. Like we misread Hindus and aborigines and other Christians . . . and sometimes, may I say it, other Mormons?"

"Meaning?"

"Just that."

"You know, in Benares something kind of nice happened just before we came home. We decided to visit Lake Dal in Kashmir, right in the foothills of the Himalayas."

"It's pretty there, isn't it?"

"It's where the Indians go to make their exotic movies. But when we got there—it was still too early in the year, I guess, already April—and we got caught in a bad snow storm. Like Bruce had in Switzerland. The planes couldn't land or get out for a couple of days. We were holed up in a little tourist bungalow. My dad caught a bad cold. So I made him stay in bed while I went down and ordered meals from the local restaurant. I met a young waiter there. He didn't have much business for a few days of course. All we had to do was talk. You know they're all Muslims there."

"I've heard that. Related to the Afghans and Persians."

"Right. Attractive people. With different language but they all speak English like everyone else in India who waits on foreigners. Well, I guess this waiter hadn't talked to too many Westerners before—just served them. The thing he had a hard time understanding was that anyone could really believe that someone besides Allah was God. He'd heard of Jesus Christ. But Jesus Christ certainly wasn't Allah. The morning we left he came out to the taxi that was taking us to the airport. He asked me once more if I really believed in Jesus Christ, that he was the *special* son of God. And for some reason it occurred to me then—I started thinking of Ganesh or the Nicene Trinity and the Angel Moroni when I said it—it occurred to me to say to him that one thing is sure."

"What's that?"

"That we all come from the same source, that we all have a common Creator. In other words, that whatever we choose to call Him, we all have the same Father in Heaven. And that that's what really matters."

"What did he say?"

"Nothing really. But he looked thoughtful—like that was something he'd never thought of before. Maybe I hadn't either. Before I got in the taxi he came up and embraced me. For a moment all the barriers between us—between a Muslim and a Mormon—had come down. They had fallen away."

"That's beautiful, Elder."

"Tony."

"That's beautiful, Tony. Thanks for the . . . lesson."

"I didn't intend it as a lesson."

"I know you didn't. That's why it was such a good one. And 'Merry Christmas,' by the way. It just turned midnight."

"Have we been talking that long?"

"Why not. I guess I'd better get back to my companion though—and leave you to yours. Do you think you could manage to give him a present?"

"A present?"

"*Speak* to him. Like you broke the ice with that Muslim waiter. And for the same reason. Because it's Christmas, I mean the season of 'peace on earth, good will toward men.'"

"I . . . I guess."

"Will you be writing your father soon?"

"Probably."

"Say hello for me."

"Okay."

"I can tell he was a good father. Let him know that."

"Okay."

"And about going home—why don't you wait another day? We can talk about it tomorrow if you want."

"I guess I can wait that long."

"Goodnight, Tony."

"Goodnight, . . . Elder Jensen."

For Larry Jensen (a pseudonym), who kept the author on his mission, then died some years later, unmarried, a restauranteur in San Francisco, of AIDS.

Curtis Taylor was born in Fukuoka, Japan and was raised in Modesto, California. After serving a mission to Japan, he attended BYU and tried his hand at writing. Two of his plays were produced by the Central Valley Players at the Golden Gaslight Theater in California. He also has three published novels, The Invisible Saint, *an LDS novel; and two novels for boys,* The Not-So-Private Eyes, *and* Treasure Hunt *(co-authored with Todd Hester). From 1982 to 1984, he was the editor at Randall Book. Currently he edits for Aspen Books. He and his wife Janet live with their four children in the Salt Lake Valley.*

ELEMENTAL WATER

by Curtis Taylor

The old man stood there, his stare digging into mine. The driving rain sparked off his forehead and dropped to the mud below. What was behind those eyes, I couldn't tell. Why he was now standing before us, I didn't know. He clenched a cane in his right hand.

We hadn't wanted to stop. Nobody wants to stop with a Japanese typhoon coming on. Our apartment was still a good fifteen minutes away, and our umbrellas were getting in the way of everything but the rain. I shivered as mud slowly oozed around my shoes. Glancing at my companion, I saw him looking back and forth from the old man to me—nervously, expectantly.

I didn't blame him for being anxious. After being in Japan only three months, he had seen more closed doors and rude good-byes than some insurance salesmen see in a year.

We had prayed and worked, planned and worked, and fasted and worked. Looking up old referrals, stopping people on the street, tracting hundreds and thousands of homes, we had worked every day's sun up and down again. My knuckles ached from knocking. My ankles were bloated from standing all day. We had tried everything we knew, but we hadn't even come close to having a baptism; we didn't even have an investigator.

My companion's green optimism was slowly melting away to bitter frustration. He could only understand a few words of the language when spoken to and could only recite portions of the lesson plan when forced to speak. He was beginning to feel that the people were cold and unsalvageable. When he tried to speak to them on the street or on trains, most ignored him, and others spoke so quickly that his brain and months of training became dumb. He couldn't understand the writings on signs, train schedules, or his own visa papers.

We had spent the afternoon tracting and were on our way back when we spotted the old man in his garden. What he was trying to do, I don't know. The row of dirt he was building up kept sliding down into the mud.

The mud. It was everywhere—in our shoes, on our faces, on walls and houses—and it seemed that the rain never washed it away. It was almost a living thing, spreading like a persistent virus.

The old man had suddenly stood up and come toward us. He was a short man, even for somebody with legs bowed like parentheses. His hair was moon white. Yellow film glazed his eyes.

I knew what my companion was thinking. We had spent months praying, fasting, and tracting, and nobody had talked to us. Now our faith was finally paying dividends.

I said, "Good afternoon," in Japanese. The man didn't move. I asked him how he was doing. Again no reply.

I turned to my companion, when suddenly the old man spoke.

"You—you kill my son." It was in broken English. "You, American dog, kill my son."

I stepped back, surprised. He was either crazy or drunk, and I didn't care to bother with him in either case.

His eyes burned with a wild rage. His face turned pale and he stepped closer to me. The cane in his hand came up a half inch.

"Why you kill son?"

"I'm sorry," I said. "You're mistaken." My Japanese was as clear as possible. "I don't know your son. Excuse me—" I stepped to get around him.

"He fight for life! You kill," the man almost screamed.

I stepped further away and spoke to my companion. "Let's go. I don't want to—"

I never finished the sentence.

The side of my head seemed to explode, and I found the ground coming toward me. In slow motion I saw the mud at my companion's feet coming closer. There were raindrops plowing into it. I could almost count every one . . . .

A faint light greeted me. I was lying on a tatami mat, still wet, but out of the rain. I tried to focus on the light and found that it was a low-burning oil lamp. The room was foreign to me. I tried to rise, and suddenly my head felt like it was too small for everything in it. I closed my eyes.

"Take it easy." It was my companion. He put a wet rag on my forehead. "Probably have a concussion, but you'll be OK. Just rest, then I'll take you home."

"Where are we?"

"In the old man's house. Relax. I'll be back in a minute."

The pain shot through my head again as I raised up. The *old man's house*? I tried to look through the doorway into the next room. There he sat, crosslegged, talking to my companion. I couldn't believe that something so ancient could move so fast, or hit so hard. He stood up and came through the doorway with my companion.

"This is Kenji Kodono," my companion said. "We've talked, and I think he wants to tell you something."

Kenji looked at the floor, his expression like steel. Samurai swords flashed through my mind.

"I am sorry," he said. "I am sorry to hitting you with stick." He raised his yellowed eyes to me. "I see you come every day. Every day I am remembering son. I remember American G.I. killing him in hole. Rain. You are much like American G.I."

His muddy hands twisted on the cane. My companion towered above him.

"I am not an American G.I.," I said in English. "I come for a church. I am a missionary. I never knew your son."

"Yes, I am knowing that. I am always knowing that. But I have many dreams. I see my son in war. He is fighting. He is great fighter. But he is not fighting American G.I.; he fighting American church missionary. He is fighting in mud, and many missionaries kill him. I dream of you."

I looked at my companion. He seemed at peace with the old man. "I did not kill your son," I said. "I want no fight with the Japanese people." I looked again at my companion. "Maybe we should go. I'm feeling better."

"No, you must rest!" Kenji said. "I am fixing you sukiyaki—you are liking sukiyaki?"

My companion spoke before I could. "Yes, we are liking sukiyaki very much." He turned to me. "This is right," he said, and followed Kenji to the kitchen.

That night, as Kenji served us bowls of the boiling food, he told how Seiji, his 15-year-old son, had died in World War II. Seiji had left home late in the fall of '43 when he found out that his father was stationed on one of the southern islands. Somehow he talked his way onto a supply ship heading for the island, borrowed somebody's old uniform, and actually entered Kenji's outfit. Kenji was brought great honor by his son's determination. The rains were unceasing as the American forces rolled ashore. Artillery devastated the terrain, leaving vast craters where troops and bulwarks had been. Kenji and Seiji found protection in one of the craters and fought until their ammunition ran out. Huddled together, knee-deep in mud, they waited for the inevitable rush of enemy soldiers. Two days later, after a cease-fire for Christmas, it came. Three marines stormed over the edge shooting. Kenji took two hits—in his right arm and right thigh. His son was hit at least as many times but kept fighting. He died, face-down in the mud with a bayonet through his back.

Kenji still felt the honor of his son's actions.

His wife died sometime during the bombings, and after the war Kenji found himself without a home and a family. He eventually found this property and began his garden. It was only a quarter acre or so, but it had given him all he needed. He talked until eleven o'clock.

Before we left, he made us promise to come back.

For the next three months, we worked harder than ever in that little village. We worked and searched and prayed, but the town never did open up.

My companion gradually acquired a working knowledge of the language and came close to memorizing all the discussions. We both learned to accept the long hours of effort as simply our duty. We were servants of God.

Then, two days before Christmas, word came that we were being transferred.

A giant storm swept in from Siberia that night. Rain seeped through cracks in the walls and roof. An east-west wind poured through the room. We were packing when a knock came at the door. Somebody poked his dripping head in, and the wind pushed the door wide open. He came—the only investigator we had ever had.

"I am wanting to baptize—*now*."

His smile widened, and I thought I saw a faint gleam in his yellowed eyes. We called the zone leaders and they said to wait, they wanted to see the only baptism in this district in the last two years.

The storm howled for another day.

Early Christmas morning we woke up to utter brilliance. Light poured in from the windows and through cracks in the walls. I got up and looked outside. Blazing snow lay over the earth like a cloud.

The zone leaders came, and we quietly, almost reverently, made our way to the church. An hour later, Kenji Kodono left his cane leaning against the wall as he stepped into the cool, clear water of the baptismal font.

John Bennion grew up in western Utah, the setting of this story. His first collection of short fiction, Breeding Leah and Other Stories, *was published this year. Mr. Bennion, who lives with his wife and four children in Springville, Utah, currently teaches creative writing at Brigham Young University.*

THE BURIAL POOL

by John Bennion

Alison dreamed that the Goshute woman stood next to her bed dressed in white deerskin. The woman's face was in darkness, and Alison panicked, rolling to her hands and knees, clutching at the blankets. Across the room Howard, dressed in his thermal underwear, loaded logs into the red mouth of the cookstove. "Can't you sleep either?" he said, grinning.

"I was asleep until you started banging around," she said. "I dreamed that the angel of death had come." She sat on the edge of the bed. "But it was only you in your ghost suit."

Howard stood with his hands on his hips. "Is there something actually wrong?"

"No." She held her hands across her belly. "Except that you're using your fatherly voice on me."

"Then stop imagining that there is. You've been frightened ever since you've been pregnant." Three years earlier the nurse had brought that other child, blue-faced and cold, wrapped in a white blanket, and laid it across her belly in the hospital. The baby had a strong, square face and Alison had wondered ever since what it would have been like to live with such a powerful child.

"I can't help it," she said. She took his hand and placed it against her. "Feel. He's awake as well, awake and kicking."

He jerked away. "It's weird to feel something moving inside your stomach."

"Silly," she said and lay down again. He returned to his mattress near the door. When he couldn't sleep, he twitched and twisted, keeping them both awake.

331

Alison woke again shortly after dawn. The clouds had blown away in the night, leaving the flat bowl of the desert valley white with snow. The only dark was the lava ridge which extended north and south behind their cabin. With the field glasses she could see the blue tarp which covered the dig, two miles north at the base of the ridge, and next to it the salt pool and stream, from which rose a mist. Alison knew that despite the sun it was bitter outside, cold as January even though it was only November. As she moved toward the table, the wind breathed through the walls of the cabin and chilled her skin.

Howard gave her a bowl of Cream of Wheat sprinkled with brown sugar. When she stirred, she brought up lumps, some an inch across. She flapped her spoon against the top of the mush.

"What's the matter?" asked Howard.

"I don't understand how you achieved such large clods."

"Dumplings," he said. "I cooked it that way on purpose." She pushed the bowl away.

Howard left to start the truck, which he ran every day for fifteen minutes in case they needed to drive her to town. She dressed and, swaying slightly from side to side, walked to the tractor. "Quack, quack," she said, but Howard was up on the haystack and couldn't hear. He was only half finished loading the wagon, so she leaned against the tractor to watch as he threw bales down, five or six at a time, and then clambered to the wagon to arrange them.

She felt the child kicking again—a son, she knew from the last ultrasound. "You are too active," she said. Her friend from Rockwood, who was into bees' pollen and higher states of consciousness, and who, for her sixtieth birthday, had changed her name from Mary to Aurora, suggested that Alison talk to the baby, give him a prebirth name. Howard suggested that Cletus the Fetus might be good. Even though she felt foolish, Alison did talk to the child, ignoring Howard's comments. For the past few weeks, without having any specific ailment she could point to, she had felt that the child's attachment to her had become uncertain. Perhaps the act of naming could hold him to her longer than the last one. "Adam," she called up to Howard. "Abraham, Aaron," she said.

"Eustace," said Howard. "Lawrence or Edgar. He shouldn't have a name which is less dignified than his father's."

"You don't have a dignified bone in your body," she said. "You don't have a dignified follicle." Howard's hair swirled at the front, a tangle of opposite turning cowlicks.

He grunted, moving another bale. Despite her better sense, she was unsettled by the fact that no name would stick. "Have patience, my hasty one," she whispered. "You have three more months."

She slid behind the tractor wheel and pushed the button to warm the glowplug. The engine started easily and, with Howard perched behind, she drove toward the cattle, which had all turned to walk toward the sound of the tractor. The wind blew from the north, a penetrating cold. She drove in a wide circle through the fields and Howard threw the hay off the back. The cattle followed, some running up to the wagon and twisting their heads sideways, long tongues extended, to gather hay from the corners of the moving stack. She never understood why they didn't just wait for Howard to throw it down.

The lane below the cabin had turned white, outlined by gray shadscale and greasewood. Near the pool it joined the main road, which also showed white, a bank of gravel which bisected the valley. She saw the yellow of the county snowplow crawling past their ranch. Suddenly she cramped, a severe low pain, and bent forward over the steering wheel. "Howard," she said, but he didn't hear. She stamped her foot down on the clutch. Her abdomen was so tight with pain that she thought she might pull a muscle. He threw off the last bale and walked up to the tractor.

"What's wrong?" he asked. She couldn't answer. "Can you get down?"

She shook her head. "Just let me sit here for a minute," she said finally.

He tried to take her hand; she didn't move to let him, so he stood, shifting from foot to foot in the cold. Finally the cramp faded, leaving a dull ache.

"Is it false labor?" he said.

"Not this hard," she said. "It shouldn't have happened."

"I'll finish, then we'll go in to the doctor. Do you want me to drive you back up?"

"I'm all right now." She drove the tractor homeward along the base of the ridge, passing the stream, so salty that not even halogeton or salt grass would grow near it. When she came to the pool, she stopped the tractor. She knew the dream woman had come to her imagination from the dig, as if the shrunken corpse which she had helped exhume had filled with life again. What was the connection between dream and life, mind and body?

The previous April Howard had decided that they should sink logs for a small pier, because the mud along the shore of the pool was pale and stinky, unpleasant to wade through when they wanted to soak in the warm mineral water. But when he started to dig the holes, his shovel uncovered a human head, white with crystals of salt, shrunken but hardly decomposed, its teeth grinning, leathery eyes closed.

Alison and the two anthropologists sent out from the University of Utah had spent the summer spading and brushing the mud and crystals from the limbs and faces of the Goshutes. They had to use a plywood frame and a pump to keep the mud and water from filling their hole. Close to the first corpse, they found more—in all, three males and a female. Alison was most interested in the woman, who had a small child fastened across her belly with inch-wide bands of leather.

One anthropologist claimed that the corpses had originally been floating in the pool before silt carried up by the shifting water channel had covered them. He pointed to the thongs tied around the ankles of all four adult Goshutes. He thought that in the burial ceremony the Goshutes tied boulders to the ankles of the dead before dropping them into the mineral-laden water for preservation. The other anthropologist wasn't so sure. Alison agreed with the first, and she wondered what the Goshutes thought and felt when they stood on the bank and lowered their loved ones into the deep water. She knew that for Navajos heaven is earthward. Perhaps Goshutes were similar; they might have believed that passing down through the heavy water was part of being reborn into the next life. The woman's friends had hoped to bind her to her child through that difficult passage.

"Dear God," said Alison, putting the tractor back in gear, "bless me not to lose this one. Bless us to stay together." She steered around the pool and drove upward toward the cabin.

At the shed Alison cut off the engine and walked slowly into the cabin. She lay sideways on the bed, waiting for Howard. By the time he returned, she discovered that she had bled. "It's starting again," she said to him. "I'm going to lose this one too." Saying it opened a dark place inside and she found herself weeping. Howard helped her dress, then walked her out to the truck.

He drove slowly at first, but the truck continually slipped into the ruts, jolting her. She felt pain low in her belly and gripped the arm rest. Howard pulled from their dirt lane onto the gravel road. "You should have called me." His face was white, frightened, and he drove too fast on the better road. She leaned across and put her head on his lap.

"I kept thinking you'd come in any minute." She turned on her back and reached upward between his arms to touch his face, which was still angry.

They drove up the long narrow valley, the last evidence of a river which had connected two parts of Lake Bonneville. From Howard's lap she could see a flat-topped butte, with huge boulders along its crown in a line, sentinels which seemed as tall and rectangular as those at Stonehenge. As they drove up around the flanks of the Simpson Mountains, she sat up and looked out at the hills below on the plane; they were rounded, knobby, so that they looked like the carcasses of huge prehistoric creatures, half sunk in mud. Finally, they crossed the pass into Rockwood Valley, down into the town.

Dr. Peterson, whose face was as broad and red as an old farmer's, wanted her to have another expensive ultrasound. Alison watched the monitor as he directed the gray, flat-bottomed instrument across her belly, which had been smeared with an amber gel. The child was curled, floating in what showed on the screen as shadows of flesh and liquid. She could see his arms and legs, his tiny penis, the coil of the umbilical cord. The image of the moving child had reassured her before, but now the tissues which were supposed to bind him to her seemed so tenuous.

"Your placenta is already starting to detach," he said, pointing to a cloud on the screen. "You should be in the hospital, but if you'll stay in bed and rest . . ." He knew they couldn't afford that cost so she knew it was his way of frightening them into obedience. "If you can keep the baby until it's eight months along, it'll have a much better chance of surviving."

As soon as they were home, Howard made her lie down. The cabin was familiar after the doctor's office, filled with the smell of wood-smoke and propane instead of antiseptic; the sight of her table and cookstove comforted her. She dozed but woke again when Howard came back in to cook. She ate sitting cross-legged on the bed—a bowl of potatoes and canned meat boiled in tomato sauce. "You believe in functional cooking, don't you?" she said.

The days through the bulk of November were like a tunnel, where she woke and dozed, keeping her body quiet. She believed that she was getting worse, that the placenta was continually loosening itself, getting ready so early that her child would die. But surprisingly, she didn't bleed again. Howard did his work and hers, seldom talking to her, moving quietly through the house: cooking, loading the fire, scrubbing the floor, fueling the generator. "You're too much of a slinker," she said to him one day. "Noise won't bother me. I'm bored out of my gourd." So he immediately made a symphony of banging pots with a wooden spoon. He sang old Rolling Stone songs to her while he boiled water in their canning kettle and started the wringer washer in the corner of their cabin. Later, she dozed to the rhythmic sound, willing the baby to stay. "Steady now," she said. "No need to be an early-bird. Stay with me."

Several times she woke to the ticking of snow against the window. She sat on the bed watching the gray-white clouds sweep across the valley. With the binoculars she watched the water in the pool, blacker than the sky. Other days the clouds blew away and the bitter wind seemed to come through the wall to her bed. On those clear, cold days the sun made the snow burn with white light. Howard moved in his dark parka across the fields below her window. When he came in, he stamped his feet and banged his hands together. "Damn cold," he said. "The truck won't start today." He drained the oil and anti-freeze and heated them in tin pans on the stove.

"Careful, you're going to burn us," she said. But by noon, he had the truck going.

The child seemed to grow larger every day, and she sat on the bed with her legs apart, her arms and hands limp. Her stomach bulged until she thought her skin would split. She no longer had the energy to change her clothing or wash her face and hair. Howard slept on his mattress, so that he wouldn't disturb her. He usually ate quickly, then left to work again.

Thanksgiving Day they ate canned quail, potatoes, sweetened carrots, and drank Coca-Cola. "When it's winter, its hard to believe that things will grow again," she said. "It's easy to believe that everything will always be cold."

"You're beastly depressed," he said. "Think about something cheerful, like sleeping." She snapped her fingers in his face, and he went outside again. When she looked in the mirror, she found that her face had become pale and luminous, like the skin of a very old person.

The morning after another deep snow, she found blood again. Howard rushed out to start the truck. The wind blew against the cabin, making a low sound like an oboe. An hour later he came back in. "I can't figure out what's wrong," he said. "Maybe it's water in the gas. Maybe the timing chain has slipped. I don't know what to do."

She dozed, woke to a slight pain, dozed again. Finally, she sat up on the bed and looked out the window. Howard, dressed in his black parka, stood in front of the raised hood of the truck. Suddenly, he dropped to his knees. Soon he rose and chained the truck to the tractor, tied the wheel of the tractor straight and started it across the flat toward a patch of field which had already been blown clear. The wheels of the truck plowed sideways through the snow, until he jumped off the tractor and jerked open the door of the truck to straighten them. The tractor wasn't going straight and the truck missed the dry patch by fifty yards.

Alison got up slowly and, after dressing herself, stood in the doorway of the cabin. Somehow Howard had turned the tractor and truck and was crossing the patch of earth. Although the wheels raised dust as they dragged, the truck wouldn't start. Soon the truck was back on the snow where there was no traction. With the binoculars she saw Howard slumped inside the still-moving truck, his head forward on the wheel. "Please, God, no," she said. But then he opened the door and unhooked the chain. He drove the tractor back to where she stood.

"You should be inside lying down," he said. She heard the faint sound of another engine. Taking his shoulder, she turned him toward the far end of the valley, where the yellow plow crawled. He ran to the tractor and drove it toward the main road. Alison returned inside to sit at the table but soon the long yellow road-grader pulled up to the front of their cabin, the door open, a small and swarthy man inside.

"*Que pasa?*" he said. "You need an ambulance?" She sat on the seat, while the driver stood beside her, steering. Howard crouched behind in the tool space. She looked down at the dig as they passed. The baby had been reattached to its mother with leather bands. "You can't beat death that easily," thought Alison. The driver, whose name she missed because of the noise in the cabin, apparently thought she was going to have her baby any minute: he kept the blade high and the speedometer at forty until they roared up to the doctor's office.

"I advise you not to go home," Dr. Peterson said later. "It's too risky to drive back and forth across bad roads in your condition. You need to use some sense. Stay in town."

Alison called her friend, Mary Aurora, who came and drove them to her house. She owned a greenhouse, one section of which she kept going even in the winter. With Alison and Howard seated in her kitchen, she strode, self-assured as a goddess, back to that steamy building and returned with a tall poinsettia, which she gave to Howard. "We'll have a good time together," she said to Alison. "A woman's time without your husband."

He looked down into the exotic leaves. If a cow or a human couldn't eat a plant, Alison knew, Howard didn't see any use in it. But she glared at him and he said nothing. He simply stood, hugged her, and walked to the door with the pot. "I'll come in every Sunday," he said. He walked down the street toward the house of a friend, who had agreed to drive him out and help start the truck.

Alison's bedroom was at the top of Aurora's white frame house, a pleasant room with a view of the mountains between the town and the deeper desert where Howard was. She stayed in bed night and day, allowing her body the space to heal itself. She lay in warm baths, talking to the child, whom Aurora had named Nicodemus because he was a waverer.

They had been friends for two years but were still unfamiliar with each other's deeper selves. Often, when they needed to talk, they instead found themselves issuing proclamations:

"You can will your body to heal itself," said Aurora.

"It's subject to powers beyond my control."

"You are majestic, an eternal being of power."

"We are transients, here a minute, then dead and buried."

"The earth is a garden."

"The earth is a cross on which we are sacrificed."

After these bold statements, they both became frightened and clung to each other on Alison's bed.

The first Sunday was warm. From her window she saw puddles melting in the roads. Although she watched the road until dark, Howard didn't have the sense to come before the roads froze again. Finally around ten, he drove up and pounded on the door. He lay his sleeping bag on the rug beside her bed and held her hand. He talked about how rough the early cold was for the cattle, the difficulty of breaking ice and hauling hay alone. She dozed until midnight, the pleasant rhythm of his voice recreating their valley for her. Shortly after light he was gone.

Although she was careful to keep herself still, she knew that resting hadn't prevented her bleeding a second time. Once the unnatural process of detachment started, she felt it would continue to its end. Aurora fussed over her, bringing dinner up and talking to her while she ate. She gave Alison positive things to read—Walden and New Age literature. She told Alison that depression could cause physical problems. Alison knew that her sadness was the natural fear of an impending death.

Contrary to both their expectations, toward Christmas Alison felt stronger again; she had a record of three weeks without bleeding. The doctor told her she should get some light exercise. She went on short walks, passing under the red and green lights on Main Street and the black-barked trees, their branches reaching up like fingers. She disliked the garish lights, but she enjoyed walking on the side streets, looking at the different kinds of houses. She walked with Howard one night, up onto the low ridge above town. They sat and watched the deer and elk come down to gnaw the stacks of the town farmers.

On Christmas Eve she and Aurora dressed themselves in heavy coats and built a fire outside in the barbecue. By the light of the flame Alison read the first part of Luke. They had finished and returned inside when Howard finally came—red-faced from having to drive with the window open because the defroster had broken.

"You need a new truck," said Aurora.

"For once I agree with you," he said. "Maybe one of our prosperous friends will float us a loan."

"You don't have any prosperous friends," said Aurora. "You are such a pair. With that truck you're an accident waiting to happen. And Alison—you spend all your time willing disaster. You believe in fate, don't you? Whatever will be, will be. You're like two pagans." She rose to bring some hot chocolate.

"How can I hold my head up anymore, knowing that?" said Howard.

"She's part right, you know." When Aurora came back, Alison turned to her. "I know we're jinxed," she said. "But we have kind friends." Aurora smiled at her and the three of them sat in a circle, their cups steaming.

Two days before New Year's Alison had another appointment with Dr. Peterson. He examined her carefully. "The placenta is firmly attached," he said.

"I'd like to go home then," she said.

"We've about made it," he said. "You're eight months and a week."

"Yes," she said. "So I can go home for a while."

"You are a strong-willed woman," he said.

"Stubborn as a mule."

That Sunday she told Howard she was returning with him. It was evening before they started back. During the afternoon, clouds had blown in, covering Rockwood like a gray, inverted bowl. The street lights and Christmas lights were blurs of white, red, and green behind them as they started back across the desert. Snow beat into the windshield. Howard drove slowly so that they wouldn't slip off the road.

When they finally came to the mineral pool, Alison reached for Howard's hand. "Let's stop for a minute and look," she said. They walked out into the snow, and she watched the flakes spin in masses above them. The wind flapped the blue plastic, shrieked through the squat brush. "I want to have a warm soak," she said, walking back toward the truck.

"Don't be crazy," he said. She quickly slipped out of her clothes, leaving them in a dark heap on the seat.

"The snow is cold," she said, walking past him toward the pool.

"Alison," he said, touching her arm. "Use some sense. It's a blizzard out here."

"It's time for a celebration," she said. "We're all alive. What's the danger?"

"Cold," he said. The wind was freezing her so she stepped quickly down the bank into the warm water. She turned and floated on her back when it was deep enough. "We won," she called. "No one had to follow." Howard stood above her on the bank as she slipped backward through the water. The water was so thick with salt that it held her buoyant. Looking down at the pale curve of her belly, she kicked herself backward; she felt like a sleek water creature.

"Howard, I missed you, Howard." She floated, arms and legs motionless. He kicked off his boots and dropped his coat. When she glanced up again he had peeled down to his white thermals and was sidling down into the water. She watched his pale face come up to her. "It's all right," she said, touching his cheek. "Swimming is not strenuous at all. My belly keeps me up. And the water's not too hot for the baby."

"There's no fire in the cabin."

"So I'll sit in the truck while you build one."

"Thanks loads," he said. He touched her hand, her head, curved his arms around her. The storm whistled above them. Floating on her back, her hand in his hand, she watched the banks of snowflakes turning in the limitless depth above them. She felt disoriented, not knowing which way was up, which down, held between by the thick fluid. She imagined those other floaters, ankles bound, sunk upright in the deep water, waiting for passage back into the sun. She could leave the pool anytime she wanted, didn't have to remain as they had for year on year, century on century. She and her child had not been compelled to join them. The water was warm on her body and limbs, the air and melting flakes cold on her face and belly. Each sensation felt like a miracle.

"The snow's getting deeper," Howard said finally. "We need to get to the cabin." The bank was slick and he scrambled out on hands and knees. When he bent backward to help Alison, he slipped toward her, and she had to come out like a crab as well. He lifted her to her feet and they walked quickly through the snow, their palms and knees marked with black mud. "That was nice," said Alison. She laughed at Howard, who hobbled barefoot, carrying his bundle of clothing.

"I've been so lonely," he said. "I'm glad you're home."

She turned the heater on full and wiped herself clean with a newspaper she found on the floor. Then she slipped her dress back over her. Before they were half-way to the cabin she was warm again. Howard, who hadn't removed his wet underwear, shivered with cold, his teeth chattering. When they came to the cabin he left the truck running and rushed inside. Soon she saw a light, and then he stood naked in the door, grinning.

"You are beautiful," she called, as she walked toward him. "He's kicking again. You should feel." She took his hand before he could step back, guiding his fingers over the curve of her belly. She looked up into his face as they both felt the bumping of a foot or fist knocking to get out.